The Flying Tigers Poker Payoff

Other Books by Author
C O Lamp

Available by getting in touch with <u>colamp@hotmail.com</u>, subject Booksale. Books marked with * may be ordered directly from iUniverse.com

Journey to a Star

Distant Love, lasting Love

The Return of Glenn Miller

The Witches who Loved Wilburn*

The Plot to Ice Governor Tea*

Flying Horseman*

Pony Trails and Puppy Tales*

Inside Lamp Confidential*

For the Love of Harlan*

The Flying Tigers Poker Payoff

✦

They Saved China

C O Lamp

iUniverse, Inc.
New York Lincoln Shanghai

The Flying Tigers Poker Payoff
They Saved China

Copyright © 2007 by C O Lamp

iUniverse books may be ordered through booksellers or by contacting:

iUniverse
2021 Pine Lake Road, Suite 100
Lincoln, NE 68512
www.iuniverse.com
1-800-Authors (1-800-288-4677)

The views expressed in this work are solely those of the author and do not necessarily reflect the views of the publisher, and the publisher hereby disclaims any responsibility for them.

ISBN-13: 978-0-595-42451-1 (pbk)
ISBN-13: 978-0-595-86785-1 (ebk)
ISBN-10: 0-595-42451-1 (pbk)
ISBN-10: 0-595-86785-5 (ebk)

Printed in the United States of America

This book is dedicated to Dottie, "child of the Lan Hua,"—Gentle Tigress —"The Real Thing!"

Contents

ACKNOWLEDGEMENT

As young men, the Flying Tigers talked freely about each other and their exploits. In the fullness of age, they hesitated and spoke with reluctance, unwilling to cause concern or consternation to the families of those with whom they fought a war so long ago.

Accordingly, several fictional characters are introduced in the manner of *roman a clef.* These characters are an amalgamation. Perhaps two or three personalities are morphed into one. Although these characters are fictional, their exploits and experiences happened to someone. Fighter pilot Hap is a name change, and Dr. A. F. Fritchen is very real. Fictional characters include:

William Bryte Booker and Donna Farley
Nathan Berry, Bobbie Kuhn, and Ann Schmitt
Barry Maskoviely Menchnikov
Billy Bob Jackson and his many girl friends.
The Chans, father and son

My gratitude is extended to the Yuen family and the kindness shown me throughout the years.

—c o lamp

1

INTRODUCTION

The jubilant cries of the Japanese invaders blended with the terrified screams of Chinese women and children. It was a slaughter beyond imagination. Nanking fell to the Japanese on 13 December 1937 and during the next three months the invaders unleashed ferocity unrivaled since ancient days. They took no prisoners. Surrendering troops were bayoneted, beheaded or machine-gunned. The Japanese rabble engaged in an unbelievable bloodbath. Of the estimated 600,000 citizens and soldiers, the number slaughtered would eventually exceed more than 369,000. 80,000 women were raped and the entire sorry episode would become known as, "The Rape of Nanking." Hearing the news over their radios, Americans were shocked and appalled for fifteen minutes. There were no on-the-spot reporters to bring them grisly accounts of unbelievable atrocities. Disbelief grew on exponential disbelief. Isolationism heightened. Who wanted to get involved with yellow barbarians slaughtering each other? Weren't there enough growing problems in Europe, the former home of most Americans?

China had not moved far from the feudal system. Warlords controlled vast areas by fear and intimidation, collecting tribute from the peasants. Following the death of Sun Yat-sen, it fell to Chiang Kai-shek, head of the Kuomintang, the Nationalist Party, to unify the warlords under his leadership.

General Joseph Stilwell was military attaché at the American embassy in Nanking from 1935 to 1939, and knew all about the atrocities. Fluent in Chinese and Japanese, Stilwell briefed his superiors. President Roosevelt again sent him to China in 1942. Stilwell became Chief of Staff for Chiang Kai-shek, in time was also in charge of the China-Burma-India Theater, and served as Deputy Allied Supreme Commander. As Deputy Supreme Commander, he was in charge of General Gifford who commanded the 11th Army Group, but as Operations Commander of the Northern Combat Area Command, Gifford was Stilwell's superior. They argued about seniority incessantly. It became a common practice for each to work around the other, a practice that became contagious for most officers. When Claire Chennault arrived, he frequently went around Stilwell, directly to Chiang Kai-shek.

"Vinegar Joe" Stilwell was not known for his tact. He and Chiang hated each other. Madame Chiang spent a great deal of time soothing out-of-control tempers. Chiang would not commit troops beyond China. He feared the Communists would take over China. Stilwell considered Chiang totally inept as a general. The US routinely denied foreign aid. Eventually, in October of 1944, Roosevelt recalled Vinegar Joe.

Chiang had no air force of consequence. The only air force of value existed in Canton, under the control of General Chen Tsi-tong. One evening Tsi-tong called all his pilots together and gave a patriotic speech. At the end, he asked his men, "All of you who are loyal to me, stand up." Every pilot rose to his feet.

The next morning, led by a Colonel, every pilot flew to Chiang Kai-shek. A young agent, Cheuk Sung-hai, barely five feet tall accomplished this coup by professing her love for the Colonel. Now Chiang Kai-shek had an air force.

Following the Rape of Nanking in 1937, Chiang's government withdrew to Hankow. In mid 1938 when Hankow became threatened, he withdrew to Chungking. With superior air power, the Japanese invaders moved forward.

Sometime between December 23, 1940 and April of 1941, "to prevent the surrender of China," President Roosevelt, the master of euphemism, signed an executive order allowing officers to resign their commissions to form a volunteer unit of pilots in China. Among those who volunteered to join General Claire Chennault where such outstanding aviators as David "Tex" Hill, Edward Rector, Frank Schiel, Robert "Snuffy" Smith and Fritz Wolf. Salaries were $500 to $700 per month, at a time when Iowa farm hands earned $20 per month plus room and board. In addition, members of the American Volunteer Group were offered $500 for every enemy plane destroyed in the air or on the ground. Pilots arrived from other branches of the military, lured in a clandestine manner. It is clear that President Roosevelt might have been impeached for violation of the 1937 neutrality act.

The AVG soon acquired planes, P-40s purchased by China from the British, less than remarkable aircraft, but planes in which Chennault had a great deal of faith. Early AVG volunteers looked down their noses at the P-40. Seeing the RAF flying Brewsters, they became disgruntled, called the P-40 "Inferior," and urged General Chennault to trade a squadron of P-40s for a squadron of Brewsters. Chennault scheduled a dogfight at Toungoo, Burma. He selected Squadron leader Lt. Jack Brandt to fly the Brewster. Chennault picked Erik Shilling to fly the P-40. They came over Kyedan at 10,000 feet. In his book, *Destiny: a Flying Tiger's Rendezvous with Fate,* Shilling remembered:

> "Each time at the top of the turn with the Brewster below, I would pull back hard on the stick, doing a one quarter turn spin cutting across the circle, gaining a little each time.
>
> When I finally locked onto his tail, Brandt in a desperate attempt to dislodge me, dropped his gear and his flap, hoping I would overrun him. I saw his flaps as they started down, so I pulled back on the stick instead of the power. I was able to conserve energy by gaining altitude, and at the same time losing speed, I stayed behind him. When he finally decided what he was going to do next, I dove back down on his tail. There was no doubt in my mind that I won fair and square with no mistake on Brandt's part. I'm certain the P-40 was the better airplane"
>
> In a later writing, remembering that contest, Brandt wrote, "How I wish I could have swapped my aircraft for yours."

Chennault knew what a P-40 could do. Although it did not have the maneuverability of a Japanese Zero, it could maintain a high-speed dive, that if followed by a Zero, the Zero would likely have its wings ripped off. Chennault coached his pilots to dive at the enemy from on high, fire a burst at the target, pass under the plane, and make a speedy getaway. "Come back from another direction, from above, with the sun at your back and fire another burst." He repeated his instructions in a nutshell. "DIVE, SQUIRT, PASS, RUN." The AVG was combat ready by late autumn.

With the US entry into the war after Pearl Harbor, Chennault dispatched two squadrons to Kunming. Two days later, ten Japanese bombers approached, their pilots expecting to bomb at their leisure, unaware they had been tracked. Up came Chennault's fighters, promptly shot down four bombers with three probables, while the rest fled. Ed Rector went after a crippled Jap bomber but Ed ran out of gas and crash-landed. It took him a week of walking to cover the mere fifty miles of mountainous terrain back to the base. Someone said, "They didn't try to bomb Kunming for a long time."

Careful records maintained, with pilots sometimes credited with a fractional one-quarter or one-third of a kill, sharing the $500 bonus, all paid by China through the Central Aircraft Manufacturing Company. When asked if he collected the bonus due, Tex Hill later replied, "Yeah. Every penny." Records show he collected a bonus of $5625. which represented eleven and one-fourth planes destroyed. Six pilots collected a bonus of more than $5000. R.H. Neale scored the highest with a $7,776.18 bonus for close computation of 15.55836 enemy aircraft destroyed. Somewhat less than 16, it is unknown how they computed that sum. Not exactly low man, Erik Shilling of the famed dogfight over Kyedan, claimed $375 for ¾ of a kill.

Often a pilot flew three missions in a day. It made the enemy think the AVC had an endless number of planes.

Broadcasting on shortwave radio from Shanghai, propagandist Tokyo Rose attempted to demoralize American flyers. "Greetings, you American bandits of the Flying Tigers, and especially you young American kids of the USAAF who have come to take their place. The invincible Japanese Air Force will utterly destroy you on your first day of activation—the fourth of July—your Independence Day!"

"We will not wait till the 4th. We'll hit them on the 3rd!" vowed General Chennault on hearing the broadcast. That is precisely what the young American kids did. Flying their P-40 Warhawks, 29 rookie fighter pilots ripped into a force of 48 Zeroes over Kweilin, chopping down 34 enemy aircraft without loss, on their first day in combat—a full day before the 23rd Fighter Group officially came into being. Tokyo Rose did not broadcast the following day.

In the five months following the attack on Pearl Harbor, the Flying Tigers shot down 300 Japanese planes and lost 12.

The AVC disbanded in Kunming on July 4, 1942, deactivated to form the CATF, the China Air Task Force. Chennault submitted a bill for planes destroyed by 67 of his Flying Tigers to Central Aircraft for $146, 999.87, a bill for 294 planes.

How did the well-paid pilots send money home? How much was lost on poker and riotous living? It would have made an interesting story of prudence and folly.

Following dissolution and reorganization, R. Rasmussen, who had been in Administration Ground Support with the AVG, approached the adjutant in Kunming, intent on banking $5000. Said the adjutant, "You have only been in the Air Corps one month. I can't take the money."

Chinese on the ground became accustomed to seeing Japanese planes go down in flames and exclaimed, "Fei hu" (Flying tiger.) However, it was the eye and teeth of a tiger shark, which adorned the Flying Tigers' P-40s.

From 1942 to 1945, the Tigers flew out of 93 Chinese air bases, which needed to be constructed. Thousands of workers laboriously built each runway by hand, often over rice paddies. First, the paddy was drained. For a base, large stones, some a big as a man's head, were placed in neat rows. These rocks were carried from a riverbed, perhaps one or two miles distant. A mortar consisting of mud and water, called slurry, was poured over them. Then came a layer of leveling small rocks, but there were only a few small rocks available. Hundreds of women with hammers sat and pounded large rocks into small rocks. Another layer of mud slurry cemented the small stones, followed by a coat of sand. A compactor, a rolling cylinder weighing 1000 pounds, was pulled back and forth by "dozens of Coolies," and now planes were ready to land.

The 90,000 workers who built one base earned a daily pay of twenty cents and a bowl of rice.

The Flying Tigers did not stand guard, did not build, did not carry, did not cook, did not clean. The AVG set the tone for those who followed. All the Chinese asked of the Americans was—"Fly and kill Japs."

2

DOROTHY YUEN

A baby girl was born in New York City on July 30, 1922 to a headstrong Chinese father and a headstrong Swedish mother. According to ancient Chinese tradition, Sandow Yuen had the prerogative of naming his daughter. When he named her Edith, his wife remembered that Edith Tong was his old girlfriend, a woman his family had arranged for him to marry. Enraged, Lillian added a couple names of her own: Dorothy Lillian. She refused to call her daughter Edith except when totally frustrated and she temporarily forgot. "Edith Dorothy Lillian Yuen, you get in here!"

As the family grew to include Jack, Edna, and Gloria, priorities altered and Sandow abandoned his studies at Columbia University and became a taxi driver and cook. One day when he came home, his long lean face appeared grave. He spread his hands. "I must return to China. Uncle is stealing my factory."

Sandow decided to take Jack and Edna with him.

"When will you send for us?" Dorothy asked. "Will it be long?"

"Who knows how long it takes a bluebird to reach the highest branch of a cherry tree? The rewards for your patience will be great."

With Sandow away, lack of money became a problem. Lillian found employment as a maid for motion picture actress Alice Brady and delighted in the high fashion hats, gowns, and jewelry the actress gave her.

Her husband wrote that he had succeeded in getting control of King Chung Engineering Company and now his wicked uncle received pay commensurate with his work. Within a year, a bluebird reached the highest branch of a cherry tree and Sandow sent for the rest of the family. An excited Dorothy knew she would never forget June 21, 1934, the day they boarded the bus for California, the first leg of their trip to the Orient.

Reunited in Shanghai, the family moved into a house near the end of Scott Road. As the years passed, in the summer of 1937, their father worried that their home would no longer be safe. The Japanese sector bristled with soldiers. "The

Japanese have moved more warships into the bay. We have to move to the Inter-national Settlement. I can't see the Japanese starting a war with the British and the French." The family made repeated trips moving belongings to the new loca-tion. "We have to be out of here by Friday the thirteenth."

By the end of Thursday, they had moved into their new home in the British sector. Dorothy knew her father was superstitious and 13 represented the worst of days. As he predicted, the next day the Japanese overran the area surrounding their old home. The Japanese battleship *Idzumo* moved up the Wangpoo River, anchored opposite the settlement, and lobbed shells in the hills beyond, attempt-ing to knock out the Shanghai-Hanchow Railway..

In their new home, on Saturday morning, August 14, 1937, Lillian donned her Alice Brady hat and announced, "I'm going to the American Consulate." She turned to Dorothy. "I want you to come along."

A representative at the Consulate advised, "You ought to return to the United States."

Outside, the streets were congested. Thousands poured into the city. Farmers brought their possessions. One carried a trussed-up squealing pig. Cars inched ahead bumper to bumper in the narrow street. Their rickshaw driver halted, blocked by a coolie carrying a crate of ducks. They shouted insults at each other. Tooting horns blotted out the rumble of distant guns. Planes in dogfights buzzed and churned overhead. A Chinese pilot in a Northrup bomber headed for the battleship *Idzumo*. Japanese fighters plunged at him, guns hammering. The engine of the Northrup stopped, sputtered and caught. Two Chinese fighters arrived to help. The Bomber pilot attempted to return to the Hungjao airdrome. Suddenly he released two bombs. They came whistling down in the plaza.

Dorothy's ears rang from the explosion. Now she heard the screams of the wounded and dying. Glass shattered and windows from the hotel started falling. A woman ran past, a shard of glass protruding from her back. Dorothy saw a detached leg. She stepped on a severed hand and fell. Her mother yanked her to her feet. She saw a clump of raw quivering flesh. Two men were naked, clothes stripped away by the concussion. Dorothy ran past a car. The driver sat rigid, his blackened hands clutching the wheel, his face charred, as flames from his burning clothes licked up around his ears.

A car upset and the gas tank exploded. Another car crashed into a building. Flame seared their lungs. They couldn't speak. Dorothy pulled her mother along. Lillian pulled Dorothy along. At last, Lillian managed, "Are you all right?"

"Yes." Gasping for breath, lungs seared, Dorothy found it difficult to talk.

"Don't look back," Lillian warned.

Dorothy looked back in time to see an escaped hog chomping on the battered body of a baby. A man hit at it with a stick and the hog clamped its jaws tighter and ran off shaking the baby like a rag doll.

Before they reached home, Lillian warned, "Now don't you frighten the other children with what you saw. My God! Bombed by one of our own! We have to get the hell out of this wretched country."

"Mother, you lost your Alice Brady hat!"

Lillian's hand went up. "I guess I did."

The death count went from 2000 to 2500. The Chinese government, "Regretted."

"The factory is lost," her father reported. "The Japs took over the entire Old Chinese city, South Station, and Nantao. I barely made it to the French sector."

"We're getting out of here," Lillian said with determination

Sandow remonstrated and pleaded. He did not want the family to leave. In the days that followed, he and Lillian argued incessantly. Beaten, Sandow finally sagged into a chair. Tears welled in his eyes.

"What are you going to do, father?"

"Chiang has asked all overseas students to volunteer for service. He offered us commissions. Some of the workmen at my factory said they will volunteer if I can be their commanding officer."

Her father was staying behind. Now Dorothy wept.

On August 2lst, 1937, eight days after losing their old house, Lillian and the children gathered on the dock and waited for an American destroyer. The destroyer transported them to the *President Hoover* and three days later Lillian and the four children were in Manila. Now began the dreary procedure of finding living quarters.

Dorothy enhanced her art of persuasion as she observed Lillian obtain housing from the American Red Cross, using bluff, bluster, cajolery, and sometimes a hint of deception to upgrade their quarters. At length the Red Cross relegated them to a cabin near the famed Wak-Wak Club. A violent hurricane bent palm trees to the earth and blew off thatched roofs of nearby cabins. Happy to have survived, they sloshed to the Wak-Wak club for safety and later a farmer took them into the city.

Lillian surged past secretaries directly into the office of the executive officer and waved an impertinent finger in his face. "Listen we've stayed in your fleabag hotels. We have rolled your bandages while the upper-crust women sat on their asses. You shuttled us out to the country where the kids would have drowned if it hadn't been for the folks at the Wak-Wak club. There is water in our cabin three feet deep."

She hesitated, glaring. "I still don't think I have your attention," she shouted. Bending forward, she reached out and swept everything off his desk. Papers, a glass holder for pencils, a flower-filled vase, a portable typewriter and a telephone crashed to the floor. "We're Americans! All of us were born in New York. Now I'm more that fed up with your gahdamned prejudice and it you don't get off your ass I'm going to call President Roosevelt."

Dorothy and Edna stood with mouths agape. They had never seen their mother like this.

"Yes, Ma'am. Yes, Ma'am," the harried Red Cross executive kept saying.

At length he placed them in a nice hotel, but there was still that prejudice. The hotel catered to Chinese.

Letters arrived from Dorothy's father. Appointed a full colonel in Chiang's army, he wanted them to return to Canton.

Dorothy and Lillian argued for days about going home to New York or going to their father. "A family should stay together," Dorothy insisted.

Lillian sniffed. "You and your father always were thick as thieves."

They left the Philippines on February 3rd, 1938 and landed at Shanghai. Their home in the British sector stood vacant but their furniture was intact in the servant's quarters. The mansion was too exorbitant, Lillian decided, and the same day they found a smaller house at 1412 Yu Yuen Road near Jessfield Park. They did not know they would spend sixteen months here before they ventured inland to be with Colonel Yuen.

One day Lillian announced, "I'm going inland to meet with your father. Then we're going home to the States."

On her return, Lillian seemed to be more at peace. She said, "One day soon, we are going to live with your father."

Dorothy asked, "When are we going to Canton?"

Lillian replied, "The situation in Canton needs clarification."

Clarification happened on October 21, 1938 when Canton fell to the invaders.

Soon a letter arrived from Colonel Yuen saying, "It is safe in Kukong. I want you to come here."

"No," Lillian objected. "I do not want to find myself in the middle of a retreating army."

In the International Settlement, the British complained about increased Japanese "Cheekiness." Taxi drivers would sometimes spirit their fares into the Japanese section, probably to claim a reward.

Jack reported, "Every time one British officer takes a cab he draws his pistol and points it at the head of the driver."

Things continued at an impasse until soon after American Independence Day, when their father's letter warned, "It is no longer safe for you in the International Settlement. I am sending a steward to guide you."

One day a jittery nervous little man appeared. "I am Ah-Chen," he said, bowing. "Your father has sent me to guide you inland."

"Are you an officer?" Jack blurted.

"No, my name is Ah-chen," the man answered, accenting the first syllable.

Dorothy guessed otherwise. The Japs would like better than getting their hands on the family of a Chinese Colonel.

Ah-chen helped them pack a bit of furniture, bedding and canned goods for the boat trip to Swatow. On arrival, they saw the city was planning for a siege. Barricades and barbed wire entanglements were everywhere.

"We can't stay here," Ah-chen said nervously. "Too dangerous."

By now, he spoke only to Dorothy because Lillian knew no Chinese. Her mother became increasingly irritated. "Where are we going now?"

"Upriver, as soon as we can get a boat."

Ten miles upstream at Chaoan, Ah-chen found a hotel and left.

"Where is he going now?"

"To see if the truck has arrived at Liu-huang to meet us. Ah-chen will be back in three days."

The hotel room was hot. Everyone felt clammy. Finally, they managed to sleep.

Dorothy wakened to screaming and shouting. A truck meshed its gears, tires squealed. It meant only one thing. Enemy! Dorothy rang for the room boy.

Ah-lau appeared, looking tense and worried. "The Japs have landed at Swatow."

Dorothy spread a map. "We are on the way to Kukong. My father is a Colonel in the army. He will find a job for you. Will you come with us?"

"Yes, Big Miss."

"What is the quickest way out of town?"

"The river."

Ah-lau, the room boy ran off and returned disappointed. "No boats. The army took all the boats to transport the wounded."

"Well, they have to let us on," Lillian said.

Gathering up their things, they hurried to the river. Lillian attempted to board a junk. The officer could not understand English when she told him her husband was a Colonel. Dorothy handed her a picture of her father who looked a great deal like Chiang Kai-shek. Behind her back, Lillian furtively waved for the children to come aboard. She kept shouting, "Look at the picture!"

Finally an officer appeared. "What's the delay?" He looked at the picture. "We can't hurt a white woman," he said and muttered something about Chiang Kai-shek.

The junk began to move under the power of eight pole-men, four on each side. Wounded men lying on the deck moaned and sobbed. The family found a place below deck.

In the early light of dawn, Japanese pilots located the sampans and junks that crowded the river. Ignoring the large Red Cross emblems painted on the sides and deck, enemy planes made a big *meow* as they came diving down, guns spitting. Splinters from the timbers fell on their heads. "I'm going on deck," Jack said. The others followed.

Now bombers arrived to blow sampans out of the water. Lillian saw a disabled man drowning, leaped in, and held his head above water. They hauled both aboard. The officer threw two dead bodies into the water. Dorothy explained, "He says the boat is so heavy we might sink. We need to lighten the load any way we can."

Another terrifying raid started midday and continued. The junk pulled into a harbor of sorts.

"Jack Yuen. Jack Yuen," a voice shouted.

"How died you find us?" Jack asked Ah-chen.

"Easy. I kept asking for a boat with foreigners aboard. They directed me here."

Ah-Chen—now Captain Chen—remained with them as they continued upstream. "One of your father's trucks will meet us."

When they arrived at the appointed place, there was no truck. "The Japanese have destroyed all the bridges," Captain Chen reported. "We will have to walk."

Along a road congested with troops, soldiers approached Lillian and touched her arm or her dress. She was the first blonde haired white woman they had ever seen and they touched her for luck. Some of them thought she was an angel. Lillian appreciated the gesture and never discouraged them. This was nothing new. It happened to her all time and left a sobering impression. Where bombs destroyed bridges, they waded streams. They sloshed through waist deep rice paddies. Lillian and Dorothy became sick and feverish. Edna became extremely ill.

Lillian fainted often during the ensuing days. Frequently strafed, they fell to the earth, fingers digging into the soil. Mosquitoes found them prime targets. Captain Chen left a message at every village they passed. Feet bloodied and swollen, they reached the bombed out town of Hsingning where only steel reinforced buildings remained. A four story hotel, with the lower two floors bombed out, offered sanctuary. They were barely able to drag themselves to the fourth floor.

The next day the manager arrived to warn them of a raid. If people suffered injury in his hotel during a raid, he would be charged.

Lillian refused to leave. "I'm sick. I have two sick kids. I'm not leaving. We will lock the door from the inside. You can say you thought we were gone."

Always in the middle of a shouting match, Dorothy wished she had escaped illness like Jack and Gloria who experienced no ill effect from drinking polluted water.

They worried that the next bomb would reduce the upper floors to rubble. Edna muttered, "I don't care. I want to die."

An insistent rapping startled them. "Don't answer it. It's the police."

Jack went to the door and listened. "Yuen family? Is the Yuen family here?"

"It's father," he shouted.

"It wasn't the Colonel. It was his servant, but the Colonel stood a few paces behind him.

"Daddy. Daddy," Dorothy cried, eyes blurred with tears. "I'm so glad to see you."

"Sandow," Lillian managed as she staggered toward him. "You're a sight for sore eyes."

Colonel Yen smiled. "This is a day for sending up rockets."

The servant carried Lillian and Edna to the panel truck. Along the way, soldiers would swarm over the Diamond-T truck like ants. "It's too dangerous refusing them a ride," explained Colonel Yuen.

Dorothy asked, "Why do so many soldiers carry puppies in their arms?"

"They are fond of dogs," said her father. "When things get tough, they eat them."

Eventually the Diamond-T halted in front of hut with a thatched roof and mud floor.

"This is our house?" Lillian objected. "In the states pigs live better than this."

"It's temporary, honey," said the Colonel.

In a couple weeks the carpenters who had come from Shanghai and were part of her father's unit had built a new house, located more than an hour's drive north of Kukong. The main room had the shape of a pentagon. Two small bedrooms were located in the rear, one for parents, and one for children. Beds for the children were hinged to the walls, and folded out the way during the day. Aspects of pride included a thatched roof and a plank floor. Lillian made Dorothy scrub the floor on her hands and knees daily.

Is this any way to treat the daughter of Colonel Sandow Yuen who is in charge of all the mechanized equipment in Kwangtung Province?

Her father commanded a fleet of trucks designed to repair and fabricate spare parts for mechanized equipment. The army could not afford to lose equipment. The Japanese knew the value of these mobile units and they were prime targets.

Mother found comfort in the house and remarked, "Too bad we'll have to burn it if there is a breakthrough. She enjoyed sending the children to a nearby stream to fetch water.

With Sandow's transfer to headquarters, he frequently received an invitation to a party for high-ranking officials. Lillian attended twice, could understand no Chinese, and refused to accompany her husband. Colonel Yuen selected Dorothy to go in her place.

The moment they arrived, Dorothy observed a young woman wearing an eye-catching red and gold cheongsam, a form-fitting gown with a tall collar. Stunning, she looked like a motion picture star, even though she stood barely five feet tall. Darker than most Chinese, her ebony curls framed a tiny oval face. Plucked eyebrows arched over dancing eyes, and smiles came easily to her red splash of a mouth.

"Don't stare," her father warned. "That's Cheuk Sung-hai."

When men entered the room, they focused on her at once. Their eyes followed Cheuk Sung-hai whenever she moved. After dinner, officers crowded around her. She paid almost no attention to the women. Nevertheless, Sandow introduced Dorothy.

"Miss Cheuk. This is my daughter Dorothy from New York."

"America," Miss Cheuk exclaimed. "Then you speak English. I am happy you are here."

"Yes, I speak English," Dorothy said, reverting to her favorite language.

"Well, I do not, but I have a sister who does," Miss Cheuk she said, speaking in Cantonese. She turned to an aide. "Have Connie come here, please."

Connie appeared as ordered and Miss Cheuk said, "Here is a chance to practice your English."

Connie liked Dorothy and invited her to spend the night. On her second visit, Dorothy again met Cheuk Sung-hai.

"I've been watching you," Cheuk said. "You have a fantastic future ahead of you. You are delightfully tall. My sister says you speak English with excellence. However, your Cantonese is that of a child."

Ashamed, Dorothy stared at her feet.

"Modesty becomes you," said Miss Cheuk "Men like modest women. I will come right to the point. How would you like to come to Chungking with me? Many important things are happening at our new capitol. Connie mentioned that you are unemployed. I am sure we can find something suitable to your talents. I understand you spent a year in the Philippines."

Taken aback, Dorothy's eyes widened in surprise, she managed, "I-I will need to obtain permission from my father."

"Of course. Have him see me," she said curtly. She hesitated. "You are so wonderfully tall. Sometimes obvious things are the most difficult to see."

Colonel Yuen met with Miss Cheuk, and returned well pleased. "The only expense will be your ticket to Chunking. With the war on, many have abandoned celebrating Chiao Nu Chieh."

Her father was speaking of the festival of the double sevens held the seventh day of the seventh month where girls displayed their skills at cooking, sewing and housekeeping. "Because you have no interest in marriage, it seems prudent for you to learn other skills. You can do that in Chunking. Miss Cheuk has powerful connections."

Dorothy remembered that she and her father had talked many times of the celebration of the double sevens and it was unnecessary for him to point out that she would soon be eighteen.

Before the day of departure, Connie had taken pains to inform Dorothy that her sister was also known as Mrs. Wu.

In their first class stateroom on the train, Dorothy apparently put on a worried frown. "Don't worry," said Miss Cheuk. "We will find you a fascinating job in Chungking."

Dorothy clung to the word "fascinating." It certainly beat scrubbing the plank floor on hands and knees.

Miss Cheuk talked incessantly. "When we reach Kweilin, we will be met by an Air Force Colonel who is in love with me. Gloriously in love with me."

Dorothy nearly volunteered, "Mr. Wu?" but was immediately glad she did not.

"Because of me—the Colonel's love for me, Chiang Kai-shek now has an air force."

Miss Cheuk—Mrs. Wu—chatted on, explaining how the Generalissimo only had a couple derelict planes, how the real air force was located in Canton under the control of General Chen Tsi-tong. "One night he made a patriotic speech and asked all the men loyal to him to stand up. Every man stood up. The very next morning they all flew away to Chiang Kai-shek, led by my darling Colonel at my request, the darling panda."

When they reached Kweilin, an Air Force Colonel met them and Dorothy could see how much he loved Miss Cheuk. He obviously wanted to embrace Miss Cheuk but because Dorothy and a manservant Ah-Fong were present, he did not. All the way to the hotel Dorothy felt increasingly awkward. It didn't help when she called Miss Cheuk, "Mrs. Wu."

On the second day Mrs. Wu explained, "There's been a change of plans. The Colonel is taking me to the airport. I'll meet you in Chungking."

The Colonel wept, tears streaming down his face. His heart had been broken. Mrs. Wu had informed him she could no longer return his love. The distraught Colonel had mutinied against his general. A Southerner, he was now downgraded to unimportant duties. Now, even Mrs. Wu had left him. He had no face to save.

Dorothy and Ah-Fong left for Chungking by bus. When Dorothy lived in Shanghai, Chungking was, "that place on the other end of the Yangtze." Ah-Fong explained that the city is, "a place where the Ancients are alive," his way of saying that civilization had not yet come to Chungking. Residents lived as they had for centuries. Ah-Fong graphically described the treacherous roads down the mountains leading to the ancient city gate. "Seventy-two turns."

By the time they reached the ancient city gate, Dorothy had swallowed seventy-two screams as the bus crazily tipped from side to side. Almost oblivious to the scenery, she did not appreciate the lush blanket of orange, banana and evergreen trees that clung to the hillsides. She looked forward to seeing roses that bloomed every day of the year in the salubrious sunlight.

Gun emplacements surrounded the city and soldiers were everywhere. Crowded with humanity, the bus slowed for two men carry a pig trussed on a rod between them. Dorothy observed coolies who carried cages of chickens. A yoked man labored along a drainage ditch. With a deft movement of one hand he raised a basket of eggs just enough to clear the head of a girl who squatted to relieve herself.

"The city has grown from two hundred thousand to a million," Ah-Fong said.

"I am glad you know the way," Dorothy said. "I would be lost here."

The stench was overpowering. Chungking was a city of filth, scattered, stacked and floating. Unbathed humanity added an offensive goat smell, enough to insure total nausea, but vomiting would as the philosopher explained, "been too pale a protest."

They found a rickshaw for Dorothy and their things, and Ah-Fong trotted happily alongside, glad he did not need to tote anything. Mrs. Wu was home and greeted Dorothy warmly. "I'm so glad you are here."

Dorothy expected a mansion but saw only two rooms. Ah-Fong disappeared to his quarters at the back.

"I have arranged a dinner party for some important guests," Mrs. Wu said. "You will be going with us."

Presently four men arrived and Mrs. Wu made introductions. "This is General Lee."

General Lee drew himself erect and spoke in Mandarin. When Mrs. Wu mentioned that she was seeking a job for Dorothy his face took on a curious expression. They group immediately set out for the restaurant.

Bombed out frequently, the restaurant had been rebuilt many times. Because boards were impossible to find, carpenters split, halved, and quartered bamboo to form boards. They lashed flattened bamboo boards together with threads of bamboo because there were no nails.

As she entered the restaurant, Dorothy saw a familiar face. "Amoy Chang," she cried. "What are you doing here in Chungking?"

His face clouded. "Do you know who you are with?" he whispered anxiously. He made a little bow.

"No. It's nice …"

"Shhh. It is nice to see you," he said with the formality of his British tutor.

Whatever was wrong with him? "Give me your address," Dorothy said realizing he did not wish to talk. "I'll visit you."

"No. I'll come to you. Tomorrow night."

With Dorothy lingering, Mrs. Wu delayed seating. "Who was that young man?" she demanded.

"Just I boy I met when I first came to China. I am so surprised to see him again. I'm sorry; I guess I'm not very worldly."

General Lee nodded agreeably. "One should always make time for old friends."

Mrs. Wu laughed off Dorothy's clumsiness and when Dorothy glanced to where Amoy Chang seated himself, she saw he had fled.

Dorothy waited for him to call the next day but he did not. Perhaps it was due to the incessant air raids that sent them scurrying to shelters. She waited impatiently the next day and toward evening heard a timid knock. It was Amoy Chang.

"Let's go for a walk."

"I can't get over seeing you here. I keep remembering how we used to race our ponies on Scott Road."

"Much has happened since we rode our ponies in the Chapei section. Do you know who you were with?"

"Mrs. Wu and General Lee, of course."

"I can see you do not." He raised two fingers as one. General Lee is right next to Dai Nup. Dai Nup is next to Chiang Kai-shek. Nobody sees Dai Nup without going though General Lee. Dorothy, everyone at your table is with Intelligence. Are you involved in spying?"

"Spying? No." Sudden realization cleared her brain and Dorothy knew that Dai Nup was really the fearsome Dai Li, the most notorious agent in the Orient. "*Me a spy?* Don't be silly."

"I am not sure I should talk to you now, but what have I got to loose? I have become involved in the New Life Movement."

When the apartment again hove into view, Amoy said, "I don't know when I will see you again." Then he was gone.

Traffic in Mrs. Wu's apartment remained brisk and men young and old came to seek favors. In China, it is necessary to have someone intercede for you. Mrs. Wu seated herself at a table to receive favor seekers, acting like an empress. If she fluttered her fan, it signaled the interview had ended. Dorothy realized favors always had a price.

Four days passed before she heard the timid knock of Amoy Chang. "What's wrong?" Dorothy asked as soon as it was safe. She had seen his hangdog look.

"Tomorrow I shall be shot for what I have done."

For a moment her breath caught. "Good Heavens! What have you done?"

He hung his head. "It began with the New Life Movement. When I didn't like the way things were going, I wrote a letter critical of my commanding officer and sent it to Madame Chiang. I should have known a mere private could not write to Madame. My letter was intercepted."

"Oh Amoy," Dorothy worried and clutched his arm. "Amoy. I can't bear it."

"If I do not see you by tomorrow at six, I shall be dead. So if I don't see you again, twenty-three skidoo."

"Twenty-three skidoo," Dorothy managed, barely able to speak.

Wracked with worry, her face betrayed her. Mrs. Wu asked several times the next day, "Why are you so gloomy?"

Dorothy could not tell her and said, "It must be the weather."

By five o'clock Dorothy was beside herself. At six a timid knock came. Seeing Amoy, she rushed into his arms. "You're safe! You're safe!"

"I risked coming to tell you I've been given a second chance. Now I must go," he remembered Mrs. Wu's stare when the door opened. "I'll be seeing you." His voice lowered. "Your friend has already seen too much. You cannot contact me. I'll be in touch."

"Who *is* that man?" Mrs. Wu demanded when Dorothy stepped inside.

"Just a friend I knew in Shanghai. He means nothing to me."

Mrs. Wu's head tilted back and she laughed. "I can see that. You do not lie very well."

"I-I have never even *dated* him," Dorothy stammered. Explanations were futile. She decided to change the subject. "When am I going to get a job? It's tiresome just waiting."

"Patience is a great virtue. Patience and a worm will make a silk purse."

The day they went to the Central Bank of China Dorothy expected preferential treatment but her eyes opened in surprise when they were ushered directly into the executive office of the bank manager.

A distinguished man, attired in a western suit, he asked, "Are you enjoying your stay in China?"

"It would be more enjoyable if I had a job."

"Excuse us please," Mrs. Wu said. Outside the office, she made Dorothy realize that their visit had nothing to do with her getting a job.

Mrs. Wu resumed her visit with the manager and when she returned, she said curtly, "What made you think our visit had anything to do with you getting a job?"

Dorothy shrugged sadly, "I don't know. I just thought." The bank manager had acted as if she could do him a big favor.

"Maybe we will see about a job in the time of the full moon."

"Full moon?"

"If you think the bombing has been bad until now, wait for the full moon. It gets much worse."

Between September and March, a London fog blanketed the city but now spring arrived. The result of the fog coated the entire city in a coat of slime.

"We're leaving the City. We're going to San Tung to visit General Yur."

The distant San Tung section provided no military target. The estate of General Yur Ying-kai became a popular meeting place for graduates of the War College. General Yur had distinguished himself at the battle of Nanking and as a result had a stiff knee and a hole in his back over a kidney. "I was saved by an American," he told Dorothy. "He found me unconscious and carried me to safety. I refused to allow the doctors to cut off my leg. Come, I want to introduce you to other officers. Do you dance?"

"Yes."

"Splendid."

Dorothy danced with nearly all the officers as the record player played *La Paloma* and *Green Eyes,* again and again, the only tunes available.

Dorothy and General Yur got along famously, trading jokes.

"You needn't be so impressed with him," Mrs. Wu said acerbically. "He can barely write. He would not have made it through the War College if young officers hadn't helped him."

Every week they visited Dr. Wong, who treated Mrs. Wu for something. He taught Dorothy Chinese whenever they sat in an air raid shelter. One day in Dr. Wong's office, they met General Chang Kai-min, commanding officers of all gendarmes in China. A pleasant meeting, Dorothy could not have guessed that one day her life would depend on him.

The next generals Dorothy met numbered six, the entire half dozen caged behind prison bars. Dorothy recognized famous generals from their photos. She was as shocked as if she viewed General MacArthur there.

Each of the six begged Mrs. Wu to help them and she promised, "I will see what I can do."

Dorothy could not refrain from asking after they departed, "How can you possibly help them?"

Mrs. Wu's eyes narrowed. "There are ways," she said with a wan smile. "There are ways."

"Why are they in jail?"

"One displeased the Generalissimo. Another burned his retreat before it was time, trapping civilians."

"Ah, he fired the city too soon." Most were southerners and Dorothy realized regional differences still existed. Some of the southern warlords resisted relinquishing their power.

It was all about power. When she thought of Amoy Chang and his warning words, Dorothy worried. *What am I doing here? Have I gotten myself in over my head?*

3

BARRY MASKOVIELYMENCHNIKOV

"Barry Muskrat is the name I go by." The young man spread his hands. "For as long as I can remember."

The recruiter shook his head. "Do you have parents?"

"No."

"Uncles and aunts?"

"Not that I know of. Not here in Cincinnati. Not nowhere."

"Didn't you have another name, when you were born?"

"Sort of."

"Well?"

"It's not something I really remember." He closed his eyes for a long moment and reached for a pencil. "I can write what I remember. I don't think it will help much." In scrawly letters, he wrote Barry Maskovielymenchnikov.

"Are you serious?" The recruiter hesitated when he saw tears forming in the young man's eyes. "Do you know your date of birth?"

"No."

"Where were you born?"

"I don't know."

"How long you been here in Cincinnati?"

"Not quite a year."

"Where were you before that?"

"New York City. More or less. I ran away."

"Commit some crime? Wanted by the police?" The recruiter did not like the name. It looked Russian.

"No, I was in a welfare home—for kids without nothing." That was true, but he had not been in a home for quite some time.

"Do you have a driver's license; social security number?"

"Not really."

"Okay, he's what I'm going to do. I'm going to put you in touch with a social welfare lady—" His hand went up when he saw apprehension and thought the man might bolt. "She is going to pull strings to see if we can find out who you are. If she cannot find out about you, no one can. When she gets a line on something, we will be ready to take you right into the Army Air Corps. However, we have to make sure you are a person first. You go to the address I am writing down and ask for Frances. I will let her know you are coming. If you want in the Air Corps, then do it."

Barry hated going to the welfare office. The lure dangled by the recruiter, actually two lures, finding out who he was, and getting into the Air Corps overcame his deep-seated apprehension.

Frances wore a man's shirt—he could tell the way it buttoned—and blue denim jeans. She had a boyish haircut. When she said, "I'll give it to you straight. If you don't give me a lot of bullshit, I won't throw any back at you," he liked her even more.

He forced a grin. It hadn't take her sixteen seconds to read his character. As they talked, she asked a lot of "Why?" questions.

"Why did you leave New York?"

"There was Bull—sort of a tough dude. He didn't like my dice."

"You didn't just run away?"

"How'd you know?"

"What did you do to get even?"

"I got accused for something I didn't do—to him. I had everything figured out to go. Ran in the fake bones, cleaned out some his lieutenants and took it on the lam."

"Now I'm going to gamble on you." Frances elicited his information and placed a long distance call to New York. "Barry Maskovielymenchnikov. You could try to divide the name in half. Maskoviely and Menchnikov. Also, try Barry Muskrat. His current age is somewhere between sixteen and twenty-five, that's my guess. Let me know anything you can find. Anything. He's almost an amnesiac."

To Barry's surprise, she replaced the receiver without waiting for an answer.

"They will send what they have in writing. It might take a week or ten days. Do you have a valid driver's license, social security number, union card?"

"No."

"Have you been working lately?"

"Not much. Off and on. Mostly scratch. It's hard to find work."

"Okay, you look like you can do an honest day's work." A laugh escaped her. "I don't have money to throw around. You will have to pay for the phone calls. This was only the first. I will get you some part time jobs. Do you remember any of the schools you attended?"

"Not really. I tried to forget."

"That was my guess. Sit down in the waiting room. I'll get back to you."

Frances placed a local call to the recruiter. "Fred. What kind of curve are you throwing me? This ABC Maskovielymenchnikov XYZ? You know he is a drop-out. I am not going to run up a big bill so you can tell him goodbye. Are you short of quota?" She forced a laugh.

"I think I can sneak him through. If he washes out after basic …"

"Fair enough. I have been talking with him. Put down he wants to go to gunnery school."

"All right."

In the days that followed, Barry worked at odd jobs, paid for the phone call and put some cash "in her bank," for additional calls. One afternoon Frances closed the door and said, "What do you know about poker? I want you to teach me your game."

God. In poker, she would be dynamite. "It's the cards, money, odds, and mental," he said, and paused a moment before he continued. "In an honest game, if two men are fifty-fifty partners without the rest knowing, each guy has twice the chance of winning—half as much, if they split. In a five or six handed game that may not be crucial, but they could still sort of gang up on the same guy. But in a three handed game, that sucker is dead, unless he's luckier than Luciano."

Frances did not smile. "If Luciano is in the game, someone might also get dead."

She knows. "Hey, I have a new game. It's complicated. It came to the Apple with a tourist from Dallas, I hear. Every player is dealt two cards only, held close to the vest. They bet to open. Then there is a three-card throw-down, face up. Each of the players uses the three cards up to make a hand. Time to ante. Now the next card is also dealt on the table face-up for all to play. Time to ante. Finally, a fifth card is dealt face up on the table for those who are still playing. It is a tough game. With six players, only seventeen cards are in play. You bet the odds."

"What do you call it?"

"Texas Throwdown. Sometimes I call it Texas Hoe-down. There is a problem with it. Nobody wants to play it."

"I can see why." Frances removed a deck from a drawer, dealt him two cards. She placed three on the desk face up. "Like this?"

He nodded, and she slowly dealt another, and another. "Like I said, Ma'am, it's not easy to learn. Maybe it's a good way to burn. But, if you are holding two hearts and the dealer turns up two hearts in the three card throwdown, you have a fifty percent chance of drawing that fifth heart on the fourth or fifth table card."

"Ah, better than in stud. They say in five card stud, only a sucker would try to fill and inside straight."

"Yeah. You win a couple hands and nobody wants to play. I guess people aren't use to betting on two cards."

During the following week, subsequent lessons involved dealing, how the dealer could sneak a peak at the top two cards while the other players looked at their cards.

Frances said, "Let me see you try to deal the second card off the deck instead of the top card. Let's see you deal off the bottom."

Frances watched. "Not good enough. My advice is, never try that when you get in the Air Corps. If you think Bull was trouble—" She left it there.

The next day a letter arrived from New York. It contained nothing helpful. "You are a smart kid," Frances said, frowning. "You should have stayed in school."

"There were problems."

"You don't think there will be problems in the Air Corps?"

She thumbed through the letter. "Hey, what's this? It says you came from Trenton, New Jersey."

Mention of Trenton revived a forgotten memory. He spoke without thinking. "Molly Craven. 4578 Washington. No. Turn around the last two numbers. It's 4587. If ever I am lost."

Her pen had moved quickly. "Molly Craven? Where did that come from?"

"I dunno. It just came out. I haven't thought of her since." He halted abruptly. It felt weird. *Why did I say Molly Craven? That was so long ago.*

"How old would she be?"

"Old."

Frances obtained a number from Information. "If we're lucky she might still be there."

She phoned and a woman answered.

"Molly Craven?"

"Yes."

"This is Social Services in Cincinnati. Does the name Maskovielymenchnikov mean anything to you? Or Barry Muskrat?"

"You found little Barry Muskrat!" she cried. "He's alive?"

"Yes, he is in my office. Would you kindly give us some information? He is trying to enlist in the Army Air Corps"

"Little Barry Muskrat? Grown up? Yes, Yes, I still have cards on all the children. If you'll hold a minute."

Molly didn't need a card to remember little Barry. She could still see him tromping around in boots three sizes too large for him. From the day he arrived, he imitated someone. He took a shine to an older boy named Barry. He wanted to be Barry, so they let him be Barry. She located a file card. The boy's given name was Sergeyovitch. She remembered his father, a ruthless villain. He had killed his wife, the boy's mother, and cut up her body, but for some reason decided to burn it instead. The fire killed a crippled old woman in the adjacent apartment. Police killed Barry's wicked father in a shootout. She remembered an officer telling her, "We ought to shoot the kid right now. He will turn out rotten like his father. No damn good. It would prevent future victims and save the state a lot of money."

Molly never believed that for a moment. Not little Barry. He was the sweetest boy. She returned to the phone. *It has to stop here.* "I found my record. What do you need to know?"

"The name of his parents to start."

"Sergeyovitch Maskovielymenchnikov," she announced, using the lad's given name as the name for his father. Continuing her false presentation, "It says he was a businessman. His wife, Alexis was a teacher. He liked driving fast cars. That's what killed him. Both of Barry's parents lost their lives in an auto accident." She decided to make Barry's date of birth a couple years younger. "He was born on July 4, 1925," she said pulling a date out of thin air. "May I speak to little Barry?"

"Yes you may. But he not little any more, he is a strapping young man, nice looking I must say." Frances extended the phone.

Barry accepted it said, "Hello" and in a moment exclaimed, "Is that really you, Aunt Molly?"

They talked a couple minutes and Frances took the phone. "He called you Aunt Molly? Are you his aunt?"

"I—I was for a while." Molly hesitated. "By marriage. That's how I happened to get Barry. After about two years, they located his grandmother in New York.

They sent him there. She died soon after. I tried to get Barry again but it was too late."

"I'll tell him to write you," Frances said, replacing the phone. She spoke to Barry. "Well, you have a living relative. An aunt. A real live aunt. Now when you get into the Air Corps, you be sure to list her as your closest—and only—living relative. You want to put her down as a beneficiary on your government insurance."

"You don't think I'm coming back?"

"Not if you deal cards like I saw yesterday."

In Trenton, Molly Craven picked up an old pen and filled out a new info card with the information she had just given to the caseworker in Cincinnati. Feeling pleased that she had given Barry a new history; she tossed the old card into the fire. There was little chance anyone would come looking, but someone had phoned, had she not? The cop was nuts. Like father, like son? The son would grow up to be a criminal? That was pure crap. Not little Barry.

Almost as pleased, social worker Frances proceeded to complete paperwork for a social security card, a social welfare registration, and an application for a union card. "It's going to take a few days to get all the records. In the mean time, I landed you a job with a trucking company. If you keep your nose clean, one of the bosses can fix you up with a temporary driver's license. If you can drive. So—Barry Maskovielymenchnikov, how does it feel to be a real person?"

"Royal flush."

In time, the recruiter looked at a handful of documents young Barry presented and wondered how he would squeeze the name Maskovielymenchnikov into the space allotted. His comment, "Holy shit," or some derivative thereof, found repetition along the line, as Barry went off to basic training. Before long, an Air Corps clerk scribbled "alphabet" above his name. It soon followed that Barry responded at muster to "Alphabet!"

"Yo"

"How's that?"

"Present, sir!"

4

DOROTHY YUEN THREATENED BY MRS. WU.

Without employment and nothing to do in Chungking, Dorothy became restless. The endless hours spent in an air raid shelter depressed her. She demanded of Mrs. Wu, "When am I going to get a job?"

"Soon. I have been talking to General Lee about you."

"I'm getting tired of all this waiting."

"Be patient. Give me some of your pictures so I can present them to General Lee."

"Why does he need my pictures?"

Mrs. Wu did not reply.

They planned another trip to San Tung at the time of the full moon and at dusk, the bombing continued unabated. Eighty Japanese planes kept up a seven-hour round-the-clock marathon that destroyed much of the city. Not long after they arrived at San Tung, a messenger appeared for Mrs. Wu and she became visibly upset. "We were lucky we went to the Intelligence shelter yesterday instead of the public shelter. Something happened with the ventilation there and three thousand people suffocated." She dropped to the sofa, exhausted. "Looting was rampant. Soldiers were cutting off fingers to get rings, hiding jewelry in their leggings, stealing watches. It was terrible."

"They never pay foot soldiers," Dorothy remarked.

"Two were shot. Before we left, I talked to General Lee," Mrs. Wu said, switching to a new topic. "He was interested when I mentioned you had been in the Philippines. Now tell me everything you did in Manila."

Another month went by and this time Mrs. Wu planned to avoid a full moon. At San Tung, General Yur Ying-kai again greeted them warmly.

A messenger came for Mrs. Wu and she said, greatly distressed, "I'm being beckoned. I must go back."

"What happened?" Dorothy asked. *Was beckoned a code word?*

"I can't tell you," Mrs. Wu said, worried.

When she did not return after three days, Dorothy thanked the general and his wife for their hospitality. "I must find out what happened to Mrs. Wu."

"No, Do-yur. It would be wise to stay with us."

"I'm sorry, I must go."

When Dorothy remained adamant, the general threw up his hands. "Go if you must."

When Dorothy arrived in Chungking, she saw Wu's apartment was gone, destroyed by bombs. *Mrs. Wu dead?* Stricken with grief, Dorothy clawed in the rubbish. Neighbors led her away. Dazed, she wandered around until the next air raid. In the Intelligence shelter, two young men known to her only as K.C. and J.B. sat down next to her. They had been frequent visitors to the apartment. They spoke without moving their lips. "Do not react," K.C. warned. "Mrs. Wu has been arrested."

"Why? Where is she?"

"She talked too much. You must check into a hotel."

Dorothy persisted and after the raid, they took her to a compound where she found Mrs. Wu in a bungalow.

"Save your questions," Mrs. Wu said. "I want you to go to the China Bank." She wrote a note for presentation to the manager.

When the bank manager saw the note, more than concern moved into his face. "Give her his," he said nervously and pressed fifty thousand Chinese dollars into Dorothy's hand.

Mrs. Wu accepted the money. "What are you going to do now?"

"I have been invited to stay with General Yur." Dorothy said.

"Good. He owes me a favor. If he asks where I am, tell him that you have not seen me. Do not tell him where I am."

"What shall I say?"

"Tell him I went on an important mission." Her dark eyes pinpointed in anger and met Dorothy's stare. He words came slowly, precisely, and with cold clarity. "Dorothy, if you tell him where I am I will have you killed."

Dorothy froze. "I-I won't tell," she stammered.

Mrs. Wu handed her a few dollars for the trip on the truck to San Tung.

No doubt in Dorothy's mind, she knew Wu could have her killed.

A week later Dorothy decided it was time to return and visit Mrs. Wu. This time a trip to the Bank of China netted sixty thousand dollars. Without thanks, Mrs. Wu said, "Here is someone I want you to meet. This is Su Ling."

After a chat, with a curt nod, Mrs. Wu dismissed the tall young woman and explained. "We sent her to Manila. She made a mess of things and came home in complete disgrace."

Wu's inflection on "She" jarred Dorothy's awareness. *She messed up, but you better not?* It suddenly became clear. From the beginning, Wu had been trying to recruit her for a covert operation in Manila. Dorothy's face betrayed the rebellion rising within her. *I want no part of this. I refuse to be a spy.* Dorothy hastened to leave.

Mrs. Wu shouted after her. "Remember what I said. If you tell General Yur where I am I will have you killed!"

At San Tung, Dorothy worried. To relive the tension, she walked the General's German police dog. Not far from the house, a soldier thrust a note into her hand and ran away. The note from Amoy Chang read, "I want you to know I am leaving Chungking. I do not know if I will ever see you again. Take care of yourself. Twenty-three skidoo."

Dorothy's mind raced. The last time she saw Amoy she had not yet met General Yur and had never been to San Tung. *How could they find me here?* Someone had been watching her!

Within a week, she returned to Mrs. Wu, who ordered her to visit another bank. This time Dorothy obtained another fifty thousand Chinese dollars.

On her return to San Tung, General Yur accosted her. "Do-yur, you lied to me!"

Dorothy shrank as she saw his shaking fist in her face.

"I know she is in custody," Yur shouted. "Why did you lie to me?"

Dorothy swallowed. Tears streamed down her face. "She said if I told you," she choked. "She would have me killed."

"You should have told me."

At length his voice calmed. "She wrote letters to some of my officers, telling them to have nothing to do with you."

"What?"

"She said she picked you off the street, a prostitute. She warned them that if they continued to see you, their careers would be ruined."

No wonder the young men had stopped coming. Now her tears came in a torrent. When her thoughts cleared, she realized Wu had destroyed the world around her in an attempt to retain control over her. Dorothy remembered that Mrs. Wu had been supporting her, but she had to get away.

General Yur saw her turmoil. "What are you going to do now?"

"Send a telegram to my father asking for money so I can go home."

When the money came, Dorothy told the General she wanted to say goodbye to Mrs. Wu.

"I wouldn't," the General advised. "You are asking for trouble."

"I need clearance. I cannot leave the city without documents. I would loose face if I did not at least say goodbye"

General Yur and Choi Kwok-yurn, a young officer accompanied Dorothy to the city. They waited in a restaurant while Dorothy went to visit Mrs. Wu.

"You lied about me," Dorothy asserted. "That was a hateful thing to do. All those terrible letters. I will never forgive you."

"Oh please forgive me," Mrs. Wu begged. "I have been under such a strain. I didn't realize …"

Dorothy cut her off. "I'm leaving!"

"Oh please don't go. You are my only link to the outside. I need you, Dorothy."

"No. I am going home. I'm going to need clearance."

"Well don't expect me to help you."

"I might have known. I will go without your help."

"If you try to leave the city you will be arrested. Remember what I tried to do for you. I gave you a chance to be important."

Important? You deceived me! "Goodbye!"

"No. Don't leave me. I, Madame Wu, forbid it!"

Madame Wu? That title is reserved for Madame Chiang Kai-shek. You are hallucinating.

With no time to lose, Dorothy hurried to the offices of General Chang Kaimin, Commandant of Gendarmes to seek clearance. He listened to her plea and began to write in his renowned calligrapher's hand.

Dorothy rattled on. I did not know Mrs. Wu wanted me for Intelligence work. I am an American. I cannot work for a foreign government."

Chang's hand halted. His head snapped and color drained from his face. "I can not give you clearance. Not if you are working for General Lee! It is not possible."

"But I am NOT working for General Lee." Completely devastated, Dorothy found herself unable to say more.

"You must see General Lee," said General Chang. He wrote directions.

Almost running, she drew up short when an air raid siren shrieked and she sought shelter. *What next?* When the raid ended, she realized she would need a rickshaw.

Intelligence headquarters were located in a huge cave that had more than three hundred steps leading into the interior. A sentry halted her.

Speaking Mandarin, Dorothy said, "I need to see General Lee."

"He will not see you."

"Yes he will."

The sentry shook his head, left, and returned with a Colonel. Dorothy gave him her name and presently she sat before General Lee.

"We are sorry Mrs. Wu has been arrested. Sometimes these things happen."

How well I know. Dorothy nodded. "It is time I went home to my father. I came to obtain clearance. And I would like to have my pictures back."

"Yes, of course," he said pleasantly, and withdrew them from the top drawer. "I never did anything with your photographs. We were aware of the situation with Mrs. Wu." He shrugged and gave Dorothy a note.

At once, she returned to the Commandant of Gendarmes. General Chang read General's Lee's note aloud. "Miss Yuen is an overseas student returning to Kukong. Please extend her every courtesy."

Dorothy hurried to the restaurant where to her surprise General Yur and Choi Kwok-yurn waited at a corner table. "I thought you would be tired of waiting."

"We would have waited longer," said General Yur. "We were making arrangements to smuggle you out of the city."

Dorothy held up her pass. "That will not be necessary."

Before long, Dorothy was on a bus, negotiating the seventy-two hairpin turns, leaving Chungking. The bus halted when night came and Dorothy realized that she had no place to sty. There were only soldiers on the bus. She had another problem. Women never traveled alone. She found a room with five beds, rented all of them, went inside, and closed the door.

In the morning, she again climbed into the bus where an officer saw her frightened look and befriended her. That night, when the bus halted, there were no rooms available and she had to sleep in a bed placed in an open hallway. "Don't worry," said the officer who spoke Cantonese, "I'll keep an eye on you."

In the morning he asked, "Do you have a place to stay when we get to Kweilin?"

"No,"

"I will introduce you to my brother-in law, the tea merchant."

In Kweilin, the tea merchant interceded and she obtained a room at the hotel. Her luck changed once more. In the morning, she learned there would not be another bus for four days. *My money will never last that long!*

"Oh no."

Frequently buses maintained a vacant seat for late-arriving dignitaries. Again, the tea merchant interceded and the man in charge assigned Dorothy to the vacant seat. Feeling relieved, now she thought her money would probably last.

Before they reached Hengyang, sentries halted the bus. "You must transfer to a train."

The rain chuffed through the countryside and halted at three o'clock in the morning.

The tea merchant bowed and asked questions. "I have a friend," he said. "She owns a hotel."

Dorothy did not wish to accompany him. Nor did she wish to stand alone in the country, five miles from nowhere. *It is getting cold.*

At the hotel Dorothy said, "I need a room for myself."

The tea merchant repeated to the clerk, "for herself."

In the morning, the tea merchant appeared and announced. "I purchased a ticket for you to Kukong. I do not go south myself. I must leave you."

Dorothy offered to repay him but he refused.

"In my country a woman alone always pays her own way. Please do not shame me. Allow me to save face."

The tea merchant reluctantly accepted and accompanied her to the station. Ushered to a comfortable stateroom, the conductor pointed to the upper berth. A military man already lounged there. "Oh no, not again."

The conductor found a stateroom with a woman and a child and allowed Dorothy to switch. She arrived in Kukong at the start of an air raid and waited hours for her father. At last, he arrived and she rushed into his arms.

"I am so glad to be home." Dorothy wept.

"Welcome home, Dorothy."

Her mother offered a restrained welcome. Dorothy hung her head. *I disappointed you again.*

Her mother ranted, "When I was sixteen I was on my own. I had a job. Here you come home, nineteen years of age and no job, just a big expense for your father."

Lillian didn't stop. "You impossible child. Are you going to work around here?"

"Yes," Dorothy managed with a squeak.

Her fears that Mrs. Wu would send a hatchet man slowly dissipated The next six months she worked diligently around the home and never once ventured into Kukong. On a day when her father paid his troops, she decided to accompany him.

In a giant arch where two roads intersected in the center of town, Dorothy stepped into the circle of light and came face to face with Intelligence agents J.B. and K.C. Her heart leaped into her throat. "How did you find me?" she blurted.

"We are not looking for you," J.B. said. "Would you like to work for us?"

A deep breath refreshed her lungs. "Work for Intelligence," she gasped. Rising above fear she said, "I am not interested in that kind of work."

"We understand, Do-yur," said J.B.

Dorothy asked, "Is Mrs. Wu still in custody?"

"Yes," KC. said without emotion.

The pair disappeared into the night.

At home in disgrace, Dorothy began a season of discontent. With her siblings in school, only Dorothy heard the scolding of her mother.

If she awakened and found herself in New York, Dorothy realized she would be a dropout. Her education was neglected. *I feel stupid.*

Dorothy confided to her father. "There is nothing as valuable as a good education."

Her father nodded. Presently he said, "A military school has started up across town. I want you to enroll Jack, Gloria, and Edna."

"But not me?"

"Not now."

Dorothy's dream shattered. Tears misted eyes. After what her father had spent on her Chungking fiasco, she dared not ask for more.

"Your mother needs you here," Sandow said. "She is so alone. She needs someone who can speak English. Your mother had so much illness we had to give her dong quei …"

Dong quei is the dark flesh of a black skinned chicken that has white feathers. Dong quei has great medicinal power.

"We took your mother to a mission hospital. A British doctor says she has malaria. I need you to be the lady of the house."

Pursuant to her father's wishes, Dorothy enrolled Jack and Gloria in the military school across town. They had to board there. On weekends, when they came home, Dorothy had to have a supply of washed and ironed clothing ready for them. Edna, who was further along in her studies, enrolled in a nearby school.

No joy in her heart, Dorothy longed for the days of leisure she had known in Chungking. In her position as woman of the house, her father asked her to be with the widow of a Colonel in the Eleventh Repair Factory, who was about to be shot. Calling her a widow was not disrespectful, as her father explained, "It will ease her burden. She has no one."

Dorothy worried that her father might face the same dire consequence. He had appropriated an Army truck used by Ah-Lau to move the family furniture from Hsingning to Kukong.

Dorothy asked her mother to accompany her and they joined a small group of spectators. The convicted Colonel hung his head in shame until he saw his family. He squared his shoulders and raised his eyes in dignity before the blindfold slipped into place. The guns fired and the Colonel's body became limp.

"That will teach him," Dorothy muttered in quiet sarcasm.

One December evening, Sandow came home with exciting news. "Sweetie, the Americans have joined the war."

"Really."

"The British too. They have lost Hong Kong. The Japs have taken over the International Settlement and interned everyone. It is rather stupid of the Japs to attack the United States. Can a stork swallow an eagle?"

"Where was the attack?" Lillian asked.

"Hawaii."

"Stork swallow an eagle," Dorothy repeated. "That is an excellent comparison."

Her father smiled. "I thought so."

Dorothy's letters to friends in the International Settlement went unanswered, except those to Tiger dos Remedios, a Portuguese citizen. He complied with Dorothy's request to send a dictionary. A section of the dictionary arrived periodically in a tightly bound newspaper. As the days passed, Dorothy received everything except section except XYZ. In her spare time, she studied to increase her vocabulary.

Six months passed after the attack on Pearl Harbor and the lives of the Yuen family failed to change in the slightest effect. United States entering the war had no effect in China.

Jack and Gloria arrived home one weekend listless and pale. They had been living on only rice and vegetables. Colonel Yuen ordered dong quei and after contemplation ordered his soldiers to build a seven-room house on the southern edge of Kukong, across the river. This allowed Jack and Gloria to commute, Edna could walk to high school, and best of all, and Lillian need not ride a truck into town to see her doctor for malaria treatment.

The hospital became Lillian's social center and she often spoke of General Pun. Generally know as General Pan, his name in Mandarin; in Cantonese to the delight of Lillian, his name was Pun. Pun had four wives. The older first wife lived directly across the street.

A British nurse complained about Pun's fourth wife. "Last year she was a servant. This year she is a wife. A person doesn't know what to call her."

One day after a relentless air raid, Dorothy stood in Au's store when an excited man ran in with news. "Three of General Pan's wives were killed!"

Her father suggested Dorothy should offer condolences. She immediately dressed in white, the proper attire, and set out on the two-mile walk. She learnt wife four and her child had come to visit wives two and three when the air raid siren squealed. Everyone rushed to the earth covered cave for shelter.

A bruised and battered General Pan mourned. "There wasn't room for everyone. I crawled under a tree. The bomb exploded in the entrance. I was almost buried."

A man ran up, gently carrying a hand. "It landed on my roof."

Not long after Dorothy returned home, a sedan chair carrying Pan arrived and halted across the street at the home of his first wife.

"Serves him right," Lillian said. "He never should have had four wives in the first place."

Another day, on the way to Au's store, a surprising encounter brought a sudden upturn in Dorothy's life.

"Do-yur! Do-yur!"

She turned, saw General Yur, and ran to him. A splendid reunion, she learned that many War College graduates were here in Kukong.

"Yes, among them, Choi, Wong, Ho, and several others."

They talked pleasantly and Dorothy asked, "Did Mrs. Wu have anything to do with your transfer to the South?"

"No," the General replied matter-of-factly, "I did that on my own. I am glad that woman no longer touches my life. She is a bomb with a short fuse."

"Is she still under house arrest?"

"That last I heard."

"I would like to visit her."

"I would not. Loyalty can be overdone. We will talk no more of her. On Saturday night, I want you to come and meet old friends. Say you will come."

"Thank you. I will."

In the weeks that followed General Yur's party, several officers came calling and asked Dorothy to marry them. Choi Kwok-yurn, who with the General had wanted to smuggle her out of Chungking, became the most persistent. Ho Hon-

si became equally persistent. Her frequent talks with Ho caused Dorothy to realize that she did not fit well in any society. In New York, she had been Chinese, a
"Chink." Here in China she was American. "I'm neither carp nor eagle," she
complained.

One Sunday morning, Edna wakened her and said, "Will you come to church
with me?"

"Only if you help me scrub the floor."

"But I will ruin my hands."

"Then I won't go with you."

"Well, all right."

Working on hands and knees, Dorothy said, "Now you know why I hate it
so."

At the Episcopal church Dorothy met May and Marion, Chinese girls who
spoke English with a British accent. A happy meeting, none of them realized that
one day, Dorothy would be responsible for saving their lives.

5

JOE REILLY VOLUNTEERS

Friends teased James and Mary Reilly when baby Joseph arrived twelve years after his brother. "Just trying to stay in practice? What was this, an after-thought?"

Joseph may have been an after-thought but at a young age, he learned responsibility from his New York City firefighter father. From his older siblings Joe learned to be adaptable. His sister married and left home when he was four. City leaders decided to rename streets. The house where Joe was born, 101 West 9th, never moved an inch, and became 14559 19th Avenue, Whitestone, Queens.

Joe attended Flushing High School until he completed eleventh grade. A new school constructed in the district and for his senior year, forced Joe to attend Bayside High, five miles away, a distance too far to walk. Because of his age, Joe could not drive a car; he had to take a bus. This prevented his participation in most school activities.

Following graduation in 1937, Joe began working for Brewster Aircraft Company, manufacturer of the Brewster Buffalo.

Aviation experts complained that the tubby little single engine fighter combined elation with disappointment. The Buffalo was a true anomaly of delightful maneuverability with poor fighter performance. Above 10,000 feet, it labored badly. Once in the cockpit, the pilot had a rather poor view because of his high position on the nose. On take-off, a pilot had to increase the throttle carefully because there was no automatic boost control. The stick had to be pushed forward to get the tail up. The climb was steep, initially 2000 feet per minute, with a maximum speed of 290 mph at l6,500 feet, but the ceiling was only 25,000 feet. The all-up stall occurred at 76 mph and the all-down came in at 67 mph. At landing, the pilot lowered the undercarriage at 95 mph, followed by slow moving flaps at 90. The approach speed of 80 mph gave a reasonable view, but required almost full backward elevator trim.

Sent to Belgium, Holland, Great Britain and Finland, the Buffalo had great success when Finland battled the Russia. Later, experts claimed it was due to the climate and the inferior aircraft and training of the Russians.

The British found the 5820-pound Buffalo to be an inferior fighter and shipped most of them to Asia where they could almost match the maneuverability of a Japanese Zeke. However, Zekes badly outclassed Buffalos in performance and firepower. In a dogfight, the initiative went to the Zeke, with Buffalo having little hope of besting the Japanese Zeke. Pilots complained of the Brewster's lack of armor plate. They hated not having an indicator to tell them when to change from one wing tank to another. At an altitude over 10,000 feet, the engine tired. The landing gear failed half the time and the tail wheel wobbled. Loss of the Brewster demanded replacements in every theater.

The September 1, 1939 German invasion of Poland brought an increased demand for the Brewster Buffalo. One day a girl named Josephine had come to visit a teammate. She brought a friend and Joseph became acquainted with Kathleen. The meeting blossomed into more. Before the Japanese attack on Pearl Harbor, the couple had decided to marry. They were married Saturday, February 14, 1942 and Joe won a Valentine for life. The war had been on for only a couple months and rationing and other restrictions were not yet in place. War was far away, across an ocean to the East, across an ocean to the West.

A baby arrived January 22, 1943. They named her Kathleen. With a wife and a family, there were really no thoughts of not going off to war. It was an unavoidable reality.

Joe's two brothers were mail carriers. Jim was already in the service, working on homing stations. Under strict orders, he dared not use the word "radar."

Tom Reilly was nearly 38 when he and Joe went to volunteer in March of 1943. "You're too old for the Navy and the Marines," said the recruiter. "You're on the border line. You can stay home if you want to."

The Reilly brothers selected the Army Air Corps and were off to Miami Beach for basic training, then to Scott Field near St Louis for radio school. By early autumn, the pair had graduated. They told Tom, "You're too old to fly," and he transferred to Madison, Wisconsin. Joe enrolled in gunnery school at Tyndall Air Base in Florida. Then it was off to Greenville, South Carolina where crews assembled for reassignment.

6

WILLIAM BRYTE BOOKER SENTENCED TO MILITARY

The Judge leaned forward with interest. His glare softened. The scruffy young man before him again admitted borrowing the police car. As the youth spoke with reasoned eloquence, the prosecutor's jaw dropped slack. When the young man finished, the prosecutor leaped to his feet. Before he could again demand a prison term, the Judge raised a silencing palm that wilted him into his seat.

"Induction into the Armed Forces in lieu of a jail sentence." The Judge's gavel banged down. "So ordered."

At once, the Chief of Police led the bedraggled youth away. "You got lucky," he muttered, staring inclemently at William Bryte Booker.

The clerk stared at the Judge in amazement.

"Say it," said the Judge.

"Nothing to say," replied his clerk. "Just surprised, that's all."

"Did you see his fact sheet?" the Judge said defensively. "His mother died when he was four. His father is a drunk … used to beat the kid. No wonder he ran away with the circus instead of going to high school."

"It wasn't a circus," objected the clerk. "It was a carnival. That's probably where he learned his thievery."

"And a lot of other things," intoned the Judge. "Did you notice his personality? He could sell refrigerators to Eskimos and swimsuits in a nunnery."

"Nuns are what he needed." The clerk remembered being rapped on the knuckles with a ruler. "Just the same, I predict William Bryte Booker is going to give the Army a lot of trouble."

"Maybe you noticed that I remanded him to custody until his enlistment is accepted and he is shipped off to basic training. The military might do him some good." The Judge suspected that without a high school education Booker would run into an economic stone wall. He would become disenchanted with his prospects and that spelled trouble. The Army was probably his last chance. There, his lack of schooling would not matter as much. If the Army needed a specialist, they trained him.

"Stealing a police car," the clerk said in wonderment.

"Joyriding," corrected the Judge. "He phoned the police as soon as he got to his destination and told them where to pick up the car."

"He is no longer a juvenile delinquent. He's a big boy now."

Seated in his cell that reeked of stale urine and Lysol, Booker did not need a lesson in reality. The surliness he felt at his earlier scrapes with the law and his last apprehension dissipated. He remembered the first couple of times he'd been jailed, when he was just a kid, and not a grown man of eighteen, he'd sat brooding, thinking of how to escape, thinking of John Dillinger, thinking how Dillinger always managed to escape. He admired how Dillinger carved a pistol out of a piece of wood, painted it with shoe polish and frightened a jailer into releasing him. For a time the newspapers called him John "Wooden Gun" Dillinger. They named Dillinger, "Public Enemy Number One." With a relentless Melvin Purvis on his trail, the FBI had been able to bring him down. Now Booker thought of his own opportunity. The corners of his mouth lifted into a grin. His lips moved. "Just like I expected. The Judge bought it." He had concentrated on extenuating circumstance to explain why he had borrowed the officer's car, how the councilman would have been disappointed if he had not appeared on time. He had sprinkled in "Your Honor," with regularity and suggested that the Army prided itself in being punctual.

The Judge had said, "I'm impressed with your presentation. Some lawyers are not as effective. So you dropped out of school during ninth grade."

"Yes, Your Honor. I did retreat from conventional education but I have continued to study. I read often. Right now I'm studying economics."

Booker was street smart—alley smart. When his father drank up his paycheck instead of buying food, he foraged in dumpsters behind grocery stores. Malnutrition, more than genetics resulted in Booker standing five feet six inches, "lean as a whip and twice as wiry." Fine boned, his gentle sensitive features gave the impression he was still a little boy. Little old ladies would want to help him across the street.

Booker graduated from scavenging for food behind the supermarket to stocking shelves inside. He had lied about his age to obtain the job. The manager frequently stood at the door at the end of the day and stared at employees to prevent them from stealing merchandise. Booker had never stuffed things in his pockets. That would have been stupid. Now and then, he would filch a candy bar, eat it in the rest room and flush the wrapper. Some nights he would scrounge boxes behind the store, a quick search, inasmuch as he knew precisely which box to examine and what he would find inside.

He heard stirring in the jail office and guessed it was the Night Watch. Booker called out, "Hey, come in here."

The deputy entered the cell area, a large shambling man with a full oval face, a broad flat brow and thick lips. A fleshy man, he had muscular arms and heavy thighs. Booker remembered that a few years back the deputy played high school football.

"What do you want? You had supper!"

"I was thinking," Booker posed slowly. "I could use that little radio I saw on the desk out there. I need to listen to quiz programs to brush up my smarts, so that I will be valuable to the Army."

"You can't have it. It belongs to the Chief."

"I know that," Booker lied. He thought it belonged to the deputy. "Those quiz programs—like Doctor I.Q. aren't just entertainment. If I apply myself I could soon make corporal."

"Not a good idea. I better not."

"Sure. Do it. It's what the Judge would have wanted. But you have tell the Chief the first time you see him, that you let me use his radio during the night and you returned it to his desk when you went off watch. Just suggest that the Judge would want me to get some training while I wait. The Chief should tell the Judge that he is giving me opportunity to study. You want to let the Chief take all the credit. It is a smart move to make the boss look good." Booker knew that the Chief could wheel in any time and they didn't need to get caught. The deputy had turned and reappeared radio in hand. "Now you get back on your bunk."

"I'm not going to try to make a break."

The deputy unlocked the cell. "I'll put the radio down. Okay, now you can come and get it. Be sure you don't break it."

Booker held up the plug and frowned.

"The outlet is over here," the deputy explained. "Let's see if the cord will reach. Stick it out through the bars. Ah, plenty long." He pushed the plug into the outlet. "Now don't break it."

"I won't. I'll be real careful."

The deputy went out to make his nightly rounds and Booker listened to his favorite stations—KDKA, WHO, WGN, KCMO, WCCO, WOW, WKBW, WNAX, and KMA. He listened to newscasts, but what he really wanted to hear was big band music—Glenn Miller, Harry James, Kay Kyser, Les Brown, Woody Herman, Tommy Dorsey, Jimmy Dorsey, and even some lesser lights.

Booker loved dancing. He had practiced with fat German ladies who lifted him off his feet during a circle two stop when a person had no idea with whom he'd be dancing. Partners changed six times, like when the bandleader said, "Promenade. Promenade." A moment later, "Dance with the lady behind you." That took care of the two-step and there was always someone willing to waltz. For jive and jitterbug, he had studied diagrams printed in the Sunday paper and eventually found Claris, a fat girl willing to learn with him. Only a little time passed before he was the most popular young man on the floor.

Dancing had its limitations, he realized. Many young girls enjoyed dancing. That's as far as it went. None of them wanted to date him, not with his reputation. None of them feared his sexual advances. Some of the girls engaged in fast and lose talk but that was as far as it went. Only one girl in the high school got pregnant—the Carlson girl—and she promptly dropped out of school and married the father-to-be. Then there was Lila Green, who had a dozen boyfriends. He had overhead Doc the Druggist say that she was responsible for ruining more young men around town …

Why am I looking back? Booker realized what had hit him. He was homesick, homesick for the town and he had not even left. It was not like when he had run off with the carnival. He and another young man who worked in the supermarket had been eating Tokay grapes. The produce manager instantly spotted the naked stems and warned them to stop. One day Booker lifted a small cluster out of a full box and the produce manager spoke to the store manager, a conversation Booker overheard from his crouching position on the other side of the display.

"I got Booker dead to rights. He's stealing grapes and eating them. I don't know what he did with the stems. He is too smart for his own good."

"I think he's been stealing right along. I didn't know he had a record till after I hired him. I will talk to the police; see what would be the best way to handle it without store involvement. Maybe I'll just fire him when he picks up his check."

Apparently, the manager had not resolved what he would do. Booker guessed he would set a bigger more important trap. When he received his paycheck Saturday night, he smiled broadly and exclaimed, "Well, I'll see you tomorrow."

They next day he was miles away with the carnival. He wondered if anyone had ever bothered to look for him.

Got to look forward. Got to make plans.

From now on, the Air Corps would make plans for him. He *had* to accept that.

A few days later, the Chief opened the cell door and said, "Time for you to enlist. My deputy will be driving you to the county seat. You will sit in front. There will be a hard case in the back seat. Don't mess with him. He will be serving prison time. That's all you need to know."

"Yes, sir."

Booker seated himself up front and watched them put the cuffs on a man, his hands stretched out in front of him. A chain extended from each cuff to a heavy ring installed on the floor behind the front seat. They locked the chain. This prevented any cuffed prisoner from reaching up and strangling the driver. A leg iron and a chain attached to the same ring.

"I guess you don't want him to get away," Booker remarked when the deputy slid behind the wheel.

The sheriff bent down to the open window with final instructions, "If he starts jawboning back there, stop the car and gag him."

"Right, Sir."

No one spoke, with Booker in a contemplative mood. He needed a plan, a strategy to avoid the infantry. He had learned at Frank's pool hall that a foot soldier had to dig his own foxhole. All a soldier had to eat was what he carried with him. In a foxhole, one dared not look out. If he did, he would have his head shot off. He had to piss and shit in the same foxhole. *I don't want to sleep in a shitty foxhole.*

After seven miles, the deputy turned to Booker. "What's the worse thing you could do right now?"

"Escape."

"You got that right."

Presently the deputy said, "You won't be leaving for induction today. You will sign up. Then you will be coming home. They will probably call you up in a week." He hesitated. "In case I'm not the one who drives you then, let me give you some free advice. Never volunteer."

"Where did you learn that?"

"From my younger brother. He's in the Marines."

"I didn't know you had a younger brother."

"Well, I do."

A voice from the back seat rasped, "Hey, these cuffs are starting to hurt."

"Shut up back there or I'll give you something that really hurts."

At the county seat, not far from the courthouse, the deputy swung into an empty parking spot.

When automotive travel was new, businessmen welcomed the east coast to west coast highway running directly through town. It would be good for business. When travelers started rushing through, businessmen installed street lights every two blocks to slow traffic.

The deputy unlocked the chains binding the prisoner to the ring in on the back seat floor. The prisoner stepped out. The had not walked more than a few steps when a large semi-truck came roaring down the highway, having cleared three green lights, the driver going for four. A young mother pushed a baby buggy, her head down, and apparently unaware of the speeding truck.

"Look out!" shouted the deputy.

The truck swerved just in time.

The prisoner shoved the deputy as he was taking a step and he sprawled, hitting the curb. The prisoner broke into a run, diagonally across the street. Booker took after him, closed the distance, and flung himself forward in a flying tackle. Caught by his legs, the prisoner fell. He rolled and began beating Booker about the head and face.

The deputy caught up with them, raised his Billy club and brought it down sharply over the prisoner's ear. The whap sounded like a club hitting a melon. Instantly the prisoner went limp.

The deputy caught his breath. "You all right, Booker?"

He reached for his handkerchief.

"I think he's still breathing," said the deputy. "I hit him pretty hard—never used my left hand before."

"Hunh?"

"I fell against the curb. I think my right arm is busted."

Two local police officers appeared and hauled away the prisoner who had not yet gained consciousness. "We'll check him tomorrow and see if he has a headache."

"Stay here by the car," the deputy ordered Booker before he followed the officers to clear paperwork. "I'll be right back. Then you can drive me to St. Anthony Hospital."

The deputy returned in a few minutes. "I thought I told you never to volunteer. You are some dumb kid."

Booker almost replied, but prudently withheld his objection.

When the deputy disembarked, he said, "Now, while I get my arm fixed, you can drive down to the recruiter. It you want to act really stupid you can take off for Denver."

Booker grinned. "I won't."

"Won't drive to the recruiter, or won't go to Denver?" the deputy asked and shambled toward the hospital entrance.

Booker located the recruiting office and when he parked, he noticed a cop car turned off a block away. *Hah. They followed me.*

He strode in with energy and announced, "I'm William Bryte Booker and I'm here to enlist in the U S Army Air Corps."

"So you want to be a pilot?"

"No, sir. Mechanic."

"Graduated from high school?"

"Not quite. Eleventh," Booker lied. If he admitted he had not finished, they would not bother to check. He had stretched the truth more than two years. A little lie was always better than a big stupid easily-checked falsehood.

"Okay, what experience have you had as a mechanic?"

"I worked on everything from a Model-T to a V-8. Some diesel. Caterpillars. Small aircraft …" He didn't mention merry-go-rounds and Ferris wheels. He had learned a great deal about engines while traveling with the Tall Tim Thomas Bombshell Shows. Something at the carney was always breaking down. A quick study, after they noticed his ability, they called Booker to see if he could make things run. As the war progressed, three separate shows had consolidated into one. He had worked some on Tall Tim's single engine plane. His boss had flown around to do advance legwork.

All right," said the recruiter. "Suppose your car or plane won't start. What is the logical cause?"

"Out of gas."

"Fuel gauge shows half full? Then what?"

"Water in the gas tank. Maybe somebody poured in something. Same thing could happen after a short start. When the carburetor runs dry of gas and takes on water, the engine sputters and dies."

"You'll do. Sign here. You are in the Air Corps."

As he departed, out of the corner of his eye, Booker noticed the recruiter reached for his phone. Not long after he returned to the St. Anthony Hospital, a squad car happened to pass. He decided the deputy was smarter than he had estimated.

After Booker spent an endless hour in the waiting room, inhaling the remnants of antiseptic, bactericide and human dissipation, the deputy appeared, arm in a cast. "Did you make it into the Army?"

"No."

"What? Why not? What did you do now?"

"Joined the Air Corps."

When they arrived at home, the Chief feigned indignation. He had phoned the police at the county seat and learned the details. "Holy mackerel. What is this world coming to when a deputy allows a prisoner to drive? Maybe I better take custody of the desperado." He turned to Booker. "I hear you tackled the hard case. He's going to remember you."

"Well, when he gets out," Booker said. "He can come looking for me in the Air Corps."

"You don't say. Just because of what you did, don't expect that entitles you to any special favors."

"No, sir."

Nevertheless the Chief brought in the radio and remarked, "You can keep it till the Air Corps calls you. We generally have a coffee pot on. You'll have to wash your own cup."

"I do have a favor," Booker said and rolled on before the Chief could object. "Would you tell the judge what I did?"

"I might," said the Chief. "If I see him."

Booker's attention drifted from Willie Swartz's clarinet an octave over the saxes in the Glenn Miller band as he reviewed the afternoon. Repeatedly he asked himself, "Why did I do that?" At length he decided he had tackled the crook because the deputy had treated him right and brought in the radio. The Chief had treated him right too.

I'm in the Air Corps now. Let the Glory Boys do the fighting. Let the fighter pilots risk their lives with dogfights. Let the bombardiers try to fly through a wall of flak. I'm going to sit back at the base, snug as a bug, and if Glory Boys come back and want to relax, maybe I can teach them a little carney poker. Sam, a pitchman, and Lady Sarina taught me to read people. They said a person could still win if he had a bad run of cards. People are predictable.

The Chief's wife had won prizes at the county fair with her baked goods. Now every night a piece of pie appeared on Booker's tray. He knew that wouldn't last. Five days later, he sat in a dusty once-retired railroad coach, headed for his first Air Corps base.

7

NATHAN LEIGHTON BERRY JOINS THE AIR CORPS

At Woodrow Wilson High School, Physiology-3 (pre-med) was available only during the second semester of the senior year. Extremely popular, classes assembled for both a morning and an afternoon session. Liberal and forward-looking for a conservative community, the Principal responded to what he viewed as potential trouble in Milwaukee's "German" community where sex education was not generously welcomed by Catholic and Lutheran parents. With a war on, and a predicted shortage of doctors and nurses, Physiology-3 had become tentatively acceptable. Nevertheless, the Principal required parental permission for any student to enroll in the class.

NOTICE

Psychology-3 is a pre-medical introductory course involving all aspects of the human anatomy, its variations and functions, including reproduction. The studies are graphically portrayed.

PERMISSION

As parent (s) of _____ we hereby give our permission for our son/daughter to enroll in this course.

Dated _____   _____

(Signature of parent or parents)

Instructor Karen Harris, a no-nonsense mother of three, held a masters degree and was more acceptable than a male instructor might have been. During the first week in April, her class prepared to study sperm microscopically. She had cleared the program with administration and previously obtained permission from student Nathan Berry to donate a sample. With a Petrie dish properly heated to 98 degrees, Nathan retired to the privacy of a supply closet. In a moment he reappeared and handed Mrs. Harris the sample. Class clowns could not resist comments.

"I'll bet ol' Berry does that all the time."

"Imagine playing with your dong to ding an A."

Pretending to be oblivious to the comments, Mrs. Harris prepared the slides for viewing. No one could have predicted the reaction.

"I don't see any movement."

"Me either."

Mrs. Harris bent down and viewed a slide. Her head came up. "Mister Berry, it appears that you are sterile."

"Old Berry is shooting blanks!"

"His gun isn't loaded."

"What do you know about that!"

"Who would like to volunteer to donate a second sample?" Mrs. Harris approached the loudmouth who talked about shooting blanks, and raised her eyebrows.

The student, reddened, squirmed a bit, and realized if he refused, he would be labeled as a dud, a less than gutless wonder.

He muttered a reluctant, "Okay."

With a second Petrie dish properly warmed, he withdrew to the supply closet and closed the door. Everyone focused on the door and after several long moments, Mrs. Harris knocked. "Are you all right in there?"

"Yeah," was the less than enthusiastic reply. Several minutes passed before the now very red-faced student appeared. The fact that his sperm was motile gave him no comfort.

"Ann, how many sperm are required creating a pregnancy?"

"Just one."

"Correct. How is conception accomplished?"

"The sperm burrows into the ovum, fertilizing it."

At the end of the class period, Mrs. Harris addressed a somewhat crestfallen Nathan Berry. "Would you please remain a few minutes?"

When the others had gone she said, "I am sorry you were embarrassed. However, knowledge can be a powerful thing. Were you ever in an accident? Alternatively, had mumps? Anything that might have caused—?"

"No—"

"It is possible there might be some underlying etiology. I suggest you consult with your physician. I understand you have been accepted into the Army Air Corps."

"Yes, I have."

Sensing his reluctance, she continued, "Think about seeing your doctor." She added as an afterthought, "The reason I didn't ask the others not to talk about you is that it would only fan the flames and make them gossip more. It might be wise to inform your parents. We wouldn't want them to be surprised."

"No, we sure wouldn't."

"Again, I'm sorry—"

"Nothing for you to be sorry about."

She sensed his helplessness but could not leave it there. "If your parents want me to know the outcome, I would be interested. I have never had this happen before."

As Nathan trudged to his next class he told himself, "At least I have something to report at dinner."

In the corridor, at three o'clock that afternoon, he heard the first mention of, "Eunuch." By four o'clock, he already had a new nickname: The Eunuch.

At home, discussion began long before the evening meal, and at dinner, his father decided he would not consult the family physician. "You're going to a urologist. We might as well start with a specialist."

The next morning Ann Schmitt paused to commiserate. "Hi. That was a tough knock you had in physiology yesterday."

"Yeah," he said glumly.

"Grandma always says, if one door is slammed in your face another will open."

"I doubt it."

Ann saw Bobbie Kuhn approaching and quickly said, "Excuse me. I need to speak to Bobbie."

"And I need to speak with you," Bobbie insisted. Her voice lowered to a whisper. "Are you thinking what I think you're thinking?"

"I don't know," Ann Schmitt said innocently. "How could I know what you are thinking?"

"You know. What we talked about it the other day. It could be that a plum has dropped into our lap. Certainly the risk is cut to practically zero."

"Well, his reputation is excellent. He is a straight arrow."

"Yeah, boy scout personified." That *is* good."

Ann and Bobbie had been classmates since kindergarten, best friends. About to graduate and enter careers as nurses, they had been talking about, just talking about, mind you, the possibility of engaging in sexual activity, "to round out their education." In order to accomplish this romantic result they decided to embark on an exciting and perilous plan that might possibly bring and end to their friendship. Neither of them lingered long on the rupture of a relationship. Without making mention of it, each decided with emphasis, "I don't want to be second."

The next meeting with Nathan Berry, carefully planned by Ann and Bobbie, also appeared to be accidental.

"Hi. Nice to see you. You're looking brighter."

"Life goes on," Nathan said.

"Doesn't it? Are you involved with anyone?"

"Do you have a girl friend?" Bobbie prompted.

"Nah," he said. "I'm not that lucky."

"Me either. A boyfriend, I mean."

"Or me. We're not close to anyone. Boyfriends, I mean."

"Well, see you." They tried to appear relaxed as they hurried down the hall.

"Why did you break it off?" Ann Schmitt scolded as they rounded a corner.

"He has enough to think about," Bobbie said. "For now. If he doesn't see something coming, his light has gone out. Tonight we plan more strategy."

The planned strategy went into effect the next day at another casual not-so-accidental meeting. They delivered their well-rehearsed speeches with rapidity. .

"Here's the deal."

"You're going into the Air Corps."

"We're going to be nurses."

"We want to make it sexually before we go into training."

"With someone nice."

"Everybody's doing it—the guys going into service—with their girlfriends."

"You're going to war. You might not come back."

"This is a once in a lifetime deal."

"You are special."

"Really special."

"There is no one we know like you."

"Special."

"There are a thousand men around here—mostly married—who would drop everything if they could make it with twins."

"We know we are not exactly twins."

"But we're willing to act like twins."

"You will believe we are twins."

"It is positively something that will only happen once in your lifetime."

"You will remember it till the day you day you die."

Nathan swallowed and managed to speak. "The two of you? Both at once? Wow!"

He noticed he stood talking to no one. The girls had turned and walked away.

"That's the bait," Bobbie said. "We won't say anything more."

"Yeah, we will make him come to us."

"If he doesn't—?"

"He's a dead stick," Ann asserted. "All the way up to his ears."

Nathan stared at their backs, remembering how they looked. Ann was tall with deep blue eyes, eyes always dancing with mirth. Broad shouldered, full figured, one day she would be a grandmother of ample proportions. Bobbie, shorter, more delicate, had hair of the darkest brown, like her eyes. She probably longed for larger breasts. She, too, had a sharp sense of humor.

Nathan sniffed in wonderment, almost in disbelief. Yet he knew what he had heard. There was a possibility the girls were joking but he did not think they were joking. All day he could think of little else. Trying to sleep that night, he kept remembering, "Once in a lifetime."

"Twice could kill a guy," he mumbled. "Twins. Geeze!"

Negotiations were less than romantic. The night—the Senior Banquet—would be ideal. Parents wouldn't think anything of it if one of the girls spent a night with the other. They planned to split the cost of the motel three ways. Three musketeers. One for all. All for one. They would not sit together at the banquet. Nathan parked where the girls could get into his car after the banquet unnoticed. They would have overnight bags. The girls would be responsible for reserving the motel a day in advance. They spent a great deal of time planning and giggling, before they decided to be Myrtle French and Gertrude Solo.

At the last minute, as the banquet began, the girls seated themselves side by side. "People would have thought it strange if we weren't," Bobbie said.

They arrived at Nathan's car as planned. He put car in gear and they headed for the motel. "So far so good." He realized his comment was lame, inane. He expected chatter from the "twins" but they remained strangely silent. He decided to wait for them to talk.

At length Ann said, "It was totally pertinent—what the speakers said. 'Dare to be different. Take a chance. Go for it.' I thought they were speaking to us."

"That's the way I felt," Ann said. 'You can't grab the brass ring unless you get on the merry-go-round. You only pass this way once.' It was almost prophetic."

Nathan Berry decided to speak. "'Don't short-change yourself.' That speaker was talking to me." Feeling nervous, he patted the prophylactics in the front pants pocket. Bobbie clutched a purse that also contained prophylactics.

At the motel, Nathan parked and the girls strolled to the office to obtain room keys. The retrieved their overnight bags and entered the room that had two full sized beds. 'Myrtle' and 'Gertrude' plunked into chairs and Nathan seated himself on the edge of the bed he had selected for himself.

Bobbie spoke an unbidden thought. "This isn't any fun."

For a long moment, they sat in silence, staring at each other. Finally, Ann and Bobbie spoke in unison. "Well?"

Another long silence followed before Nathan reached into a canvas bag that looked like an ordinary grocery bag with handles. He brought out a bottle of bourbon. "I lifted it from Dad. It will take off the edge." He knew he had to limit his intake to one drink, not more than two, if he expected to perform. He learnt that from people at Frank's Pool hall. He brought out picnic cups, said, "Disposable," and poured generous drinks for the girls, a small drink for himself.

"To us."

"To us."

He brought out an Agfa camera equipped with flash. He had started the roll at the banquet.

"I don't want my picture taken," Bobbie said sharply.

"It won't be like that," he said. "Just the two of you girls together. It won't mean anything to anyone else. If you get tired of it as a memory you can dump it in the trash."

"Well, all right," Bobbie agreed.

"How about one of each of us with you?" Ann suggested. "That would be another secret memory."

Bobbie snapped the photo of Nathan with Ann and said, "I'll pass on having my picture taken with you."

"So you don't want to know me," he taunted.

"I'll know you soon enough," Bobbie said and giggled. "Okay, I'll take a picture of you alone." She glanced at the room keys on the table. For a fleeting instant, she wished they were car keys. She felt like grabbing the car keys and making a break. Then the liquor heated her insides and she said, "Say cheese."

In the years ahead, Nathan would learn that when some women giggled, laughed or grinned, it was to cover the fact that they were frightened. He poured another round of drinks, large ones for the girls.

Ann raised her paper cup. "I, for one, am not going to let the banquet speaker's advice go to waste."

The room had warmed and Nathan started to disrobe. *I need to be the man.* He stopped when down to his shorts. The girls halted at bras and panties.

"We did agree to leave the lights on—for science. But not so bright?" He extinguished the overhead light, leaving a single floor lamp illuminated.

Ann removed her clothing and flopped down on the bed. Bobbie quickly pulled off her things and lay face down. Nathan dropped his shorts and slid between them.

Bobbie turned her head toward Ann. "We haven't kissed since sixth grade—at camp. The play—remember? I feel like doing it again in this play."

"Sure," Ann agreed. "Why don't we make it a three way kiss? "We're all in your play."

There was barely enough space for faces but they managed a three way kiss.

"Like three musketeers. One for all and all for one, Nathan said. "Ann, you're beautiful." He spoke to Bobbie, "You're beautiful too."

Bobbie regarded him. "With all that between your legs isn't it awkward?"

"Not really. About twice a year, my shorts bind and I sit on a testicle. That really hurts. I usually yelp."

"Aren't you supposed to be—" Bobbie hesitated. "Erect?"

"Probably. I guess I'm overwhelmed."

Ann chortled. Don't be afraid. "C'mere."

He slipped on a prophylactic and decided to have sex with Ann. He immediately encountered resistance. He pushed hard and flexed his hips. He thought he felt something tear. His penis felt suddenly warm. He and Ann made the discovery at the same time.

"Oh hell," he muttered. "The rubber broke."

Ann tossed back her head and prodigious laughter rippled forth. "That's what happened on Mom and Dad's wedding night. It's the reason I am here."

"How did you find that out?" Bobbie asked. "Certainly they didn't tell you."

"Grandmother did. It part of our family history."

The word wedding suddenly paralyzed Bobbie's thoughts. *You are giving up too much for science.* The word science opened a door. "I hope I don't have that problem. Can I look at you?" Bobbie asked, "I mean really look? For science?"

"Why not? I'm not much to look at."

"That's the way I feel too," Bobbie said, as she reached up and turned on the other reading lamp.

She viewed him critically. Now she decided to feel him. She touched him timidly at first, checking the foreskin that moved. Her hand gently closed over his testicles. "May I put on the new rubber?"

"Why not? If you do it scientifically." *She's rather brave.*

Presently they discovered the same resistance. "You're dry," he observed.

"Did anyone remember to bring Vaseline?"

"No."

They settled for Ann's cold cream. Sex with Bobbie was about the same as with Ann. Bobbie felt tense. It did not feel pleasant.

"My turn again," Ann said after a couple minutes and held her arms outstretched. "I suppose there is a book telling how twins are supposed to make this interesting. I'm not going to Paris to get a book."

Ann held him close. He was soon out of breath, spent.

"Well, we did it," Ann said.

"Yeah, we did it."

"Yeah," Bobbie said. "Personally I think sex is over-rated."

"It's supposed to get better over time."

"You were both wonderful," he said. It worked. In spite of our inhibitions."

"I was totally uninhibited," Ann said.

Nathan rose, walked to the bathroom, returned and plunked down on the other bed. In minutes, he was fast asleep.

"For your scientific record," Ann said. "This proves that females are the stronger sexually. I was just getting started. What about you?"

"Just getting started," Bobbie affirmed and buried her face. *Screw science.*

Nathan had fallen asleep earlier than usual and awakened early. In the gloom, he saw Ann in the next bed, facing him, with Bobbie cuddling Ann, also facing him. He rose, peaked through a crack in the blinds to welcome a new day. He walked to the bathroom, urinated and flushed the toilet. He feared the noise would waken the girls but neither awakened.

He lifted the cover over Ann, noticed she had donned pajamas, and slid in beside her. His breath on her face or his hand on her abdomen wakened her.

"Good morning," he said cheerfully.

"Hi," Ann said sleepily. "What time is it?"

"I think it is time for your turn again."

"For sure."

He helped her out of her pajamas. Their movement snapped Bobbie awake. He reached across to her and began massaging her buttocks. He had been reading everything he could get his hands on and learned a gentle buttock massage would be a great turn-on. Last evening, he hadn't followed any of his recently acquired information..

Bobbie reacted. "Don't you touch me."

It's not working! Maybe it was the pajamas. He hand moved beneath the layer of cloth to cup the soft worm skin of her buttocks. He heard her sniffing and sobbing.

"You're crying!"

"Am not!"

"You are too crying," Ann said.

"I'm not." Bobbie snuffled.

"It's okay, Bobbie," Nathan consoled. "It's okay. I'm here." He continued his gentle massage. He moved to kiss her. His parallel position over Ann altered to become an X. Bobbie turned away and now his fingers slid into pubic hair.

She murmured, "Don't."

Nathan fumbled open the buttons of her jacket and his part of the X figure over Ann became a +. He swirled his tongue around her Bobbie's nipples. He used his nose as an encouraging prod and her mouth opened. The tips of their tongues met tentatively and withdrew.

"You're so good," he whispered. He rocked up and away from Ann and came down parallel on Bobbie. "You're so good," he sang in her ear. His tongue found hers.

My mouth must taste terrible. Bobbie ignored the unbidden thought and began responding, animated, returning motion for motion, emitting sounds now, ohs followed by ahs, then little squeals of delight.

Ann stared in wonderment at the sounds and action.

"Oh my! Oh, God," Bobbie exclaimed in delight. "Wowie!" She gasped for breath. "I—I just had an ORGASM!"

"Well, I didn't," Ann muttered irritably. "It's my turn now."

Nathan couldn't continue He was totally limp. He remembered a time-honored line and admitted ruefully, "This dog won't hunt."

Bobbie screeched. "You didn't wear anything." She leapt up and with one hand on her crotch, awkwardly hobbled to the bathroom. "Look what you did to me. Yuck!"

The moment she reappeared, Nathan said, "I'm going to shower."

Ann smirked. "So, Miss Kuhn, scientist, what did you learn?"

Bobbie said, "I learned a great deal about male anatomy. Males are inferior to females sexually. I learned that sex could be painful and pleasant. I learned that sex is terribly messy. Yuck."

"It's my turn to have an orgasm," Ann said matter-of-factly.

Bobbie rattled on. "I also learned how easy it is to forget protection. I know that if any one of us has a disease, each of the others is prone to contract the same dreaded disease. If our friend is sterile due to inactivity, with all the action early last night, if he began producing sperm at midnight, then I will be gloriously, wretchedly pregnant. I think I am going to be sick." She amended, "I mean guilt-ridden forever. You know we did something so absolutely outrageous that it boggles the mind. And we can tell absolutely no one." She noticed Nathan had reappeared with a towel wrapped round him. "If either of you betray me, I shall absolutely positively kill you both. Quite dead. I hope I never hear the word 'twins' again!"

Smile for the birdie," Ann said. She had retrieved Nathan's camera and now the flash bulb winked the moment he appeared.

"Hey. Cut that out."

"You better not have caught me on that picture, "Bobbie warned.

"I didn't. You were off to one side." Ann continued abruptly, "Inasmuch as I am owed one orgasm, when are we going to do this again?"

"Never!" Bobbie shouted. "Never! Haven't you heard a thing I said? There will be consequences."

"No more." Nathan said. "Never again."

Half dressed; Bobbie raised her arm in a preachy benediction. "I'm with Voltaire. Once is interesting. Twice is depravity."

"I don't want to be depraved," Nathan said.

Bobbie glared directly at him. "I'm going to trust you to destroy the negative and photo if I'm shown."

"I'll give you both," he promised.

Bobbie frowned. Her little hand dropped from her mouth. "There's going to be consequences," she predicted gravely. "There are going to be consequences."

When he had dressed, he drove to the little restaurant next door. The girls checked out and walked to the restaurant, all part of the ruse to make it appear the two had spent the night alone.

"There's still one photo on the roll," he said. "Maybe we can get the waitress to take our picture. There should be nothing wrong with a picture of us in a restaurant."

"Sure," Ann said.

Bobbie merely sulked.

The waitress snapped their picture.

"I wonder what I face coming home, dragging in at this hour?"

"Hah. Me too."

Worries about parental questions never occurred. They all made to the ten o'clock Physiology class.

Without warning, Ann asked Mrs. Harris, "I understand the orgasm in the male, but how does a female know? How?"

Bobbie and Nathan exchanged quick surprised glances.

Amid subdued snickers Mrs. Harris said, "Ah, the singing whistle of boiling teapot. Like birth control, orgasms are not a proper discussion for this class. We have already pushed the envelope as far as we dare. That is why I have taken care to use the term ejaculation in very limited detail." Karen Harris hesitated. "A woman knows."

Nathan noticed things had changed. Talking to each other, the girls now and then used the names Annette and Roberta, and the formality of "Excuse me" and "Thank you." Each demanded to see the pictures first when developed.

"We will view them together, for better or worse. You will have to be patient. I couldn't risk having them developed locally. I sent them to a mail order place." That was true as far as it went.

When she encountered him alone, Ann remarked how simply wise he was to send the pictures away for developing. She invited him to her house when her parents were away in an attempt to achieve an orgasm. "But don't tell Bobbie."

Nathan tried but Ann didn't soar. She did not have an orgasm the second time. He began to feel used and feared her parents would arrive early and catch them in the act. After the third attempt and failure, during which time Ann insisted he keep his shirt and socks on, "in case they show up unexpected,"

Nathan said firmly. "That's it. Fini. The end."

He could see where Ann was headed and he did not want her to get involved with man after man in search of an elusive orgasm. He knew she valued her grandmother's advice. "Listen Ann, I was talking with my Grandmother, off the record, you know." Actually, he had not spoken to his grandmother. If he had said "orgasm" in her presence, his grandmother would have slapped him silly. "We were just gabbing about our psychology class and how Mrs. Harris wouldn't talk about orgasms. Grandmother mentioned that Mary Rose Murphy had eleven kids and still had not had an orgasm. Maybe you will never have one. Like I will never have sperm."

"I'll have to learn to fake it," Ann said.

It took forever for the developed pictures to arrive. He had ordered several copies of each. In the meantime, he mentioned to Bobbie that Ann felt somewhat left out because she didn't have an orgasm. They decided to bring up the subject gently when they viewed the prints.

The day before graduation, he called the girls together to view the five different poses. Bobbie snatched up all the prints and the negatives that showed her half clad in pajamas, looking at Nathan partially wrapped in a towel,

"We got away with it," Ann said.

"Yeah for now," Bobbie said. "You really blew me away when you asked about orgasms the first time we were in class. I've been studying. Some women never have an orgasm. There were studies showing that some women only experienced orgasm after marriage and being deeply in love."

Nathan smiled wanly. "Sorry, you didn't obtain that high, Ann."

"Not your fault," Ann said. "Fault runs both ways" She clutched the four photos allotted to her, absent the one showing a half-clad Bobbie and Nathan in a towel, and without another word, marched away.

"There are consequences," Bobbie said. "We are now going to different nursing schools."

"In case I don't see you at graduation. I wish you the best." Nathan reached out and shook her hand.

She tilted forward and quick-kissed his cheek. "Bye."

Later, in the quiet of his room he studied a remaining set of prints. In addition to the dated prints, he had ordered five-by-seven enlargements of the last five pictures on the roll. He placed them in a leatherette folder, some new kind of material that came out as a substitute for leather. Not in the order they were taken, they told the story of (l) him and two girls meeting in a restaurant, (2) the two girls seated in a motel room, (3) a picture of him and Ann, (4) a photo of him alone and (5) a photo of a half naked Bobbie with him coming out of the bathroom partially wrapped in a towel.

They would kill me if they knew I had them. Especially Bobbie. Once is interesting, twice is depravity, indeed. He decided not to take the enlargements with him into the Army Air Corps. The little photos would be enough. He placed the folder containing the enlargements in a metal case, locked it and slid it under the bed. It would be there when he came back—if he came back.

8

DOROTHY YUEN MEETS JOHN BIRCH

Meeting May and Marion had given Dorothy a new circle of friends. She and Edna began singing in the choir at the Episcopal Church. Dorothy never imagined that another circle of friends would lead to both joy and embarrassment.

Lillian returned from a treatment for malaria and sat before the faded mirror. She parted her hair in the middle and created a roll that extended from ear to ear like a crown. "I learnt that an American Consular representative is at the hotel. I'm going to see him and I want you to come with me."

"Why?" Dorothy asked.

"You are twenty-one now—although heaven knows you certainly don't act like it. You are still on my passport and I want you to get your own. I sure do not want to loose my citizenship. As soon as this bloody war is over I am going straight home!"

Dorothy realized that within her mother's statement cradled the idea that her mother suspected that she might remain in China. "All right, I will go with you." Dorothy had learnt a word her mother used, and the value of credentials. Certainly, she wanted her own passport.

At the hotel, when they knocked on the door designated by the manager, a man responded and said, "I'm sorry, I am not the representative. My name is Smith. Perhaps you might come back later?"

"It is a pleasure to meet you, Mr. Smith," Lillian said. "It is such a joy to converse with someone who speaks English."

"If you like to speak English, perhaps you would like to meet some American soldiers who are here on R and R. Follow me." He led the way down the hall and knocked.

"C'mon in. The gahdamned door is open," bellowed a gruff voice.

Smith stepped inside and observed that he interrupted a poker game. To combat the July heat, the men had unbuttoned their shirts, which hung over their trousers. One soldier's fly stood open in a large V.

"Straighten up! Button up!" Smith shouted. "These are American women. They speak English. This is Mrs. Yuen and her daughter."

With mouths agape, trembling fingers rushed buttons into their holes. One man spun around as he tucked in his shirt. Another yanked his belt to lock it.

"I-It's b-been months since I talked to a girl who spoke English," said a man, with face aglow. His hand raced forward. "I'm Bob Yarano."

"Yer gahdamned right. It's been months. Jesus Christ, you damn neart caught me with my pants down." A brawny man came forward, hand outstretched. "Cannon, Ma'am."

"Yogi," said another.

"His name isn't really Yogi," said a fourth man. Hi, I'm Lonnie."

"His name isn't really Lonnie. It's Lonneman."

"Please to meet you," Dorothy said to each.

"I imagine you boys get lonely. How would you like to meet an American family?"

"We sure as hell would," said Cannon.

"Fine. When we have an air raid, why don't you come across the river to our house? It is only three miles. We have been there two years and the bloody Japs haven't hit us yet."

"Wow."

"Americans."

"You want some wine, girly?" Cannon swallowed and reddened. "I mean Missus."

It would be the last time Dorothy would see the hard swearing, heavy drinking, cigar smoking Cannon embarrassed by anything. Dorothy covered his embarrassment. "I think the gramophone needs winding."

"We don't wish to interrupt your party," Lillian said.

"Hell it ain't a party. It's just a gahdamned card game. Sit right down. Make yourself to home."

"Sorry. We are running late. We only stopped in to extend the invitation." Lillian drew a map and handed it to Lonnie.

"Poor boys," Lillian said after they exited. "They don't have a friend in the world."

"They are so big,"

"Americans," Lillian said with pride.

The four were attached to the 96th Fighter squadron, one of three squadrons established when the AVC, the original Flying Tigers volunteer group disbanded a year earlier to become part of the Air Force.

Dorothy awakened early the next morning and began the wretched task of scrubbing the floor. When she finished with the floor, she stepped outside to mop the porch. She saw four men lounging there—the four Air Corps men they met the day before. With a startled scream, Dorothy dropped mop and pail and fled inside.

Completely humiliated, Dorothy knew they had seen her acting like a coolie scrubwoman. Mortified, she couldn't face them. After an eternity of shame swirling within her, Dorothy risked cracking the door. One of the men had spread a puddle and was busy mopping. Lonnie noticed her. "It's okay. C'mon out."

"I'm too embarrassed," Dorothy managed, cheeks aflame. I have completely lost face. I can't bear to face you."

"Aw, come on out."

"Yeah. It's all right."

"Shit yes," Cannon said gruffly. "What's to worry about? My old lady always mops the damn floor."

Dorothy didn't realize that when he said "old lady," he was talking about his mother. "How come you came so soon?"

"Early air raid," Yarano said, grinning.

Yogi said, "We didn't see a thing."

"That's the gahdamned truth," said Cannon. We seen nuthin'."

In the days that followed, the four frequently borrowed a Jeep and drove from their base for a visit. Lillian Yuen thoroughly enjoyed the rough talking Cannon. Dorothy and Edna devised schemes to make the men take them around town in the Jeep, moments of fun in a dreary war.

Mrs. Au, an irrepressible woman of boundless energy operated a store where she sold rice, beans and other difficult-to-obtain staples. She invited Dorothy to a party, and Dorothy accepted, unaware that the store served as a center for covert activities.

Dorothy fastened her gaze on an American officer and realized she was invited because she spoke English. At first, she thought he was part Chinese. His sleepy eyes were small dark and satiny in a lean handsome face. A midnight lawn of hair swept from a lofty brow. On second thought, Dorothy decided, he was too pale for Chinese.

"Hello," Dorothy said.

"Hello," he answered.

"Are you enjoying the party?"

"You speak English."

"I should. I'm an American citizen from New York. Dorothy Yuen."

He laughed. "I'm John Birch from Rome, Georgia."

They exchanged histories of their formative years and soon were talking about church. Dorothy mentioned that the Episcopal Church needed a piano.

"I come across one now and then. Maybe I can get one." Captain Birch hesitated, as if he dreaded an answer to his question. "Does it matter to you that I am a missionary?"

"No," Dorothy replied, puzzled by his question. Then she noticed no one asked him to play the finger game. One person called out a number and thrust out some fingers on one hand. An adversary would call out a number and try to extend the same number of fingers. If he did not match the same number of fingers, he lost and had to take a drink. The point of the game was to get people drunk. No one would ask a missionary to get drunk.

Birch asked to walk Dorothy home later and Dorothy introduced him to the family. Everyone liked John and he asked to return the following evening and the next. He invited Dorothy to dine at a restaurant on a boat. She widened her eyes in surprise when he ordered the entire meal along with instructions in flawless Mandarin.

"Dorothy do you know how really beautiful you are? I have had my mind on you all day. In my business that may not be prudent." He spoke of his home, Birchwood, and Dorothy said, "I'm confused."

He explained, "I have not put aside my faith and being a missionary just because I work for the Army."

Dorothy realized John Birch was a complex person.

Returning Dorothy to her home, he visited with the family and asked Dorothy to walk him down the path. Suddenly his strong arms closed around her. He drew her close and kissed her firmly.

"Captain Birch! I thought you were a missionary."

He tossed back his dark head and laughed.

As Christmas of 1943 approached, the girls asked the four men of the fighter squadron to go with them to church. "You can meet May and Marian. They are British subjects and speak English. Their parents live in the West Indies."

Cannon chewed his cigar. "I can talk Limey."

"I got mine," Lonnie said," placing an arm around Dorothy. "You guys can share the Limeys."

Yogi and Yarano whispered back and forth but Dorothy heard, "What if one is fat?"

"Neither one is fat," Dorothy assured them

"Are you going to church?" Lillian exclaimed, looking at Cannon. "Hah! If you show up the roof will fall in." Lillian particularly appreciated Cannon.

"Hell yes," Cannon said. "I've been to church before."

"C'mon, I want to meet those Chinese Limeys."

The six piled into the Jeep and drove to church for the midnight service. The girls sang in the choir. Half way through *It Came upon a Midnight Clear,* Dorothy and Edna heard a loud crash.

The weight of the four large Americans on the balcony had been too much. It crashed to the floor.

"Dorothy's mother said the roof would fall in if you went to church." Yogi teased.

"Aw, shuddup," growled Cannon.

When Lillian heard what happened she erupted in unrestrained laughter.

9

BILLY BOB WILLIS JACKSON JOINS AIR CORPS

Willis Beauregard Jackson Jr. of Birmingham, Alabama, started life as Junior. He did not like the name as he grew older, and for a time used Beau, Bubba, and Willie, names of which neither his mother nor grandmother approved. They preferred Billy-Bob, a name readily adopted by the community. He could not outdistance Billy Bob.

Billy Bob grew up to hate Blacks, Jews, Catholics, Arabs, Republicans, most teachers, and anyone else with whom he disagreed or appeared to be different. An uncle became a dragon in the Ku Klux Klan, an organization his storeowner father liberally supported.

In Billy Bob's view, the law worked much too slowly and often failed to achieve the desired result. It was much easier to get a desired result by personal intervention. By the time Billy Bob was ready to join the Yankee Army Air Corps, he had sown more than his share of wild oats, rolled enough snake eyes for ten men, and bluffed his way into winning and losing countless hands of poker.

What he had not accomplished was convincing Jennifer Kay Longstreet to "go all the way." That did not prevent him from trying.

"You know there is a war on," he whispered in his syrupy southern drawl. "Ah mat nevah cum home agin."

"Well that is it precisely," replied Jennifer of the ample bosom. "If you think I want to be a widow with a baby, sitting here in Birmingham, when you go down in flames, well, Bubba, your head is full of corn meal mush."

"Aw, don't be that way."

"No!"

"Aw c'mon. Once won't hurt anything."

"Will so. Will hurt you most of all."

"Hunh? How do you mean?"

"I will positively never speak to you again as long as I live. You will lose the best woman you have ever met. It will show you don't love me."

"I do so love you."

"And I love you. We can wait until we are married, when you come home and we start a family. You will be glad we waited."

Won't neither. Billy Bob knew he would never be glad he waited. He thought of drastic action, forcing here then and now, but quickly abandoned the idea. There was something about old family honor. His grandmother called it "Noblesse oblige." If he went ahead, if her father did not kill him, his own father certainly would. When all his blandishments failed, Billy Bob went off war to kill flat-faced slant-eyed Japs.

He had already cleared one hurdle with the Army Air Corps. He had presented documents showing his name as Billy Bob Willis Jackson. He had shed the Jr., and no damnyankee outfit would want a Beauregard. It had been a matter of looking ahead and being prepared. When questioned if Billy Bob was his real name, he said "Yes Suh," and plunked down documents including an Alabama driver's license.

He decided not be fooled by the sergeant who assembled the recruits. "Okay, you meat heads, empty your pockets. You have no need for pogey bait, candy or gum. Brass knuckles and switchblade knives go into the box. Pictures of legs and tits—toss them into the box. Pictures of your wife, mother, daughter or best girl may be saved, just don't try to pull a fast one. Dice and playing cards, get rid of 'em. Rubbers go into the box." The grinning sergeant would probably take a breath and finish, "Okay now, get rid of that stuff. Into the box."

Billy Bob knew that's how it would go down. He'd be smart. He wouldn't be caught with any of that stuff. He knew the guys in charge of the company nabbed some of the stuff. Decks of playing cards might make it to a USO club. It was weird, taking away rubbers on the first day, and showing movies about venereal disease and on graduation from boot, practically ordering the men to carry rubbers.

It came down that way. When he had nothing to contribute, the sergeant scowled at him and said, "Clean living kid, huh?"

Billy Bob had plans. He would put in for gunnery school after basic, and just before he shipped out, he would pick up three dozen Trojans, a handful of dice and six decks of Bicycles. During the down time between missions, he would be ready.

When Pfc. Billy Bob came home on leave after Basic Training, Jennifer Kay Longstreet complained, "You didn't write me very often."

"I was busy, Darlin', sunrise to sunset. There wasn't time to write."

Jennifer knew that when other men entered military service, in the beginning, they frequently wrote, but she allowed the matter to pass. Perhaps the drill sergeant had it in for Billy Bob and assigned him extra duty. She knew Billy Bob often rubbed people the wrong way.

He drew himself erect. "Did I tell you that I am going to gunnery school?"

"You didn't mention it."

"Well, I am, Sweetie. If those Slant-eyed apes try to attack my plane, Blam Blam Blam. I will shoot them down in flames."

"It sounds dangerous. You know they shoot back."

"It is really dangerous."

"I'm proud of you. We should go and celebrate. Mabel's Roadhouse would be nice. I hear the place rocks."

"Where ever did you hear that?" he said quickly. He did not want her to go there. His hands came up and he shook his head. "I already made a reservation at an Italian restaurant."

"Aren't you a dear?" Every time they were together, she expected him to urge, "Let's do it. Let's go all the way." Surprisingly, Billy Bob had been a perfect gentleman. He hadn't suggested it one time. He finally realized going all the way would be foolhardy—out of the question.

At the Italian restaurant, he kept filling her glass with wine. "You know it's my last night of leave. Let's check into a comfortable motel. We can do it one time. You know I am going in harm's way."

"Billy Bob Willis Jackson! I'm surprised at you," she said with the courage of too much wine. "You know we decided to wait until we are married. After we are married you will be glad we waited."

I doubt it. "If you say so."

"I do say so." Jennifer smiled. The military had been good for Billy Bob. He looked handsome in his uniform. "Have I told you how handsome you look in your uniform?"

Jennifer was not the only woman impressed by a uniform. In all his life, he never had an easier time picking up chicks. It had never been easier to score.

Billy Bob directed his wandering thoughts to the woman across the table. "Did I tell you, you are pretty cute yourself?"

On the home front, girls, young women, middle-aged women, and older women answered a patriotic call, and in some cases found emancipation in factories engaged in war production. Jennifer mentioned in her letter to Billy Bob that she had started work in a factory.

Before she received his reply, he arrived home, a graduate of gunnery school.

"I wish you had told me you were coming," Jennifer said. "I have to work the swing shift. I won't always be available. It's too late to try switching on such short notice."

"It came up suddenly. We were so good at destroying targets that they moved us out early. I will be all right."

"I wish you had phoned me."

"Never mind, Darlin'. I will say goodbye to friends. When I go back, we are shipping out, headed overseas."

"Maybe we could go to Mabel's Roadhouse after my shift."

"Not that place again. It's too wild. Before I forget, where I am going censorship is tight. I won't be able to tell you. Here is a code I developed. In my letter look at the third paragraph. It will always be paragraph three. If I write, 'Remember the classes we had in English and Algebra. I didn't appreciate it then, but I'd like to be in class right now."

'We never were in English and Algebra class together." she objected.

"You and I know that! Do I have to write it out for you?" he said impatiently. "It's a clue. In that paragraph is the word, English. That means I am in England."

"Oh yeah, I get it."

"No don't forget. Paragraph three."

If you remember to write. "Now you take care of yourself. I want you coming home. As soon as this war is over, we can get married." Maybe telling him that, Jennifer decided, would stop him asking her to go all the way.

He understood her ploy. There were other women around. She wasn't the only pebble on the beach. "Right now, marriage seems a long way off."

For Jennifer, long hours at work brought the added reward of budding friendships. The knowledge that they were doing something to promote the war effort facilitated bonding. Jennifer expressed a reluctance to join other women in their after hour celebrations. At length, Martha convinced her to join the group at Mabel's Roadhouse.

Mabel's, a slightly rundown structure near the factory, was located about a block beyond the city limits. That meant law enforcement fell to the county sheriff and his network of thinly spread deputies. As a result, management ignored mandatory closing hours.

Jennifer recognized several of the women seated around the table. Introductions were casual. Martha announced, "I finally convinced Jennifer to come with."

"I wanted to come a while back," Jennifer countered. "In fact, I asked my date, Billy Bob Jackson to bring me here, but he had already made a reservation at the Italian restaurant"

"Do you know Billy Bob?" exclaimed a woman introduced as Irene Daniels.

"Everyone knows Billy Bob," Alice Tucker said dully.

Jennifer realized at once that if she wanted to obtain information she had to remain unperturbed. "He is quite a handsome figure in his uniform."

"Aren't they all?"

"He's full of bull," said Susan Grimes.

"What a line he throws."

"Oh, he's smooth," said Irene. 'You get the room while I find a place to park the car,' he said. You know what? He stuck me with the paying for the room.'"

Amid squeals and raucous laughter, Jennifer bit her lower lit and struggled for control. *I have been such a fool.* She felt color diffusing across her face.

"That man sure loves his lovin!" said a woman who had not previously commented.

Jennifer forced a wan smile. "I guess you could say that." She refused to allow herself the privilege of righteous indignation. She would wait until she reached home for revenge.

Later, during a quiet moment, Jennifer spoke to her grandmother in hypothetical terms. Her grandmother said without emotion as she stared vacantly across the room, "Honey, it goes with the territory. Men are no damn good."

Jennifer tried to be reasonable and not totally vindictive. After all, Billy Bob was fighting for his country. She could realize that if she was unwilling to jump into bed with him that he might go looking elsewhere for a willing partner, but she did not need to accept such behavior. She embarked on a one for one letter writing policy. If he wrote a letter, she would write one letter.

She wondered what kind of mischief he might be doing at this very moment. Until now, she had not considered that he might not have a role in her future. Indeed, she might possibly have a future—with someone else.

10

DOROTHY YUEN WORKS FOR 23rd FIGHTER CONTROL

Lillian Yuen was pleased with the military men her daughter invited to the home. The next time she ventured out and about, she returned with two. "Dorothy, I want you to meet Jack Hartell and Willie Hershenfeld. They are radio operators with the Twenty-third Fighter Control."

Willie gulped. "Wow, you're beautiful."

Unable to reciprocate, Dorothy found Willie unattractive, but he had a pleasing personality. Within days Willie and Jack invited Dorothy and Edna to a Chinese restaurant.

Edna watched them in amazement. "Do you always eat so much?"

Jack Hartell said, "You are accustomed to Chinese cooking where one pork chop feeds and entire family. At home I always eat two pork chops, sometimes three."

Willie clasped his arms and exclaimed. "Oy Vay, I never eat pork chops!"

"You don't know what is good, Willie." Jack laughed.

Dorothy knew something private had passed between them but did not understand the significance. "I know a place that serves hamburgers," she volunteered.

"You do?" Willie exclaimed. "We're going there right now."

Within minutes, Willie stuffed his mouth with a ground beef patty, deep fat fried, and covered with sweet-sour sauce. "Mother wouldn't believe this."

Jack teased, "She doesn't know there is anything west of New York. Make a note so we can find this place again."

"My girl can find it," Willie retorted. "Right, Dorothy?"

Dorothy enjoyed hearing New York talk and a few days later stopped to visit the pair at their radio shack. Willie introduced her to stern-faced Lieutenant Lynn.

"I heard about you," he said without emotion. His face remained placid-sour.

Surprised, Dorothy asked, "From whom?"

"Captain John Birch. He said to say hello. He was very insistent about it. He sends his regards."

Captain Birch had finessed it so that Dorothy would need to send him a letter. She started, ruined a page, and realized she could not waste another.

January 19, 1944
Dear Captain Birch,

I am writing to let you that we are all fine. Even Mother had a couple good days. We enjoyed your visit. Every once in a while one of us will remember the singing of hymns and Gloria will pipe up about your promise to look for a piano. I think she wants to be grownup like Edna and me. I am sending the address of the church in case you find one. I confess my father drew it for me.

Things are happening very fast here in Kukong. More Americans have arrived. I have two new friends, Willie and Jack. They visit our home all the time and take Edna and me out to eat. We are having a lot of fun. They are radio operators. They introduced me to their Commander, Lieutenant Lynn. Was I ever surprised! He said that you had told him to give me your greetings. How nice it was that you thought of me. I was sure surprised.

I caught a glimpse of some other soldiers I thought were Americans. I suppose I will be meeting them soon. That is, if they are staying around here.

Please excuse my writing. I'm sorry I am not very good in English or in writing letters.

Your friend,
Dorothy Yuen

Willie and Jack continued to visit and Willie kept calling her, "My girl," and several times he exclaimed, "I just love you." Like many young men she met, Dorothy realized Willie was falling in love with her. It wasn't love. The young men were only lonely, far away from home and she happened to be the only girl around who spoke English. With their friendship, they had all shown her respect. She did not realized that was about to change with the suddenness of rain out of a clear sunny sky.

Dorothy heard her mother and an American coming up the path, laughing and carrying on as friends who had stopped too long in a tavern. Dorothy recognized the Navy uniform.

"Commander, this is Dorothy."

"Hi, Babe," said the Commander, leering at her with X-ray eyes. His too-small collar sent the lapels out like wings. "Are you sure it is all right if I take Babe out for dinner?"

"Of course. Dorothy has a lot of friends. She will go with you."

Dorothy took an immediate dislike to the Commander.

"Get your hat, Babe." His eyes roamed over her and turned to Lillian with a short burst of laugher. "I shouldn't have told you that story."

"I enjoyed it," Lillian said. "It's been too long since I heard a good story. I used to have this friend Riley." She broke off suddenly and shot a glance at Dorothy when she remembered her daughter had caught her in bed with Riley the Undertaker. "Riley used to tell some good ones."

"Say, didja hear the one about the traveling salesmen?" His voice went low but Dorothy managed to hear, "Out came the farmer's daughter."

Her mother erupted in laughter. "You're a real card."

"Is it all right if I smoke while I wait for Baby?"

"I'm ready now," Dorothy said, none too pleasantly.

The Commander led the way to a café-bar. At a table for two, he sat reeking of sweat and flatulence, blowing smoke in Dorothy's face. "I run a tight ship. There's room for a smart girl like you. Know what I mean, Baby? Wanna 'nother drink?"

"No, thank you."

"That's a good egg. Easy on the booze. The last floozie I had, got skanked and could drink a barrel. Whatd'ya say, Baby, wanna come with me?"

"Mother isn't well. She needs me."

"What's wrong with her? She looks all right to me."

Dorothy felt his clammy hand on her knee and moved back quickly. "What are you doing? Remember that you are an officer."

He guffawed. "That's rich. Look, don't play coy with me, Baby. Not with an old lady like you got. She has been on the road. Now spin your legs back under the table."

"No."

"Have it your way, Baby. I like a challenge. Picking plums can get old. Your old lady told me that you went to Chungking for six months. They say that place really rocks."

"Yes. The city is circled with small mountains, pointed rocks. It must be the most bombed city in the world."

The Commander roared. "That's more like it. I knew you were a live one." He called out, "Waiter, hit me again. You're my type, Baby."

"No, I am not. I'm not even white."

"Close enough. So what if your father is a sloppy. I don't see a Chink married to a white woman very often."

"My father is a Colonel in Chiang's army in charge of—"

"Yeah-yeah."

Dorothy tried to speed up dinner and the Commander finally agreed to take her home. "Not your night, eh? Mine either. I didn't mean what I said about your old lady. Well if that's the way you want to play it. Okay."

On reaching home, Dorothy attempted to leave him at the front door but he followed her inside. Now, reeking of Sen-Sen, he sidled to Lillian. "I been tellin' Baby, it's two hundred dollars a month as long as she wants it."

That is all Lillian had to hear to become his willing conspirator. She turned to Dorothy. "It is just the job you have been looking for."

"No mother it isn't. I am not at all interested."

"Not interested," Lillian objected loudly. "What is the matter with you? You have been moping around the house, wanting to get away from me. Now a job drops right in your lap and you turn up your nose." Lillian turned to the Commander. "I don't understand her."

"Yes, Ma'am."

"Have you explained the job?"

"Yes, Ma-am," the Commander said silkily. "I explained about the money. The job has lots of time off. I will keep an eye one her."

"There." Lillian said.

"No. Mother, can't you see?"

"She is a stubborn one. Let me talk to her." Lillian passed a wink to the Commander that Dorothy detected. "You stop tomorrow."

"Aye aye. But that's the last call. I'm shaking the dust of this burg off my feet." When he had gone, Lillian continued to rave. "You have to take the job."

"Oh, Mother."

"Don't Mother me. That's the first decent offer you have had. Edna is old enough take your place. When he comes back tomorrow, you are going to take the job."

"Can't you see what he wants? Don't you understand anything?"

"I understand you are too old to have your father support you."

"So you are going to throw me to the wolves."

"You wouldn't know a wolf if one bit you."

Dorothy sulked to her room, utterly defeated, knowing not where to turn.

No long after daybreak, a knock on the door catapulted Willie Hershenfeld and Jack Hartell into her dilemma. "The Commander only wants to get me into bed," Dorothy blurted.

"You are not going with a Navy man," Willie insisted. "I'm going right back the shack. We need a translator. I am sure we can use you."

Dorothy forced a smile. At that moment, Willie's chiseled features looked beautiful.

"Let's go right now," Willie said.

Soon, as she stood before the stern-faced Lieutenant Lynn, Dorothy mounted a confident smile with no substance behind it. She stood tall they way Jack instructed and allowed her friends to do most of the talking.

Lieutenant Lynn listened and said, "Oh, yes. You are a friend of Captain Birch. I think we can use you."

Dorothy drew in a breath and her shoulders sagged in relief.

"Dismissed," Lynn said curtly.

The moment they were outside, Dorothy hugged Jack and Willie and Jack and kissed each of them.

She told her mother that if the Commander showed up to tell him she had taken another job.

Fearful on her first day as a translator, a young Chinese man with the American name of Robert gave her confidence. "You will catch on in no time."

When radio messages came in, Dorothy translated them into English and phoned them to the floor above.

"Why don't I just run them up?"

"Off limits," said Robert, laughing. "Military rules. They won't allow Chinese up there. Mysterious Caucasians."

"We might sabotage their transmitters," Dorothy said.

Soon Dorothy became proficient and managed a shift on her own. One Sunday morning a bird colonel and a lieutenant colonel appeared.

"I'm Dick Wise and this is Chuck Hunter," said the Colonel. "We are here to see Lieutenant Lynn."

"Captain Lynn now," Dorothy corrected. "I will tell him you are here."

If she had known that Dick Wise would someday be her entire life she would have treated him with more than polite indifference.

A few days later, Dorothy received a letter on stationery headed UNITED STATES ARMY AIR CORPS.

Changsha
27 February 1944

Dear Dorothy;

Your kind note of the 19th reached here yesterday. Thank you for not waiting until my tardy one went to you. Just the word that you have not forgotten me means much.

Dorothy, you have not left my thoughts since the first night I saw you! You must be a witch,—a beautiful witch,—to cast such a spell. The reason I have delayed in writing (I did start several times, but lacked time to finish, then was dissatisfied with what I had written and destroyed the poor beginnings) is that I have been increasingly busy; since leaving Kukong I have been in Kweilin, Kunming, Changsha, Leiyang, and then back to Changsha day before yesterday. I expect to go north to the Yangtze River very soon, but will return to Changsha after that journey. I wish I were going to Kukong instead!

Glad to hear that your folks are well. I inquired as to pianos for sale in Changsha, and learned to my regret that a mission school here had sold two before I arrived! If I can locate any more, I'll do all I can for you and Gloria.

Am happy too, that Lt. Lynn passed my regards on to you. I hope you're not seeing too much of the American boys down there, Dorothy! I know this is a selfish thing that I have no right to say, but I am horribly jealous of those fellows who have opportunity to see you.

Enclosed is a photograph made here in Changsha. I hope you will send me one (a snapshot will do) of yourself. I admit such a bargain would be entirely to my advantage,—to "swap" something ugly for something beautiful and rare. If you don't care to give me the pleasure of keeping your picture, feel free to keep mine, anyway, to scare the rats away!

Don't ever apologize for your English writing! I only wish I could do as well! Please write soon again; the address you used is O.K.

Please extend my best wishes to your family. Remember that, while I dare not hope for more than your friendship, still I want to be yours, as much as you will have of me, my lady!

P.S. Please don't call me "Captain Birch"
    This is my name---------------------------John.

Dorothy put down the letter and a sigh escaped her. Captain Birch was falling in love with her. Military men always fell in love when they were far away from home. It wasn't really love, she knew.

"John," she whispered. "It's isn't love. It isn't love."

Sandow Yuen noticed the handsome Lonnie Lonneman who frequently appeared with a Jeep was falling in love with Dorothy. That did not disturb him. He worried about Willie Hershenfeld. "Don't become too deeply involved with him."

"I see him every day at work," she reminded her father. Seeing Willie daily changed suddenly when he and Jack ventured into the field with little more than their transmitters.

That same day, Captain John Birch appeared in one of his surprise visits.

In an enthusiastic mood, he said, "Have dinner with me, Dorothy. Where I will be tomorrow, you wouldn't believe."

"Very well."

"You can't imagine how many times I read your letter. I hope you received mine."

"I did. I love the way you write. At the end, you called me, 'My Lady.' I thought of your home in the South. The phrase has a Southern flair."

After dinner, which John ordered in flawless Mandarin along with extensive instructions, John lead the way to a secluded spot near the river. "I am glad you are a serious person, Dorothy. You are not always pulling in two directions. In you the East and West has blended. You will be able to appreciate what I am about to say. You aren't a person who cannot make up her mind, pulling first in on direction then another. As a missionary, I know that marriage is a serious undertaking. You understand the—"

"John," Dorothy said with sudden force. "You have been speaking about another woman." She halted, embarrassed. "Forgive me. I had no right—"

"I *was* thinking of someone else. She couldn't commit to my way of life. That is over now. You are very perceptive. You affect me."

"Really?"

At night, when I am alone out there, you are constantly in my thoughts and prayers. Your face comes to me out of the mists. Today when I saw you again, I realized I had your face pictured in my mind, correct in the most minute detail. The curls, the dimple in your cheek. Do you know the Chinese call a dimple a 'wine hole'? There is so much I want to tell you. I don't know where to begin."

"You could tell me what you do—out there."

"It's terribly secret. With your work in the radio shack, you know I am involved in communication. I move around a great deal. I have been up north with the Communists, with the Nationalists, and frequently behind enemy lines."

"I didn't know that." *He is with Intelligence!*

"There is danger in my business. One never knows when he might say too much. Well, I told you a secret, now you must tell me one of yours."

Dorothy thought a moment. I have a friend, Tiger dos Remedios. He sent me a dictionary in installments, concealed in a newspaper. I study it."

"Bravo. Studying a dictionary. You have captivated me with your charm and beauty, and also your intelligence. No wonder I have fallen in love with you."

"John—"

They talked for a time about his home in Georgia, about his hopes, about life with a missionary.

Captain Birch continued, "I know I have no right to ask for your affection but when I go out in the field I take you along in my heart. There is something I want to give you so that you will remember me. He brought out a pin the size of a twenty-five cent piece, the emblem of the Flying Tigers. "Mine once, now yours. It isn't exactly a fraternity pin, and this certainly isn't the campus of Mercer College in Macon, but the bond I have with these men transcends—oh here, let me pin it on you."

When he had it pinned, he held Dorothy at arm's length, admiring his work, and drew her near. He kissed her warmly. "Dorothy, I love you."

She returned his emotion. "John …"

"There. Now you are pinned to me."

"I am not sure I should wear it. After all, I am not a Flying Tiger. The military will object."

"Tigress," he corrected. Forget the objections. Out in the wilderness, I have heard the majestic roar of tigers. If you roared, it would be beautiful. You are the finest tigress in all of China."

Exhilarated, he placed his arm around Dorothy and walked her home. He kissed her again and said farewell.

Lillian was up and stirring. Dorothy asked, "Mother, does the phrase 'pinned to me' mean anything to you? John said I was pinned to him."

"It doesn't mean anything to me. I suppose it is something those military boys have dreamed up."

The dictionary gave Dorothy no help. Deep in her heart she knew 'pinned' had a special meaning. Was it one-step short of an engagement ring?

Off from work, on a day or rest, her father summoned Dorothy and she assumed it was to counsel her about the amorous attention of Willie Hershenfeld. There was no one else in the house.

"I sent the others away," he said, despair lining his lean thin face. His sunken eyes filled with anguish. "Sit down, Dorothy. His voice trembled. "An owl has come to rest in my pear tree."

She knew an owl was an evil omen. According to legend, owls devoured their mother. Mothers devoured their owlets. "Pear tree?"

"A pear tree is the symbol of long life, purity, and justice," Sandow said.

His hands moved across the table. "Here is all the money I have. On this paper I have written my other assets."

"Why, father?"

He raised his gaze, averting his face and stared past her. "You remember the Colonel of the Eleventh Repair Factory? I-It's-It's the same t-thing."

"No," Dorothy shouted, as a knot twisted her stomach. "Not the firing squad!"

"Who can say? It is in the hands of the gods."

"For using an Army truck to transport your family from Hsingning? For having Ah-Lau use a truck to get our furniture? For this you will be shot?"

"No." He attempted to smile. "Those things are permitted a person of my station. They say I sold spare parts."

"What? How can they say that?"

"I am not guilty of what I have been charged."

"If you are not guilty, how can they charge you?"

"The bird chooses its tree, not the tree the bird. There is nothing more to be said. I must report to headquarters now."

She watched him go. He stopped at the door and turned. "Dorothy, tell the others I love them."

Stunned, frozen, at length Dorothy broke lose and started to run, sobbing. She realized that instinct more than reason sent her in the direction of General Yur Ying-kai. Her lungs cried out for breath. She kept hearing the crack of firing squad rifles, remembering the victim's body going limp. She strained for composure. This was no time for tears. "Damn the Chinese and their stupid final solution."

General Yur's pleasant greeting gave her hope. "Hello, Do-jur. I sense you are in trouble. How may I help?"

"It's father," she blurted, running on about his dire circumstances. "I know he is not guilty. This man who refused to allow his vehicles to go to Kukong until there are many reasons—whose troops cannot use vehicles except once a month on payday—is not guilty. How many times have I heard, 'Every ounce of gasoline is a drop of blood for China'?"

"Your problems are never small ones," General Yur said. His brows had come together like the wings of a duck hawk as he listened to her plight. Now he forced a grin. "I have little power with military justice but I will look into the matter. Go home and don't worry. I will see what I can do."

Dorothy returned home, heavy hearted, no joy in her soul. Even Willie Hershenfeld could not cheer her up. The gloom dissipated the day her father came home and said, "You may return my money."

"What happened?"

"On close inspection they found no evidence against me."

Dorothy knew it would be necessary to thank General Yur. "Ah," Dorothy said, "It is observed that the owl has flown out of your pear tree."

Her father bowed, clasped his hands together and said, "Let us share a pot of tea and speak of happier times."

The leached-out tea had grown cold when Lillian called, "Dorothy, Ho Hon-si is here to see you."

"I had to tell you my good news," he said. "I am now a Colonel."

"Congratulations. The tangerines of your New Year are hanging high and bright."

They went for a stroll and Dorothy knew Ho Hon-si would again ask her to marry him. He did not disappoint her. With a twinkle in his eye he said, "If I could get your mother mad enough at you, I would have you as my wife."

"I have news as well," Dorothy said. "I am working for the Americans. I have a job at 23ʳᵈ Fighter Control as a translator."

A sober expression moved across his face and disappeared in an instant. He changed the subject to a familiar one, comparing the customs and traditions of Chinese and *Meghwa,* the word for Americans. Then he added, "I wish you wouldn't run around with Americans. They will get you into trouble."

"I can take care of myself. Don't forget that I am Meghwa."

"I could easily forget." He enjoyed bantering. "Are you sure your mother isn't mad at you?"

"Not enough to send me into your arms." She did not know that some of his words would soon be prophetic.

That weekend the men from the 76ᵗʰ Fighter Squadron appeared and Dorothy extended an invitation to her sister Edna. "There is a grown-up party in town and you can come with us if you wish."

"Yeah, I can see she is grown up," Lonnie said approvingly when Edna appeared.

Yogi reminded her, "Other guys will want to dance with you. Remember that you are with us."

"Damn right," said Cannon.

A drive of fifteen minutes took them to a pre-war home where the party occupied the entire second floor. Chinese students from Lingnam University relocated after the fall of Hong Kong, played mah-jongg, and at one table, four Americans were playing poker. In an adjacent room dancers whirled to jivey gramophone records.

"Turn over that Bluebird and play it again."

Suddenly the downstairs door popped open and gendarmes with drawn weapons charged up the stairs.

"You are all under arrest," the leader shouted. "Don't move."

Dorothy managed to duck into a closet. She heard a gendarme scolding. "Gambling is illegal. Dancing is prohibited by the New Life Movement."

In their search, a trooper discovered Dorothy cowering behind the door. He directed her out with a wave of his bayonet.

Prisoners had their wrists bound and the two dozen violators attached to a rope. The line included Chinese military, an officer, a Colonel, students, and several women, one of whom was heavily pregnant. Ordered to march to headquarters, Dorothy looked around and saw Edna clutching Cannon's arm. At first sign of the raid, she had run to him. Gendarmes would not touch American troops or anyone with them. Dorothy wanted to kick herself. She should have known that. Why hadn't she used her head?

Yarano and Lonnie stood by helpless and Dorothy shouted to Edna, "Get Ho Hon-si."

All along the street, the prisoners were humiliated. Dorothy wondered which of them would receive a blindfold and hear the crack of rifles.

Several hours in detention, Dorothy heard her name in Chinese. She stepped forward and the guard gestured toward the exit.

There stood Colonel Ho Hon-si, resplendent in his new uniform. He saluted curtly. "I will take charge of the prisoner."

Not until they were well outside did he relax. "So you can take care of yourself," he scolded. "I warned you not to get involved with Meghwa."

Dorothy could not answer.

"I don't know what I ever saw in you," he fussed. "I would not want a wife of mine to be a common criminal. Dorothy, Dorothy!" He tossed back his head and laughed.

"Thank you for getting me released."

"Why didn't you tell me you were going to that place? I would have warned you not to go. We planned that raid for days. You and the Americans are a constant embarrassment to me. Now there is one thing you must do."

"Yes?"

"In the morning you must visit my commanding general and inform him what I have done for you."

"I will."

"I suppose I can release you how. I shouldn't. I should never let you go."

In the morning, Dorothy went to the commandant of gendarmes and explained what Ho Hon-si had done. She succeeded in obtaining the release of her friends from Lingnam University.

As they were discharged, they became extremely irritated with Dorothy. "If you have influence to have us released now, why didn't you do it last night?"

None of them ever spoke to Dorothy again.

On the way home, Dorothy stopped for some sweet tarts for her mother. Lillian launched into a scathing tirade. "Well, it has finally happened. You landed in jail. I always knew you would."

"It was a mistake."

"I knew the cops would get you sooner or later. Ever since I saved you from jail for starting fires in the streets of New York."

"You saved me?" Dorothy shot back. "That is not what happened. You were hanging out of our second story window shouting, 'Take her away, I don't want her.' Some saving that is. It if had not been for that kind-hearted policeman I would have been arrested—no thanks to you."

"You were always able to wrap men around you finger. Some day, my girl you will find out that trick will not work."

11

CHAN AND TANG GUARD FLYING TIGER PLANES

If a Wall Street tycoon returned home and discovered that a bomb reduced his house to rubble, he still has his bank account, brokerage account, his Cadillac, Country Club membership, professional license, and his reputation. His family probably made it to an air raid shelter.

Chan Fu-lim survived the bombing with a son and daughter, who mourned the death of their mother and two younger siblings. Japanese fighter planes, attracted by the fleeing refugees that were no more than a horde of insects, enjoyed strafing them, and stitched to death the only surviving daughter where she lay hugging the earth. Father and son had only the clothes on their backs and a small bag of rice. The father pulled his son away from the crowd and headed for Kweilin. It would only be a matter of time before the military saw them and pressed his son into service. Becoming soldiers in Chiang Kai-shek's army guaranteed short-term survival, if not a salary. Chan decided to volunteer them both. There were obstacles to surmount. He sat and thought deep thoughts, and formulated a plan.

Before they volunteered, Chan explained to his son, "Americans sometimes act backward. The do not read from the bottom of the page to the top. They read from the top to the bottom. They place their family name last instead of first. In America I would be Fu-lim Chan." He paused and said, "The tea leaves tell me that we must change your name. We must become friends, not father and son. I have decided to give you a name—not Ong, a country name, but Tang, a respectable city name of which you may be proud. You shall no longer be Chan Che-lue. You shall be Tang Hong-tsi."

He paused and when his son did not reply, continued. "A son cannot serve two fathers. In the army, a father and son are suspected of putting family interests ahead of the Generalissimo. At the least, army officers will suspect us of favoritism, of first looking after each other. In any case, they would separate us. Merely changing your name does not halt the sunrise." Chan waited for his son to speak.

The young man said, "A snake in a rice paddy is worth more than a snake on the table."

His son knew traditional words of wisdom. "How so?" Chan asked and allowed his son to explain.

"A rice paddy without snakes becomes the home for a thousand rats. Rats will eat all the rice."

Chan bobbed his head. "Americans are not skilled in ancient wisdom, but in America even a poor man has a radio. A poor man has a telephone. Perhaps a poor man has an auto. Not only people of wealth fly planes. Women fly those large birds—but not in war."

"Perhaps one day we will visit *Gum San,*" Tang suggested.

"You cannot see America until after the war. Perhaps never."

Tang wondered why America had crept into the conversation. His father—now his friend—had learned rudimentary English while employed by a hotel Americans frequented. Tang could not understand why his father had insisted on teaching him some of the backward language but he often said, "Two tongues are better than one."

Tang had been tempted to say, "Like a snake," but that would have incurred his former father's wrath.

Deep in concentration, his father spoke his thoughts. "It is good that I became a father at a young age. If I tell the Army you are a little older and I am a little younger, they will not suspect we are father and son." He stopped and outlined his plan. "We shall see if we can serve China by watching the nest." He saw puzzlement on the face of his—friend. "The place where the mighty American birds gather is in nearby Kweilin. How would you like to guard the *Meghwa Fei hu?*" Suddenly he asked, "Who am I to you?"

"Father."

The young man earned a sharp cuff to the arm and quickly amended,

"Friend." He did not make the error again.

Chan's plan became elaborate. "My family is gone. Your family is gone. We met on the road and recognized each other. We lived on the same street. You made deliveries to the hotel where I worked."

They located a command post and received directions to headquarters. Interrogated by a Lieutenant, a Colonel happened to pass. Chan interrupted, "Permission to speak to the Colonel." He saluted sharply.

Immediately impressed that the speaker was not an uneducated serf, Colonel Fong asked, "Starving?"

"No," Chan lied, and added with a smile. "Not until tonight."

More impressed, the Colonel said, "What is on your mind?"

Chan did not waste the Colonel's time and launched into his plan to guard American warplanes. "I speak their language and will be able to report on their activities. That intelligence might be extremely helpful. If we remain together, as a team, my friend and I will be able to report, even if one of us is detained."

"Say something in American," said Colonel Fong.

"Don't call me Joe. My name is Kelly."

The Colonel raised his brows at Tang indicating the same question.

"Yes sir," said Tang. "Don't call me Joe. My name is Arthur."

An American might have thought he said Otto instead of Arthur.

They stood ready to explain what they had said but the Colonel knew no English and merely nodded. "Hao. You are in the Army. Can you use a rifle?"

"Yes," Chan said.

"Assign them to Yang Tong," said the Colonel. "You will report to me personally."

Chan saluted. Tang saluted.

Chan mused as they followed a guide. "Perhaps the tree has selected the bird."

In due course, they received second hand uniforms, small caps and leggings, and a broad Sam Brown belt of fabric and lastly, a rifle. Tang fingered a small round bullet hole in his shirt and wondered: had a Japanese sniper killed the previous owner?

Eventually they arrived at their duty station. "I forgot to tell you," Chan told his friend. "If you fall asleep on guard duty at night, you will not be wakened. You will be shot."

With the passing days they became accustomed to seeing Americans gather in a hangar they called the "alert shack" to await the return of their flyers. Early one morning, Chan heard the stuttering of an aircraft engine and immediately identified it as a Japanese fighter in trouble.

The pilot knew he would not survive. If he lived after the crash, the Chinese would cut off his head. To do honor to himself and his Emperor, he aimed his stricken plane at a structure.

Americans poured out of the alert shack in time to see the pilot crash into one side of hanger and out the other, trailing smoke. Running to the wreckage, Chan immediately pried open the canopy and with a long hook pulled out the pilot.

Tang jerked off the man's boots. Chan removed the pilot's sword, insignia and identification. They tossed his body back into the burning plane.

By the time they reached headquarters and Colonel Fong, Chan wore the dead pilot's boots. Tang wanted to keep the sword. Chan reasoned that they would soon eat the rice obtained for it in trade, but favors from Colonel Fong might continue for a long time and be extremely valuable. "Sometimes a debt acknowledged is greater than a small bird in the hand. "The Colonel has already granted us the favor of remaining together."

Chan saluted, presented the sword with ceremony and said, "The Son of Heaven will have no more use of it." He surrendered the dead pilot's identification. "Some day you may have the welcome opportunity to return it to a live enemy." Chan made a slashing motion with an imaginary sword.

The Colonel bowed and uttered a word of thanks. His trust in Chan was not misplaced. His brows lifted. "I see you have retained the pilot's boots for yourself."

"The honor belongs to my young friend Tang. He approached the burning plane at great risk to his life. Tang lived on my street and I told his mother I would look after him. He has no family now. He shamed me with his bravery. After a reasonable time these boots will be his. If something happens to me, I beg the Colonel to honor a dying mother's request—and mine—to look after Tang."

Colonel Fong nodded. The flickering idea of confiscating the boots dissipated to his joy and approval of receiving a sword. He would claim he obtained the sword minutes after the enemy crashed into the soil of China. He decided to exhort his troops. "Bring me an enemy. This swords needs to be returned." Then he would thrust the sword, sometimes putting a nearby soldier in peril.

Chan withdrew. "Nothing more to report, Sir."

"Hao."

Away from headquarters, Tang said to his friend. "I see what you mean about storing a favor. It can be a treasure. You were lucky the Colonel did not take your boots."

"It is wisely written on tablets of jade that luck does not seek a fool."

12

JOE REILLY IN KWEILIN

The first time he saw the hostel for the 11th Bombardment Squadron at Kweilin, Joe Reilly realized it had a practical advantage. While other hostels clustered near the runway in areas long ago denuded of trees and timber, this hostel lay two miles from the south end of the runway in a grove of tall straight evergreens on a knoll overlooking rice paddies. It reminded him of the evergreens back home. If enemy bombers attempted to destroy the runway, they would need to be two miles off target in order to damage the hostel.

Rice paddies surrounded three sides of the hostel and a tall bamboo fence rose on the fourth side. During summer, when coolies flooded the rice paddies, from the air it appeared that the hostel was on a wooded island. In winter when frozen over, it became an oasis. Reilly appreciated the significance of the location.

A single dirt road led to the airfield, and when the rice paddies flooded, the inundated road sometimes halted traffic for a couple days. Floods sometimes left the road cratered.

A mess hall, recreation hall, two administrative buildings, two barracks for officers and six for enlisted men formed a compact group of twelve. Split-bamboo laths held the mud plaster on the walls. Beneath thatched roofs, plaster ceilings created garrets where a prodigious amount of huge rats had their quarters. In one administrative building were offices for the Commanding officer, Executive Officer, an orderly room and squadron supplies. The second administration building held the mailroom, special services office, and dispensary and photo lab.

The large barracks had six rooms approximately twenty feet square. There were no hallways. All rooms opened to a porch and had windows front and back. Photographs and magazine pinups of girls with endowed bosoms and lovely long legs completely covered the walls. Ten or twelve occupants assigned to a room made it crowded, even with double or triple-decked bunks. Four laced-backed chairs and two small tables provided for card playing and letter writing. Each man had a clothes locker. It everyone converged at the same time, several had to find refuge in their bunks. Likewise, reading, writing, or playing cards necessitated that seating at the tables occur in shifts.

Each barracks room had a single heater cunningly constructed of a converted oil drum that supplied limited heat for a couple yards. Remaining warm in cold weather was a continuing a problem. Unable to crowd around the stove, men shivered in their bunks. Often charcoal became the fuel and sometimes the flimsy outrageously priced furniture, allegedly acquired by the US government for more than Ethan Allen prices, found its way into the stoves. Each room had a single outlet and one 60-Watt Chinese bulb. Supplying electricity, two generators, installed by engineers valiantly attempted to keep up with demand. Two nights a week, men enjoyed movies shown in the recreation hall, which plunged the barracks into darkness. Then the men resorted to tung oil lamps, no different from those used a thousand years before. They consisted of a wick stuck into a metal container. With no chimney, and without a way of regulating the wick, the candlepower gave off light equal to two fireflies and the stench of a small civet. According to plan, the men played poker in their rooms—if several crawled into their bunks. A close watch of the time resulted in making sure the game ended before ten when the lights went out.

Reilly lay in the upper bunk watching the bombardier betting as if he held four aces when all he had was a pair of nines. The guy was an idiot. As Joe predicted, he lost.

The recreation hall did not have heating facilities. In cold weather, the men sat on the rows of benches without backs, watching the movie in their boots and flight gear. More interesting than the movie to many were the reports of Intelligence Officers on the progress of the war in Europe and General MacArthur's island hopping campaign.

Behind the screen, in a small alcove, a snack bar operated by a Chinese concessionaire, served coffee, Chinese pastry, peanut brittle, and sometimes hot dogs of dubious content. Prepared in a small lean-to attached to the outer wall, the men thought the snack bar also served as a listening post for Japanese intelligence.

The free laundry, collected by houseboys, always returned with numerous items missing, not exactly what President Roosevelt meant in his Lend-Lease program.

A washroom at the end of each barrack provided two shower stalls and two or three water taps. Coolies carried in buckets of water to fill the overhead tanks. If the water came from a rice paddy nearby it might be rather muddy. The mess hall, located in a remote corner of the hostel, had a single door. On entry, enlisted men turned to the right, officers to the left. A kitchen divided the two eating rooms. Here labored Chinese cooks clad in dirty ragged clothes, spitting and blowing their noses at random. American men avoided peering into the kitchen.

When Joe Reilly arrived on the base, meals did not include milk, powdered or canned. There was no jam, butter, fruit, fruit juice, Army rations, yeast, cornstarch, baking powder, or beer. The meat, vegetables, flour, sugar, coffee, salt and pepper were of local origin, mostly produced within sight of the hostel.

All "good" food was flown in over "The Hump." Coffee from India, due to scarcity, was available only at breakfast. Water buffalo, the major meat source, utilized animals slaughtered due to old age or disease, young animals being far too costly for food. As prepared, buffalo meat had the consistency of old shoe leather. Pork, a high-grade delicacy, was too expensive. Even poor grade pork was rarely served. Chicken became a gastronomic delight, served about twice a month. The men did not like to see meat brought in by carts from Kweilin, exposed and covered with flies and road dust. Nowhere in the area was there any refrigeration. Of all the meat served, estimates ran as high as ninety percent for the portion that the men refused to eat.

Substituted for wheat flour, readily available in India, rice flour might have been suitable if there had been any yeast or baking powder. Without leavening, the only way to eat bread was as French toast; even then, toasting did not render it digestible unless it was soaked in gravy. Members of the 11th Bomb Squadron were impatient when they heard of men located in other areas complaining about Spam. One of the guys said, "I'd give a week's pay for one damn can of Spam."

Fifty years after Kweilin, men remembered the sugar. So-called sugar contained bits of human hair, straw, string, and flies, and fermented rapidly to become sludge with the color and smell of a G.I. blanket

Japanese air raids occurred often in a waning moon, frequently in early morning hours. Aviators knew enemy planes were coming due an elaborate warning system. *Jing Bao,* less frequently stated as *Ching Pao,* a variation of Chinese dialect, meant "air raid." Translated more accurately Jing Bao means "to be alert." The Chinese hung a lantern in an easily viewed place when planes were an hour distant. Two lanterns meant the planes were fifteen minutes away and three lanterns meant, "They are here!" Lighted lanterns, they soon realized, attracted the enemy, and in some areas, they quickly extinguished the lanterns. Along with the lantern, came the slow beating of a gong. Two hits, repeated in a few seconds, accompanied two lanterns. The frantic pounding of the gong accompanied three lanterns. For Flying Tigers the lanterns became "balls," and there were three predictable reactions as well, four if one counted the Adjutant.

At the sound of a one ball, Lt. Williamson would leap into his personal vehicle, roar down the highway and not be seen until the next day. Half the men joined his example, donned gas masks, grabbed carbines, and hurried to the hills or caves. About one-third of the men arose, dressed fully, and headed for slit trenches. The fourth group, made up of "old hands," doubters and cynics, remained in their bunks, reminding each other the Jap bombers would need to be two miles off target in order to hit the barracks. Anyone dropping off to sleep was an actor. Each of the heroes remained awake, listening for the sound of bombs dropping or the familiar warning sound of a Maytag engine. At the first sound of a washing machine engine, they would leap out of their bunks, often stark naked and dive into a slit trench.

Learning the day of the week became important. Monday and Thursday night, the enlisted men went into town. Officers took leave on Wednesday and Saturday nights.

The first man to reach a Jeep or truck became the driver and everyone piled on board for the trip of seven miles to the ancient city of Kweilin. Formerly sleepy, the influx of refugees brought with them the higher standard of living they had known in Hong Kong, Canton and Shanghai. They brought with them their trades: merchants, bankers, doctors, accountants, teachers, students, architects, engineers, lawyers and manufacturers. More cosmopolitan than New York, Joe could see Chinese exiles from every province, British, French, Russians, Filipinos, Burmese, Eurasians and Anglo-Indians. With patience, one could find treasures of every description.

Most of the men sought excellent restaurants, such as found in the Lok Chong Hotel, located in the North part of the city. The Lok Chong sprawled across and spacious courtyard adorned with flowering trees and large stone images of animals.

For men interested in soup, the Lok Chong had a full-page menu of soups creamed and clear, some featuring lily pad blossoms. The best of Chinese cuisine, served in "family style" began with a large bowl in the center of the table. Diners received small bowls of rice and chopsticks. To sterilize the oft-used chopsticks, wrapped in brown paper, diners would immerse the chopsticks in boiling water supplied for the purpose. Following the cleansing ritual, one reached into the large bowl or tray to obtain morsels of chicken or duck, exotically seasoned, sweet and sour pork, chicken liver, mushrooms, bamboo shoots and bean sprouts, which were then stirred into the individual rice bowls. Starving men soon became more or less proficient with chopsticks. Hot tea, without sugar, served in tiny cups without handles, continued to be available all during the meal.

Anne and Yvonne, enterprising sisters from Hong Kong owned the Central Café. They spoke excellent English and knew what Americans wanted. They featured roast chicken, fried pork chops, potatoes mashed or French fried, coffee with sugar and cream, and banana pie and custard pie.

Catering to servicemen, the Lido Café offered a similar menu. Because the Air Force had little food, poor variety, "really bad chow," as one flyer exclaimed; these restaurants were extremely popular and captured a large portion of an airman's salary.

Assignment to the crew of a B-25 thoroughly pleased Joe Reilly and gave him a measure of pride. The Mitchell, named after pioneer air advocate Billy Mitchell, possessed many exciting features. Three bladed propellers spun in a 12 foot 7 inch circle on twin engines that developed 1700 horsepower and could send the plane along at a speedy 300 mph. The plane burned 150 gallons gas in an hour of flight. To check the oil level, a member of the ground crew climbed upon the wing and pulled out the dipstick to ascertain the presence of 30 gallons. Capable of carrying 6000 pounds of bombs, the B-25 boasted fourteen forward firing .50 caliber machine guns. As the war progressed, variations in the B-25 included moving the top turret and space for the waist gunner. Radioman-gunner Reilly enjoyed firing out of both sides.

On the runway, the only guards were Chinese. A rag-tag lot, many did not wear shoes and slid their toes into sandals. They wore leggings reminiscent of an earlier war. Ruled by fear, the enemy forced captured men to serve. If an escape attempt failed, they were shot. If they were caught stealing or trespassing inside aircraft, they were shot. Frequently the Chinese sentries would sit on the front wheel of a B-25, leaning forward in a relaxed position, the butt of their rifle on the ground. If during the night they became heavy-lidded and fell asleep, the roving corporal of the guard would not bother to waken them. He would simply place his pistol at their temple and pull the trigger.

Always eager to show an American their weapon, some of their rifles were so rusty Joe doubted they would fire. The Chinese guards were genuinely proud to have a rifle.

The young Chinese guards had a practice Joe did not understand. When a plane taxied for take-off, they would suddenly run across the flight path "to ward off evil spirits." Sometimes they did not make it and a propeller would split their head, even their bodies and they would lie writhing into death beneath the roar of aircraft engines, victims of the evil spirit.

Since meeting his crew back in the States, Joe learned more about them. Lieutenant Bob Russell, the pilot, claimed to be an engineer, a college graduate, who invented a coat hanger that employed a spot weld near the hook instead of a twist. Sold to a manufacturer, Russell claimed he received 2/10 of one cent for each of the stronger hooks sold. Russell always had some invention cooking on the back burner.

Co-pilot Winthrop Dada turned 21 in China. He had a flash temper and punched out a Navy Officer in Washington, D.C. They bailed him out of jail before coming to China. Joe predicted he would get into more trouble.

Carlton Doyle, the other officer who used the name, "Buck," served as bombardier-navigator. A crack salesman, making $1000 per month with Remington-Rand, his ability did not incidentally include navigation. From Day One, Buck could not tell North from South.

Tail-gunner Robert Mongello had served in the military long enough to draw "fogey pay." He used the name Mongell whenever possible because he wanted to be French instead of Italian. Teased about that deception, during poker games crewmember Polinsky called him Mon-Jello and a few times, Mon-Jelly.

Philip Polinsky, turret gunner had the look of a man aged 40. He told more lies than Errol Flynn. Joe figured the truth had eluded him since age five. Whenever he met a man, Polinsky always pretended he knew someone in his town. "St Louis? I dated a girl in the jewelry section of Kreske's in St. Louis." If he met an airman from Denver he might say, "Do you know a girl named Shirley who waits on tables in that little restaurant?" Earlier Polinsky pretended to be a doctor and wanted to be called "Doc." That request didn't fly. Joe started to think of Polinsky as "the man from everywhere."

When Airman Blaine won $7000 playing poker, Polinsky advised. "Put the money in U S war bonds. When you get home, study hotel management. Cash in the $7000 and buy a hotel in the Catskills."

Polinski had a sense of humor. "We're the best crew in the entire Air Force, absolutely fearless." Paying more attention to his drinking than poker, out of the hearing of officers, he added, "Of course if a Jap fighter comes up to greet us, from that moment on we are in big trouble!"

"My queens beat your jacks, smart guy."

13

WILLIAM BOOKER, COUNTERSPY

Booker strode into the office of Colonel Wise, commander of the Service Group and saluted sharply.

Wise looked up wearily. "Yes, Sergeant?"

"Sir. I am a mechanic with the 23rd Fighter Group. I heard scuttlebutt that we lost a B-24 due to bad fuel. About the alcohol we have been getting—I took a small sample; put it in a tin pot I made, held it over the fire, and boiled off the alcohol. I had at least 25 percent left, mostly water, some oil and sludge. It is getting dangerous to pour that stuff into our planes."

Colonel Wise gave Booker a weary look and brightened somewhat. He knew the sergeant had a suggestion and listened.

"If we can get some large funnels, an outrageous supply of chamois, and some old fashioned clothes pins, we could make filters. The chamois, placed inside the funnel as sacks, would act as strainers, removing the water and probably a lot of the oil. It would take time to stain all the gasoline. It might be slow going but it would take out a lot of water." Booker hesitated. "It we use welding equipment, we can make the funnels."

Wise shouted to Lt. Ed Cabelka and ran it past him. "See what you can do."

"One more thing," Booker said hesitantly. "I may have messed it up. The other night, about oh-two hundred hours, I was out among the planes when I heard a man call out something in Chinese. From the second plane nearby came an answer in English. The older man continued running though words in Chinese, and the younger man responded in English. I caught, "Tienchi boo hao," and the young man called back, "Bad weather." I couldn't understand all of it. "Yu," said the older man. "Fish" replied the younger. After some word the young man didn't know, the older man said, "Wrong. You got it wrong."

"What did I do? Like an idiot, I walked up to the older man and asked, "Where did you learn English?"

"I worked at a hotel frequented by Americans," he said.

"'Good,' I said. 'We appreciate you guarding our planes.' So there I am three days late and six pounds light in the brain department. I could have stumbled onto some Chinese spies. Or worse, Japanese sympathizers. That English speaking Chinaman is not standing out there all night guarding our planes for his health, the way I figure it. I may have blown something for Intelligence."

"Maybe. Maybe not. The soldier didn't hesitate to admit he knew English." Wise frowned and rubbed his jaw pensively. "He already knows you. If he is after information, you would be the most logical person to supply it. Would you be willing to make contact with him? It could be something, or it could be nothing. Your life might be in danger. If you agree to do this, I do not want you to talk to anyone but me. If Chinese or American agents follow you, I want to know about it. Be careful what you say and listen closely to everything he says. It may be difficult to remember, but do not put anything in writing. Well, what do you say?"

"I'll do it sir."

14

NATHAN BERRY TRADES LETTERS WITH BOBBIE KUHN

Nathan Berry sometime wondered if the two classmates who were now nurses psychologically raped him. Ann Schmitt had not answered his letter. He assumed that her disappointment in not achieving an orgasm with him had led to anger. Well, that was her choice.

He remembered people saying, "Sex is all in the mind." If that happened to be true, he certainly had the brains to control the impulse. Despite his age—old enough to be in the military—he had the nagging feeling, "I'm too young for sex." On second thought, he was not really too young, but it was certainly too soon. On the other hand, it might be the wrong setting. There were not many choices.

He weighed alternatives—Chinese prostitutes or nothing. He decided chastity offered the best answer for him. All he had to do was guard himself against popular psychology.

He waited until arriving in Kweilin to send Bobbie Kuhn his address. If she replied promptly, several weeks would pass before he received her letter. In the meantime, he contented himself reading old letters he saved.

Dear Nathan,

It has taken me quite a while to answer your letter. Do you believe in fate? Ann and I were best friends practically forever—until a man came between us. Not that we aren't friends, but we have drifted a world apart. Each of us selected a different nursing school than we originally intended. I started thinking of becoming an Army nurse.

My parents objected. They said I was too young. They didn't want their baby in the Army. They said if I discovered I didn't like nursing, I couldn't get out of the Army. I had to honor their request.

In the meantime, I had a chance meeting with a nurse. Was this fate? She told me I had to be 20 before I could be an Army nurse.

My parents had their way, and I started nursing school where I had the brilliant? idea of adding a couple years to my age in case I wanted to join the military. So far so good. You cannot believe how mature I have become. Ha ha.

I do like nursing. When I get a little more experience I may become a Navy nurse. I'm dealing with the Navy now of see if I can enter a program where I will be able to earn a gold stripe. Ensign to you.

Love, Bobbie

Nathan nodded. Although Bobbie had not stated it directly, he surmised that she had not received a letter from Ann Schmitt. He remembered they had been close friends up to graduation. Perhaps there was something more. Had he really come between them? He was glad Bobbie continued to write.

Dear Nathan,

I am in the Navy working my tail off. This old woman of "20" was worried in case the Navy obtained my record from Wilson High that showed me to be 18. I was ready to explain that Mom fibbed to the school so I could be with kids who were my friends. But the age thing never came up.

My nursing school experience has served me well and an officer says he wants me to teach volunteers coming in. That means a lot of extra work for me, trying to keep ahead of women older and smarter than I am.

Well, I'm out of time. Must run.

Love, Bobbie

Nathan admitted that Bobbie wasn't really his girlfriend. Well, she was a friend and she was a girl … and if he wanted the relationship to blossom into something more … it would be up to him to make a move in that direction. He heard stories about military nurses. He had seen Air Corps nurses whooping it up … usually with officers. Why not? There was something else. That little *ménage a trios* on their first date—if it was a date—did not strike him as an ideal foundation for a serious relationship. What made Ann and Bobbie do that? Still, there was something about Bobbie that was clean and fresh. It might be crutch reasoning to believe that Bobbie been talked into it by her long-time best friend Ann. One thing for sure, ground floor reasoning—he could not get her out of his mind. He decided the thing to do now was keep corresponding.

Dear Bobbie,

One of the first questions a guy will ask when he meets another is, "Where ya from?" It would make an interesting study of personalities of those who ask that question and those who do not. Are there any distinguishing character traits?

When I said I was from Milwaukee, one of the men called me Schlitz. Schlitz Berry sometimes becomes Schlitz Beery, but I don't mind.

There is a fellow here, who uses his first name, which is Barry. You would never guess his last name. Maskovielymenchnikov. A waste of space, hah?

I am turning into a great mechanic. If you are flying by, please drop in. Not much news, bye for now,

Good luck,
Nathan

Dear Nathan
It's not the Island breeze
that is calling to me
it's the U S Navy
sending me out to sea
to a hospital on shore
in a place I adore
it's Aloha Hawaii to me!

Maybe my poetry is not so good, but as you can see I am delighted about being sent to the Naval Hospital at Pearl Harbor. It is going to be a challenge to repair what the war has done to the men. It is hard for me not to feel their pain. I think I will put in for surgery.

Thanks for wishing me luck. It paid off. By the way, if you ever see me again, you will owe me a salute.

Sign me Ensign Kuhn.

Nathan delighted in receiving her letter. He decided to reply at once and selected a time when the usually crowded barracks were deserted. It was enlisted man's night on the town and most of them had left to chase whores, go sight-seeing or seek a fine restaurant.

Nathan started his letter with a more amorous, "Dearest Bobbie," decided he had come on too strong, scratched it out and wrote "Dear Bobbie." Not satisfied with that he decided, "Yes, Ma'am!" would be appropriate as a literary salute. By now, he knew he would need to rewrite the rough draft.

"Congratulations on your promotion and your posting station in sunny Hawaii." He did not use the line, "I wish I was sick there so you could take care of me." That was stupid. Air Corps personnel did not end up in a Navy hospital. "How I would love to be with you and enjoy fun in the sun. I am not making light of your work." He had to make sure she understood that.

"I remember all the Hawaiian movie settings, scenes at the Royal Hawaiian Hotel, the sea, the surf, the outriggers, the pineapple drinks—mai-tai's. Hollywood certainly knew how to get us longing for the islands. Now you are there."

He wanted to get her reaction. "I spent a great deal of time thinking of you. I suppose it is beyond wishful thinking—that you spent any time thinking of me. Not where you are now. Do you ever think about after the war? I am headed for college … probably to get a degree in psychology. I don't suppose you would like to be my favorite co-ed. With Love and Kisses, Nathan." He had mentioned love. When he had sealed the envelope, he brought it to his lips and kissed it. He noticed he was grinning.

15

BARRY—BECOMES MASKOVIELY MENCHNIKOV

The Group Commander stared at the file. *Only a corporal. Square peg in a round hole. He must have screwed up in gunnery school.* The Commander remembered something he learned in OCS. "The men in your command do not need to like you." That had to run in reverse as well. He did not need to like Barry Maskovielymenchnikov. He only had to be fair. He shouted at the orderly who could hear him through the flimsy bamboo curtain. "Send him in."

A man of five feet seven entered, gave him a sloppy salute, and received a careless salute in return. "I'll get right to it, Corporal. You cannot spend the rest of your military career being Airman Alphabet. Some low-level clerk penned that over your name. I have done extensive research on your name. Fortunately, I had a professor in college who came from Russia. He maintained contacts with the Russian Embassy. He checked out your name. Somewhere along the line, your two names merged. My proposal is that we un-merge it and correct your service jacket by cutting your name in half. We are in China where that is possible. Once you return stateside, that opportunity is lost. Hell, if the Japs shoot you down, the way it is, you cannot even get your full name on a tombstone. You would probably end up as the Unknown Airman of this war. It is your call. Would you like me to make a correction and amend your service record to reflect your true name is Barry, middle name Maskoviely, last name Menchnikov?"

Barry Alphabet, AKA Muskrat, did not need ten seconds for a decision. "Yes sir! I would like that!"

"Consider it done."

"Thank you, Sir."

The officer's tone softened. "Forget what I said about a tombstone. Go out and shoot a Jap in the ass for me."

"Yes sir." Barry saluted with enthusiasm and received a lackadaisical salute in reply.

The Commander stared in the Corporal's wake and allowed a grin to build. He never had a Russian professor. It was all so much bull. Wasn't cutting red tape one of the privileges of command? He spoke his thoughts. "Maybe now you will make Sergeant."

As he walked away, Barry decided that not much had changed. He would still tell his friends to call him Barry. At muster, officers would now call him Menchnikov. If anyone asked, he would tell the men headquarters had finally discovered his true name.

At the moment, he looked forward to playing poker. Every Friday night two or three marathon games began which lasted until Monday morning. Small games, like on the one in Master-Sergeant Bratty's quarters. Space limited the game to one table and four chairs. There might be room for one spectator and usually a couple guys tried to sleep in their bunks. Out of respect, the card players tried to keep the noise to a minimum. If some player tired at 2400 hours or 0300, someone waited to take his place. In that manner, the game continued without interruption all weekend until Monday morning.

Candles flickered at each corner of the table and as they burned down, Bratty pressed a new candle over it, and when it burned down, he pressed another candle in its place. By Monday morning, each corner of the table held a large pile of wax.

All evening the cards had not been running in Barry Menchnikov's favor. At 0100, a crew chief withdrew and a Lieutenant who had been waiting asked, "Is it all right if I sit in with you?"

Master-Sergeant Bratty said, "Fine with us. Five card draw poker. One dollar to ante, no raise over two dollars—three raises max."

The Lieutenant seated himself on Barry's left and received the first card. With all five cards were dealt, while the others were arranging their cards, Barry managed to sneak a peak at the corner of the next card to be dealt—the king of clubs. He had to do something to change his luck.

The Lieutenant opened. "I'll bet two dollars."

Master-Sergeant Bratty said, "I'll call."

When the next player, Sergeant Bill Booker, pushed two dollars toward the center, the Lieutenant placed a .45 caliber pistol on the table. His steely eyes came to rest on Barry. "The next time you deal those cards, when you get done dealing, you immediately put the deck right down on the table."

Menchnikov swallowed. "Are you accusing—" he managed.

"I make no accusations," said the Lieutenant in a voice of Solingen steel. "I let my friend do the talking." He patted the .45.

Barry's mind raced as he searched for the right words. "I-I believe m-my integrity has been challenged."

"He didn't accuse anyone," Master-Sergeant Bratty cut in. "I call."

"Play cards," Booker said. "I call the Lieutenant's two dollar bet."

Barry's mind continued to race. If he folded, he would look guilty. If he drew cards and won the hand, he would look guiltier. If he folded now, he would only lose the original dollar ante. "These cards are hopeless," he said calmly. I fold." He turned to the Lieutenant. "How many?"

"I'll take two." The Lieutenant flipped out the throwaways and watched Barry use only his thumb to slide the top two cards off the deck.

"Three for me," said Bratty.

"I'll take two," Booker said.

"I'll raise two dollars," said the Lieutenant.

Bratty put on a theatric frown. "Are those pearl handles? I don't remember seeing pearl handles on a .45."

"No. Pearl handles are for pimps," the Lieutenant said tartly. "Those are pure ivory. I had them custom made in Bombay."

"By me," Bratty said and tossed his cards. He had not drawn anything to go with a pair of queens and decided the Lieutenant was a splurge player.

Booker said, "I'll call your two dollars and raise you two."

"Right. I'll see you." The Lieutenant added two dollars to the pot. "What do you have?"

"Not much," Booker said. "Three fives."

"That beats me." The Lieutenant put down a pair of queens and two kings.

The Lieutenant dealt and Bratty opened with a quarter. Booker raised fifty cents. Barry Master-Sergeant Bratty took his time when the Lieutenant asked, "How many?" Even if he drew another ace, it would not matter when Bratty analyzed where the Lieutenant was headed. He needed winning cards and did not have them. "Fold." Bratty threw down his cards.

Booker held a 2-3-4-8-9 unsuited, discarded the 8 and 9 and called for two cards. He needed an A-5 or a 5-6 to complete a straight. It didn't happen. He picked up a pair of 4s. Booker raised two dollars.

Barry Menchnikov muddled his cards. "I'm out."

The Lieutenant raised two dollars.

Booker called.

The Lieutenant showed two pair. "Aces over tens."

"No good enough," Booker said. "Three little fours."

"Do you always get three?"

"Not usually," Booker said.

Before Master-Sergeant Bratty dealt, the Lieutenant announced, "My last hand coming up, win or lose. It's getting late."

Booker checked his hand and bet one dollar.

Barry Menchnikov muttered softly. "Shit," and raised two dollars.

The Lieutenant raised two. Bratty raised two. Booker covered the raises and tossed out a lone card throwaway. The bid returned to Barry. He couldn't believe he held a straight 10 high flush. *Holy cow! This beats four of a kind.* "I will play these and do what seems to be popular. Raise two."

The Lieutenant discarded two cards and received two. As expected, he raised the bid two dollars.

Bratty discarded a pair and called. Booker called. Barry M said, "I'll raise another two bucks."

The Lieutenant raised two.

Barry called and waited for the Lieutenant to make his third raise. "I'll raise you two."

Barry had his two dollars ready. "And I will call."

The Lieutenant showed a pair of kings and a pair of queens."

"Kings and queens again," Booker said to no one in particular.

Barry spread his straight flush. "I have you covered."

The Lieutenant said, "It's not my night. I told you this was my last hand. I had better leave before I lose my shirt to you enlisted men. He holstered his ivory handled pistol and dispatched a stern look at Barry. "Keep your nose clean." He walked away.

Master-Sergeant Bratty called after him. "Were you AVG?"

"Yeah," the Lieutenant replied and the door closed.

He had not offered his name and in the years ahead Barry Menchnikov would inflate his rank and his name became Ed Rector, Tex Hill, Casey Vincent, or one of the Pappys—Boyington or Herbst. As things stood, he felt he had to clear the air. He hoped to quash a possible rumor. "What was that pistol on the table all about?"

"He thought you were sneaking a peak at the deck," Master-Sergeant Bratty said. "If I thought you were doing that, I would shoot you myself."

"I wasn't," Barry insisted.

"This is worth telling," Bratty said. "About two years ago, in a place like this in Chanyi, in a game like this, Sergeant William B. Reichmann of Atkins, Arkansas woke up in his bunk and said, "Hold it down. I'm trying to sleep." One of the poker players, an AVG civilian worker, drunk at the time, raised his pistol and shot him."[1]

Barry's eyes widened. "For real?" he exclaimed in disbelief. "Killed him?"

"Yeah. I had one of the few dress uniforms available and they put me in the honor guard. We buried him in Kunming."

Booker asked, "Did anything happen to the AVG civilian?"

"He served one year and paid a thousand dollar fine."

"That Lieutenant," Booker posed. "What do you make of him? I work with a man from Milwaukee. He is always analyzing things. I wish he had been here."

"The Lieutenant? Hotshot. Showboat. He is used to a high stakes game. He was bored with us enlisted men."

"A good dealer," Barry said. Did you see the fantastic way he handled cards? You don't suppose he was doing something funny?"

"No. I watched him like a hawk," Bratty said. "Just like I watched you."

Menchnikov played another hand and quit. He concluded he made a miraculous escape. From now on, he would play it straight.

His Aunt Molly, by marriage, and current beneficiary, might have told him that no good deed goes unpunished. Barry Menchnikov embarked on a heroic losing streak. He began to leave markers. The men called them jawbones because a player jawboned his way into the game instead of putting in cash.

To accomplish that, a player needed a make-believe friendlin instead of a pesky make-believe gremlin.

The same friendlin accompanied Barry on a flight over Lingling. A Japanese fighter attacked the B-25 and tail-gunner Barry fired burst after burst dead center. The Jap kept coming, closing the distance. Barry kept firing. *He is going to ram us!* Suddenly the fighter's canopy disintegrated and Barry saw blood streaming from his enemy's forehead. Still he kept coming … faster. "Pull up! Pull up!" Barry shouted frantically. By the time the pilot pulled back the stick, the Jap pilot fell forward and his plane nosed down sharply, trailing smoke, missing the B-25. However, the Jap's shots had not all missed.

"There is something wrong with the landing gear," said the pilot as he approached home base. He ordered the engineer to crank it down.

---

1. In a reprise, the *Atkins Chronicle* of October 29, 1943 printed: Sgt. Wm. B. Reichmann, U.S. Army Air Forces, son of Mr. and Mrs. Albert Reichmann, gave his life in the performance of duty in China on August 16, 1942, a native of Atkins.

"You let that damn Jap get too close," complained the engineer. "He shot up our landing gear. The next time you're going to crank it down."

"I was not too late. I was on him all the time. I got him, didn't I?" Barry said proudly. "Besides, the skipper gave you the order to do it."

16

DOROTHY YUEN JOINS FLYING TIGERS IN KWEILIN

Sandow Yuen warned Dorothy again not to become involved with Willie Hershenfeld. "He is from an entirely different culture."

"Willie is from New York."

"He may be from New York but he is from an entirely different culture. His family would never accept you."

Dorothy did not understand her father's reasoning. There was something special about Willie. He had a heroic face of carved teakwood, a face that in time that would be craggy and appear to need sanding. When Willie held her in his arms, Dorothy felt her heart quicken. Could she be falling in love?

"Darling, I love you so much, "Willie said, enraptured.

She had to push him away, she knew. When he tried to kiss her again, she turned sideways. "Not so much."

"I have a surprise for you." He reached into his pocket and brought out a jewel box. The sun's rays caught the green jade and it appeared like a robin's egg in his hand.

"It's beautiful."

"Like you. It is an engagement ring." He grinned. "I love you and I want to marry you."

"Oh Willie—"

He swept Dorothy off her feet and kissed her soundly. "I can't wait to take you home to mother."

"Your mother might not like me."

"I'll make her like you."

Willie had often spoken of his strong-willed mother. "I am glad you remembered her." Dorothy said. "If you brought home a wife, a foreign looking woman, your mother would not be happy. With a culture so different from yours—where the twain shall never meet, I would not fit in." Since her father's recent warning, she had spoken to Edna, and her sister remembered a quote from Kipling. Edna also stated she did not agree with it. "Willie," Dorothy continued, "You need to know that the odds of a successful marriage are insurmountable." She pronounced the long word slowly. "I cannot accept the ring, Willie."

Crestfallen, a dark shadow crossed his face. "I am not going to give up. I have written all about you to my mother, described you in every detail. She will like you."

"I haven't heard such a pipe dream since my uncle smoked opium. You need to get a hold of yourself. I expect soon your mother will contact the Red Cross to look after you."

"Was there ever such a woman! I absolutely positively love you."

Dorothy's outstretched stiffened arm prevented him kissing her. "And don't call me this weekend. I have some friends coming."

"Oh," he said his voice hollow. "That bunch of crew chiefs again. Stay out of trouble. Don't get arrested again."

The men from the 69th Fighter Squadron arrived as expected and this time Yogi was not with them. Apparently he had rotated out, replaced by a young man with hair the color of corn in the sunlight.

"We brought you a little ol' country boy from Pennsylvania," loveable Lonnie said, "This is Fred Ifft."

"Yeah, his home town of Evans City is so small that even the town rat left."

"He's a chicken-plucker," Cannon said, chewing his cigar.

"Hello Fred." Dorothy shook his hand.

"Dorr-thy," he acknowledged in heavy rolling Pennsylvania twang. "I'm not stationed here. I am stationed Kweilin, just here on a visit. The guys decided to let me tag along."

"I'm glad they did," Dorothy said.

"Have you lived here long, Dorr-thy?"

"A couple years. Why do you ask?"

"Scuttlebutt at headquarters is that the Japs are mounting a summer offensive and this is a prime target. The line has held for a couple years. Maybe the Chinese army can hold it. Headquarters is not sure."

No idle gossip, her father had heard the same disquieting rumor and a couple weeks later, when the thunder of Chinese guns echoed, her father decided the family must move instead of waiting for the enemy to come charging down the nearest hill.

Willie Hershenfeld appeared when they were packing to leave for Kweilin. "Oh my God, you are leaving." He collided with Dorothy in a kiss. "I'll move heaven and earth to see you off. I'll come to Kweilin to visit you."

"We had better say goodbye here."

"I'll try to be at the train to see you off," Willie called back as he departed.

The night grew dark when Sandow and two his men transported them to the station. With their suitcases and bundles of goods, there was barely room in the stateroom. Saying goodbye to her father had become a ritual. Sandow pressed a note into Dorothy's hand. "This is the address of my friend in Kweilin. He will look after you. Now Dorothy, you take care of your mother and the children. I am counting on you."

The train was about to leave. There was no sign of Willie. Dorothy stationed herself on a platform between cars, peering into the gloom. She heard him call out before she saw him. "Dorothy! Dorothy! Wait!"

Willie jumped aboard. "Made it! Jack covered for me."

She felt the strength of his arms.

His voice rustled in her ears. "I love you so much I can't bear the thought of us being apart."

Dorothy felt his body trembling against hers. "I don't want to leave you either."

"Will I ever see you again?"

"I hope so."

"Without you, life is nothing. Nothing!"

"Don't say that, Willie."

The train lurched forward, threatening their balance. They clung tighter.

"Tell me you love me," Willie pleaded.

"I do love you," Dorothy whispered, unable to hold back tears.

The train began to inch ahead.

Willie fumbled in his pocket. Out came the jewel box. You would not take this as an engagement ring. Your birthday is coming in a few weeks. Accept it as a birthday present."

"I can't."

The train gathered speed.

"Yes, you can. You said you love me."

"I know, but we cannot marry."

"Take the ring."

"The train is moving."

"I know it. Take the ring."

"You have to get off!"

"TAKE THE RING!"

"Oh, all right."

"Gotta go. One more kiss." He drew her close and kissed her hard.

I will love you forever," he said, getting ready to jump. He flung himself off the train. When he gained his footing he called, "Write me." A rush of air and the click-clack of wheels on rails swallowed his words.

The train puffed into Kweilin, a city surrounded by grotesque mountain peaks. Disembarking, Dorothy approached an MP. "Excuse me; do you happen to know Fred Ifft?"

The soldier did a double take. "You speak English!"

"He is stationed at the air base. Could you get a message to him? Tell him Dorothy Yuen has arrived." She copied the address her father had given her.

"Yeah, sure," the soldier said, still in disbelief.

The next day a Jeep screeched to a halt at the address and Fred Ifft and several friends approached. "Dorr-thy," Fred sang out.

Soon she told Fred she desperately needed employment and the next day Fred returned with a grin. "It's all arranged. I got you an appointment with the Colonel."

With Fred's assurance, Dorothy managed to summon courage to meet the Colonel. Trembling with fright, when she raised her eyes she recognized Colonel Wise who had come to visit Captain Lynn at the radio shack one Sunday morning.

"So we meet again," said the Colonel.

Dorothy admitted she lacked skills in office work. "But I am willing to try."

"Can you type?"

"A little," she fibbed, feeling her knees shake.

"Okay," the Colonel said. "When can you start?"

"I-I'll need time to get the family settled … perhaps by the end of the month …"

"All right. We can wait a couple weeks. When you are ready, get in touch. I will send a man to get you."

Outside, Fred waited and listened to Dorothy's melancholy complaint. "I can't type."

"You can learn. I'll take care of it."

The next day Fred appeared with a typewriter and an official Army training manual. Buoyed by his enthusiasm, Dorothy sat down and began to memorize the keyboard. As the days passed, she felt sorely disappointed in her progress. Every time she viewed her work, she groaned in disgust. It would be easier if she did not try numbers. Why did the Army need numbers?

17

CHAN AND TANG, SPIES

"Today you will have the privilege of wearing the boots," Chan told Tang. "We go to headquarters."

When Colonel Fong called him, Chan lost no time in getting to the point. "We were standing sentry duty. I have been teaching young Tang. I speak a word in Chinese. He must respond with the same word in English. Late one night, the American heard us. 'Where did you learn English?' he asked. I told him I had worked in a hotel patronized by *Meghwa*. I made a blunder. The American knows …"

"… knows he has found a vital contact for his spying activity," the Colonel interjected. "You have found a splendid source of information. You must follow where it leads. You must cultivate his friendship. Remember always to listen more than you speak"

"I have been listening."

"So?"

"The Meghwa chatter like monkeys. They suspect spies and enemy agents are among us."

"The Meghwa are not fools. There may be traitors among us. I have thought so." *Including you and Tang.* The Colonel emitted a disruptive, "Ho!" and sobered at once. "Had the American caught you speaking Japanese you would not be standing here."

Chan nodded. "Our lives are not without danger."

"Do you suspect any of our troops? What have you discovered?"

"Nothing definite. There is a man—Jung Kin—that I do not trust. He once spoke of a new regime when this war is over. He said the rich will be forced to share with the poor and the state will own everything."

The Colonel waved him away. "I should speak to Tang. Have him come in."

Chan risked saying, "A word of encouragement."

Tang stomped in wearing the dead Jap flyer's boots.

"I hear many fine things about you," Fong said. "It is my order that you make friends with the American who wants to be the friend of Chan. To listen is golden. To speak is not without risk. If Chan is killed, you must bring me the message. What did you observe about the American?"

"He has kind eyes."

"The kind eyes of a mongoose?"

"I understand. Keep my eyes open."

"Do that and stay alive." The Colonel waved him away. His eyes focused on the boots as Tang withdrew. In a sudden burst of command decision he shouted, "Stop. Bring in Chan."

Chan reappeared and tried not to look perplexed.

"I am issuing an order that Jung be placed between you on guard duty. That way you both can keep an eye on him. Keep up the English lessons. Go."

Colonel Fong allowed himself a satisfied smile. Soon he would call in Jung and ask if noticed anything strange about Chan and Tang. "Hao!" If his plan worked, he would soon be a general.

As important as it was to become acquainted, when they met, Chan and Booker projected an air of practiced indifference. Booker finally began the conversation.

"I see you put on the Jap's boots. I wish I had been that brave. The whole plane could have exploded."

Chan remained impassive. Not fluent, he nevertheless understood the gist of conversational English and merely nodded.

"Do you still have the Jap's sword?"

Chan shook his head. "Used to pay debt."

Booker left it there until he approached Chan with an invitation. "Do you have chopsticks?"

Chan patted his chest and nodded. "Hao."

The word 'Good' was used frequently. "You come to where we eat tonight. You can eat with me, outside. Understand?'

"Yes," Chan said. "Tang too?"

"Sure," Booker said. "Bring Tang."

The pair arrived early while Booker and some of the men engaged in sunshine poker. The warm sunny weather offered better light than candles. When Chan and Tang joined the spectators, to prevent them seeming impertinent, Booker waved a greeting. "Boys, these are my friends, Chan and Tang. I asked them to stop by."

"What?" sang out Billy Bob Jackson. "Charlie Chan and Poon Tang. Are you really Charlie Chan?"

"Knock it off," Booker ordered.

"Are you Poon Tang?" Jackson persisted.

Several of the men snickered.

"Yo, Charlie Chan and Poon Tang." Billy Bob taunted.

"I said knock it off," Booker said sharply, his brows drawn down in anger. Unless you want to go a couple rounds."

"Aw. Don't blow a gasket. I didn't mean nothin'. I was only funnin'.'"

"Are we gonna play cards or what?"

Booker said. "Play cards. Play 'em like you got 'em."

Billy Bob raised, the other three called. He put down a full house, three jacks and a pair of fours, and raked in the pot.

"Don't spend it all on hookers," teased a member of his crew. "Every time we go into town and the truck makes the rounds to go home, the last stop is always the pro center. There we find Billy Bob. We always have to wait for him. He can never get enough. He's a real Casanova."

Billy Bob smirked. "Man cannot live on bread alone."

"Is he really an expert?

"Expert? Hell, ol' Billy Bob is the undisputed world champ-peen!"

Nathan Berry identified a threshold opening. Booker had put down Billy Bob about his insensitivity. He had won a pot and a crew member had dubbed him an expert. A prime opportunity for Billy Bob to pontificate, Nathan asked almost dispassionately, "By the way, have you ever made it with twins?"

"The perfection over perfection? Hell no. I had a chance once. They were supposed to be real pros. A booking agent said he could arrange it but it would have cost me as much as a new Chevrolet. I didn't have the money …" Seeing he had the crowd's attention, Billy Bob rolled on. "Listen, your grandfather dreamed of making it with twins. So did your father, the Chief of Police, your preacher and the neighbor next door. Only one in eleven hundred thousand ever pulls it off. And none of you have ever met anyone who did. Not even Chennault with …" He halted abruptly, aware he had entered forbidden territory. "Right, Charlie Chan?"

"Right," said an impassive Chan.

Nathan marveled at the way Billy Bob turned it around. He had marked his territory—at least temporarily. Chan would be Charlie Chan, at least for him. "Listen," Nathan posed. "There is another possibility. If not twins, they could be sisters. Or you could just have a couple friends, out for a real good time."

Billy Bob looked afar and beamed. "It could be just as good, maybe better."

"What would make it better?" Nathan Berry asked. Men around were becoming fascinated with the conversation.

"What would make it better, Mister Philosopher is a double freebie, nothing held back. Dream on. It. won't ever happen."

"We are imagining. What then?"

"Well, son, when it's over those broads would hate each other for life. It would spell disaster and you can take that to the bank."

"Hell," interjected a spectator. You could get three Chinese whores for little or nothing—"

"And that is what it would be worth," said another.

"You sure know a lot," Nathan acknowledged. He thought of the distance between Ann Schmitt and Bobbie Kuhn who had been friends. That was before they became Myrtle French and Gertrude Solo. "Hmmnn."

"What are you murmuring about?" Booker said. "Don't believe a damn thing he says."

When the men went in for chow Billy Bob Willis Jackson accepted a minimal amount of food, retired to a corner, took out a neatly folded piece of paper. His pencil slowly moved. "Dear Jennifer. Well, Darling, we returned from an extremely dangerous mission, safe and sound." Jennifer Longstreet had made it clear that she was busy with defense work and would discontinue bombarding him with letters but would continue to reply when she received a letter from him. "I don' know what's gettin' in to her," Billy Bob whispered. He noticed her last letter did not end with the usual, "Love, Jennifer." She ended with, "Take care of yourself, Jennifer." At least she realized how dangerous were the missions he continued to mention.

Outside, Booker told Chan, "Wait here. I will be back with something to eat. He ordered double and triple his usual quantity, heaping the tray full. He asked for three bowls and carried the food outside.

"Bad food," Booker said, forcing a smile. "The water buffalo died of old age and tastes like the leather of your boots. The bread has been run over by a hundred trucks."

"Thank you," Chan said.

They ate in silence until Booker said, "I invited you for a reason. Do you know hamburger?"

Chan said, "Hamburger. Yes, I know hamburger."

Can you get me some ground beef patties? Ready for the pan? Fresh. Ready to fry. We cook it here. Can you get hamburger?"

"Ready to go? Ready to fry? Yes. Will be a mixture."

"That's right, some beef, some pork, some of this, some of that. Okay?"

"Very Okay."

"You bring it any time. Wake me if you need to." He handed Chan Chinese National currency equivalent to ten dollars.

18

BOBBIE KUHN MEETS COMMANDER FRITCHEN

In 1941, the U.S. Naval Hospital at Pearl Harbor sat on the south bank near the entrance of the harbor, where the channel forked north and south to surround Ford Island. This patch of land was Hospital Point. Just to the southeast of the hospital was the Navy's tank farm, a storage facility for oil needed by the Pacific Fleet. Behind the Tank Farm, a half mile away, stretched Hickham Field. The hospital's Commanding Officer enjoyed a well-manicured beachfront home, almost unseen by low-level personnel.

The bombing on December 7, pointed out the folly of having a hospital near oil tanks and a runway. In early 1943, a new hospital rose in Aiea Heights on Red Hill. From the hospital, one had a panoramic ninety-degree view of sugar cane and pineapple fields and the not too distant ocean.

Ensign Bobbie Kuhn drank in the sight and gorged on fresh pineapple to such an extent that a colleague warned, "Better tone down on the fresh pineapple or you will get a mouth full of canker sores."

With time available after orientation, Bobbie sat down and wrote a letter to her friend Nathan Berry, with the Flying Tigers in China. She read the last part of his letter again. "I suppose it is beyond wishful-thinking—that you spent any time thinking of me. Not where you are now. Do you ever think about after the war? I am going to college … probably to get a degree in psychology. I don't suppose you would like to be my favorite co-ed. Love and kisses, Nathan."

When Bobbie finished reading his letter, she sat beaming. She raised his letter to her lips and kissed it.

Presently, she received a message that the Captain wanted to see her.

"Nurse Roberta Kuhn," he began. There were no commissioned officer nurses prior to the war. Of the old school, the Captain sometimes continued to address them as nurses. "You wanted surgical experience," he said in a surprisingly avuncular manner. "I'm not sure I am doing you any favors by sending you to Commander Fritchen."

Bobbie raised her eyebrows in a gentle question. She learned not to interrupt. Why speak when a gesture would do as well?

"The man is a legend. When the bombs were falling on Pearl Harbor he was the first surgeon to operate and later continued four on and four off for days. He is entitled to a medal, but will probably never get one. That can lead to frustration—for you. Never complain about long hours. The only reason you will not be working twenty-nine hours is because there are only twenty-four hours in a day."

The Captain paused and relaxed, as if about to relate a mystery. "Commander Fritchen has a wife, a son and a daughter. They were out here, but less than two months before the bombing—as if they knew what was coming—his family bugged out for Iowa—leaving the Commander alone. The entire family became unpopular. This leaves a man who is moody, frustrated, lonesome, and a damn fine surgeon, with no one to take it out on but the nurses. Thank God, he respects patients. You may have heard that there is the right way, the wrong way, and the Navy way. There is one more and this will be paramount for you—Fritchen's way. Whether you make it will be up to you. I could give you a written recommendation but I chose not to do so. The first time you screw up, I don't want the Commander jumping all over me. Any questions?"

"No sir." *Jumping all over an officer who seriously outranks him? Fritchen must be a terror.*

When she reported to Commander Arthur F. Fritchen, Bobbie chose not to wear dress blues. She saw a face filled with authority, designed to command. His jaw was firm, eyes widely spaced and piercing.

"You are not in uniform," Fritchen said, aware of her scrubs.

"I came to work, not to parade."

She's got a smart mouth. "Very well, follow me. I want you to hold a penis while I try to insert a catheter."

She allowed the physician to take his position and she took the side opposite. He noticed she did not hesitate a moment to grab hold of the man's limp penis. She did not move it into an erect position but held it at a lowered angle, squeezing not too hard to obstruct the channel, and used two fingers to support his testicles. Fritchen had never experienced such competence. *She might be a whore but I can use a nurse who knows her business. Why was he thinking like that? After the bombing, a bunch of prostitutes came to help. Nothing mangy about them, they were tremendous help.*

Back at the office he continued his orientation, his right leg and right arm rising in unison as he warned, "You have heard there is a right way, a wrong way, and the Navy way. Now you will learn a new one. Fritchen's way."

She would become well acquainted with his rocking back, his right arm and right leg rising in unison and falling in cadence as he scolded, in this case someone named Mahoney. "Mahoney, you are so God-damned dumb."

"May I ask a favor," Bobbie said.

"No time off. No leave till you earn it."

"Right, sir. Would you come with me to surgery and show me how you want the instruments laid out. What I learned to call them may not be helpful. I want to learn what YOU call them."

The gruffness drained from him. He had never seen a nurse like this. He peered at her intently. *Obviously sharp, young enough to be my daughter. She might just work out.* He decided to give her the benefit of the doubt. *She seems willing to learn.* "You will be on call. Don't waste time putting on lipstick."

In the days that followed, she decided to learn if any nurses were present December 7, and if not, she would discover those willing to repeat scuttlebutt.

Careful not to be caught prying, she used a phrase that became a model. "Commander Fritchen was bear today. I think he would be in a better mood if he had a family."

"But he does have a family …"

In this manner, Bobbie learned a great deal about the intrepid commander. She learned not to exacerbate his moodiness and listened intently whenever he became professorial. She did not hear nurses gossiping that Ensign Kuhn had a salutary effect on Fritchen.

"You know," the Commander said to Bobbie. "Surgery and commiserating with the men takes a lot out of me. I go home to nothing. Life gets tedious. I do not intend to presume on your own time, but I wonder if some night you would accompany me to dinner."

"I would like that very much, Sir."

A puzzled Bobbie wondered later if his probe was all talk or real. It did afford her time to prepare a response if the invitation presented itself.

Two days later, Fritchen finished closing an abdomen and the grin that lifted the corner of his mouth told her he had something on his mind. As they strolled down the hall he said, "I think you would enjoy the Alexander Young Hotel."

"A hotel?" Bobbie said without emotion. "You are taking me to a hotel?"

"The dinning room, Miss."

Bobbie accepted the "Miss" as mild scolding. "That's a splendid invitation," she said. "But I have a request too. First, let's drive down to the old hospital where it all began. You can tell me all about the attack, what you did, how it felt. Maybe you do not know that some day I want to write this history. I hope for publication, but maybe it will only be for the family. You are a big part of it. The Captain called you a legend. I desperately need your story."

He tried to swallow his grin and failed. He pumped modesty into his tone. "I think that can be arranged."

19

JOE REILLY AND CREW IN TROUBLE

"Reilly's crew" made bombing runs daily on the 7th, 8th and 9th of July. The crew expected the night run on July 10, 1944 would be no different. The briefing officer spoke tersely. "You have been there before. You will hit the airfield at Hankow."

"Routine," Lt. Bob Russell thought. *Same as before. Follow the river, the tributary, and there it is.*

Tail-gunner Bob Mongell would rather miss the flight, stay home and play poker. "Hankow again," he whispered.

"You will carry fragmentation bombs," said the briefing officer. "The goal is to destroy all their planes on the ground."

Dada, the co-pilot nodded. *Makes little sense. If we blow holes in the runway, they make the Chinese prisoners fill them in before we get home.*

Reilly covertly scratched an itch.

They casually strolled to their B-25. Hours of darkness remained. Lt. Russell revved the engines and the plane lifted off with ease. The flight to Hankow was uneventful. In the darkness, the river rippled below. They followed a tributary. Then they were over the target. A searchlight illuminated them at once.

"What the hell!"

Usually searchlights stabbed the night sky. In previous runs, the lights had sprayed the sky in vain, usually a mile or more away. Lights continued to pin them.

Lt. Russell spoke his thoughts. "Have the bastards got radar? Look out!"

They started their run.

An ear-splitting explosion rattled their brains. The upper turret shattered, flinging shards and splinters of metal and Plexiglas everywhere. The plane lurched and rolled. Men inside were flung against walls and ceiling.

"We're getting out of here. We're going home! Pilot to Reilly. Check the bomb bay. See if any bombs are hung up." Sometimes a bomb would hang up and need to be worked lose.

Reilly crawled on his stomach to the bomb bay and made a report. "The bombs are still all there."

"Damn!"

"The bomb bay is shut. Looks like it never opened."

"Buck forgot to open the bomb bay?" exclaimed Russell. "Son of a bitch. Now we have to go back."

Searchlights picked them out again. Flak exploded all around, as their frag bombs stitched down the enemy field.

Reilly inhaled. *Still in one piece.*

Polinsky prayed. "Let's get out of here."

The B-25 labored and lost power.

We've been hit. We're going down!

Russell's voice crackled in the earphones. "Time to hit the silk. Abandon ship!"

Tail gunner Mongell made his way amidships. At the hatch, he fingered the pins that held the ladder they used to climb in and out of the plane. The pins gave way and the ladder dropped out of sight. He leaped into the opening. The slipstream caught his legs and he hit his head on rim before he dropped out of sight. Joe Reilly heard the bone-shattering thud that sounded like a club hitting a melon, and decided, "He's dead for sure."

Joe made his way to the opening and sat on the edge. The rushing wind caught his legs and whipped them back along the fuselage. His brain raced. He tried to remember parachute training. They hadn't had much. Training consisted of jumping off a six-foot platform and learning to roll. He remembered Mongell telling about a friend who bailed out. The ring of his chute kept hitting him in the face, breaking his teeth, breaking his nose, mashing his cheeks. Joe eased out of the plane and pulled the ring at once. He remembered he was supposed to count to ten. *Now it won't open. I am killed. I am dead.*

The chute opened. He felt his body snap. He kept holding the ring. He suddenly realized he had no feeling. There was no motion. *Am I dead?* He kept clutching the ring. All was still. He couldn't feel anything. He couldn't see through the clouds. He wasn't moving. He had to get moving. He had to get feeling. He unsnapped his holster. If he shot a few holes in the shroud, he would start dropping. Now he saw a cloud. *I am moving. I'm moving!*

He re-holstered his .45. *Got to unhook the chute.* He started the unhooking procedure. Then he remembered this was supposed to be done only over water. Was he over water? *No. There is no water here.* Now he was afraid he would fall out and started re-hooking. He snapped one lock, hit a tree, and hung there upside down.

He managed to pull the chute clear and cut a shroud line. He dropped to the ground. He looked around. He could not see much in the darkness. He dug into the emergency pack and located a folding machete. He dug a hole and buried the chute, saving some of the shroud lines.

He looked around furtively, relieved that he saw no one. His thoughts reverted to a time a few months ago when the briefing officer reminded them that the enemy shot down football player Tom Harmon behind enemy lines. During the month it took Harmon to return to base, he was aided by the Chinese underground. Reports of his exploits appeared in *Liberty* magazine and the *New York Times,* which identified those who helped him. The Japs sought them out and killed every one. "Knowing that," said the briefing officer, "We cannot predict what kind of reception you will get."

In the early morning gloom, he saw a mountain and decided to climb. He heard the Japs liked to stay low; they did not like high places. It made sense to climb the mountain.

At the end of the day, he had reached the top. Disoriented, he thought a rice paddy ought to be in the lowlands, but here was a rice paddy.

He knelt and drank deeply of the water. Now he remembered that the Chinese fertilized their fields with human wastes. He fumbled into his escape kit and found a Halozone tablet used to purify water. He popped it into his mouth and swallowed.

Horse out of the barn. He removed a canvas bottle from the emergency pack, filled it with water and dropped in a Halozone tablet. He drank again and waited for his guts to burn. Nothing happened. Did his belly feel warm?

The second day he walked down the slope on the far side and into a village. A man carried an umbrella. That meant they were going to walk together.

The people in the village provided a shower, donned him in a shawl and coolie hat. A man led him to a promontory and pointed down into the valley where he could see their crashed plane. The man gestured for them to go down to the plane.

"No," Reilly shook his head and refused to walk in that direction.

Joe wondered if the rest of the crew survived. Was Mongell dead? Had anyone in the village heard anything about his crew? He brought out the little book they called Lookie-Talkie and made his requests known. He learned nothing. The Chinese man tried to use the Lookie Talkie in reverse and had no success at that whatever. The Chinese man became extremely frustrated. Joe saw down to rest. He thought of his wife Kathleen. Any time now, she would be getting the dreaded telegram that he was MISSING IN ACTION.

As predicted, the dreaded telegram arrived.

WESTERN UNION

NYTC JUL 29 AM 4 L4
WU 72 44 GOVT=WASHINGTON DC 29 23 9A
1944 July 29 AM 3 54

MRS KATHLEEN M REILLY=

3023 92ND ST JACKSONHEIGHTS LI NY=

THE SECRETARY OF WAR DESIRES ME TO EXPRESS HIS DEEP REGRET THAT YOUR HUSBAND STAFF SERGEANT JOSEPH J REILLY HAS BEEN REPORTED MISSING IN ACTION SINCE ELEVEN JULY IN ASIATIC AREA IF FURTHER DETAILS OR OTHER INFORMATION ARE RECEIVED YOU WILL BE PROMPTLY NOTIFIED=
    ULIO THE ADJ GENERAL.

20

DOROTHY YUEN BECOMES DOTTIE

Lillian interrupted Dorothy's typing practice. "We can't live on greens and water. You will need to find your father and get some money."

Kukong still had not fallen.

Dorothy boarded the train carrying a chart of a typewriter keyboard she had drawn. She continued to practice. People stared at her moving fingers. *They think I am crazy.*

In Kukong, she went directly to Mrs. Au's store and asked to send a message to her father.

Sandow Yuen met her, face drawn, weary from lack of sleep. "I don't know where the Japs are getting all their equipment." He gave her all the money he could assemble.

Dorothy worried. "Will the city fall?"

"I don't know. I have to get back to my post."

Their meeting had lasted only five minutes. The train would not leave for hours. Dorothy decided to visit Willie and Jack at the radio shack. Willie was not there.

"After you left, Willie became despondent," Jack said. "He is terribly depressed. He asked for extra-hazardous duty. He is out in the field somewhere with his transmitter."

When Jack had a break, they walked to the restaurant under a darkening sky and a drizzle. By the time they had eaten, the drizzle became a heavy mist.

Jack had to return to the radio shack and Dorothy hurried to the station, still worried about Willie.

She saw no line at the ticket window. An officer said, "This train has been confiscated by the military. No civilian passengers allowed."

Brain numbed, Dorothy panicked when she thought what might happen to her, alone and helpless. She halted, sucked in a deep breath, and pushed unbidden thoughts to the back of her mind. She began to run. She saw a rickshaw and shouted, "Headquarters, please." She desperately hoped Colonel Ho Hon-si would be there. She reminded herself not to tell him she had visited the Americans. His back would stiffen with anger.

Ho appeared weary. His uniform looked slept-in. He listened and said, "I think you may be in luck. General Zung is in charge of troop trains. You met him at San Tung. Maybe he will make an exception for you."

"Would you write a note for me?"

"I'll do better than that. I will take you there myself. I need to get out of this office."

Enroute, Ho asked, "How are you getting along with your mother?"

Dorothy gave him a playful punch.

He said, "That is the most fun I have had in weeks."

At the station, confusion reigned. Soldiers ran back and forth. Many more were present than could possibly board the train.

"There is a possibility," General Zung said gravely. General Fong has a small roomette. Maybe his is willing to share. I will ask him on your behalf."

Something deep inside Dorothy wanted to cry out, "Don't," but she managed, "If you would, please." She had met General Fong only once, in Chungking. He had a great fondness for girls. Did she dare ask Colonel Ho or General Zung to inform General Fong that she was not that kind of girl?

General Zung returned presently and informed Dorothy, "General Fong said you are most welcome, but there is one thing …"

Dorothy held her breath. Her fingers clenched. "Yes?"

"He pointed out that the train only goes to Hengyang. You will need to get another train there."

Dorothy resumed breathing.

Troops clustered like flies on mooncakes atop the hopelessly overloaded railroad cars. In open boxcars, soldiers stood crammed together. In the tiny roomette, General Fong nodded and appeared tired. He lapsed into silence and Dorothy thought of Chungking and San Tung. Without Mrs. Wu, she would not have met so many generals.

Dorothy remembered a letter she carried. In the gloom, she could not read what Willie's mother had written, but she knew the words by heart. "We have picked out a nice Jewish girl for Willie." Before going to Kukong, Dorothy had sent a letter of reply. "Don't worry. The matter is already settled. I have refused the engagement ring" Had she really intended to share his mother's letter with Willie?

More depressed from losing her than from the hell of war, Willie faced a hell of his own creation. Unable to cope with her refusal to marry him, he had placed his life in danger. Dorothy now realized the wisdom of her father's advice. She could not marry Willie now or ever. One day, Willie's mother might face a hell of her own. The son who went to the Army as an obedient boy would return as an independent man. No way would she be able to pick a wife for Willie.

Arriving in Hengyang, Dorothy scolded herself for not having prepared. She should have known this train was also been commandeered by the military.

"I must get to Kweilin," she pleaded with an officer. Her words had no effect until she said, "I am an American and I must get to Kweilin."

"An American?" he said gruffly. "Then you must see an American officer."

"Where?"

"In a hotel across town."

"But I will miss the train." Already she heard the hiss of steam from an impatient engine. She had no choice. She hailed a pedicab.

At the hotel, the Lieutenant, a short, sour-faced swarthy man, eyed her with suspicion. Dorothy kept pleading and at length he relented and said, "Okay, if you don't mind sharing a roomette with a bunch of men."

"Americans?"

"Yeah. Take it or leave it."

Americans are civilized. "I'll take it."

At the station, the Lieutenant pointed at the rail car. Unable to board, a cluster of men filled every entrance. With a closed fist, she pounded on the side and shouted, "Excuse me. I am assigned to this car and I can't get aboard."

"Grab on," someone shouted. Arms reached out and hauled her through the window.

"I'm Whitey," spoke a platinum haired youth.

"Dorothy Yuen."

"You're a friend of Willie Hershenfeld and Jack Hartel," he exclaimed, face animated. "I'm with the Twenty-third Fighter Control too. We radiomen talk about you all the time."

Before long, everyone encountered a problem. The men relieved themselves by standing on the platform between cars.

Whitey offered a solution for Dorothy. "The train is so loaded it almost stops going up a hill. Jump out."

At the next hill, the men lowered her out the window. Dorothy squatted behind a bush, and as the train gathered speed, she ran for the waiting arms that hauled her aboard.

The men indicated they wished the trip lasted longer but Dorothy felt happy to return home. When her mother heard of her adventure, Lillian remonstrated. "You and your generals. It would not surprise me if you received an invitation from Chiang Kai-shek."

"I hope not," Dorothy said. "If Chiang sent for me I would be shot."

Dorothy busied herself with the 'liberated typewriter.' After two days of intensive study and practice, on July 29, she sent word to Yang Tong that she was ready to go to work.

The next morning, lanky Lieutenant Willett called for her in a Jeep and deposited her at a building near the edge of the runway.

"This is your billet," he said. "You will be living with nurses."

Two nurses were present, both tight-lipped. They each uttered a restrained "hello." Before they closed her room door, Dorothy overheard, "What is she doing here? She isn't a nurse."

"Hell, she isn't even white."

While unpacking, Dorothy heard a screech of brakes. A Jeep skidded to a halt. Looking out, Dorothy saw two men she would later know as Colonel Tex Hill and General Casey Vincent. The horn beeped. The nurses came running. The roar of the gunned engine drowned out giddy voices and giggles as the Jeep raced away.

Now an air raid warning shrieked. Running out, Dorothy looked for a shelter. Why hadn't the nurses told her about the nearest air raid shelter? That is the first thing people did when visitors arrived. Dorothy saw a B-25 gliding between a gap in the peaks, a Jap bomber hot on its tail. She flung herself to the ground, fingers digging into the earth. *Woom!* The earth shook. *Woom!* Too close—only a couple hundred feet away. *Woom! Woom! Woom!* A string of explosions stitched down the field. Steel fragments rained down behind her. Far down the runway, the B-25 landed safely.

"Bitches," Dorothy screamed, beginning to sob.

She returned inside and cried into her pillow. "You white bitches. May the salt of a million tears pour into your wounds." No one had told her the location of the mess hall and she missed supper.

In the morning, Lt. Jim Willett called for her. "Is there a place to eat around here?" Dorothy asked.

"Mess hall. No time now. The Colonel is waiting to see you. He will explain your mess privileges."

Willett marched her into the office of Colonel Wise. The Colonel explained, "Dorothy, you are a civilian employee of the Army Air Corps. Although a civilian, you are considered an officer. You are entitled to eat in the officer's mess. I understand that you have a billet in the nurses' quarters. Nurses are officers. Any questions?"

"Yes. May I eat in the enlisted men's mess?"

Wise hesitated, somewhat perplexed. "Yes ... I guess so ... if you wish."

Willett directed her to a typewriter at the far end of plain paneled room without heat or lights. On her right, Colonel Wise sat facing her. West Point trained and born to lead, his great-grandfather as governor of Virginia had signed the order to hang John Brown. Commanding the Third Sector, Colonel Wise was responsible for logistics and obtaining supplies for nineteen air bases.

As if his shadow, at the next desk, sat Lieutenant Colonel Chuck Hunter, then Lieutenant Ed Cabelka, formerly stationed in Africa. At the last desk in the row sat Sergeant Moore. In the center row were two desks. Dorothy sat facing Master-Sergeant Shirley's back.

Presently Lt. Cabelka approached Dorothy's desk. The tiny black moustache on his upper lip did not move when he spoke. "I want you to type an endorsement on this."

Dorothy flustered. "I don't know what an endorsement is."

"An endorsement," Cabelka said didactically, "is a terse usually one-line response to correspondence, indicating approval, or disapproval, or whatever action is taken. It is typed on the bottom of a communication, headed by the words, 'First Endorsement,' unless it is a Second Endorsement. The signatory officer signs above the typed name, rank and command authority."

Dorothy mumbled, "Yes," and spun the letter into the typewriter. Perspiration broke out at her armpits. A nervous spasm flashed across her back and burned there. Pulling herself erect, she inhaled and punched at the keys. The result was total chaos. She mangled Cabelka's name.

"Cavekla? My God!" exploded. "You didn't even leave a margin. Don't you know anything about margins?" He stormed to his desk and returned with a manual. "The first thing you need to learn is to leave proper margins. Read this. It will tell you all about margins and spacing. The Air Corps is fussy about form."

"I think her for is just fine," Sergeant Shirley intoned softly.

"Okay, you don't know how to type, but you will learn. I want you to type this endorsement until you get it letter perfect. I don't care if it takes all day.

When you get it right, we will cut it out and paste it over this—this—this" He flung up his hands in disgust and retreated to his desk.

Cut and paste became standard procedure. Soon Dorothy encountered a problem not listed in the manual. "Sergeant Moore, I need help," Dorothy pleaded.

Moore smirked and bit out, "Just because you are the only girl here, don't expect to get special attention."

"B-But—"

"Don't think we are going to do everything for you."

"I only—"

"I haven't got time to answer your dumb questions. Do your own work. Don't ask me to help you."

Sergeant's Shirley's eyes widened in disbelief. Lt. Cabelka frowned. He said in a gentle voice. "If you need help, Dorothy, you come to me. Do not worry about things you do not understand. This is your first day, and you are nervous. You will be fine in a couple days."

She had been wrong about numbers. It seemed everything involved numbers: 14th Air Force; 23rd Fighter Control. P-38s, P40s, and B-25s needed gasoline ordered in a quantity of 25,000 gallons. They dropped 500 pound bombs, destroying a total of 12 locomotives, 87 railroad cars, 164 trucks, 29 bridges, and 193 sampans in an area where massed 7500 enemy troops.

Without supper the previous evening and no breakfast, Dorothy eagerly waited for the noon meal. Ravenous as she walked into the officers' mess, a cheer rose above the din. Men whooped, hollered, and stamped their feet. Powerless to control the rosy flush that spread across her face, on the verge of tears, Dorothy wanted to run but her feet seemed glued to the floor. Clenching her teeth, she found a seat. "I'm not a star," she mumbled.

"Out here you are," said the officer seated nearby.

She managed to eat the double portion of everything she had been served and when she approached the office she heard an unidentified voice say, "I don't give a damn if she can't type. She stays!"

She identified the voice on entry. Lt. Cabelka stood laying down the law to the rude and impertinent Sergeant Moore.

Colonel Wise raised his head. "Ma'am."

Dorothy rose and hurried to his desk. He gave an instruction and by the time she reached the desk of Sergeant Stan Pillsbury in the adjacent wing, her mind blanked. "Oh God," she exclaimed. "The Colonel sent me to get a Special Order, but I can remember a thing."

"Don't worry," he said quietly. I'll help you."

Formerly a librarian in New York City, he popped he head into the Office from which Dorothy had come. "Colonel, what was the subject of that Special Order you wanted?" He returned, pulled the order out of the file and allowed Dorothy to carry it to the Colonel in triumph.

At the end of the day, Dorothy looked at the cardboard container near her desk, a cigarette box filled with rejected paper, a monument of her mistakes.

"Don't worry," Cabelka said, as he nudged the container with his toe. "Tomorrow there will be only half a case of Lucky Strikes."

Dorothy tired of the attention in the officers' mess and entered the mess for enlisted men. "I'm tired of eating eggs all the time," she complained to a freckle-peppered, red-haired Irishman from Boston. "I can't stand all this commotion."

"Leave it to me, Dorothy," Sergeant Denehy said. "When you want to eat alone, you see me."

"Next time."

When time for the next meal arrived, Denehy intercepted her and led Dorothy to a storeroom piled high with crates. There they dined in peace on K-rations, pork and beans and matzo balls.

Red Denehy raised a warning finger. "Don't say nothin' if you like it here. Let the enlisted men think you are eating with the officers and let the officers think you are eating with the enlisted men. Man," he exclaimed, "I'm putting my life in jeopardy. If they caught me, they would kill me."

Denehy stared into the distance. Amusement flooded his face. "I was jus' thinkin'. I had a civilian car in Kunming, a Nineteen Thirty-seven Plymouth. When I transferred here, I had to sell it. I wish I had that Plymouth here. I'd give you a ride. Lots of rides. Guys would sit up and take notice. I'd be the envy of the base."

"No," Dottie said. "They would envy that Thirty-seven Plymouth. Knowing you, I can guess where you obtained the gasoline."

"Right you are darlin'." Denehy's thunderclap of laughter revealed his devilish nature.

Dorothy learned that one reason for her popularity was due to Whitey, of the Twenty-third Fighter Squadron, with whom she had shared a roomette on the train from Hengyang. He had announced her arrival on the radio.

Ten days after arrival at the base, Colonel Wise said curtly, "Let's step out back."

A plowed area, for a moment he paced back and forth. His stern look told Dorothy there was trouble. "Dottie, you remember I told you to consider yourself to be an officer. Maybe I didn't make myself clear. An officer has a certain duty, an honor to uphold. That honor must be upheld at all times, even before duty."

"Yes, sir."

"Let me say what you do with your personal life is you own business" His voice sharpened. "Still we positively cannot have enlisted men in your quarters!"

Dorothy's mouth opened in dismay. "Enlisted men in my quarters? I never—!"

"It has come to me on authority."

"I never did."

"High authority."

Tears rushed to her eyes. Dorothy's shoulders shook to her sobbing. "I never had any men in my quarters," she managed. "When someone calls for me, I am always ready. When I see them coming up the road, I meet them outside. The only man who was ever in my quarters was Lieutenant Willett the day he dropped me off. He carried in my footlocker. He was gone in a minute." She couldn't stop crying. The Colonel's hand went to his chin. A pensive frown lined his brow. "I believe you," he said at length. "Now stop crying, Dottie."

Dorothy dabbed her eyes and felt him touch her arm. "Come."

No sooner inside, Wise issued an order to Lt. Cabelka. "This is another one of Casey Vincent's deals," he said. "Dottie is cramping the boy general's style with the nurses, otherwise he wouldn't be feeding me this bullshit. I hate to play into his hands and give him what he wants, but I want you to find a different billet for Dottie. We will put a stop to his spreading these God damn rumors."

"Now?" Cabelka asked.

"Right now!"

Cabelka returned in a short time and announced. "Dottie, I found a place for you in the officer's quarters of the Twenty-first Photo Reconnaissance Squadron."

Dorothy moved into barracks directly opposite the hospital on the opposite side of a narrow mountain range that snaked along the edge of the field.

The decision to place Dorothy with Photo Recon led to the men shooting an inordinate number of photos of her posing against various backgrounds. She guessed they were selling the pictures or trading them for favors.

An officer complained, "You are slowing our speed around here. We usually run around nude or maybe in a towel. Dorothy recognized the problem. Toilet and shower facilities were located in a large room and every time she locked the door, the entire battery went out of commission. She opted for using the ladies restroom in the base hospital across the street. She acquired a chamber pot for night use.

One night the Blam Blam of anti-aircraft guns shattered her sleep. She leapt up and saw at once that all the men had fled. Major Leo Brown was supposed to knock on her door to waken her in case of an attack. He hadn't.

Dorothy accosted him in the morning and he said sheepishly, "I didn't remember you until I was half way up the hill to the shelter. Then I was too scared to come back."

Dorothy arched scolding eyebrows. "Really?"

He never forgot again.

In a few days, Lt. Cabelka lifted the ban on rolling original correspondence into Dorothy's typewriter. The ordeal of pasting ended. Now the officers barked commands, and Colonel Wise would say, "Dottie. Take a letter to base commander. Tell him to—"

Dorothy's responsibilities increased. When Sergeant-Major Pepin's crew became stricken with dysentery, she was placed in charge of certain files and learned the Air Force was running a brothel.

"I know it's not by the book," Colonel Wise complained, "But I can't have the entire base laid up with clap. All the tarts, hookers and prostitutes in China have turned up here in Kweilin."

"Every other one is an enemy agent," Cabelka added. "Every now and then we round up the girls from the Bamboo Club and have Doctor Shaner examine them. That's the best we can do. Slit Alley is Off Limits."

At lunch, Dorothy learned from Red Denehy that Slit Alley was the area north of the bridge. "A lot of good Off Limits does," he scoffed. The girls mince over to the Ledo, the Red Plum, or the Central Café."

"I understand how the boys feel, "Dorothy said. "Every time they fly out on a mission they think it may be the last time."

"Yeah. They don't give a damn. If they did, more of them would come to Supply and get a pro-kit."

"Well, it's a problem for the Colonel."

"You think he's got problems? Every time I go to confession, Father Buckley says, 'What are you going to do now?' I tell him I'm going back to Supply and hand out contraceptives." Denehy titled back his head and laughter boiled from his depths. He focused on Dorothy eating her favorite part of the K-ration. "Dottie, if you don't stop eating those things you are going to turn into a matzo ball."

One evening Ken Kesterton knocked on Dorothy's door. He handed her a 'Dear John letter' he just received. It began, "Dear Ken. Relax. I'm married."

The next morning Ken took off on a photo recon mission. Unable to gain altitude, he aborted the flight and attempted to return to the field. The P-38 plunged, hit the ground, and exploded in a glowing ball of flame. Sirens shrieked, fire engines and ambulances raced to the spot, all arriving too late to be helpful.

One officer remained at quarters when someone came in looking for Kesterton's footlocker. It had already been removed and the man left. The officer had been asleep and couldn't render a description. Colonel Wise sent an urgent directive to the Commander of 21st Recon and together they examined the locker. They found three markers, probably from poker games. "Get those bozos in here," he shouted.

Soon three airmen were standing at attention at the Colonel's desk. He wanted to demand, "Which of you tried to get into Kesterton's foot locker?" Instead, he said, "We can't send these markers to his family. They have suffered enough. How long is it going to take you turnip-heads to make good on these?"

"I will redeem mine right now," Sergeant Booker said. He fished ten dollars out of his wallet and handed it to the Colonel.

The other two shrugged. "Not till next payday," Billy Bob Jackson said.

"Yes," said Menchnikov.

"Very well. You will have until the next payday. Lieutenant Cabelka, see that a lien on is placed on their wages." He whispered to Cabelka, "Have Booker come back to see me in an hour."

When Booker returned, Colonel Wise led the way outside. "We lost a good man and a good plane. Do you have any ideas why?"

"Pilot error, mechanical malfunction, bad gasoline, maybe sabotage."

"Have you been keeping an eye on Chan?"

"Nothing out of the ordinary, so far."

Did you go to Kesterton's room and try to get his foot locker?" Wise asked suddenly.

"No," Booker said, maintaining eye contact. "No."

"What about those two—Menchnikov and Jackson?"

Booker shrugged and rolled over both palms.

"I want you to keep an eye on them too."

Colonel Wise issued an order. THIS COMMAND HAS MORE TO DO THAN COLLECT MARKERS FROM EVERY LOSER WHO PLAYS POKER, EVEN IF THEY DESIGNATE THE SUM OWED IN BOTH NUMERALS AND LETTERS, EVEN IF THEY BEAR THE PRINTED NAME, RANK, SERIAL NUMBER AND SIGNATURE OF THE LOSER.

BE WARNED THAT MARKERS ARE DEBTS OF HONOR. COLLEC-
TION MAY BE DIFFICULT AFTER SEPARATION FROM SERVICE.

If his warning did not deter the use of markers or jawbones, Colonel Wise set
the standard for the required information on them, and made the men aware that
it would not be prudent to try to evade payment. Rumors ran rampant. Wise
would collect on markers if someone complained. In spite of the warning and
outrageous rumors, men seemed willing to risk court martial, being tossed in the
stockade, or assigned extra duty. The prudent among them became more wary;
the schemers refined their tactics.

"Have you heard the scuttlebutt on jawbones?"

"Oh look, here comes Dottie."

"I was already looking."

21

GAMES, THE BOOKER BOOK, AND A FUNERAL

Colonel Wise may not have foreseen that his order gave markers legitimacy. As markers increased in popularity, Sgt. Booker rehearsed a presentation he would repeat many times.

"Record your markers—jawbones—with Booker. There is no charge until you wish to verify the recording, and then the fee is nominal. Do not risk misplacing or losing a marker."

Recording consisted of making an entry in a small shirt-pocket book and adding his imprimatur to the marker. Booker l, Booker 2, Booker 3. When paid off, Booker drew a line through the book entry. If he witnessed the payoff, he added a "D." and if he saw the marker destroyed, "DD." If a grantor acknowledged the debt, he added a V. He did not explain his code to anyone.

Booker grinned as an idea blossomed. If recording became popular, nothing would prevent him from creating a bogus marker for $500 or $1000, allegedly made by someone recently killed or rotated home. Such a ploy afforded him entry into a high stakes game. After a long moment of amused contemplation, he abandoned the idea.

God apparently does not limit His protection to mad dogs and Englishmen. It may have been fate or a great comet impinging on the second house of Jupiter.

Not long after Booker spread the word at Yang Tong and the adjacent base, Ehrtong, a pilot soon to leave for home accosted him. "I have an eight hundred dollar marker to register. What will you give me for it?"

"Obviously you think it is worthless. I'll tell you what I will do. It's your choice. I will pay you half—if and when I collect—or I will give you a hundred bucks ... as soon a I get the cash. Tomorrow."

"I'll take the hundred."

"Okay. Because I am running the book, I will have you sign the transfer when we complete it. Tomorrow."

"At the latest."

Booker found a well-heeled pilot willing to trust his favorite mechanic with a hundred in exchange for a marker.

The transaction with the man going home, completed the next day, gave Booker an $800 marker. His eyes narrowed as he grinned. If he sold it for $200 or $300, he would garner a nifty profit. That might be better than pushing it out in a high stakes game.

Scuttlebutt about jawbones became rampant and Booker decided to run the "Booker Book" past Colonel Wise before some misbegotten rumors reached him. The Colonel listened to Booker's explanation and said, "As long as it's legitimate and doesn't interfere with your duties, I have no problem with it."

"It does give me an excuse to come and see you. I have noticed one thing about Chan and Tang. Now there is always a man stationed between them named Jung."

"Better keep an eye on him too."

As sunshine games became more popular, Hap, an officer and fighter pilot, sat in with the enlisted men. "Ah, recorded in a book," he observed when he heard Booker's speech. "You are one more obstacle to eliminate if someone wants to steal a jawbone. Now a rat has to eliminate two roadblocks. You could become a marker, I mean marked man. No pun intended."

At least I'm not a fighter pilot, constantly in danger."

"You could be hit in the head with a wrench."

"I see what you mean. While you are shooting down Zeros, some scumbag steals the markers out of your footlocker. Then I become a target."

"They won't get anything out of my footlocker," Hap said arrogantly. Any jawbones I have stay with me in Bouncing Beulah. They are safer in my plane than in a footlocker. There are the Chinese guards. If I get shot down, I lose more than some damn markers that may not be worth crap."

Booker did not take the banter lightly. He decided to secure a duplicate book at headquarters. The next time he went into town, he would purchase more notebooks.

Hap continued to tease Booker. "A guy could pull a Capone—take you for a ride."

The spectators laughed. Booker grinned and nodded. A duplicate record had become essential.

Booker carried the duplicate record to headquarters, intent on giving it to Colonel Wise, until his eyes halted on Dottie. Booker decided Dottie was a safer depository than the Colonel. Anyone harming Dottie would live about ten seconds—maybe five."

"You have enough on your mind," Booker told Wise and the Colonel agreed Dottie would be a better choice.

"I spoke to the Colonel, Dottie," Booker said. "Guard this book with your life. If something happens to me—" He left it there.

Now Booker let everyone know that he had safely secured a duplicate record at headquarters. They way he told it, the duplicate book had been the brainchild of Colonel Wise.

Booker reacted to suggestions to grow his business. He sought the assistance of another mechanic, Sgt. Nathan Berry.

"Schlitz," he began. "I need help with this recording gig. My weakness is a lack of cash. I know you have been saving for college—"

Berry cut him off. "And I am going to continue saving for college."

"I don't intend to dissuade you. What I need is a deputy to go to the 11th Bomb Group and to Ehrtong—and do some recording. If you want to buy any markers at rock bottom price that is your profit—money for college."

At length, Berry agreed and Booker showed him how to endorse the marker, assigned him some numbers to use in case he needed them, and created a code letter S for entries he created.

Several enlisted men accumulated enough money to risk playing for higher stakes. Hap, the fighter pilot accepted the deck and joked, "I'll be glad to relieve you of your cash."

Hap shuffled the cards with the élan of a casino dealer. Barry Menchnikov noticed and said, "You are obviously a more skilled poker player than we are. Officers make more money too. You will have to let us use markers."

"Jawbones? Sure," Hap said easily. He dealt to Menchnikov, Billy Bob Jackson and Booker.

Menchnikov, overjoyed with a pair of deuces, opened with a five-dollar bid, repeated by Jackson who held J-J and Booker with Q-Q. Hap glanced at his K-K and said, "Match your five and raise you a hundred. Cards?"

Menchnikov and Jackson requested three cards and Booker held up three fingers. Menchnikov added Q-2-Q and Billy Bob 7-7-5. Each of them stayed in with a call of one hundred dollars. Booker received three cards, unsuited.

"Let's separate the men from the boys," Hap said impishly, viewing 9-9. "Raise you four hundred more."

Presently, Menchnikov pushed out a marker for four hundred. Jackson raised an additional hundred and flipped in a marker for five.

"Five hundred?" Booker questioned. "Okay." He dropped in a marker for eight hundred and withdrew three hundred in cash. He suppressed a grin. *I paid a hundred for it and have already turned it into three hundred cash.*

"That's the idea men!" Hap exclaimed. "Two hundred for me to get even and a bump of another two."

"I call," Menchnikov said and contributed a two hundred dollar marker.

"I call," said Jackson and plunked down a marker.

Booker noticed that Menchnikov did not bite his lower lip as he usually did when he bluffed. He hadn't nervously tugged once on his left ear lobe. That meant he was holding something. The pair of queens he held wouldn't bring anything home. He had already dumped in a marker and pulled out 300 in cash. He would come out of the game three hundred dollars ahead of two players. "I fold," he said with weary pretense.

Hap presented two pair, K-K-9-9. Billy Bob had two pair, J-J-7-7. Barry Menchnikov felt nervous excitement ready to explode within him as he exclaimed, "Full house," and spread 2-2-2-Q-Q.

"You call deuces a full house?" Jackson muttered.

"Yeah!" He raked in the pot.

Booker saw the two queens he needed ended up with Menchnikov—not a good omen. While he ceremoniously muddled his cards, Booker quickly calculated that after the opening five dollar bids, $2800 had come into the game. There was $2200 in markers. If Hap had won, he would have had $600 in cash after having contributed $800. Before that dawned on him, Booker rose and said, "I have to tune up a Lightning."

Hap called to one of the many spectators. "Jerry. Get in here. These enlisted guys are killing me."

As soon as the Lieutenant seated himself, Barry Menchnikov shuffled the cards and stopped. "We are going to play a different game that I learned from a Texas tourist who came to New York. I call it Texas Throwdown. Everybody pays two dollars to buy two cards, which are held close to the vest. Time to bid. Then I deal three cards, face-up on the table. Everyone uses these cards as part of their hand. Time to bid again. I deal one more card face-up. Bid again. Then one final card face-up. Bid again. To recapitulate,"—he spoke the word deliberately. "Everyone will be using three of the five cards on the table to make their hand. Everyone can guess at what you are holding. It's a no limit game, four rounds of bidding, so be reasonable.

Holding a pair of aces, Billy Bob stifled placing a large bet and muttered, "Five bucks."

"Same from me," said Jerry the Lieutenant. "This is a crappy hand." He frowned at his mixed suit 9-10. "How the hell do you bet on only two cards?"

Menchnikov explained, "I guess we are betting on hope—getting more hearts, something like that. Just wait for the action on the three card throwdown."

Hap resisted an urge to raise the ante when he picked up a pair of kings.

Menchnikov said with a flourish, "Time for the Texas Throwdown." He slid cards off the top of the deck and spread a K-K-J

"A pair," Billy Bob cheered as if only he held the kings on the table to go with the aces in his hand. He started the serious bidding. "One hundred."

Jerry the Lieutenant went along with the hundred. "So we are all holding a pair of kings."

Hap grinned at his two kings and at the two kings on the table. "And a hundred for me."

Menchnikov delighted that he had dealt himself a pair of aces. For the next table card, he turned over a jack.

Billy Bob Jackson saw only the pair of aces in his hand and the pair of kings on the table. Maybe the dealer would turn over another king or another ace for himself. Jackson raised another hundred.

Jerry the Lieutenant wondered—hoped—the dealer would turn up a queen on the last card, giving him a straight.

Impressed with his four kings hand, Hap said, "Hundred to get even and five hundred more."

Menchnikov sucked in a breath. Two aces and a pair of kings were getting to him. He shoved in a $500 marker and turned over the last table card. "Deuce."

Jackson said, "Five c-note marker."

Lieutenant Jerry didn't get his queen to make a straight and folded.

"Going easy was for openers," Hap said, and looked at Menchnikov. "Now I'm going for blood. I know you still have that eight hundred dollar marker from the last hand. Up eight hundred."

Menchnikov tossed in the marker and said gleefully, "Call."

Jackson plunked in a marker. "Call."

Hap looked at Barry. "What do you have?"

"Aces over kings," Menchnikov said proudly.

"What?" Jackson objected somewhat indignantly. "I have aces over kings. "What the hell is going on? This is a crappy game. It ought to be outlawed like hearts." Early on there had been so many heated quarrels by men playing hearts, that hearts was ruled Off Limits for the entire base.

"I agree Texas hoedown is a crappy game," Hap said, "I think it was designed for hoes. But Gentlemen, I hold kings over kings" He raked in the pot.

"It looks like I have a deck of jawbones. Where did that Booker go?"

"He went to tune up a Lightning."

A sadness gripped Menchnikov. The game he held back as a big gun had failed him. Crowd reaction did not favor Texas Throwdown. It did present an outrageous a problem. The guy with the most money had an edge. He realized another problem. If Hap got shot down, with Booker's Book and a spare at headquarters, his paycheck would be attached forever.

Moments before first light of dawn, a one-ball *Jing bao* sent pilots racing for their planes. Left on the runway, the planes would be sitting ducks.

Hap gunned the engine and gained altitude quickly. He veered to the east. He kept his head and eyes moving. He looked around.

Below, not far off, he saw a lone Zero and dove in for the kill. He fired a burst and the gun died. Frantically he pulled the trigger again. Nothing. *Jammed!*

Sweat broke out at his armpits. *I'm unarmed!* In that split second he knew if he climbed the Jap would get him. He pushed the stick forward hard and poured on maximum speed. The Zero rolled and followed.

Hap twisted left, straightened and feinted slightly to the right, just as the Jap pilot expected, but Hap twisted left instead, gathering speed in a surging power dive that he worried he could not control. Could he pull out of the screaming power dive? He had waited until the last minute to pull out before the ground swallowed him. Hair stood up on the back of his neck. His heart palpitated. He thought he stopped breathing. He could not look back. He had to keep his eyes on the ground. He waited until the last minute and gave it a split second more before pulling out at much too close to jagged peak level.

Now he looked back. Did he imagine the Zero had ripped off its wings? It hit the earth and exploded on impact in a glowing ball of fire. "Separate the men from the boys," he whispered.

By the time he returned to base, his cigar chewing irritation ripened to gut-ripping anger. "What the hell happened to my gun?"

A cursory inspection and the armament chief said, "Easy to figure. Look. Somebody reversed a couple cartridges in the belt causing it to jam."

"Who the hell would do that?"

"Some sonofabitch who is more Jap than Chink."

Fighting a war demanded a higher priority than a routine investigation. Chinese Colonel Fong quickly discovered that Jung Kin had been assigned to guard the ill-fated plane. Jung denied seeing anything. At a separate meeting, Chan reported he had not seen anything suspicious. Nevertheless, Fong assigned Jung to guard a different plane.

At the suggestion of Colonel Wise, Booker spoke to Chan, who said they sometimes marched around the plane to keep awake. "I don't think Jung had time to get in. Too much risk."

Rumors quickly spread and pilots decided to check the ammo belts prior to takeoff.—if they had time.

Late in the evening, Booker paid a call on the sentries and spoke to Chan. "Everything in order?"

"Hao."

"Where is Jung?"

"He was moved."

The night remained calm and without event until almost the first light of dawn. Then the glint of a small flashlight attracted Chan. He saw someone coming out of Hap's plane. "Stop! What are you doing …?"

A loud shot shattered the silence.

Tang ran to where Chan fall. "Who did this?" he cried.

Chan managed one muffled word, "Birry," and died.

Tang glanced around. He saw no one. He had often seen death and knew what he had to do. He removed the Jap pilot's boots from the feet of his friend. Now several sentries and the roving guard appeared.

Tang moved to retrieve his rifle. He had placed it on the ground when he ran to his stricken father, and now it appeared pointed in a different direction. As guards crowded around the body, Tang turned his back and checked his weapon. *Who unloaded his gun?* He quickly reloaded.

Presently an officer appeared and took the weapon from him. He checked the breech and looked surprised to find it loaded.

Tang attempted to find words in English and could not. He gestured frantically toward himself and said repeatedly, "Sergeant Booker. Sergeant Booker." Colonel Fong had suspected Booker might be a spy, but Booker had been a friend. He had kind eyes. If Booker was involved, Tang thought it would be wise to bring him close.

Ordinarily, finding someone's billet might take hours, but because of The Book, Bill Booker was popular enough to be located quickly. Awakened, he hurried to the scene.

An interpreter arrived and Booker learned that no one had observed the mysterious shooter. Tang pleaded to be excused in order to report to Colonel Fong and asked Booker to guard the body of his friend.

Booker ordered two American guards posted while he made a report to Colonel Wise.

"It's that plane," Wise opined. "Someone spiked the gun before. Now someone wants to spike the guns or some other sabotage. You are a top mechanic. I want your crew to go over that plane with a fine toothed comb."

"Will do, Sir. In the meantime, I think the American government should arrange a funeral for Chan."

"What?" Colonel Wise erupted. "I have more to do than arrange a funeral for some obscure Chinese infantryman. We are trying to fight a war and losing. I can get enough of anything!"

Dorothy stared in surprise.

Colonel Wise read her expression.

Dorothy spoke up. "He did save a plane—probably the life of the pilot."

"Bad precedent," Wise said, speaking more slowly, lowering his voice. He saw Lieutenant C. K Wong had entered and wondered. *How much had he heard?*

"It would show that Americans value every life," Dorothy continued.

"There is a precedent in thanking China for saving a plane."

Colonel Wise raised his eyebrows at C. K. Wong. "Can you arrange a funeral? Check with Lieutenant Cabelka re costs. You will need to locate Chan's commanding officer."

"Colonel Fong," Booker supplied.

"Can do," Wong said. "Mama foo foo."

When Wong and Booker departed, Wise muttered. "Wong, Fong, Tang. Does every name have a ring to it?"

"Not Dottie Yuen," Cabelka said without emotion. *She can get a ring for every finger without batting an eyelash. Different kind of ring.*

The plane, Bouncing Beulah, checked and rechecked, idled at length. The idling proved that the fuel remained safe. The idling revealed no damage.

"Good to go," said Sgt. Nathan Berry.

Tang reported to Colonel Fong what he had not seen relative to the earlier sabotage. "I did not see Jung Kin on the wing of the plane. I did not see him jump, but I saw him in the air, coming down, about this far off the ground." He spread his arms wide. "When he landed, he bent over and picked up his rifle."

The Colonel said, "Chan reported seeing nothing that night."

Tang nodded. "If someone started at the tail of their plane and someone else started walking in the front their plane at the same speed, they could go round and round for a long time and not see each other." He used both hands in circular motions to demonstrate what he meant.

"This morning, when Chan guarded the plane, did you see who shot him? Even a shadow?"

"No."

"What did you notice?"

"After the shot, I saw Chan fall. I put my rifle down to help—my friend. After a while, I retrieved my rifle. Someone moved it. I checked my weapon. It was unloaded. I quickly reloaded and now an inspector asked to see my weapon. He was upset to discover it loaded."

"Did you see Jung there?"

"He arrived with other spectators."

"Hao. Go back to your post. I will assign a new guard."

Presently, American Lieutenant C. K. Wong arrived and promised the Chinese Colonel a funeral for the guard, financed by the Americans. Fong could not believe that Wong Chew, the American Lieutenant, would go to all the trouble to arrange a funeral for a lowly guard. Yet, it was happening. He would lose face if he did not capture the offender. Fortunately, he had an excellent clue. He ordered the appearance of Jung Kin.

Colonel Fong spoke to a junior officer when they observed Jung approach. "Are you sure that is the man who told you to check Tang's unloaded weapon—told you that Tang probably shot Chan?"

"Yes. He is the one."

"Go now."

The Colonel left Jung standing at attention. "I have some questions about recent events. Did you ever climb on the wing of an American's plane?"

"No, never."

"Did you ever see Chan associating with the meghwa?"

"No."

"Did an American sometimes come and talk to Chan?"

"Not in my sight."

Fong drew his pistol. "You should have been more observant." He fired. The bullet made a hole between Jung's eyes and he toppled backward. Fong quickly searched the body for jewelry and money. He found a small purse and called to an aide. "Throw this lying Communist traitor in the garbage."

Fong remained impassive. He would report to the General that the culprit who nearly destroyed an American plane had been captured and executed. The General would be pleased. He would report to the Americans that the traitor had been executed. The Americans would be pleased.

A saddened Tang returned to the Yang Tong base. The body of Chan now lay at the edge of the runway. As Tang knelt near his father, with the butt of his rifle on the ground, the muzzle pointed in the air, he noticed an unusual scratch on the weapon. He recognized the scratch. *This rifle is not mine. It belonged to my father.* Tang's thoughts came in a flurry. *No wonder I thought the position was changed. Someone switched rifles!* He forced his thoughts to slow. Instead of fleeing, as a criminal might do, he changed rifles. Why had he unloaded his father's gun? Although Tang's thoughts came deliberately now, her knew the killer possessed the cartridge—unless—unless it was ejected onto the runway. It came to him like a giant gong. *THE EJECTED CARTRIDGE WAS A SHELL CASING—AN EMPTY. CHAN AND HIS KILLER HAD FIRED AT THE SAME INSTANT!* Tang squeezed shut his eyes and remembered. Yes, it echoed, a loud bang, two shots fired as one.

He rose and his eyes eagerly scanned the runway for a shell casing, expanding the circle, searching. He did not find a shell casing. They were ready to start the plane.

Hap, the pilot bantered with the mechanics. "Is she ready?"

"Yeah. Fit as a fiddle and ready for love. You gonna take her up?"

"Nah? I'm just going to taxi around for a while, see if Bouncing Beulah has a bellyache."

Tang focused on the plane. *Fool. Instead of searching for a cartridge from your father's gun, you should be looking for a shell casing from the murderer's gun.*

The engine of the plane revved. Bouncing Beulah slowly began to move. Tang saw it. The glint of metal. *Shell casing!* He ran forward.

Mechanics thought it was another crazy Chinese ritual. Chasing a plane?

Tang warned himself. *Don't pick it up.* Was he some dumb coolie fresh from a rice paddy? He had read detective stories. He knew about fingerprints. He pulled piece of paper out of his pocket, quickly placed it over the casing, closed his fist, and thrust it into his pocket. He turned and ran to the body of his father.

In that moment before his hand closed over the shell casing Tang saw it could not have come from Jung's rifle, or his father's, or his own. It was the spent brass casing of an American .45 caliber pistol. Jung Kin must have stolen a .45. Now Tang had to inspect the wound.

Booker approached and saw Tang pulling aside Chan's clothing in order to see the entry point of the fatal wound. Booker stared at the hole, saw Tang hastily recover the garment. Booker gestured to emphasize his words, "Stay here. Stay here."

Tang nodded his understanding and Booker hurried to Service Group headquarters. "Did C. K. Wong get back, yet?"

"Not yet, "Dorothy said. "He should back soon."

Everyone waited for Lieutenant Wong. For Tang, it became a day of endless hours. Finally, C. K. Wong arrived with a group of funeral directors. Booker had left word to be notified the moment Wong arrived, and came running. He drew Wong aside, saying in a low voice, "Colonel Wise wants the bullet removed from the body prior to cremation. He wants to see all of us at headquarters. He wants to hear from Tang."

With interested parties assembled in his office, Colonel Wise explained, "We need to make a report so this matter can be closed. Interpreted by C. K. Wong, Tang realized the questions were more detailed that those asked by Colonel Fong. The American Colonel wanted him to repeat what he heard, especially the last words spoken by Chan.

"He said, 'What are you doing …?' Then I heard a loud shot. I ran to my friend's side. I asked, 'Who did this?' Before he died he uttered only one word."

C.K Wong interpreted, "Say his last word just like you heard it."

"Birry. Bir-re," Tang repeated.

Colonel Wise thought a moment and said, "If Chan understood Tang's question, in his dying breath, he named the shooter. That includes every Barry and Billy we know. Barry Menchnikov, Nathan Berry, Billy Bob Jackson—"

The Colonel's recall surprised Booker. He cleared his throat and said, "You can add one more. Billy Booker."

Tang's brain jarred to a sudden realization. What hadn't he realized it before? *Dumb son—not worthy of Chan.* When his father called out to the intruder, if it had been Jung Kin he would have spoken in Chinese. Chan had recognized an American! He spoke in English!

Tang stiffened and put on an impassive face. He dared not show emotion. He wanted to cheer at the discovery. Why hadn't he realized sooner? Why hadn't Colonel Fong realized it? He must be very careful not to accuse an American or the American Colonel would have him shot. *Remain calm. There is time to think later.* The killer is still loose!

"That's all," Wise said. "Dismissed."

Everyone saluted and Wise said, "Booker. Please remain." When the others had gone, he said, "There is going to be a funeral for the Chinese soldier. On my authority, you may invite the Billys and Barrys and a couple others. We can spare a few men for a funeral. Remember there is a war on."

"Will do."

Outside, Tang asked Wong to repeat conversation. *Booker is clever. He put his name forward with the others.* He acted like a friend, but he is not beyond suspicion.

The joy of suspicion, the realization of an unidentified new murderer hung as a dark cloud, diffused with rays of indecision. Tang decided to wait with his revelation. They had arranged a funeral for Chan—a very great honor.

Colonel Fong dispatched a message to Colonel Wise, thanking him for arranging the funeral, relating, "The traitor who sabotaged the plane by reversing the cartridges has been apprehended and executed for his crime."

When Tang received the news, most of his indecision disappeared. Colonel Fong had made a decision. American Colonel Wise had spoken. Neither dared lose face. It is wisely written on tablets of jade that if one seeks revenge, he should first dig two graves. Tang subdued his anger; he delayed digging two graves—but he would never forget. He would not forget the names, Barry Menchnikov, Nathan Berry, Bill Bob Jackson, and Billy Booker. Booker had taken pains to include himself in the list of suspects, precisely what a clever spy would do. He remembered Wong's words about Booker. "He is very much respected. He maintains the records of every poker debt. On this his word is law."

Chan had been cremated, his ashes placed in a decorated urn. At the appointed time, in a local Kweilin cemetery, Colonel Fong and Colonel Wise met, bowed low, and shook hands. A crowd of local dignitaries clad in white, a few in light blue, gathered with representatives of Chinese and American military. The priest burned fictitious money to help the spirit of the deceased pay the entry fee for the door into the spirit world. Mourners lit numerous punk candles. Chinese music failed to drown out the nose of many firecrackers. Colonel Wise, Lieutenant Cabelka, Lieutenant C. K. Wong and Dorothy placed small bowls of rice at the grave to sustain the departing spirit. An American bugler played taps. Throughout the ceremony, Tang wept quietly.

"I wonder when the spirit will come back and eat the rice," Colonel Wise said on the return trip to headquarters.

Dorothy replied, "About the same time an American spirit would return to smell the roses."

The moustache on Lieutenant Cabelka's lip almost moved.

22

COMMANDER FRITCHEN AND BOBBIE KUHN

Commander A. F. Fritchen sat waiting for Ensign Roberta Kuhn to arrive. Protocol of rank mandated that she call for him. Nurse Kuhn wanted to detour to the old hospital. She wanted to hear about the beginning of, 'a day that will live in infamy.' He tilted back in his chair and stared vacantly at the ceiling. Early that Sunday morning, he remembered shaving when the phone rang. The hospital wanted him there immediately. "We are being attacked."

During the ten mile drive from his cottage on the Elks grounds near Diamondhead, through the business center of Honolulu; local Polynesian police stopped all vehicles. "Go back to your homes." Wearing civvies, he expected they would halt him, but when they saw the P H license plate, they waved him on. He turned on the radio. A KGMB announcer frantically shouted, "This is not a drill. It's the real McCoy."

War! It starts again!

Now, as he waited for Ensign Kuhn, his thoughts reverted to the First War. He had graduated from the Chicago College of Medicine and barely completed a year of internship at Cook County Hospital when he found himself in France. As a Captain, an Army doctor, he treated the wounded and sat with the victims of poison gas and gangrene for two years, from the summer of 1917 until July 31, 1919. He never would forget the date they released him. That war had taken too much out of him. After the war, he started a practice in Decorah, Iowa and later joined the Naval Reserve.

As he drove to the hospital that morning of December 7, he could not stop remembering. *It has started again!*

Approaching the hospital, he almost parked under a tree. Everything was chaotic, enemy planes dropping bombs, small arms fire from the ground, larger guns booming in the distance. Fearing the tree would topple on his car, on sudden impulse, he parked on the pier and glanced up at the white clouds of smoke from anti-aircraft guns.

A loud voice came from the screened-in lanai. Captain Frank Ryan, executive officer, shouted, "For God's sake, Fritchen, get up in the operating room." Ryan had been Chief of Surgery until November 5, and since becoming the Executive Officer, he orally appointed him the Chief of Surgery.

A smartly dressed Ensign Kuhn stode into Fritchen's office and interrupted his reverie. "Ready to go, Sir?" Bobbie Kuhn asked pleasantly.

"Very well."

"You wanted to know about the beginning," Fritchen said when they reached the car. He allowed her to open the passenger door and seat herself.

"The beginning is different for everyone," he said didactically and shifted the car into gear. "For me it goes back to the time when we were a family—together—enjoying tropical Hawaii. We had dinner on the Battleship Arizona. Commander Roehow, the senior medical officer on the Oklahoma invited my family to dine in the wardroom of the Battleship Oklahoma—heady stuff for my eleven-year-old son, Dean. We were constantly meeting people. My wife Ann said, 'You have an affinity for strays.' Joe Tulis wasn't really a stray. He was different—an old sea dog. He spent a lifetime in the Merchant Marine and managed to wangle a Lieutenant's commission with the Navy.

"Joe Tulis was certainly interesting. He marveled at the way Japan built up their navy. He called their navy awesome. 'It's Awesome,' he insisted. 'Any day now they are going to attack Hawaii. The Japs really want to hit L A and Frisco, but then they would be caught between the coast and the Pacific Fleet. They will settle for a strike here at Pearl.'"

Now, as Commander Fritchen and Ensign Kuhn neared the old hospital, he said, "I nearly parked under a tree but at the last moment, I parked on the dock. The dock took a direct hit, blew up, and my car went into the drink. Later, when it was safe, I had a diver go down and retrieve the license plate." Something about the memory of parking on the dock bothered him. Maybe he should not have told her that. Yet, there were still staff members around who probably told her that already.

The Commander stared into the water and his somber expression told Bobbie he was visiting a grave. She chose to venture a well thought-out comment. "If you had been at Lexington and Concord—if you had been at Gettysburg. If an Admiral pinned a Navy Cross on your chest. If you had dinner with President Roosevelt or shook hands with Winston Churchill, none of it is as important as your seminal experience here at Pearl Harbor on December Seventh! It will prove to be the singularly most important moment of your life!"

Fritchen swallowed. His eyes misted. He wanted to take her in his arms and draw her to his chest. He forced himself to look away.

Bobbie asked, "So where did you originally want to park your car?"

Her question dissolved the spell. He would ask himself dozens of times why he wanted to hug this clairvoyant grandmother in a girl's body, and never found an answer. He knew it was not sexual. It was dispassionately mental, almost as if some mysterious force—heard by whatever controlled his conscience—spoke her words.

"Under that tree over there," he managed, pointing. He hadn't intended to tell her about the family, but she probably heard scuttlebutt. Negative gossip always circulated more quickly than compliments. "Ann was thoroughly fascinated by Joe Tulis's prediction of a Japanese attack. When Marjette left to attend the University of Iowa, the idea became an obsession. Tension between us increased. We had words."

Bobbie did not desire a further explanation and diverted him. "What is your daughter studying at the University? Following in her father's footsteps?"

"Oh, hell no. She takes after her artistic mother. She is taking English and drama. As I was saying, for Ann it became an obsession. One evening Ann declared, 'I had a premonition. There is going to be an attack soon. Dean and I are going home!' They left on the navy transport, Wharton."

"Not too popular, I imagine," Bobbie said softly.

"You can say that again. Getting closer to the day, on the evening of December 5, a Lieutenant Colonel invited me for penny-ante poker. At the end of the evening, I gave an Ensign a ride downtown. He told me that on Wednesday night the 3rd, when they were out on maneuvers, they came across a Japanese submarine. The captain of the battleship called all the officers together to determine what action to take. They did nothing. There is plenty blame to go around. On Saturday night, the Sixth, I had the duty and stayed near the phone. That is the only night since I arrived that we had no surgery. Truly, it was the classic lull before the storm. That is when I had a premonition of the attack. Still it surprised me when they attacked the next morning."

"I know you were extremely busy in surgery." Bobbie removed a small notebook from her purse.

"Yes," Fritchen said. "I am certain that I am the first surgeon to operate at the start of hostilities. My first patient already lay on the operating table. Something nearly amputated his left arm at the shoulder. I quickly completed the amputation and sent him to the ward. I ordered him treated for shock.

"Between operations, I had a couple seconds to peer out the window. An enemy plane passed so close I made eye contact with the pilot. A terrific explosion in the direction where I parked my cart blew out hospital widows. Not that close, it was the Destroyer Shaw blowing up. A Jap plane came down and skidded off the roof of the laboratory building, across the tennis court, into the petty officer's residence. I heard later, a sharp-shooting Marine rifleman had brought down the plane.

I kept operating for more than five hours and during that time only lost one patient. Lt. Commander Gross relieved me. We went on a schedule, four hours on and four ours off. That doesn't sound difficult, but a person has to eat, sleep and bathe on the four off. Soon, we were so beat we could not get to sleep and we dared not take sleeping pills for fear of falling asleep during surgery. It was pure hell.

"I hear you did some outstanding surgery."

"I operated on a patient with a rent in the terminal end of the bowel which allowed feces into the abdominal cavity. I sutured the rent, cleaned out the feces, and was about to close, when the lights went out. Tracer bullets from a machine gun flashed past outside the window. I placed my head on the operating table and waited until the lights came on again to resume suturing. I completed closing. Thanks to the sulfa powder that I sprinkled inside, the patient did well. We were thankful for sulfa powder."

"And I am thankful I took shorthand in high school, Bobbie said. "Don't stop."

"That night a young man came in, hit by shrapnel. The shard entered one side of his thigh and exited the other, leaving a funnel shaped wound. I picked out pieces of bone and realized the femur had been completely severed, a section missing. I debrided the wound, shook in sulfa powder, covered the wound with Vaseline gauze strips and immobilized the leg. Bone grafting needed to be undertaken later. It turned out this patient was Ensign Taussig, either a son or nephew of Admiral Joseph Taussig. Later, I received a letter from Lt. Commander Roehow, who invited us to dine with him on the Oklahoma. He was now a patient at Mare Island Naval Hospital in California and stated that Ensign Taussig was there with him, getting along fine, and sent his greetings. The Ensign didn't lose his leg."

"That was nice."

"It made me feel good."

Commander Fritchen continued to talk as they briefly toured the old hospital, now an auxiliary facility. "I did two surgeries that I will probably never repeat. I completely reconstructed two rectums. You may omit that from your report. I am nevertheless proud of the accomplishment.

"The nurses were exceptional. Only one nurse broke down, became hysterical, and could not stop crying. I remember surgical nurse Lillian Banks from Hampton, Iowa, lying here on the tile floor, trying to get some much needed rest. I particularly remember people from my home state."

"I do too." Bobbie said. "I'm from Wisconsin. Milwaukee."

"I was born in Wisconsin. Racine."

At length, Bobbie said, "Thanks for showing me around the old hospital. I appreciate it."

When they set out for the historic Alexander Young Hotel, the Commander said, looking straight ahead, "I remember something else. They invited us for dinner on Battleship Oklahoma. After dinner, a young priest came up to me and asked, 'Are you Dr. Fritchen from Decorah, Iowa?' I said I was. He hailed from St. Lucas, about twenty miles from Decorah. I remembered operating on his sister. We delayed surgery in order that he could be there. He offered me a cigar and we went out on the spacious deck of the Oklahoma and enjoyed a movie. That is the last time I saw Father Aloysius Schmidt."

The Commander swallowed. "During the attack, the Oklahoma capsized, turned upside down, and looked like a huge injured whale diving for the depths. Father Schmidt's hips were too wide to squeeze through a porthole, but he kept shoving slimmer men through to safety as long as he could. He went down with the ship. I had to get that out before we reached the hotel."

Military men crowded the large dinning room of the Alexander Young. Most were officers, predominately Navy.

"What would you like to drink?" Fritchen asked.

Bobbie said, "Vodka Collins—and just one." She wanted to set a guideline early.

When the drinks arrived, the Commander told the waiter, "We will start with papaya sprinkled with lime juice."

He turned to Bobbie. "I heard the broadcast by President Roosevelt. He downplayed the damage here, as if the enemy had barely scored. In reality, thousands died. Bodies were stacked up like cord wood. We had a total blackout on photos. They said the American people couldn't take it. I think that was a big mistake. The American people should have been told."

Bobbie sipped her drink. She could barely keep up with his continuing conversation. When she saw his drink glass nearly empty, she said. "Excuse me. I need to make a trip to the head." She did not return at once and spent a couple minutes writing what he had told her at the beginning of the evening When she returned she saw he had a fresh drink.

When he emptied the glass, Bobbie said, "Alcohol runs through me like a sieve," and returned to the ladies room to transcribe more of his recollections.

On her return, she saw the Commander had a fresh drink.

"I think I should have talked to someone about this sooner," he confided. "It feels good to get it off my chest."

His unburdening, Bobbie realized held more than a hint of disappointment. Several times, he repeated, "She should have stayed till Christmas." Many of the Navy wives boarded ship and departed for the Mainland on Christmas Day. Bobbie debated and refrained from saying, "Having an independent wife must bring many advantages." She cut a piece of steak and popped it into her mouth.

Fritchen covered the awkward moment with a solemn pronouncement. "Sometimes Ann is too damn artistic."

"I am so glad you shared your memories of that terrible day," Bobbie said. "You have been extremely forthcoming."

He stared at her glass. When you say one drink, you mean it. "Do you have a young man?" he asked suddenly.

She smiled. "Well, that is a positive maybe. We were in high school together. It is a rather low flame on the back burner. He is a mechanic with the Flying Tigers. When this war is over, he plans to go to college and study psychology. He wants me to be his coed. I think I will."

Fritchen nodded, muttered, "Good," and became pensive.

Bobbie guessed his thoughts focused on something far away. "I am enjoying this fabulous pineapple pie."

Fritchen ordered an after-dinner drink and said, "This evening is more fun than I had in a long time. That is why we cannot do it again for a long time."

Bobbie listened and allowed her inquisitive nature to question, "Would being seen with me generate a rumor about favoritism?"

"Certainly. More than that. As things appear, they are—even when there is no substance."

Bobbie did not comprehend that he worried more about her reputation than his own. She tried to define him and jotted down, "Beyond category." She had the vague impression that the Commander was not thinking of her but of someone else.

When they returned to the car, Fritchen said, "Hilo Hattie came to entertain us. She taught some of us to hula. She kept saying, 'Watch the hands, boys. Watch the hands.'" Now he began to sing quietly, "The Princess Papuli has plenty papayas …"

"I know that song," Bobbie exclaimed and joined him.

"She loves to give them away—and all the neighbors they say—oh me-oh, oh my-oh, you really ought to try a piece. Of the Princess Papuli. Papayas."

They laughed together.

At home in the nurse's quarters, Bobbie reviewed what she had written and added notations. She thoroughly enjoyed the evening. Spending time with the Commander allowed her to think of someone other than herself. Wracked with guilt, she wondered if there was more to life than a bundle of secret longings, secret feelings, and secret emotions, shared with someone who had his own cluster of secrets. Sharing might not occur if the secrets did not remain secret.

If you want to share a life with Nathan Leighton—'the latent'—Berry, Ensign Robert Kuhn, you better get off the tuffet and grab the shy boy. You had better go for him.

Her thoughts continued to focus on the man in China. *If he wants me to be his coed while he studies psychology, I'll give him something to psycholize.* Soon, she decided, she would write with enthusiasm, restrained enthusiasm, "Yes, I will be your coed. I do nylons but I don't do socks."

23

JOE REILLY AND CREW TRY TO GET HOME

Alone in a Chinese village, Joe worried: had everyone been able to get out of the plane? They should have. Where were the others? Were they safe?

A day after he landed, Joe heard voices filled with excitement. Then he saw them approaching—the rest of the crew. Mongell was with them. "I thought you were dead," Joe said. "The way you hit you head."

"It still hurts," Mongell said.

Reilly looked at them. "Where are your pistols?' No one carried pistols. He directed a sharp gaze at pilot Lieutenant Russell.

"We gave them away," Russell said sheepishly.

"I would never relinquish my sidearm," Reilly said. "I see he has a forty—five." He directed his gaze toward their guide, a short young man who delighted in waving a .45 pistol, ordering the villagers to do this and that, as if he was a commanding general.

"Yeah," Polinsky said. "He acts like a big wheel. We call him Little Wheel. You got a cigarette?"

"Sure," Joe said. "Where are yours? Didn't you get any in your pack?"

"What pack?"

"The back pack of your parachute. It had lot stuff in it ... medicine. Halozone to purify water ... Atabrine to ward off malaria. There was a little compass ... a folding machete ... a wire saw ... and cigarettes. Where is your stuff?"

"I didn't know it was there."

"What about you?" Joe asked. He asked each man.

Not one of them had saved the pack. Reilly viewed them with disgust and rising irritation. "Weren't you guys ever listening when we were briefed?"

"I'm glad somebody else is catching hell," Buck Doyle said. "Mongell and Polinsky have been giving me hell for not turning out the light in the nose cone."

"And not opening the bomb bay," Lieutenant Russell added. "If the bomb bay had been open we wouldn't have had to go back."

"Yeah," Polinski said bitterly. "If we didn't have to go back we wouldn't have been shot all to hell."

"And forced to ditch."

"I'm the one who had to crawl to the bomb bay on my belly," Joe said. He looked at pilot Russell. "The next time you want the bomb bay checked; you send Doyle."

"Sounds reasonable," Russell said.

"That's water under the dam now," Dada said. "We aren't out of the woods yet."

"If we ever get back, we ought to trade Doyle to the Athletics—or whoever is in last place."

"They wouldn't take him."

"All right. All right, you guys."

Little Wheel kept waving the pistol, ordering around the village peasants like a major domo. They dined on eggs and more eggs. The crew felt like they were eating a week's supply for the village. They heard someone killing a pig. The village cooks served chicken and when a villager reached for a serving, they learned to divert him in order for a crewmember to grab the piece.

Villagers paraded past with large pieces of pork. The crew received the heart, lungs and liver. Joe said, "I hated liver since a kid when my mother fried liver and onions."

Little Wheel stashed the crew in an attic over a Chinese School. The School was far different from what the men had known. There were apparently no questions or answers, no silent times. Everyone talked at once, all the time. The men found it difficult to sleep.

Again, they were fed. They hate heartily, and wondered what they had eaten. Reilly used his book, the Lookie Talkie and learned they had eaten Dog. "It was dog," he announced.

Mongell immediately became nauseated and threw up.

With Little Wheel leading, they walked along narrow trails for sixteen days. Little Wheel remained with them waving his pistol, getting them food. A Japanese plane noticed them. Buy the time it began its strafing run the men had flung themselves behind boulders or rocks. Seeing nothing more than peasant's garb, the Jap pilot decided not to waste his ammunition.

Later, another Japanese pilot sprayed the rocks over their heads, apparently hoping to start and avalanche. When it didn't happen he failed to make a second pass. When they were about forty miles from their base, they climbed aboard a bus. Soon they transferred to a train and didn't need tickets.

When they arrived in Kweilin, they could not send lengthy explanatory Western Union telegrams. They sent standard greetings like, "Merry Christmas," and, "Happy Birthday," And adding the words. "I am safe and sound."

Joe told the briefing officer, "I sent fourteen of those telegrams to every member of the family I could think of. I hope one of them got the message that I am all right."

At the base, all the men except Reilly drew sidearms and became acquainted with the emergency packs in their parachutes.

Lieutenant Russell added an additional command. "Nose cone dark."

On the next run in their newly assigned B-25, when Russell ordered in a tense loud voice, "Bomb bay door open," someone was heard to mutter, "If it ain't open, we'll throw out Doyle."

Riley said, "If it ain't open, somebody else can crawl on their belly and open it."

24

WHEN LUCK RUNS SOUR

Lieutenant Cabelka waved his arms and fussed. "I don't know what he expects. He appears out of the blue like a phantom, and wants everything on a minute's notice. I need a case of cigarettes to pay his radio operators. I need some CN. He expects to pay them in advance. Doesn't he know that is prohibited by Air Corps regs? All right, Dottie I want you to type up the request, the voucher and disbursement forms. I'm headed to payroll."

Dorothy grasped his problem. Cabelka always had to take American greenbacks to the local black market and trade it for Chinese National currency in order to pay everyone. Dorothy read the order. Her head snapped when she read, "Captain John Birch."

The moment Cabelka returned he exclaimed. "A newsman on the base gave me the same rate for CN as the best black market downtown."

Dorothy stopped typing, ran to the mess hall, and asked excitedly, "Have you seen Captain Birch?"

"You just missed him. You know what he did? He ate one meal including dessert and started over and ate another whole meal."

Dorothy ran to fighter headquarters, failed to find him, and hurried to medical supplies. She did not find Birch there and returned unhappily to the office.

"You just missed him," Cabelka said.

"Oh damn. I wanted to see him."

"Maybe you can catch him before this plane takes off."

When Dorothy arrived at the runway, the plane had begun to taxi. Crestfallen, she returned to office. Seeing her distress, Lieutenant Cabelka said, "Let's get a cup of coffee."

In the mess hall, Cabelka drew two cups of coffee and seated himself. "So you know the living legend."

"Yes, we are friends."

"I would say a little more. We have to keep the lid on about John," he said soberly. "Can you imagine some correspondent getting wind of him? He is one of the biggest heroes in the Pacific."

"Really?"

"Really. The man is absolutely fearless. He is behind enemy lines half the time. When one of our planes get shot down, the peasants put what remains on ox carts, on railroad cars, and we get them back. Eighty percent fly again. When a plane went down, in the early days flyers who survived were pitch forked. Today, we get them back. That's because of John Birch. One tiny slip would put him in danger."

"Well, I'm glad no one knows."

"And probably never will. Folks will remember Colonel Jimmy Doolittle's raid on Tokyo back in Forty-two. They might remember Doolittle was forced down inside China, but will they know it was John Birch who saved his butt and got him out? Hell no." Cabelka lit a cigarette and laughed. "The irony of floating our entire payroll through the black market. I finally found some use for a newspaper correspondent."

"We had better get back," Dorothy said.

Efficient little Dottie, that's you. Since Colonel Wise started calling you, Dottie, the whole base has picked up on it. Incidentally, the Colonel likes you."

"Really?"

"He had me put though a raise for you. I'd say that proves it."

"A raise? For me?"

"Oh, c'mon, Dottie. Don't you know the influence you have over him?"

Dorothy knew not to under-rate the influence of Lieutenant Cabelka He had created an entire squadron out of thin air and managed to release information about their missions and exploits, all in order to obtain additional much-needed supplies. No one ever uncovered the fact.

Every day held something interesting. An enlisted man operated a still behind the barracks and produced alcohol. When the still exploded and killed him, the base chaplain, Father Buckley joked, "I sent a letter to his family stating that he had been killed in action." Those who knew Father Buckley knew the truth could be elastic.

Father Buckley enjoyed playing poker. At the start of a marathon weekend in the quarters of Master-Sergeant Harry Bratty, Jim Denehy and Fred Ifft joined him in a spirited game. Father Buckley was a fierce competitor. Whether playing baseball—he covered second base—or playing poker, he hated to lose. Idle banter became personal.

Red Denehy emitted an evil laugh. "Prepare to lose your ass, Padre. I'm going to win back my bucks."

"That will be the day."

"Now, now," Bratty said. "Remember the first law of poker. Leave emotion at the door."

"It's not emotion," Denehy objected. "This is reality. What is your second law?"

"Learn to draw out a bluff."

"And the third law?"

"If someone tries to buy the pot with an outrageous raise—" Bratty halted.

"Well, what's the rest of it?"

Bratty chuckled. "No one has figured out the answer to that one yet."

Father Buckley spoke. "Well, maybe I will just teach a certain red-headed sinner the fourth rule. Never mess with Father Buckley."

The others laughed politely. They remembered another of the priest's inadvertent pronouncements often returned to haunt him. "Little white lies don't count."

The daily grind of endless missions, the need to squeeze in eating and sleeping, resulted in poker losing some of its luster. Nathan Berry realized certain players had an obsessive urge to win, to accumulate money. Others exhibited a similar obsession to merely survive. He wondered if this reflected how they viewed their role in the military. Did obsession always eliminate fun?

Billy Bob Jackson had lost consistently. He knew his luck had to change. Soon. The next hand would be different. The next deal would give him blockbuster cards. *C'mon, hit me with a couple aces to start.*

His breath caught when he picked up an ace. Then he received an unsuited 4-5-6-7. He dumped the ace and could not believe his good fortune when he added an 8 to his hand. He swallowed hard and allowed the corners of his mouth to turn down in a misleading scowl. He closed his fan of cards. One player had folded; the two remaining players had each called for two cards. What were the odds of them getting a full house or drawing four of something? Playing it cool, he raised the bid twenty dollars.

Menchnikov raised fifty dollars.

Booker raised fifty dollars.

One of them is bluffing, probably both. Billy Bob flipped in a marker and called.

Menchnikov laid down a heart flush and reached out to rake in the pot.

"Shit," muttered Billy Bob.

"Not good enough," Booker said and displayed a full house, Kings over Jacks.

"Shit is right," Menchnikov said and stopped reaching for the pot.

"Mail call," shouted the clerk. "Ives, Jackson, Jones...."

"Jackson here," shouted Billy Bob. "I can't win a damn thing at cards. Maybe my luck has changed. He ripped open the envelope he recognized. He read hastily and paled. He forgot to breathe. Now a rosy flush of anger ascended his neck and diffused across his face. "The bitch sent me a Dear John letter," he cried. "The bitch is married. This is one crummy day!"

He read her letter:

To Billy Bob Willis Jackson, Often when I write there is little news. This time I have news!! Little did I know when I worked at the factory what might happen to me.

Do you remember how we agreed to communicate? Paragraph 3?

3. This is where you are or HAVE BEEN. Irene Daniels, Alice Tucker, Susan Grimes, Karen Lee, Trixie, and numerous Chinese prostitutes.

Ah ha ha, can't you see,
As you read paragraph three,
of the last letter you'll get from me.

By the time you finish reading this letter I will be MARRIED. Call me Missus, but don't you ever write or speak to me again!

Several days in the future, Billy Bob would realize that he should have done nothing. Instead, he set out on enlisted man's night on the town. He drank heavily from the get-go and ultimately engaged a prostitute. Morose and deeply intoxicated, alcohol inhibited his ability to function. Enraged he began beating on the nearest substitute for Jennifer Longstreet. "You two-timing bitch, I'll kill you"

He kept swearing at the prostitute, beating on her. Her terrified screams drifted through his alcohol-fogged brain. He had to get out. Racing into his clothing, he made his legs move. He left without paying. "Go to hell!"

His failure to pay, converted a community service entrepreneur into an unwilling volunteer. She tasted blood in her mouth and she tasted revenge.

In the morning, after-thirst drove Billy Bob to water. He became nearly as drunk as the night before, and staggered around.

"Get this idiot a skin full of coffee," said his pilot. "He is in no condition to fly with me." Against his better judgment, he allowed Billy Bob to assume his position as tail gunner.

The drone of the B-25 lulled Billy Bob to sleep. When the Captain learned of his dereliction, he ordered the waist gunner to take his place. Friendly fighters provided cover and the plane escaped without incident. On landing, the pilot drew Jackson aside. "If you ever pull that crap again I will have you up on charges. Unless you accidentally-on-purpose fall out the bomb bay."

"It won't happen again, Sir." Billy Bob knew that being respectful paid off.

Two nights later, a sober Billy Bob walked the streets of metropolitan Kweilin, and determined to remain that way. With an evening dedicated to friendliness, it nevertheless surprised him that his presence generated so much attention. Various girls approached him. "You say how much, Joe."

He waved them away—until he saw a comely prostitute whom he patronized before—her lithe body triggered a delightful memory.

"You come my place," she said.

He followed. He would remember later the tiny voice in the back of his head warning him. "Don't go with her." He looked around furtively for the woman who had instantly become the wicked Jennifer Longstreet, the object of his uncontrolled rage. He didn't see her.

The room appeared sleazy, reeking of perfume. The woman did not talk much but he had not come to talk. Already the thought of her heightened the desire within him.

"Drink," she murmured engagingly and pressed a glass into his hand.

"Thanks. Just one." *One won't hurt. He had never had trouble with just one drink.*

In the gloom, he watched her disrobe and sipped his drink. The room felt warm—suddenly too warm—almost hot. He mopped his brow. *Did I eat something bad?* He felt unsteady, dizzy. The wall moved. "Hey!" he shouted and lapsed unconscious.

He did not feel the fingers that removed his trousers and slipped them back on. They returned his wallet. Women appeared and lifted the inert form onto a small cart. Covered with a sheet and surrounded by vegetables, the cart drew scant attention as it moved through narrow streets. When Billy Bob groaned and showed signs of retaining consciousness, a man pulled him off the cart and placed him in a sitting position, his back against a wall. The man approached two enlisted Air Corps men and led them Billy Bob. They checked for signs of life and detected shallow breathing. When they turned around and looked, the Chinese man had disappeared.

Eventually Billy Bob regained consciousness. The two Airmen raised him up and walked him between them. Wincing, Billy Bob had the mother of all headaches. He fumbled for his wallet. On inspection, he discovered it contained a single US dollar bill. "I've been rolled," he muttered, unaware that he had been relegated to the lowest form of humanity, one so low even prostitutes refused to take his last dollar.

The airmen placed him on a bus that returned him to Yang Tong. The thunder in his brain subsided after a medic gave him something to combat the knockout drops. In the barracks at last, he flung himself into his bunk fully clothed. He slept until dawn. Rising unsteadily, he stumbled toward the toilet and made a startling discover. His penis was covered b y a prophylactic. He blinked. "Hunh?" *I don't remember this.* His attempts to roll it off met resistance. On closer inspection, he saw it had been put on inside out. He managed to roll it under and slide if off. He saw puss and slime in the end of the condom that smelled of rotten fish. *Geeze. What hell is this?*

He washed repeatedly, and could not rid himself of the putrid stench. Although he received no clue as to the identity of the foul-smelling exudates, he learned to an unusual extent the undeniable purpose. He developed a genital itch that heightened to irritation. His penis began to drip. His testicles were swollen.

"Hmmm," declared Dr. Shaner, as he pronounced his diagnosis. "You got a dose and a half."

25

CHAOS

In a well-thought-out presentation, Tang said to Colonel Fong, "The burden of obligation for the impressive funeral for my good friend Chan hangs heavy, like a noose on the neck of a goose."

"Well spoken."

"I request—beg—to be allowed to go with the *Meghwa* if they decide to leave Yang Tong." His words made it clear he placed no blame on the failure of the Chinese army to halt the Jap invaders, a position in opposition of Generalissimo Chiang who often hastened to blame. "I would save face if allowed to continue to serve the *Meghwa fei hu.*"

Fong's brain raced. With Tang at a different location, a dangling thread disappeared. "What you say has merit."

"I would like to leave with the *Meghwa*. I hear it will be to Liuchow."

"Not possible." Fong softened his tone. "They will take all the vehicles. We have none to spare. We remain here to fight."

Tang decided it was time to depart. "As you say."

Fong allowed him to reach the door when he shouted, "Chan!"

Tang halted abruptly. He knew immediately he had made a mistake, his identity uncovered. He struggled for an idea. *What do I say?* He slowly turned.

Fong asserted, "Chan was your father."

Tang remained impassive and acknowledged, "Chan was my father."

"Sit," Fong said sharply. "I need to think." After a long moment he said, "Your name is Chan. What is the rest of it?"

"Chan Che-lue."

Fong's eyes narrowed. With Tang—Chan—gone, there would be no loose ends in case the General had questions. He dipped a brush into ink and wrote an introduction, a pass, a recommendation.

Chan Che-lue is hereby detached from this command. He has served as an important guard for the Fighting Tiger planes of the American Army. His sharp eyes led to the capture of a traitor to China. He is to be given every consideration.

Colonel Fong signed with lavish letters to show his importance. "You will continue to guard the planes."

"I shall continue to do so," Tang—now Chan—said with a smile.

Chan returned to Yang Tong and sought C. K. Wong to interpret his request to Sergeant Booker that he travel with the Americans to their next base. Lieutenant Wong puzzled why he made a request to Sergeant Booker and not to him.

Booker said, "I do not know how that can be arranged."

"No way," said Wong. He remembered Booker made the request to recover the slug from Chan's body before cremation. A few days ago, he had gone to headquarters and dropped the slug into Colonel Wise's hand. He had not thought it necessary to say, "As you ordered."

Colonel Wise looked surprised. He had not remarked, "What do you want me to do with this?" He simply placed it in his desk drawer.

Those who have opportunity are often unaware of opportunities missed.

Lieutenant Wong glanced at the "passport" given to the man he knew as Tang, and failed to notice the name, Chan Che-lue.

Booker remarked, "The first time you present this recommendation to a new command they will take it away from you. This is something you should keep. Why don't we go to headquarters and see if Dottie will go with us to Photo Recon and have some copies made?"

At headquarters, Booker repeated his request. Young Chan tagged along to Photo Recon like an obedient puppy. He marveled at the way Dottie gave instructions. A man photographed his document. Dottie turned to Tang and spoke in fluent Cantonese. "We can go now. The copies will not be ready until tomorrow. Come to my office in the afternoon."

Her Chinese disarmed him and he blurted his thoughts. "Were you captured?"

"Yes," Dorothy said with a chuckle. "Many years ago."

"Can you take me with you to the new base?"

"It will be difficult. I will see what can be done."

Returning to headquarters, Booker said, "Now that I am here, I might as well update my marker records. When you receive photocopies of Tang's order, please save several copies for me. It might be important. By the way, did Wong ever bring in a slug from the autopsy of Chan?"

"Yes. Colonel Wise has it. It's in his desk."

Booker asked Colonel Wise to see the slug. "Ah," Booker said upon examination. "It's a .45 caliber all right. Does that fact give you any ideas?"

"No. Should it?"

"Not everyone has access to a .45."

The Colonel said, "Anyone in the U S Air Corps does."

"But certainly not everyone in the Chinese Army. What are you going to do with it?"

"Give it to you," said the Colonel. "I'm tired of it rattling around in the drawer. I don't know why they sent it to me in the first place. Take good care of it." He turned and said in frustration to no one in particular, "Now where am I going to get that?"

With rumors rampant about evacuation, it was a time of exhilaration, exaggeration and excess. With extra sorties flown, short on supplies, it was a hectic and crazy time. Actors went out of character and did things they would not ordinarily do. Men found time to relax wherever and whenever they could.

The next afternoon, Dorothy returned from Photo Recon with numerous copies for Tang and Booker.

"Sergeant Moore is gone and won't be back," Lieutenant Cabelka said, fingering his moustache. "That ought to make you happy."

Dorothy raised a quizzical eyebrow.

"Moore fouled up. Casey Vincent's Intelligence reported the Japs are still sixteen miles from Paoshan. I told Moore to message, 'Do not—repeat—do not—blow up the base.' He left out the 'not' and ordered it blown. Wing thought it looked odd and contacted me prior to sending. I was able to straighten things out. I told Moore he could stick around and be court-martialed or transfer his ass out. He grabbed the transfer. He won't be bothering you any more, Dottie."

Dottie worried about the evacuation. Since the fall of Kukong, her father had not yet reached Kweilin. He had ordered her to take care of the family. If he did not arrive, she would not be able to go with the men, and would need to stay behind and care for the family.

When Tang called for his photocopies, Dorothy remembered Booker saying there was something mysterious about him. Remembering some of the mannerisms of the notorious Mrs. Wu, Dorothy spoke in a low voice cloaked in veiled meanings. "I will keep your secret."

Chan assumed—erroneously—that she could read Chinese as well as she spoke it. He nodded impassively and said, "Yes, I am Chan Che-lue."

"And the late Mr. Chan—?"

"—was my father."

"I find it almost impossible to get a ride for you to Luichow. However, I shall speak to Sergeant Booker. We will see what we can do. In the meantime, guard your plane."

"Hao. It shall be done."

When he called for his copies, Booker agreed to search for transportation for the young man he now knew would be Chan on arrival in Liuchow. In the rush of pre-evacuation preparation, Booker spent more time monitoring poker games than playing. He kept looking for sweet deals—markers at bargain prices. He paused to watch a game.

Hap the fighter pilot paid scant attention when he drew a pair of black eights. A club ace widened his eyes and when a spade ace followed, he paled. He hoped desperately the next card would not be a diamond but he knew it would be a diamond before the picked up the diamond jack. *Dead man's hand!* A hot tongue of fear—anger—ascended his spine; a crimson flush spread across his neck and diffused over his face. *I can't fold. I have to play it fair and square.*

He breathed in relief when Jackson and Menchnikov raised.

"I'll call," Hap said abruptly.

Menchnikov raised. Billy Bob raised.

"I'll call," Hap said. "What do you have?"

Jackson spread jacks over fives.

"A pair of kings and a pair of sevens," Menchnikov said.

Hap spread his cards, his face solemn.

"Yipes," Menchnikov exclaimed. "Dead man's hand!"

"I'm out," Hap muttered. He waved at the pot. "I don't want it. Each of you take out what you put in. Split what is left, equally." He strode away, his back stiff with anger.

Booker caught up with him. "What was that all about?"

"Dead man's hand, dead on. I'm done for. Some Jap sonofabitch is going to punch my ticket. Sure as hell."

"You don't know that."

"It's damn near certain. Even that fifth card confirms it. The best historical evidence says it was diamond."

There is room for a different result. You seem to know a lot about it."

"Listen, Wild Bill Hickock never sat with his back exposed. One day there in Deadwood, the vacant chair in a game attracted him. His back was to the window and Jack McCall shot him in the back of the head—twice. Hickock was holding black aces and eights—and a diamond."

"You never had the hand before?"

"Hell no. I'm still here."

"Have you been playing poker lately?"

"Not much."

"I thought so," Booker mused, searching for an idea. "Who dealt the hand?"

"Menchnikov."

"Have you been playing with him lately?"

"Not for quite a while."

"There is your answer."

"Huh?"

"That hand should have been dealt to you quite a while ago. When your gun was spiked, that was the bad omen. When they caught that Chinese Fifth Columnist, that took care of it. He was shot. The way I see it, this is just a delayed response to something that has already happened."

"You think so?"

"I'm damn near positive."

"I hope you're right."

"If you want to ward off some evil spirits you might consider giving a lift to that Chinese trooper to Liuchow when we go. He saved your buns once, maybe twice."

"There's no room in a Lightning."

"You have been doing some close-in protection for B-25s. They owe you big time. I heard Chiang Kai-shek issued the order. Leave it to the Chinese army to issue orders without means of implementing them." Booker showed him a photocopy in Chinese.

"May I have that?"

"Only if you work at it."

"Okay."

Booker felt like shaking his head in disbelief. He felt the .45 caliber slug in his pocket. Maybe it was not a Jap pilot Hap needed to worry about. *A superstitious fighter pilot. Who would have thought?*

Dorothy sat in poker games with the enlisted men, briefly. If she won a hand she would say, "I don't want to take all your money. I need to get back to work." If she lost, she said, "I can't let you take all my money. I need to get back to work."

Master-Sergeant Harry Bratty had a plan to utilize more of her time. "You need to come out on the firing line with us and learn how to use weapons."

"Shurr," Fred Ifft, agreed in his heavy Pennsylvania twang. "You need to be able to perrtect yourself in case the Japs break through."

Bratty said, "You need to be able to shoot back."

They gave Dottie a crash course in firing pistols, carbines, automatics and machine guns.

Everyone had cause for concern. Hengyang fell and Lingling was lost. Kweilin stood in the path of the Japanese assault. Nurses and wounded had been evacuated. Correspondents Clyde A. Farnsworth and Teddy White popped in for final stories.

"Are you going to let Dottie stay?" asked Lieutenant Willet.

"Hell yes," exclaimed Colonel Wise. "She has been at war seven years. You don't see her cowering behind a desk or pissing in her pants every time a bomb goes off around here. This is a hellova lot more than I can say for some of my officers and enlisted men." He turned to Dottie. "Do you want to stay with us?"

Dottie bobbed her head. "Yes. Unless my father doesn't get here."

She ripped a sheet out of her typewriter and winced. Her hand instinctively flew to her shoulder.

"Hurt?" Willet asked.

"Yeah."

"Firing cannons will do that."

"They weren't cannons."

As evacuation fury heightened, men were restricted to base. Billy Bob Willis Jackson wangled a special pass two nights, strapped on his fully loaded—one in the chamber—Colt .45 and went looking for the prostitute who drugged him, rolled him, and inoculated him with a sexual disease. He had to be clever. First, he had to remain in the shadows, watching. If he found her, he had to act friendly. He had to watch for covert signals to anyone following them. He would not be lured into a room where he would be trapped. If he found her, he would tell her, "Eat first." He would lead her to an upscale restaurant. He would make her give him what money she had. In a back alley littered with junk—something to cover her body—he would remove the pistol and quietly shoot her in the head—twice if necessary. In two long evenings of searching, he did not see her. *Uppity bitch* Lately the cards were running his way. With his luck turning, maybe he would find someone at the next base.

At headquarters, Dorothy received permission to take time off to visit the family. She observed shop owners boarding up their stalls. Some pasted patriotic red and black messages on the boards. Many used red and black paint to post dramatic price cuts of one-half or two-thirds on items GIs might purchase. Among the bargains were signs hung by prostitutes. "So long, boys." A couple girls signed their names. Sanitation services were suspended. Dead and dying accumulated in the streets, many victims of cholera. The stench burrowed into one's nostrils and clung there. People with death on their faces trudged toward the railroad station. There, activity heightened as engines puffed back and forth. Inside the station, men shouted, waving their arms to determine priorities, deciding who would receive space on the train.

Arriving at their home, the family clustered around Dorothy as she inquired, "Any word from father?"

"No," Lillian said; face ashen. "I'm worried sick. People are leaving sooner than they did in Kukong. Like there will be a breakthrough any minute."

Jack interrupted, "Do you think old General Ironpants can hold the line?"

"For a long time yet," Dorothy said, although she had no idea.

"How are we going to carry our things?"

"You will only be able to take what you can carry."

"I hate to leave your father's chairs—after bringing them all this way."

"There is no other choice."

"We must depend on you, Dorothy."

"I know. I hope Father gets here."

"I must get back now. Try not to worry. Father will get here." Dorothy prayed that he would. She desperately wanted to remain with the men of the Fourteenth Air Force.

On her way to headquarters, she passed a hangar where a small group played poker. She saw Booker and gave him a subtle wave. He responded with an upraised palm and continued to watch.

The entire strategy of poker had changed, depending on whether players accepted markers. Men tired of winning only their own money. Some men refused to play in games allowing markers.

Barry Menchnikov raked in a pot of more than two hundred dollars. Standing behind him, Nathan Berry leaned forward and placed his hand over Menchnikov's. "I'll take my cut of that. I'm here to redeem your jawbone."

"You can't do that. That' isn't fair!"

"Do you want to take it up with Colonel Wise? You know he will attach your pay." Both had stood before him. "Don't you remember he said a marker is a debt of honor?"

Menchnikov reluctantly allowed Berry to remove two hundreds dollars. "The marker is for three hundred," Berry said. "You will need to give me a marker for one hundred."

"The hell I do," Menchnikov flared. "I don't have to do any such thing. If you want to swoop down like a hawk, you will have to settle for what you get."

Color heightened in cheeks as tempers simmered. Menchnikov turned to Booker.

Booker knew Berry had paid only one hundred dollars for the marker. "Well," Booker said. "If you attach a house or a car for a debt, you cannot make the debtor give you another car. You have to settle for what you get."

Menchnikov's temper cooled. He redeemed a $300 marker for only $200, saving $100. Berry made a handsome $100 profit on his investment. Nevertheless, Menchnikov's eyes narrowed and he muttered, "Some day I'm going to get even—" He dropped it, but Booker remembered his tone.

The tactic quickly spread. Men who stood around and tried to collect winnings became known as "marker sharks," or "jawbone jerkers." There were a few other unsavory names. Players maintained a sharp lookout for anyone they suspected would attempt to make a collection.

The base continued to be on edge. The Chinese Sixty-second Army became swallowed up in a week as the Japanese churned through the hills toward the Chuanhsien Pass, the strategic gateway to Kwangsi Province. Command ordered the Ninety-third Army to bottleneck the Japanese there. A ragamuffin army, the Ninety-third had pillaged government rice stores at Liuchow before going to the pass. According to American OSS reports, the Ninety-third was so disorganized one field commander didn't know where the next unit operated. Some men had Chinese rifles; some had Russian. They had either no ammunition or the wrong ammunition. Old distrusts between commanding generals and Generalissimo Chiang Kai-shek surfaced and flamed into hostility. The Ninety-third retreated from the pass without firing a shot, whereupon the Generalissimo ordered the commander shot. By then it was too late. The Japanese strategy was simply to push on south to join forces sweeping up from Indo-China, giving them a road from North China all the way to Singapore.

At Yang Tong, Operation Alert remained in force for two weeks before the final order to leave. Men frantically packed their gear. Dottie typed a flurry of last-minute orders.

Colonel Wise received an urgent message. "Rescind the order," he said. "We are staying."

Lieutenant Cabelka muttered and swore. The landing strip at Paoshan, which he had saved from destruction earlier, had to be destroyed, their planes diverted to Chihkiang.

Bombs rained on Kweilin. Fires broke out with volcanic fury, glowing red, with black smoke billowing into the autumn sky. It hung there, an enormous cloud, waiting for a *kwang mo* wind, the acrid smell added to the already overpowering stench of death.

Dorothy considered it a miracle that phone lines were still in operation when Edna called. Interference on the line caused both to yell. "Repeat that," Dorothy shouted. Could she believe what she heard?

"FATHER—HAS—ARRIVED. FATHER—IS—HERE!"

"Good," Dorothy hollered. "*Hao.*"

The next day the order arrived, "Abandon Yang Tong." They ordered bomber crews, sent on missions, to return to Liuchow or alternate bases. Fighter pilots were assigned to various bases. During the last minute rush a UC-64, a high wing monoplane dropped in.

Colonel Wise groused, "What the hell does he want?"

Lieutenant Cabelka checked and reported, amused, "He came to pick up *General* Casey Vincent's flush toilet. It is the only one in the area. It's probably an art treasure."

"Then it ought to go to the Smithsonian," Colonel Wise grumbled.

It did not go to the Smithsonian; it went to Luliang where General Vincent had his new headquarters.

"Dottie, can you run these papers over to fighter control?"

"Yes, Colonel."

Dottie was half way there when someone shouted, "Look out, Dottie." A bullet spanged into the building and Dottie flung herself to the g round.

A concealed sniper was not hitting anything. He kept pecking away, probably with iron sights, Dottie thought. Cursing, she scooted around the corner on hands and knees and ran out of the line of fire.

She saw Major Huang, Chinese liaison officer, scolding an aide. "My shoes are gone," he screamed as he punched the aide. He wrenched the man's rifle out of his hands and began beating him with it. "Idiot! Imbecile! Bring back my shoes or you are a dead man."

Pale, shaking with fright, the aide hurried off to find the Major's shoes. He had lost his weapon, an offense for which infantrymen were often shot.

Later, Lieutenant Cabelka told Dottie the Major spared the aide's life. He returned with six pairs of shoes; one pair belonged to the Major. However, Major Huang retained all of them.

Captain Gibbens walked into headquarters and asked Colonel Wise, "Can I borrow Dottie for a while?"

They conferred and Wise said, "Just don't get her blown up."

Dottie followed him to a Jeep and Gibbens said, "There are more than five hundred buildings on this base that must be destroyed before we leave. I want you to get in on the fun."

In each building, demolition crews had placed a gasoline drum. Captain Gibbens halted the jeep in line with the open door and handed Dottie a .45 automatic. She fired once. Gasoline gurgled from the drum and spread across the floor, sending up fumes. The Colt bucked in her hand again, igniting the building. Gibbens floored the Jeep raced to the next building and Dottie fired again. Sometimes a thatched roof would heave into the air with the explosion, and then settle gently into the flames. Often tongues of liquid fire dripped down on the roof from the apex to the eaves, creating burning patches on the ground. Some buildings burned slowly. Others were gone in flash. Evil black clouds belched forth from the petrol.

"Anyone can hit them sitting still," Captain Gibbens said. "How about trying some wing shooting?"

"Okay."

"I am not going to stop. You must shoot each can once. Then I will circle and you can light them off on the second pass."

He drove slowly but Dottie had to snap two shots at some of the drums. Increasing his speed on the second pass, some of the buildings failed to *wump* into flame."

"They are not so easy to hit when you are speeding," Dottie said. "It's my turn to drive."

"I see what you mean," Gibbens said when Dottie went speeding past the targets. He touched off the last few with well-aimed shots from a carbine.

First Lieutenant Norwood Wilson, a veteran ordinance officer, called "Whiskers" by the men, led a demolition crew. A high stakes poker player, Whiskers carried a brief case filled with more than one thousand American dollars and two gold wristwatches. He ran into a building, fused a hundred pound bomb and hurried out. He drew up short. He had forgotten his brief case! Before he could turn, *Wooom!* The brief case, blown to smithereens, scattered burning money in all directions as flame consumed the currency.

Wilson's shoulders sagged. His arms went limp. He shouted something appropriate, pulled himself erect, and ran to fuse the next bomb.

Harry Bratty rushed to board a C-47. The plane took off and returned in minutes. In the race to evacuate, someone forgot to remove the pins in the landing gear, which prevented retraction. The pins hastily removed, the C-47 took off a second time.

As the sun began to set, a single wing of fighter planes, retained as air cover, took off for Liuchow. Demolition crews placed thousand pound bombs in the runway, wiring them in clusters. Out of the bomb noses came the fuses; in went C-Compound. When detonated, the blasts made craters twenty to thirty feet deep.

The sky darkened and the headquarters staff could see silhouettes of the demolition crews frantically working in the eerie glow of headlights. Rows of flaming buildings lit up the area with the brilliance of noon. Suddenly they heard a crackling sound like Chinese firecrackers.

"Who forgot to remove the ammunition?" Lieutenant Willett demanded as bullets whined in all directions. Tracers arched left and right adding a weird comedic touch.

"Mount up."

The thirty-vehicle caravan moved into the hills; Jeeps, command cars, trucks and an ambulance. Colonel Wise, Lieutenant Cabelka and Lieutenant C. K Wong were in the last Jeep. Everyone turned for a last look at the monstrous pow-wow.

The Jeep of Colonel Wise drew up with a flat tire. Troops from the truck ahead leaped out, armed with machine guns, and stood guard until men bolted the spare in place. Colonel Wise delighted in driving the Jeep, racing up and down the length of the convoy like a shepherd dog herding a flock of sheep. Most of the men enjoyed driving Jeeps. More versatile than the hotrods they remembered from teenage years, they could "express themselves," in Jeeps and many vowed to get one after the war.

A hundred miles out, they came to a river. A pontoon ferry operated manually by pulling ropes, allowed only two vehicles to cross at a time.

"What's the bottleneck?" Colonel Wise demanded as he reigned up and dismounted. "If the Japs catch us bunched up, there will be hell to pay."

Everyone stared at the clouds. Men became nervous.

A sergeant ran up. "There is an earthen dam down stream a short way. If we blow it, the water level will drop. Maybe we can drive across."

"Blow the damn thing," ordered Colonel Wise.

The men paced a land mine in the center of the dam. Crouching behind vehicles, they heard a thump. Yards of earth hurled skyward and clods rained down on them. When the water dropped to hubcap level, a single Jeep started out and made it safely across.

"Head 'em out!"

Thirty miles later the convoy arrived in Liuchow and began setting up new headquarters.

With no place to stay, base facilities already overcrowded, Colonel Wise solved the problem. Standing at the wheel of his Jeep, he waved the convoy into a turn and every vehicle followed him. In the city, he appropriated a two-story hotel in a compound surrounded by a wall. Immediately, Chinese sentries guarded the gate. Hotel workers and Army cooks began carrying in supplies. The retention of hotel employees greatly boosted morale. The Colonel assigned Dottie a room of her own.

At dawn, as if planned for days, a wing of fighters roared off the runway to engage the enemy. Chan, now using his real name, proudly guarded Hap's Lightning. Several people who might have been involved in his transfer asked how he arrived. No one knew. For the record, no one ever discovered how he arrived from Kweilin.

26

DOTTIE IN CHARGE

"The boy general doesn't have anything on us," Lieutenant Willett declared when the staff assembled in the newly established officer's mess. "Do you know we have flush toilets?"

"Don't tell Casey. He might come back from Luliang."

Lieutenant Cabelka rubbed his moustache. "How does if feel to be prisoners of the Japs?"

He answered their quizzical expressions. "Yeah. We must be prisoners. Teddy White jumped the gun on filing his dispatch. We were in Kweilin days after he declared the base destroyed."

Colonel Wise emitted an oath.

"Teddy had some deal cooked up with Casey Vincent," Cabelka explained. "After the control tower was wired, Casey was supposed to fly over and set off the detonators with well placed bursts. Tower detonators were supposed to be synchronized with the thousand pounders in the runway—one big grandstand play. I guess Teddy wanted some pictures of the whole thing going up. But demolition couldn't wire it that way. The deal fell through."

Colonel Wise swore again.

"Isn't that terrific," scoffed Lieutenant Willett. "Casey Vincent and Teddy White all alone on the base after everyone else left—with the Japs closing in. Hell, not even a schoolboy would believe that."

"A school boy WOULD BELIEVE IT! That is the stuff heroes are made of."

"Bullshit."

"Precisely."

"That's what is wrong with correspondents. They make heroes out of the wrong people."

"Why can't they send us somebody like Ernie Pyle?"

Cabelka drained his cup. "The feedback I am getting indicates that Teddy is saying that he and Casey hung around after we left."

"Man there wasn't anybody around when we left."

"Did you see anyone?"

"Hell no."

"You're base historian, Cabelka," the Colonel said. "Straighten it out."

"I can't. It doesn't fit into military history. What do you think I am writing, a Hollywood gossip column?"

"That's what I thought you did," Willett said.

"Dottie," the Colonel brightened. "I'm making the hotel our headquarters. I want you to stay here and man the phones. We need to go to the base a lot. If none of us are around, you are in charge."

Me, a West Point graduated Colonel? Ho-hum.

Every change of location brought a reunion with one or more friends. It surprised Dorothy the day Jack Hartell approached. She ripped off her headphone and embraced him. "How did you know I was here?"

"I have my ways," he said impishly and explained, "Are you kidding? You have the most popular name on radio. 'Dottie Yuen is leaving Kweilin. Dottie is enroute Liuchow. Dottie has arrived.'" He sobered to a request he knew Dottie would make.

"What do you hear from Willie?" Dorothy asked expectantly.

He came out of the field with a whole skin. When Kukong fell, they pulled him back to headquarters for reassignment. He must be about ready to point out for home. I'm on duty. Got to go. See you later."

We'll get together."

"As Willie would say, 'Right.'"

"Right."

The following day, Dorothy hugged another Jack—her brother. The family came to headquarters to visit her. They had managed get aboard a hopelessly crowded train from Kweilin. Everyone looked thin. Lillian's dress hung on her bones like a sack.

"I have never been through anything so miserable in all my life," Lillian said. Her face took on a pained disagreeable expression.

"The conductor sold the toilet for one gold bar," Jack exclaimed, wide-eyed. "Nobody could go to the bathroom."

"People went where they lay," Lillian said. "What a stink! The smell alone was enough to kill. I never want to go through that again."

"It was really bad," Edna said. "We were human sardines packed in a sauce of our own filth. I hope the conductor chokes on his gold bar, the greedy bastard.

When I saw all the pots and pans on the train earlier, I didn't realize that most of them would be potties before we reached Liuchow."

Jack said, "There was a rickshaw on top of one car. And a pig. One boy hugged a rooster all the way." Jack's eyes widened. "One woman had a baby!"

"Ten people died, "Lillian said wearily. "When the train stopped, people didn't move. They were afraid they couldn't get on again."

Gloria spoke up, "Can you get me some candy bars out of K-rations?"

Dorothy clasped her hands to her cheeks. "Shh. We can't talk about that here at headquarters. I'll see what I can do."

Before the family left Dottie,—being a Colonel in Charge—raided the commissary and sent each of them home with a treat. "You can't stay," she said. "I am too busy on the phones."

Lillian marveled, "Not only does she know all the Chinese Generals, now she is running the American Air Corps."

In her scant moments off, Dottie sought out First Lieutenant Norwood "Whiskers" Wilson and asked to watch him play poker. He acknowledged, "You certainly would bring me luck."

With his briefcase full of money recently exploded and burned, Whiskers put markers to good use, which allowed him at once to start rebuilding funds. "You want a rule?" he asked teasingly. "Play 'em like you got 'em."

At first, Dorothy assumed Whiskers meant to bluff, as if one held winning cards. Soon she altered her interpretation to mean—Don't bet on expectation, what you think you will draw. Play the cards that you hold!

She watched Wilson win three hundred dollars holding three queens. He won another hand with two pair, aces over jacks. "See, you bring me luck," he said, and at once redeemed a marker.

"Thanks for the lesson, Dottie said. "I need to get back to headquarters."

"Thank you for the luck."

"Now that your luck is gone, Whiskers," said an opponent. "Maybe I can whip your ass."

"In your dreams."

"You can't know what I was just dreaming."

"I think I do. Play cards."

"Glad you're back," Cabelka said when Dottie returned. "I have an appointment. We just got here. Now we need to move again."

Presently Jack Hartell raced up to the hotel in a Jeep. "I came as soon as I could, Dottie," he said, out of breath. "You are in big trouble. I know it was your voice coming over the air. What were you doing on the radio?"

"Radio? I wasn't on any radio."

"Yes you were. I recognized your voice. Man, it was critical. We were talking down a gut-shot tanker. The pilot was shot to hell and the tanker was coming in for a belly landing. Your voice kept coming on, 'No, I can't go out with you tonight.' Every time an officer came near, I made static to cover your voice. God, I couldn't cover it all. Where the hell were you broadcasting from, Dottie?"

Dorothy's hand flew to her mouth. "I know," she cried, panic stricken. "I went for a walk with Sergeant Korowski. He asked me aboard a B-25. 'Go to the gunner's section,' he said. 'Put on the headphone.' He stayed up front and said, 'How about a date tonight, Dottie?' I said, 'No, I can't go out with you tonight.' We talked quite a while."

Jack frowned and shook his head. "That damn Korowski. He didn't have it closed off. He threw the intercom switch too far and it all went out on the air. If the brass asks me, I'm gonna know nothing. Maybe you can say it was an accident—blame it on Korowski. Let him answer for it."

Dorothy knew she was in for trouble, but the trouble received was not what she expected. Major Frank Gleason of OSS and Colonel Wise kept up a running charade that had her worried for days. The ailing plane had landed safely, unhindered by the voice interference.

At length, Major Gleason admitted it was all a put-on. "It's a gag. You are not in any trouble. Colonel Wise and I were just having a little fun."

Dottie shook a fist at him. "I am so damn mad at you. You are as bad as Sergeant Denehy. No, worse! A lot worse!"

She was still angry with the Colonel when he told her, "Dottie, there are some females at the end of the runway. I want you to go over and find rooms for them. Don't they know we are on evacuation alert?"

At the end of the runway Dottie found Hollywood stars—Jinx Falkenburg, Pat O'Brien, Ruth Carrell, Jimmy Dodd, Harry Brown, and Betty Yeaton.

They put on a splendid show in a hangar and the men were delighted. Later, Dottie had officers double up to make room for them. It was midnight and officers still crowded around Jinx with adoring eyes.

"The enlisted men feel bad about you being with the officers," Dottie told Jinx.

"I have no way to get to the enlisted men," Jinx said. "If you can get them together, I will talk with them."

Dottie ran to the enlisted men's wing and began pounding on doors.

"Come meet Jinx Falkenburg," Dottie shouted.

"Stop kidding."

"On the level."

Finally, some men in shorts stumbled into the corridor. Dottie convinced them Jinx wanted to meet them. They rushed into their uniforms. Jinx engaged them in pleasant conversation until two in the morning.

"Dottie," a Sergeant said, "You can wake me up any time."

"If I had something like that waiting for me back home—" a man said dreamily.

"I thought you did, George,"

George muttered a one-word epithet.

Too dangerous for the entertainers to remain in Liuchow, Dottie arranged for them to fly out, and embarked on a project of her own. When they evacuated—which would be soon—she had to take the family on the military caravan. She could not allow them to suffer on some train—if they could get on a train.

"Out of the question," bellowed Major Bull, the transportation officer. He glared at Dottie though round glasses. "We can't take civilians. This is strictly a military convoy. Strictly military."

Dorothy importuned Colonel Wise. "They are all American citizens," Dottie argued. "As senior American officer around, you owe some responsibility to them, to help if you can. They are destitute."

"What about your father?"

"He is an ally. Married to an American. He wants to go on the convoy too."

"A foreign national. That's more difficult."

"He is really a member of the family."

"It's a little unusual."

"Americans. They need help."

"Very well. I suppose it is permissible in an emergency. All right, I will issue an order to Major Bull. "Have a truck available for the Yuen family."

Dottie could well imagine the expression of the face of 'The Bull.'

The Bull had his revenge when he learned the family planed to take their chow. "No dogs. No dogs on the convoy."

Dottie pleaded with Colonel Wise. "Major Bull won't let us take our dog. The Chinese Army always has a dog."

"*A dog!*" Wise erupted.

"Yes, a nice little chow dog, all white. It is really a wonderful little dog and part of the family. I just love it. It won't take up any room at all. On the same truck."

"Dammit to hell, Dottie! What do you think I am running? A kennel?"

"It's just a tiny thing. A little dog."

"Oh, all right, take the damn dog. Only don't bother me."

The issue of the convoy settled, Dottie found time to visit a friend. Less than four hours earlier, she learned Livia Lung was in the city. Dorothy had become acquainted with Livia in Kukong.

When Dorothy arrived at the Lung home, the family busily prepared to flee to the hills, hoping to find refuge in a mountain cave.

"You can't take Livia with you," Dorothy remonstrated. "Don't you know what the Japs do to girls like her?"

"What else can I do?" her brother said, spreading his hands helplessly.

"There is a chance," Dorothy said. "I might be able to get her on the convoy with my family. I will ask the Colonel. Can you stay until morning?"

"Not a minute longer. If you think there is a chance."

"I'll get in touch."

Dottie knew she could not see the Colonel until morning. She found him having an early breakfast. She slid up a chair and greeted him in a gentle voice. "This war sure is terrible," she said tentatively.

"We are all sick of it," he said.

"Bad times make having a friend all the more important. I have this friend, Livia Lung. She is a fragile thing. The Japs will get her unless I get her out on the convoy with my family. It's absolutely vital."

Colonel Wise gulped and choked on his coffee. He slammed down the cup and continued in a paroxysm of coughing. Recovering, he stormed, "God dammit, Dottie, what the hell do you think this is, some tour bus?"

B-but she's such a frail thing," Dottie stammered. "She is delicate. She can't live like an animal in a cave. She will die. All she needs to take with her can be carried in a bandanna. She won't take up any room at all."

"No."

"I can't bear to think of what the Japs will do to her when they catch her. I mean, do you have any idea?" Sniffing, tears welled in Dottie's eyes.

"Yes, God dammit, I do know," Colonel Wise growled, bear angry. He glared with eyes of blue flame. "Oh all right! She can go, but hear this! No more girl friends. No more family. No More dogs. No more, God dammit of anything." He pounded the table, face livid. "I have a war to fight. You are going to cost me my eagle. How did you get into this outfit? Can't you go over to Chennault, Stilwell, MacArthur—anybody?"

'"I-I'll g-get you a fresh cup of coffee."

Wise regarded her sheepishly as she put down the cup. "I'm sorry about the cusswords, Ma'am." He glowered again.

Certain she had exhausted his patience, Dottie murmured, "Thank you, Colonel."

"Do you always get your way?" he demanded, shaking a finger at her. "There is a limit to some things." He waved her away with a disgusted look. "Now get the hell out of here."

Originally, Major Bull assigned a 6 by 6 truck for the Yuen family. Unlike most Chinese, the Yuens packed everything and an irate Major Bull allocated a second vehicle, an ambulance.

Overcome with gratitude, Livia Lung kept bowing, repeating, "I am most grateful. Thank you."

Lillian picked up on it and said, "Dorothy, I am proud of you. When I think what it would be like on a wretched train—if we could get a train."

Sandow leaned forward and whispered to Dorothy. "A messenger came for me during the night."

Following his inclined head, Dorothy saw the man lingering outside the gate. She recognized him as an employee of her father's factory from Shanghai. He had long been in her father's command and helped build several homes for them in Kukong. "Is there some way we can get him aboard?" Sandow asked.

Dorothy ran over to Major Bull and described his peril. "My father just received an urgent message. His runner his here. Can he come aboard?"

The Bull's head snapped imperiously. "Of course not! We can't take Chinese Nationals. It is forbidden, completely against regulations."

"Not even part way?" The family would be leaving the convoy at Kweiyang, because Colonel Sandow Yuen had been ordered to Chungking.

"Out of the question!"

At that moment, Colonel Wise passed by. "What's holding things up?"

"She wants me to take a Chinese National," said The Bull.

The Colonel wheeled on Dorothy. "You again! God dammit, Dottie, what is it this time?"

"A runner, a messenger came for father during the night—big surprise—totally unexpected—didn't know he was coming—can't leave him. Been close to the family for years. Practically family."

"God dammit, get him aboard. And get the God damn convoy moving."

"Move out," shouted The Bull.

"Move out," called a Sergeant.

Dottie remained behind with the headquarters staff. Overhead, the *mee-oww* of diving planes attracted her attention. A new P-51 Mustang and a Jap Zero were tilting in battle.

"Get him," Dottie shouted.

She ran around a corner to watch. The Mustang came streaking down, all six of its fifty caliber machine guns spitting. The more maneuverable Zero rolled on its broad wings, peeled off with right rudder, throttle full on, and dived into a loop, intending to come out on the Mustang's tail.

Deprived on a quick kill by split-second evasive action, the Mustang burrowed up into a cloud, rolled, and came roaring down, screaming, under full power, guns hammering.

"Get him! "Dorothy cried. "Get him!" Suddenly she felt herself bowled over by strong arms and carried into a trench. Behind them, rows of bullets from the planes kicked up dust.

"God dammit, Dottie, what the hell are you doing?" Colonel Wise scolded. "Standing out there in the street. You don't even have on a helmet."

A thin pencil line of smoked trailed from the Zero. Its engine faltered and the Zero began losing altitude in a graceful arc, and then plummeted. It crashed over a nearby hill, the explosion sending up a dark cloud.

"Atta way!" Dottie cheered.

Colonel Wise regarded her, shaking his head. A grin slowly spread across his face and a twinkle entered his cold blue eyes. "Dottie," he said, continuing to shake his head. "Are you trying to get yourself killed?"

Dorothy dusted herself off and noticed his eyes were very warm. "No," she answered, but if you keep using me for football practice I am liable to get hurt."

"Dottie," he whispered, slowly shaking his head.

The next time she saw her mother, Dottie learned that she should not have been concerned about bending the rules. Lillian reported, "When our convoy was three miles out of Liuchow, trucks and Jeeps halted for assorted tarts, prostitutes, and girlfriends stationed along the route. It was all prearranged." Unwilling to be deprived of creature comforts, our men were leaving Liuchow in style.

The order to evacuate arrived the next day but an early winter fog kept planes grounded. Everyone feared the Japs would overrun the base before they could get airborne.

"Don't leave the phone," Colonel Wise ordered. "I want to know where you are every minute. The first three-foot opening in this soup and we are out of here. I'll send someone to get you."

Within hours, the clouds parted and a Jeep rolled up to the hotel. "Get in," said the crew chief of a C-47.

"You speak English," he marveled as they sped toward the plane.

"Don't all Americans?" Dottie said.

"Yes, but—but I don't see many girls—I mean—"

Dottie seated herself in the cargo area and presently the co-pilot came back and introduced himself. "The Captain wants to know if you would like to come up front."

"Yes, Lieutenant."

Both were exceedingly happy to be speaking to an American girl and they had a fine time. Hours later, as they approached Kunming, the Captain said, "Put on the headphones and request landing instructions."

"I don't know what to say."

"I will tell you."

He briefed her. The airwaves cracked with the incessant chatter and abundant static. Adlibbing a bit, Dottie spoke into the mike. "This is Flying Tigress on C-Forty-seven, ATC, approaching field. Request landing instructions, please."

At once, everything went silent.

Dottie repeated the lingo. "Request landing instructions, please."

The network remained ominously silent.

At length she told the pilot, "You better do it. I am not getting a response."

"They probably think you are Tokyo Rose." He chuckled and took the mike. The moment he repeated his request the entire network came alive. The crisis was over.

"What if General Chennault happened to be standing in Operations?" the Lieutenant asked, looking worried.

"What if he was?" the Captain said nonchalantly.

After touchdown, Dottie went directly to her he assigned billet and never learned if the Captain took any flak for putting her on the air.

At an early opportunity, the staff assembled to celebrate their safe arrival. Glasses clinked together over the table, "*Kampei,*" Dottie exclaimed.

Attempting the Chinese version of "bottoms up," the men managed, "Gam-bay" or "Gumbuoy."

"Dottie," declared an amused Lieutenant Cabelka. "You should have been there. You should have seen Willett. There we were, the last two planes of out Liuchow." He raised his palms to represent the planes. "A DC-3 takes off ahead of us and Willett says, 'How come I never get to light of any buildings? You guys always have all the fun. I want to light off something.'"

"Shut up," Willett scowled, giving Cabelka the evil eye. "I don't want to hear any more about that!"

"Now I MUST HEAR IT," Dottie said emphatically.

Cabelka chuckled. "Sure. We were boarding the last plane. 'Go light off the latrine' Colonel Wise told him. Willett goes over and applies a torch to one corner. Just then, the old Chinese Revenge catches up with him. The side of the latrine is only smoldering so Willett figures he has time. He pops in and sits down. Suddenly—*pow!* What happens, the fire snakes into the pit below. The oil down there flames up against Willett's ass; he lets out a scream and comes tearing out with his pants flopping around his ankles."

"Shut up about that!" Willett muttered.

The group guffawed and snickered, enjoying his discomfiture.

Colonel Wise, who had been silent, banged down his glass. "This place is chicken—" He broke off when his eyes reached Dottie.

Startled, they turned to him. "Lieutenant Cabelka," Colonel Wise said firmly. "I want you to pass the word that officers and men will need to get used to saluting again. We are in Chennault Country—China headquarters. Get the word out." He rose and stalked away in a discontented mood.

"That's surprising coming from a West Pointer," Willett observed.

"He prefers to get things done instead of going by the book"

"He is getting a lot of heat from the top."

"I'm with him. This base is chicken shit."

27

THE PERSONAL ASPECT

Since arriving in Kunming, the group from Liuchow suffered a drop in morale. No one appreciated the emphasis on military regulation and the uncertainty of war. Formerly they were Third Sector, but not enough of it remained to be a separate command. As a result, Colonel Wise took command of Sector One and the Sixty-eighth Service Group, now responsible for supplies and personnel west of the one hundredth third meridian. Absorbing new bases from the inactivated Third Sector, their responsibilities included logistics for nineteen bases.

Lieutenant Cabelka read the list aloud. "Namyung, Anshun, Mangsheh, Szemao—" He halted. "Paoshan? I thought we lost that." He checked and reported, "What do you know, it is another Paoshan."

There were personnel changes. The fierce looking Major Bull became Base Commander at Siuchwan. First Lieutenant Norwood "Whiskers" Wilson now commanded Tsingchen.

News continued bleak. Since leaving Liuchow, the base at Nanning had fallen. This did not affect Colonel Wise as much as the November 20, 1944 issue of *TIME.*. Officials in the Pentagon fired off inquiries to General Chennault and the ripple became a tidal wave when it reached the desk of Colonel Wise. Hands shaking, face drained, he sat stunned. After a moment of shocked silence, color began to flow into his features. "He wants to court martial me," he got out. "I don't know anything about burning a million gallons of gasoline. Dammit!" He leaped to his feet. "Cabelka. I want you to get to the bottom of this. Get me a copy of *TIME.*"

Cabelka secured a transcript of the offensive part of the article.

The dreary process began all over again at Liuchow, 100 miles to the southwest. Colonel Richard Wise, commanding the Third Sector, China Air Service Command, worked around the clock to get out all the men, equipment and supplies which he had worked the year around to get in—up to 3000 planeloads flown over the Hump route; a million gallons of aviation fuel, torturously accumulated and stored, now impossible to save.

"I didn't destroy a million gallons of gasoline," Colonel Wise raged. "We never *had* a million gallons. Who the hell wrote this crap? Teddy White? I'll deck him."

"I don't think it was Teddy," Lieutenant Cabelka said. "Anna Jacoby was hanging around the hotel. She is the only one who had access."

"I'll kill her," Wise shouted.

"You Okayed the dispatch," Lieutenant Cabelka said quietly. "After Third Sector passed it, her dispatch had to be released by headquarters of the Fourteenth."

"I didn't pass it. Not a million gallons. God dammit. We never had a million gallons. If I ever get my hands on her—"

An incipient smile played across Cabelka's face. "I will dig into fuel consumption records. We could not have burned over five thousand gallons."

"What are you grinning at, dammit?"

"It is rather funny."

"I don't think so. It could cost me my eagle."

"I have the fuel consumption charts. Do you want me to call Chennault, take them over for him to see?"

"Hell yes. Get him off my back."

Wit a chuckle Cabelka set out to convince General Chennault that the gasoline consumed at Liuchow was five thousand gallons, not a million.

Much later, Colonel Wise encountered Anna Jacoby and despite his wrath, she offered to produce her notes. She maintained her editors could not read her shorthand and had added two zeroes to her report. Wise was less than satisfied with her explanation. "That would still make it ten thousand gallons, twice what we had."

Perhaps the cold November limited outdoor poker games. More than likely it was the "chicken-shit" atmosphere found at headquarters. Games in the barracks received little publicity.

A whimsical expression on the face of his friend Nathan Berry prompted Booker's question. "What's eating you, Schlitz?"

"I have a fantastic idea. Everyone in the Fourteenth Air Force kicks in five hundred bucks to buy chips in a gigantic poker tournament. At the end of the competition, the Poker King has his choice—one million bucks or he can marry Dottie."

"What?" Booker erupted in a shout. "Are you nuts? Have you run that past Dottie? She will kill you."

"Of course I have not. It is big, really, really, big. They will broadcast it on sports radio. Studios will film motion picture shorts, shown in theaters all across the country. It is fantabulous. The breathtakingly hyped question is, "Will he take the million bucks or Dottie's hand in marriage?" Flying Tigers are hooting and hollering. The cameras are grinding. The winner speaks with a mouth full of cornmeal mush. 'I think I will take them both.' He drops on one knee. 'Dottie, will you marry me?' America goes positively wild. They will eat it up. It is psychologically serene."

"Everything is serene except what Dottie will do to you when she hears about it. It is so fantastic, I think I will go over and run it past her right now."

"Don't you dare," said a fearful Berry. "Don't you dare!"

Booker broke out laughing. "I think I will win that tournament."

"Spoil-sport."

"You have a basic problem with your idea. Now that we are in Kunming, Chennault will probably see Dottie. You know what will happen then."

Berry said, "He doesn't marry them."

"He will change his tune with Dottie."

"Kay-ripes. We have to keep them apart."

"Of course," Booker twitted. "I could run right over and ask Dottie to marry me. That would make it academic."

"Where did you learn a word like academic?"

"Same place you learnt psychological."

More than vaguely aware of the role she played in men's conversation, Dorothy remained unaware they brought Chennault into their conversation, which proved to be almost prophetic.

The explosive clash between Chennault and Colonel Wise fresh in her mind, Dottie reacted to panic as she set out to see General Chennault. *You have seen dozens of Generals. Don't be afraid. This will be no different.* She knew in her heart that it would be different.

An aide halted her. "Is it possible to see the General?"

"He always has time to see a pretty girl," quipped the aide, a mischievous sparkle in his eyes.

The aide revealed no secret. Chennault's love for Chinese girls was well known. Dorothy had observed him at a party and knew what people said was true.

Seated at his desk, Chennault looked up wearily. His eyes widened as he saw Dorothy.

She studied his face. His eyes were narrow, covered by thick arched eyebrows, his nose long and probing. A pugnacious jaw came jutting out beneath a straight slash of a mouth. Much revered by the Chinese, they called Chennault *Chennote Chiang Chung.* The General had so often looked trouble in the eye and stared it down that his face wore a resolute expression even in repose. The Chinese had another name for Chennault—"Old Leatherface." His leathery, weather-beaten skin came because of open cockpit flying. Like the Americans, the Chinese venerated their heroes with diminutives, usually employing the prefix, "Old." In the office, Dorothy had sometimes heard the General called, "Old Hatchetface."

"I am Dorothy Yuen," she said. "I have been working for Colonel Wise since Kweilin and I am hoping you will help me."

"If I can," Chennault said. "First, I need to hear what it is. What is the problem?"

"It is my Grandmother. She is trapped behind enemy lines and I want to get her out. We need a plane. Can the American Air Corps help?"

He cleared his throat as if he had bronchial trouble. "It's extremely dangerous landing behind enemy lines."

"Grandma says there is an air strip near where she lives. She sees American planes coming in and taking off all the time. It has to be a secret strip."

"Where did you hear that?" he recoiled. His face became grave.

Grandma was able to get a message to my father. He is a Colonel in the Chinese Army. I received Father's letter from Chungking yesterday."

His yes narrowed. "I don't know any landing strip. Show me on the map." He swiveled around, rose and stood at a map that dominated the wall behind him. "Show me where."

"In Honan Province. Right here," Dorothy she said, pointing to the spot.

The General blinked. "We have no landing strip in that area. There must be some mistake. We have nothing there."

"But Grandma saw them."

"Could be," he said, speaking loudly because he was slightly deaf. "Maybe the Japs are using the field. They might have painted our emblems on some of their planes for a surprise raid. I would not put it past them. I'm sorry. I can't help you. I would if I could, but we have no strip there."

"Thank you anyway," Dorothy said sadly.

Outside the sky darkened, the gloom of night started to sweep down over the mountains as she walked toward the mess hall. Her thoughts resonated with General Chennault's words. His statement were definite, his denials emphatic, but she did not believe him. *He lied to me.*

She became aware of footsteps behind her and tensed. On a shortcut, she did not wish to meet anyone in the darkness. The footsteps continued ominously. At the mess hall door she turned.

"Captain Birch!"

"Dorothy!" He drew her into embrace and lifted her off the ground. "It's so good to see you," he said releasing her. "I didn't know you worked for the Air Force." He swept off his overseas cap and opened the door.

"Then you don't know we missed each other in Kweilin by less than a minute."

"When was that?"

"A couple months back."

"Oh-h-h." His face went long and sad. "If I had known that I would have been blue for weeks. Seeing you is wonderful. I have been hoping I would see you again. After Kukong fell, I worried about you."

"We evacuated by train. Father joined us later." How handsome John looked in his uniform.

Birch led the way to a table in a corner. "Dorothy, what is troubling you? I sense something." His hand came over hers in a consoling gesture.

"It's Grandmother—she is behind enemy lines." Dorothy related her disappointing meeting with Chennault. "I can't understand his denying the existence of the air strip. Not after Grandma saw it with her own eyes. It has to be common knowledge in the area."

"General Chennault is concerned about security. Maybe the strip is no longer in use."

"I'm worried for her."

"I will help if I can. Right now, excuse me; I'm going back for seconds. Would you like something?"

"No, thanks."

John returned from serving area with enough food for another meal. "My Lady, you are as lovely as I remember."

"I'm surprised."

"That I remember you? You shouldn't be. You have ever been in my thoughts and now that I have found you again I am going to make sure that you don't escape me."

Soon they were in the barracks. No one else was present and Captain Birch spread a map and said, "Show me where your Grandmother says there is an air strip."

Dorothy indicated the spot. "Right here."

"Yes. I have been to Chengchow several times. I am acquainted in Honan. Don't worry, Dorothy, I will rescue your Grandmother for you."

"I hope you can. She is a nice grandma."

"When I rescue her, how shall I contact you? I may not be able to bring her where you are."

"Bring her to any air base and ask for Colonel Richard H. Wise."

"All right."

"She has bound feet, little feet no larger than my hand. She cannot run for a plane."

"I understand."

"She's a Baptist, you know."

"Imagine that! That's wonderful. The Lord works in mysterious ways." He folded the map.

"I never saw a silk map before. Where ever did you get it?"

"At Liangshan Air Base, from Ong Hong June."

"Is he a famous topographer?"

"No. Captain Albert Ong of Arizona is with American Intelligence. Actually, he gave me three maps. Here, take one of them. Silk maps are very practical. They don't fall apart when wading a stream."

"Thank you. Printed in three colors, I will treasure it. Are you sure you want me to have it?"

"I still have two others. When you look at it I hope you will think of me and know that I am somewhere in China."

"Really?"

His shoulders shook to his laughter. "You're precious. Do you still have my Flying Tiger pin?"

"Of course. I don't wear it. The other men would not understand."

"You're right. There are so few girls out here. I am sure you would rather be friends with all of them instead of being pinned."

"I'm not entitled to wear it. I do try to be friends with all the guys. At Kweilin and Liuchow, I was the only woman in the outfit. I feel responsible ..."

"A sense of mission! Wonderful!" His lean face brightened like a teenage boy. "I am learning a lot about you and I like what I discover."

"I am learning about you too. They tell me you rescued Colonel Doolittle. Tell me about that."

"There isn't much to tell. I was only doing my patriotic duty."

"Go on."

"All right. It happened in western Chehkiang Province along a river. A friend of mine had to get to Shanghai and I took him as far as Sing Teng. I was returning to Shanjao when I stopped to eat. Sitting in a little restaurant someone crept up and whispered, 'Are you an American?' I nodded and he said, 'Follow me.' That is Biblical. The man led me to the river, not far from where I left my boat. There, hiding in a sampan was Colonel Jimmy Doolittle. He had been forced down after leading the raid on Tokyo—this was back in Forty-two. I helped get Colonel Doolittle out safely, also some of the other flyers who ran out of gas of parachuted down. That was some raid. They were just told to bomb Tokyo and head for China. One thing led to another and before you know it I was involved. I mean *involved.*"

"I realize how important the work is you are doing now."

"We can't talk about that."

Suddenly an air raid siren shrieked.

"*Jing Bao*" Dorothy cried, rising, attempting to pull him along.

"Let's do something daring," he said calmly, refusing to release her. "Let's stay right here. I think it will be safe, unless the night-time precision of Japanese bombers has dramatically improved." He laughed heartily.

They sat in the darkened barracks holding hands, speaking Cantonese and a few words of Mandarin, sharing thoughts in English as they listened to the steady *blam-blam-blam* of anti-aircraft batteries and the dull thud of distant shells.

His leg was warm and reassuring against hers and his free hand moved to link with her free hand. "What are you going to do in the future? Have you given any thought to your life?"

"When this is over? Yes. What are your plans, John?"

"I think I am back on track. For a while, I was running down a dead-end street. Just because you admire someone very much, it doesn't follow that that someone has the same goals, or that they are willing to share—"

"I know. Sometimes I have been unable to return the affection some men say they have for me."

"It can be painful, first, an outpouring of love, the aspirations for the future, the joy of sharing, then suddenly comes the realization that those feelings are not returned or shared. Then comes loneliness."

Dorothy realized he had fallen in love but now it was over. Somewhere in China, there had been another girl. "I am glad you know what you want."

"Actually that's the problem—trying to fit my private desires in with my calling. What about you, Dorothy? Have you decided whether your real life is in the United States or here in China?"

"More and more I keep thinking of New York. Perhaps if I visited, if I could *feel* New York again, I would know then that my heart really belongs here in China. I know I love being with the Fourteenth more than anything. It is the most exciting thing I have every done and I enjoy the gaiety."

"You are looking at a dream, My Lady. When the war is over the excitement will be gone. The men will return to their wives and sweethearts. Hey, there is the All Clear."

"Yes."

"I want you to think about your future, Dorothy. I believe there will be a happy future for you here in China with the right man."

An incipient laugh rose in her throat. "You are fun even when you are serious."

Holding, hands, they talked far into the night, dreaming of a time they could not see, a future that lay beyond the next air raid. Then it was time for him to go.

"I had a nice evening, John."

"So have I. And I wasn't haunted by ghosts." He often remarked that ghosts haunted him.

Talk of ghosts caused Dorothy concern. She felt him draw her close. His voiced hushed, like wind rustling oak leaves.

"Dorothy," he murmured. "I don't know anyone I enjoying being with as much as you."

His lips pressed against hers in a swirling passion. She dared not think of tomorrow. Her legs threatened to lose their strength until she remembered this is wartime. Then he was gone, faded into the night, ghosting all over China, only to materialize somewhere behind enemy lines. Sitting in darkened barracks, staring beyond their immediate situation was utterly absurd. It would have been, but for hope—and faith.

If Kunming had only one short block where prostitutes paraded, Billy Boy Willis Jackson would have found it. He strolled along nonchalantly and suddenly his eyes widened. Did he see the prostitute who drugged and rolled him in Kweilin?" He fell in behind a couple taking long strides. *It is her! She is definitely the one who robbed me!. No doubt about it.*

Identification positive, he halted and moved into the shadows near a building. Too late to accost her, she stood arranging something with a Captain. Billy Bob followed them discreetly, taking pains to remain out of sight. They entered a door in an alley.

Billy Bob waited. When the Captain reappeared, he would burst in on the woman. He resigned himself to a long wait. The Captain did not at once appear. Billy Bob waited.

A man arrived with a cart. He entered the same door. Presently, the man and a woman exited carrying the Captain. They placed him on the cart and covered him with a sheet. The man proceeded down the alley.

Billy Bob moved. He tried the door and charged in, .45 caliber pistol drawn.

"The Captain's money," he rasped.

The woman turned. He followed her to a dresser. She pulled out the drawer and reached inside. He suspected she was reaching for a knife. He saw a glint of a blade and savagely raked the barrel of his .45 diagonally across her face. In a continuing motion, he brought the butt down on her hand in a bone-crushing blow. She yelped and dropped the knife. As she bent forward, he brought down the closed fist of his left hand with tremendous force striking the back of her neck. She dropped.

Pain dizzied, by the time she focused, he noticed a half filled glass with liquid. He guessed the Captain only drank half.

"You drink," he said sneering. "Maybe I let you live." He handed her the glass and menaced her with the pistol.

She drank.

He found some garments in a drawer and rolled her over on her stomach, keeping her down with his foot. He tied her arms behind her, tied her legs, and placed a gag in her mouth.

He found money in the drawer, Chinese National currency, American dollars and some bills he didn't recognize. "The Captain's contribution," he told himself. He came across her purse and dumped its contents. He shoved more bills into his pockets. *Don't dawdle. Her friend will be back.*

He found shoes and rattled them for contents. A small leather pouch dropped out of one. He did not look inside. Between his fingers, the contents felt like gemstones. He dropped the pouch into his trouser pocket. He looked at the woman. She appeared to be asleep. He decided against continuing the search.

Outside, he took five steps and whirled around, .45 at the ready. He saw no one and continued toward the street. He looked around and saw no one following him, peered into the street, and stepped out.

"Are you going to war?" asked an enlisted man.

Billy Bob realized he was holding a thin-bladed knife in his left hand, a cocked .45 in his right. "I guess so," he said sheepishly. "There are some toughs following me. Are you going back to the Air Force Base? I could use a friend."

"Good God!" Colonel Wise exploded. "Of all the damn stupidity. The Chinese army had fifty-three tons of ammunition hoarded at Tushan. Two dozen warehouses full! Major Gleason got there three minutes before the Japs overran the place. Gleason blew it up right under their noses. I wish I had an army half as efficient as OSS. Who's in charge of Chinese logistics?"

A bundle of energy, Colonel Wise had difficulty dissipating his frustrations. Dottie hoped the inspection tour of the Burma Road, might relax him.

On December 22, Colonel Wise, Major Maurice Hollman, Lieutenant Cabelka and American Vice-Counsul Richard M. Service set out in a command car for Mangshin, 880 kilometers distant, in Yunnan Province. They returned on the 29th and reported the Burma Road capable of handling increased truck traffic.

"How is our base at Tushan?" the Colonel asked.

"Nearly evacuated, Sir, according to radio from Kweiyang. The belly tank factory at Kweiyang has been ordered to Kunming."

"A mobile engineering crew has been dispatched to Paoshan," Lieutenant Cabelka reported. "The weather is so bad; I can't get supplies into Suichwan."

Look at these reports," Colonel Wise said gravely. "Chinese Intelligence is completely broken down in the Kweiyang area. They are in a state of utter confusion. I'm worried about Suichwan. We may have to pull Major Bull out of there"

"I wouldn't do that," Dottie said. "I think you should leave him there. Send him forward. If he could just glare at the Japs—"

"What?" he said sharply. Slowly his features drained of rigidity, the corners of his mouth turned up, and a rifle report of laughter rang out. He slapped his desk, his body shaking with glee. "Send Bull forward … to glare at the Japs." He continued to laugh as if he had been hoarding laughter for weeks. "Now I know why I keep you around. You are precious."

Cabelka chose the moment suggest sending additional personnel to Louhuanping even though orders had come through halting construction there. "We can still use it for fighter staging operations."

During the night, the Japs bombed Yunnanyi Air Base and destroyed two A-3 refueling units badly needed in Paoshan.

At the New Year, a letter arrived from May and Marion Shim, who Dorothy had met at church in Kukong. The girls managed to flee and were in a village near Namyung. Their letter held a poignant plea. "Can you help us? May and Marion Wilson."

Dorothy assumed Wilson was the name of an early family employer in Jamaica. Chinese people sometimes did that in colonial countries.

"Colonel," Dottie posed, "I just received a letter from dear friends in Namyung."

"I was just thinking of Namyung. Lieutenant Irwin Mohr is over there."

"Is there any way the girls can be flown out? It is more than a month since they wrote their letter. I know there is trouble in the area."

The Colonel's chin came up. His upper lip drew down in petulance. "God Dammit, Dottie. Do you think I am running a shuttle service?"

"No sir."

"Do you realize that is nine hundred miles?"

"But there is a constant stream of planes coming to headquarters. Everything comes here."

"Namyung is in danger. Japs are moving all around there. We will need to blow the runway any day." He lit a cigarette. "Mohr doesn't have time to go looking—"

"The girls won't be hard to find. They speak English with a West Indies accent. The village isn't all that far from the base."

"I'll look into it. I can't promise anything. I am going to leave it up to Lieutenant Mohr. If he wants to risk his bar it is all right with me."

"He will if you ask him."

"Yes, yes," Wise said irritably. "I said I would look into it, Ma'am. Haven't you got some work to do?"

Retreating to her desk, Dottie knew there was nothing more she could do to help May and Marion. Bases continued to fall. The irascibility of Major Bull did not save Suichwan. An order came down to blow the runway at Namyung. Dottie did not know if Irwin Mohr found the May and Marion in time, and she continued to worry.

"Look at this report," Colonel Wise called to Lieutenant Cabelka. "The Japs are freezing to death in their cotton uniforms. They are stripping bodies to stay warm. Everything is covered with ice. It's a crystal wonderland. They can't live off the land. The have run two hundred miles past their supply point. The Japs will soon stop. They will never get to Kweiyang. I'd bet on it."

"I almost would," Cabelka said slowly.

A brilliant tactician, Colonel Wise attacked a problem directly, sometimes too directly. A few days later Dottie heard an amalgamation of voices as she approached the office. As she entered, she heard Wise shouting at General Chennault, "You'll have to give that to me in writing!"

Chennault's face froze, the muscles in his neck tightened, he jaw jutted forward. He stormed out, his back stiff with anger.

Cabelka, sporting new Captain's bars bent down and whispered, "Not too diplomatic."

Later in the club, the staff discussed the incident. "One reason Wise is rebellious is that he is not in line to make Brigadier General."

"Yeah, he wants to make Bee-Gee so bad he can taste it."

"I like his style. Let's drink one for the Colonel."

"To the Colonel, who won't accept mediocre work or mediocre thinking."

"Or mediocre drinking."

"Gambay."

"Gambay."

Not only the Colonel drank too much. All the men were drinking too much.

The order to evacuate Namyung had been sent when a radio message arrived from Lieutenant Irwin Mohr. He found May and Marion but the airstrip had been destroyed. It was too late to fly them out. He put the girls on a Jeep and sent them over mountain trials to Kanchow to catch a plane there. However, on reaching Kanchow the base was in flames. He put May and Marion on a 32nd Troop Carrier plane with 20 British soldiers and took a different plane to Chihkiang.

Dottie waited for May and Marion now and asked a man at headquarters to calculate the ETA. She walked to Chennault's headquarters where the staff eyed her with indifference and suspicion. Dottie felt they might call the military police. At bases commanded by Colonel Wise, she had been accepted by radiomen. Here in Kunming, no one knew her. She could not even get inside Chennault's control tower. Rejected and helpless, she returned to Sector headquarters and asked a friendly Sergeant for help.

He jangled the phone and asked for a report. He put down the phone, his face somber. "The plane is lost."

Dorothy's breath caught. "Shot down?"

"No. Lost. They don't know where they are. They are flying around in circles."

In a few minutes, Dottie asked him to call the tower again. "No more news. Maybe it's compass deviation."

Dottie said pointedly, "How come every time one of these farmers turned navigator gets lost, it's due to compass deviation. If it was daylight, they could at least see haystacks. You know they navigate by haystacks."

"They will be all right, Dottie. "Want a cup of mud? It could be a long night. Let me get you a cup."

An hour later, Dottie agreed to accept a cup. She nearly gagged. "Standard Air Force Coffee," she muttered. "How many spoons have dissolved in this?"

At length the phone rang. The Sergeant listened and appeared dour. "Bad news, Dottie. The plane ran out of gas and they are going to ditch. Maybe they will hit the silk."

A curtain of gloom settled over Dottie as she trudged back to the barracks. Lieutenant Mohr came in one day and exclaimed, "Thank God for last-minute orders. When May got on that plane, she received the last parachute. If I had gotten on, I would not have had one. I would be dead. I sure don't want to explain to the family why I died saving one Chinese girl." He snickered, enjoying his gallows humor.

No news arrived, not even the report of a crashed plane. Three weeks passed, when Dottie heard that two English-speaking Chinese girls were on a plane coming to Kunming. It had to be May and Marion.

Tense and anxious, Dottie waited for the plane to taxi to a halt. The hatch opened. Seeing May and Marion, she heaved a sigh of relief. *They are walking!*

They hugged and everyone spoke at once.

"The Jeep ride over the mountains with Lieutenant Mohr was terrible. My heart was in my throat half the times." Wide-eyed, Marion clasped a hand over her mouth.

"No, no, not the Jeep ride," Dorothy said impatiently. "What about the plane?" She turned to May. "Tell me about the plane."

"The first thing I knew, they took the plane up to twenty thousand feet and had us check our parachutes. 'Buckle up,' said the crew chief. I thought he was kidding. It was for real. We didn't know if we were over enemy territory. 'When you land, don't call out. It might be the enemy. Wait for daylight.' Then the crew chief threw me out. My scarf was ripped off. Suction tore off my shoes. I yanked the ripcord. The chute came open and shook the daylights out of me."

"We are so light," Marion interrupted. "They were afraid we would get caught in the slipstream and smash into the tail."

"I landed in the snow," May said. "With no shoes. After a minute, I realized I was unhurt. I wrapped myself in the parachute and waited for dawn. When the sun came out, I saw someone in the distance. Luckily, it was a British soldier. We weren't in enemy territory after all. We met some Chinese. I tried to communicate with them but their dialect was different. They didn't even know there was war on. They were strange people. Little by little, we re-grouped; everybody except Marion."

"I came down over the ridge and they couldn't find me," Marion said.

May shrugged. "We had to set off without her. Luckily, we found her. The next day we passed through a small village and a little boy came running up, wide-eyed. "We also have a girl who came out of a bird.""

"I sprained my ankle," Marion said.

Dottie said, "It's a wonder you didn't break a leg. I am so glad to see you both. It is a lucky thing that Lieutenant Mohr didn't get on the plane with you. Did you know that May got the last parachute?"

They followed Dottie to her quarters. Eventually May and Marion obtained jobs on the base.

Men accumulated points for months of service and many were ready to 'point out' for home. Nearly everyone had a nest egg they planned to use to marry, to buy a car, or buy a house, or start a business. Preparing to leave China, presented a 'last clear chance' to 'go for broke' in enlarging that nest egg with poker winnings. Men became reckless; other issued markers with reckless abandon, knowing that once they left China, efforts to collect on them would be generally unsuccessful.

Studying cards became less important that evaluating the player—how long did he have before he 'pointed out?' Allowing a player to use markers early in the game became a strategy until an opponent understood his ability or technique. Once understood, the use of markers might be summarily suspended with a demand for cash. The abrupt change rattled some. Succumbing to uncertainty, they were off their game, which gave the advantage to their cunning opponent.

"There is more than one way to skin a cat," said Hap. "And the cat hates every one of them."

"There will be no new markers in the next game," Hap said didactically. "Like in Old Maid, only old markers previously issued by players at this table will be accepted." He chuckled. "Menchnikov, I have some of yours that are so old they have grown whiskers."

"That isn't fair," Menchnikov said with a squeak. "I can't put in markers but you can throw my old markers at me!"

"Well ..." Nathan Berry paused.

"You will just hoist the bid with my marker," Menchnikov charged, "and try to freeze me out. I have to match it or fold."

"That doesn't make any sense," Nathan Berry said quietly. "If you are froze out, as you say, or if Hap wins, he gets stuck with your markers again. The only way he really wins is to have someone else take the hand. I have an amendment. No old markers come in with a value of more than the bid and no drag of cash out of the pot. The marker is in for the bid. That's it. The player can't make change." He looked at Hap. "Agreed?"

Hap nodded pleasantly. "That's fair."

Billy Bob sat serene as a pimp, flush with the earnings of a prostitute. After robbing the prostitute, he decided to stay away from that part of town. In fact, he never again went into Kunming unless accompanied by friends.

Billy Bob liked to have things come his way; he hated a dilemma. On the one hand, he felt tempted to double the Captain's money—had he not recovered an unknown Captain's money taken from him by an evil prostitute? On the other hand, common sense dictated something else. *Don't piss money down a rat hole.* The battle before him was between Hap and Menchnikov. He would allow them to fight it out before coming in with his winning hand—he felt his full house of queens over 6s was a winner. He opened with a meager two dollars.

Nathan Berry drew three cards and added an ace to the pair he already held. He stayed in the game but did not raise.

Menchnikov unwittingly signaled by his mannerisms that he "had good cards." When he raised twenty-five dollars, Berry felt sure of his analysis and closed his card fan.

Hap had a Menchnikov marker ready. "I will meet your twenty-five and raise you a hundred." He tossed in the $200 marker.

Billy Bob wondered if his Q-Q-Q-6-6 hand was good enough. It was too good to fold. He reluctantly shoved in cash.

Nathan Berry decided his three aces were fodder. "Fold."

Menchnikov thought if he raised, Hap would merely toss in another of his old markers. He swallowed. "Call."

Menchnikov's full house, jacks high, topped Hap's straight, but fell to Billy Bob's queen high full.

Billy Bob regarded the Menchnikov marker he acquired with disdain. Billy Bob's turn to deal, when Nathan Berry tossed in his cards they flipped, revealing three aces. Billy Bob quickly turned them over. *Geeze, he is playing it close. He folded early.*

Menchnikov glowered. Now two guys were poised to toss in his markers. Maybe his best strategy would be to fold. He requested three cards and exclaimed with energy, "Yeah." Mercifully, he held a nothing hand. When Berry opened,

Menchnikov bumped up the bid slightly as if eager to go. When he folded on the next round, it would be a surprise.

Hap raised. Billy Bob raised. Berry folded. Menchnikov said, "I fold too."

Hap quick-glanced at Billy Bob and raised. Billy Bob called. Neither played a Menchnikov marker. Billy Bob scored with two pair.

"That's all for me," Nathan Berry said, rising. "Luck is not with me today."

Menchnikov seized the opportunity to avoid receiving his own marker. "I'm done too. Till Next time."

Hap beamed and waved a marker at Billy Bob. Billy Bob picked up a Menchnikov marker and waved it back at him. "Well, you got rid of one."

28

THERE IS A FUTURE

Momentous changes were taking place. Captain Cabelka and Captain Gibbens, Dottie's pistol shooting friend, transferred to a new base more than two hundred kilometers distant, near the Indo-China border. They returned near the end of March.

"Am I glad to see you," Colonel Wise said. "We are set to transfer to Chanyi. I am sending you two ahead. I got wind of a plot to raid my staff. They want you, but if I transfer you to Chanyi; when they discover you are already at Chanyi; I doubt that they will call you back. Dottie cut the orders." He halted and turned to the men. "Unless you would rather ship out of my outfit."

"No sir!" they shouted in unison.

The Captains departed at once and in a couple days, the rest of the staff boarded a C-47 called the "Thunderhead Special." The plane had flipped over during a storm in Kweilin; the wings replaced, and the plane sent ahead to Liu-chow prior to evacuating Kweilin. Despite being officially "destroyed," the plane continued be used in spite of there being no record of it.

"Dottie, this is the life," Colonel Wise proclaimed as he removed a cigarette from his aluminum case and lit if off the butt of the last. He mused, "Some day I will need to account for this plane. Maybe I can do what Captain Cabelka did. You know he destroyed two trucks on paper and gave them to the Chinese Army as we fled Kweilin."

Dottie nodded. She realized they were in two wars: the real war and the paper war. One frequently bore no relation to the other.

The Colonel smiled. "Cabelka made his trucks disappear. I will talk to him someday, about making this plane appear. I am sure he can do it." An amused laugh boiled from within his depths. "I even have two Lieutenants to fly this bucket."

Dorothy's thoughts wandered. Somewhere far below, in a remote area behind enemy lines, her grandmother waited and prayed. She hoped John Birch reached her in time.

For its size, Chanyi was extremely busy. A record number of planes landed, bringing supplies. The Japanese presence in the sky dwindled.

Although she had been with the Fourteenth for some time, the increasing confidences the men shared with her surprised Dottie. She listened to their hopes and fears, their innermost thoughts, even their indiscretions with women. She thought it might be because she was the only woman on the base and had become a mother figure to them. "Wrong," she decided. "I am more of a big sister."

Captain Cabelka brought news. "You can start packing, Dottie. "We are moving out. Cut orders for all of us to Peishiyi."

"Peishiyi? That's wonderful." Peishiyi was not far from Chungking. Maybe she would be able to visit the family.

All of the staff was in high spirits as they boarded the Thunderhead Special bound for Peishiyi. This time they were not fleeing the enemy and were leaving the base intact, running smoothly. A month to the day after arriving in Chanyi, they landed at Peishiyi.

At the first opportunity, Dottie caught a ride with a Jeep heading for Chungking. The trip of 35 miles over rough and bumpy roads took well over an hour.

The family delighted in seeing her and at once Edna drew Dorothy aside. "I can't stand Mother. She is after me all the time. Just the way she did with you. Remember?"

Dorothy made a face. "How could I forget?"

"The harder I work," Edna complained, "the more difficult she becomes. All I hear is, 'When I was sixteen I had a job. You are still laying around the house.' I have got to get away."

"What does Father say?"

"When I reminded him that you were only eighteen when you came out to Chungking alone, he gave me one of his all-knowing nods and said, 'That's true.' Daddy won't object if I get a job."

Dorothy grimaced as she remembered her fiasco with Mrs. Wu. Her mind lingered on failure, until she heard Edna saying, "Besides, I am nearly nineteen. Can you get me a job at the air base?"

"I don't know." Dorothy hesitated. *Do I want a younger sister at the base?* Was Edna ready to meet the world in the person of the Fourteenth? Still, if she remained at home, she would not be any more ready a year from now. At the base, Dorothy realized, she would be able to keep an eye on her.

"You *will ask?*" Edna pressed.

Dorothy knew all too well Edna's situation at home was hopeless. "I will see what can be done."

"I'll be eternally grateful."

Dottie lost no time in taking up the matter with Colonel Wise. Had it not been for Cabelka's chuckle behind her, she would not have realized the Colonel started a cat and mouse game with her. She returned her averted eyes to scan his face an instant.

"I didn't know there were any more like you at home," Colonel Wise said without expression.

Dorothy nodded. Of course, he knew.

"At least this request of yours won't get me court martialed—right away."

Dottie remained silent.

"You are beginning to show promise. On that basis I suppose I can take a chance on Edna."

"Thank you."

"I don't know if I can stand two of you pressuring me. How long before Edna comes in here demanding that I hire her sister?"

Dottie made a phony bow and said in a squeaky voice. "It is in the hands of the gods."

The Colonel chortled and cleared his throat. "No, it is in the hands of Mother." He called Sergeant Pillsbury, Mother. Okay, Dottie, when Edna arrives, have her report to Mother. He is an extremely patient man. We will see if you sister can learn filing."

"Yes, Sir."

"And one more thing—"

"Yes—?"

"She cannot ask me anything. No dogs, no frogs, no hogs, no nothin."

"Right."

The Colonel need not have worried. Dorothy gave Edna instructions of her own. "You are going out in the world before you are ready." She dispatched a penetrating stare. "You will be the second woman on the base. That involves responsibility."

"But I am nearly nineteen. Next month—"

"No!" Dorothy snapped. "You are eighteen! That is what you will tell them. It sounds better. And listen, young lady, there are some strict terms."

"Anything, Dorothy. I will do anything."

"You will not do anything! First, you will obey all the rules and regulations of the United States Army Air Corps. When you are with a man, you will not allow him to touch you below the shoulder or above the knee. If they try, you made them stop immediately. Understand?"

"Okay."

"And when you go out with men, you will be in by eleven. No exceptions."

"B-But."

"Furthermore, what I say goes. I have asked the Colonel not to speak to you about this, but technically, you are in my charge. What I say is final. One word from me and you are off the base."

"I'll be good Dorothy. I will try very hard. No job can be as bad as Mother."

Dorothy nodded. "You will be working for Sergeant Pillsbury, a very intelligent man. Learn all you can from him."

Dorothy knew Sergeant Pillsbury would watch over Edna like a mother hen. She worried what might happen after work. Weeks passed before Dorothy began to repose a confidence in her sister.

Speeding in a Jeep, sometimes they would hear a thud, look back, and see a ball of feathers fluttering, rolling like a tumbleweed. Frequently a youngster would dart out and pick up a chicken dinner.

While shopping, Dorothy glimpsed General Zung. She stopped to thank him for allowing her to board the train at Kukong.

"You know Big Brother is here," he said.

Big Brother was his name for General Yur Ying-kai. "No I didn't know he was here."

"He is at a hotel nearby."

"I would like to see him."

General Zung accompanied her, and after telling General Yur, he had a surprise, departed.

General Yu nodded to a woman who peeked into the room. "This is my wife."

The lady was not the wife Dorothy met previously. She had to be the country wife of the marriage arranged by his mother.

General Yur appeared gloomy. His eyes were heavy lidded. A shadow as dark as his closely cropped hair spread across his face.

"Forgive me," he said. "I am in a melancholy mood."

"You appear troubled."

"It is my mother," he said wearily. "The doves have flown. She will soon meet her ancestors. At this critical time, it is my duty to be with her." He broke off as his voice caught. Eyes misting, he continued. "She is in Hunan, behind enemy lines."

"The area is yet free?"

"Yes Do-jur. But it is isolated. It will require a plane." He sagged into a chair, defeated.

"The Fourteen Air Force has many planes."

"And a goose has wings," he said hopelessly.

"I will see what can me done." Dorothy raised a cautioning finger. "My influence is not great."

"I will be most grateful."

She left General Yur in a better mood and feared she would catapult Colonel Wise into a worse mood when she made her request.

Wise remained strangely calm. "Dottie, that is a twelve hundred mile round trip."

She expected the Colonel to refuse.

The Colonel explained, "If he was an American General instead of a Chinese national, there might be something we could do."

"He is a dear friend who often helped me. He saved my life." Dorothy realized she could not tell the Colonel she had been mixed-up with Chinese Intelligence and the notorious Mrs. Wu. "Colonel, without his help, I would not be here." Could she tell him General Yur saved her father from a firing squad?

"He saved your life?"

"Yes."

"I can't drop everything. I have a war to fight." The sleeping tiger awakened in his voice. "You know what you are asking is patently illegal, Dottie." His voice intensified. "You are going to get me court martialed."

"Yes sir," she said and quickly amended, "No, Sir."

His hands came down smartly. "I will need to arrange something. I can't just go winging down there. It has to look good."

A couple days later, the Colonel called to Dottie. "Ma'am?"

She strode to his desk for instruction.

"I find it necessary to make a trip to Hunan," he said with a lopsided grin. "Tell your friend to be ready. I do not want him on the base until I am ready to take off. If people see him, they will start asking questions. I will taxi over near the road; then he can climb aboard. And one more thing—"

"Yes?"

"I know he has aides and servants. He can bring two, but not the whole God-damn Chinese Army. Understand? I am flying a C-47. I cannot take the whole kit and caboodle."

Dottie could not wait to give the good news to General Yur. When the driver dropped her at the General's hotel, Dorothy was so excited she forgot her purse in the glove compartment.

General Yur was elated. His eyes sparkled beneath is crew cut. "Do-jur, when you are here, magpies build nests at the front door. Truly you are a child of the Lan Hua."

"You have meant more than an orchid to me," Dorothy said, nodding formally, almost bowing.

"Come," he said, "Let us share a pot of tea." He did not invite his country wife to join them.

When her driver called for her, the first thing Dorothy looked for was the purse she had placed in the glove compartment. "It's gone," she cried in dismay. "I had three hundred dollars in it."

"I'm sorry, Dottie. If I had known you left your purse, I would have taken it with me."

"Not your fault, Sergeant." Disgusted and angry with herself, everything she had managed to save since coming to work for the Fourteenth was gone. In the depths of despair, Dorothy visualized herself pushing a large bag of money across a giant ledger marked, "Owed to General Yur." Specious reasoning, Dottie concluded. A mere three hundred dollars would not extinguish the debt she owed General Yur.

At the appointed time, Colonel Wise's well-dented plane taxied to the end of the runway. A car rolled out of concealment. General Yur stepped out, saw Dottie and bowed low. He limped toward the plane as fast as he could. Without a ramp, he had difficulty getting aboard. He grimaced in pain as he twisted the stiff leg he injured at Nanking. Aides scrambled aboard after him. The hatch closed and the Thunderhead Special revved and rolled for takeoff. As the prop-wash tousled her hair, Dottie felt warm and happy that she had been able to assist General Yur.

On April 13, Captain Cabelka departed for Washington, D.C., followed by a leave to Wisconsin. Not expected to return for two months, office staffers were pleased Edna had come to work, especially when Sergeant Pillsbury came down with malaria. Dottie visited him in the hospital located behind headquarters.

"Sergeant Pillsbury, how are you—" Mouth agape, she cried in wide-eyed surprise when she saw his roommate. "John! What are you doing here?" Captain Birch looked thin and pale.

"Malaria," Birch said weakly. "Really I am all right."

"You know each other?" Pillsbury said, surprised.

"Yes," they said in unison.

Very discerning, Pillsbury soon excused himself and left them alone.

"Dorothy, I am so glad to see you." His hand came out to touch hers.

"And I you. This is a wonderful surprise."

"Seeing you is the best medicine I can get."

"You allowed yourself to get run down. What you need is a vacation. Why don't you go home on leave to Georgia?"

"I can't. Not until the war is over." He managed a rueful smile.

"Yes, you can. For many men the war is over. They pointed out for home. You have been here longer than most. A vacation is long overdue—and richly deserved."

"My heart cries out to see Birchwood, but I can't leave. Who would do my work?"

"Who is doing it while you are here? Surely the war can do without the Phantom Mandarin for a couple weeks."

"That's just it. It can't. My people depend on me. In many places I am the only link. No on else can speak with these people. I am the only liaison. I can't be wasting my time on vacation—or waiting for a relapse that might never come."

"Or might return with a vengeance."

"About your grandmother," John said abruptly. "I have not forgotten my promise. I am working on getting her out. The strip she is near is seldom used—it is only used to drop in supplies or a new transmitter. It's going to be touchy, but my friends are working on it."

"Grandmother Poh-poh will be happy to get on this side of the Japanese lines."

"Don't worry, Dorothy."

"Somebody has to worry. You said it would be touchy. Just like I worry about you needing a vacation."

A dimly adventurous sparkle came into his eyes. "I'll tell you what. Just as soon as this war is over, we will go back to Birchwood together. You will be my guest."

"That might come sooner than you think."

"I know. Have you noticed how our troops are pouring up through Italy and across France? When Germany collapses, the Allies will concentrate on Japan."

"It's time for me to go."

"Come back and have dinner with me."

During the following days, Dorothy visited Birch two, sometimes three, times a day. When she scolded him again for not taking a vacation, his face became coolly composed, his voice impassive.

"I may never leave China. Maybe I should not pay attention to the voices in the mists. I am sure it is not a premonition."

"John, what do you mean?"

"My Lady, do you believe in ghosts?"

"Of course not."

"I hope you do not think any the less of me if I tell you—"

"Nonsense. I recall you have several times mentioned ghosts. Do you really believe in ghosts?"

His voice lowered to a whisper. "It is not a matter of believing. I heard them on many occasions."

"You have? Tell me."

"One night in a deserted house, I rested and heard footsteps. I went to investigate and there was no one there."

"Perhaps someone left."

"No. I heard noises. I found no one. The ghost was the ghost of a Chinese military man. That wasn't the only time. By the look on your face, you don't believe me."

"It isn't that I don't believe you. I know you must be constantly on guard. Could it have been a dream? In that ephemeral zones between wakefulness and sleep …?"

"No."

"Perhaps your imagination … playing tricks on you."

"I considered all these things. I lashed myself fully awake. I walked around. Then I heard the voices again." He hesitated. "I think it's time for the movie."

They took their stools and watched images on a large white bed sheet. Not long after they returned to his hospital room, Sergeant Pillsbury popped in. "Am I interrupting?"

"No," Birch said. "Your timing is perfect. I was just telling Dorothy she would make some man a wonderful wife."

"That she will," Stan Pillsbury said. "Of course, the selection process may take some time. She probably dates a dozen guys every week."

"Oh?" John said seriously, a dark shadow moving across his face. "Tell me about that."

"I already said too much. With all the people on the base, I should have said two dozen. Captain Birch, you should see this girl dance."

They continued to banter. The next time Dorothy visited Captain Birch, he took up the same point. "Dorothy, do you think you could stand being a missionary's wife? There is a tremendous challenge for a Christian woman. I think you would make a wonderful helpmate."

"I don't know, John."

At that moment, a pilot stuck his head in the doorway. "Hey, Dottie." He turned and shouted. "Hey Guys! Dottie is here."

Within minutes, the room filled with eager faces. Men began to relive not their war experiences, but happier times.

"Dottie, do you remember that party in Liuchow? There stood the Colonel, three sheets to the wind ..."

After a cackle of laugher, another began at once. "There was Chennault with this little Chinese gal. How the hell was I to know? He wasn't wearing any uniform. How could I know who he was?"

Dottie glanced at Captain Birch and saw displeasure hardened his expression. As their eyes met and he looked away.

"Yeah," a pilot rambled on. "In Kweilin—that was before the Bamboo Club burned to the ground. I was going—"

"Knock it off," a voice commanded. "Pipe down!" A male nurse appeared and cleared the room. "This is a hospital, not a bar."

"Dorothy," Captain Birch called after her as she prepared to leave. "Thanks for coming. Goodbye, Dorothy. Thanks for everything."

His somber tone meant more when a messenger hand delivered his letter.

---

9 May

Dear Dorothy:

I don't know why I'm writing this; maybe it's because I have failed to find an opportunity to speak with you alone in the last few days.

It makes little difference now, as I expect to leave Peishiyi in three days, but until then, please don't waste any more of your time coming to see me. You see, dear, your visits have come to mean too much to me. I'm afraid I'm falling in love with you, and this I intend to stop.

Even if I thought I had a chance with you, I should still want to stop running the risk of looking into your eyes. You want a life of city lights, gay parties, many friends, and much excitement. I want to find my pleasures where sunlight dances on grassy meadows, where blue mountains tower into the sky, or where ocean waves break on moonlit shores. I prefer a few old friends to many new ones.

I should have learned my lesson a year ago, when after leaving Kukong, I wanted you so badly I couldn't sleep. In spite of my intention not to see you any more I guess I'll always have a perverse longing to see you again,—it's a queer life, isn't it?

Anyway, Dorothy, I want always to be your friend. If ever you can use my help in any way, please command me.

Forgive me if this note seems to you foolish or annoying. God bless and keep you.

Good-bye
John

P.S. I shall always be grateful for the kindness you have shown me the past two weeks. J.M.B.

As she read, Dorothy's hands trembled. How could he say that? How could he? Something within her flamed in her depths, ascended in anger and enveloped her heart. She struggled to hold back tears and succeeded. *How can he know so little about me? I'm not like that.* How can he say such things?

Unaware that she had started running toward the hospital, she realized it now and drew up short. *John no longer wants to see you.* As proof of his intentions, she read his letter from the beginning. Her spurt of mindless anger subsided and calm returned, leaving only her pride injured. Shaken, she watched a lonely sun melt into the skyline, knowing that a certain future had slipped from her grasp. As the shadows lengthened on distant bluffs and darkened the land, so had the dark shadow of being unwanted darkened her future. Her heart in turmoil, she found it difficult to sleep. In the morning, she thought John felt miserable too and timidly decided to visit him. As Dorothy approached, John's head came up sharply. "Didn't you get my letter?" He broke off and forced a sickly smile.

"Yes, I received your letter. *Xiang-nian ni.*"

"I miss you too," he repeated in English.

"I couldn't stay away." She swallowed the constricting lump in her throat. "I am not going to allow you to banish me so easily."

"I do not want to—"

Instantly, they flung themselves into each other's arms, trembling, clinging to each other tightly.

"Darling, I can't let you go," he said. I have been so miserable, riddled with guilt, for sending you a way. It has been agony. I am so glad you are here."

Dorothy's heart lifted as she waited for him to find the words she knew he would select with care. "Dorothy, I am not sure we can—or should—go on this way. There are dangers—"

"I know. One who rides a tiger cannot always get off. But if there is no danger of falling off, it is wise to considerer a course of action before leaping off."

"Excellent. Let's talk. You first."

"You said you wanted to be friends, but your letter tore my heart. You wounded me deeply and I became very angry. You don't know me at all. Wherever did you get the stupid idea that I want a life of city lights and gay parties? I am not like that. You hurt me."

"I am truly sorry I hurt you," John said with compassion, his great brow furrowing. Perhaps I was wrong. I see you carefree and gay, always in an airy mood. You are so popular with the men. How could I not think of you other than the life of the party?"

"I am the only woman on the base. I must spread myself very thin. But that has nothing to do with my future."

Birch sat down and drew up a stool. "Well, then, tell me what you would like."

"I don't even want to live in a city," Dorothy said. "I want a home in the country ... near a stream. On the hillside is an orchard ... cherry trees ... apples ... plums. There are birds—larks, thrushes, magpies. And children. There are two cows for milk, a hive of bees for honey ..."

His palms flew up to silence here, his eyes widened in amazement. "Except for the specifics, do you know what you just described?"

Before she could say "No," he exclaimed, "Birchwood! You just described Birchwood! I am overwhelmed!"

'Really?"

"You certainly have given me something else to think about."

"I know you have thoughts about continuing as a missionary."

"I do. It might mean making a break with the missionary society. I do not agree with everything they do. They send missionaries out here who can't even speak the language."

"You speak it well."

"When I learned Mandarin my tutor accompanied me wherever I went. I had more of an introduction than just 'hello" and "thank you." I intend to be an intense missionary, to live among ordinary people. I'm tired of missionaries who live comfortable lives, who sit around a mansion in splendor right in the midst of poverty. He stopped. I guess I have been carrying on. I'm enthusiastic. That is why asking any woman to share my life would mean surmounting obstacles. I care for you so deeply, on the one hand I cannot think of offering you anything less than a comfortable life."

"I am glad we are friends again."

"That is certainly an understatement, sweetheart."

"I must go. The Colonel will think I have become a patient."

"Goodbye, My Lady."

In was not goodbye. On his date of discharge, the walked her to a large tree overlooking a tranquil valley. "My thoughts are with you constantly. I cannot get you out of my mind. My mind is made up. I am asking you to marry me."

"John," Dorothy said helplessly. "I thought we decided—"

"I can't go on without you. I may be a missionary, but you give me courage and hope, and sustenance. There is no longer any way that we can't be together."

She pressed a finger to his lips. "As friends." Lying in the grass, looking up at him, with a blue heaven in the background, she murmured, "John," and he bent down and closed her lips with a kiss.

"Don't say anything more," she gasped. "I am not sure...."

"Darling, Sweetheart, this is the happiest moment of my life. I love you. I adore you. I cannot go on without you. There is nothing else to be said. Say that you will marry me, Dorothy."

He kept kissing her and kissing her. Her wildly racing heart wanted to cry out, "Yes," and brain told her now was not the proper time. The world was still at war. At length he released her.

She rolled and sat up, "Captain Birch," she said, putting up a restraining arm. I thought we agreed not to spin ourselves into a cocoon of passion. You know what my immediate answer must me. Don't make me give you that answer. If I forced them now, they would not be the true words of my heart."

"Oh darling—" He kissed her repeatedly.

"Please—we must stop. Now. A future requires a solid foundation. You told me that in Kukong. Even now, there is talk of the war ending. We need to me patient. We can be patient."

"I suppose so," he said reluctantly.

"This time when you are alone beyond the outposts, I hope you will remember I am your very closest friend. Surely we can find each other as soon as there is peace …"

"We shall, I promise we shall, My Lady. God has sent you my way, I am sure of it. Although this time, I didn't hear what I wanted. Dorothy, I love you so much."

The suns warm rays filtering through the leaves dappled the turf with their shadows. She heard him say, "It is time for me to go." He helped Dorothy to her feet.

"I have a favor to ask."

"I'm yours to command."

"Would you just leave? Let us say out goodbye here. I want to remain and meditate, and remember this moment."

"Of course."

He held her in his arms. "Goodbye, Dorothy. Just remember that I love you."

"I love you too, John."

She watched him go. *Did I say I loved him? Did I speak those words?"* Dorothy bit her lips, still feeling his kisses. Her legs lost strength and she sagged into the grass and watched him leave in long loping strides. Suddenly he turned, "My Lady, you have not heard the last of Captain John Birch."

"Laughing, he ran down the hill, soon lost from sight. Rising, Dorothy knew she had made the right decision, for the moment. There was still a war on.

Ten minutes after she returned to the office, Sergeant Pillsbury thrust an envelope at her. "Captain Birch wanted me to give you this."

Dottie tore open the packet. Inside there was no message, only three hundred American dollars!"

"He felt badly about your purse being stolen," Stan Pillsbury said.

"I never told him about that," Dottie said adamantly.

"I did, casually. We were just talking and I happened to mention it."

"Gossiping, you mean."

Her routine shattered, due to spending so much time with John Birch, at noontime she wandered into telephone central. She spoke to the signalman. "That looks interesting. I have never worked a switchboard."

"You haven't? Sit right down here. I will show you how to run it."

A call came through and a voice rasped, "Let me speak to the Duty Sergeant." Dorothy recognized the voice of Captain Dell. From his expression, she could tell the Sergeant was receiving a dressing down.

The Sergeant flustered. "Yes, that was Dottie." He pulled the plug and said, "Uh, this is a classified area. You are not supposed to be here."

"I hope I didn't get you into trouble."

"That all right. It is time Captain Dell noticed me." He sniffed and grinned.

Dorothy hurried to report her error to Captain Wise, but Captain Dell reached him first.

"That girl works for you," Dell charged. "Do you know what she was doing? Working the switchboard. That is a sensitive area. Highly classified. I want her reported."

Colonel Wise issue a short dry laugh. With a supercilious reproving looked, staring over his spectacles like a grandfather scolding an errant and beloved grandchild, he said slowly, "Don't be silly, John. Dottie is cleared for Top Secret."

Captain Dell shrugged. "Uh," he muttered. "Just doing my job."

"No doubt about that."

Dell nodded stiffly as he stalked past Dottie in the doorway.

Colonel Wise looked up. "One thing about your sister Edna. She didn't cause me any trouble."

Edna had transferred out with the Chinese American Composite Wing, an integrated group, where American pilots taught combat skills to Chinese counterparts. The CACW had flown to Chihkiang, taking Edna with them. Once again, Dottie was the only woman on the base.

Since early April, elements of the Fourteenth supplied coordinated support for troops landing. Colonel Wise had been greatly interested in Okinawa. "He grew fond of saying, "Only three hundred miles to go," the distance from Okinawa to Japan.

A bell jangled and Colonel Wise scooped up the phone. He listened and his face to on a perplexed expression. "Two Chinese women, an old woman and her daughter? Asking for me. Hell, I don't know any old Chinese woman and her daughter. Tell them to get lost. Where did you say they were" Chihkiang? I don't know anybody over there."

"Colonel Wise, Colonel Wise, "Dorothy interrupted excitedly. "That must be my grandmother." She ran to his desk.

"God dammit, Dottie, what are you saying?"

"I-I d-didn't have a chance to tell you—"

"Hold on Sergeant. I'll call you back." The Colonel put down the phone. "Now what he hell is this, Dottie?"

"I didn't think it would happen so soon. Captain Birch is trying to get Grandma out. If she made it, she was to report to any air base and ask for you." Dorothy stared wide-eyed and breathless.

"My God, Dottie. What are you going to pull next? This is top-secret intelligence! What am I supposed to do now? We can't transport Chinese nationals and I can't leave her standing on the runway at Chihkiang."

He did wait for her to answer. He phoned base operations. "Ah, Sergeant, tell command over at Chihkiang to make the ladies comfortable. And ... as inconspicuous as possible. And get my plane ready at once."

Colonel Wise turned to Dottie. "I have to get them out at once. The sooner I do fewer will know. Dammit, Dottie, this is the living end! You are going to get me court martialed." As he was going out the door, he barked instructions. "You know what to do. Just like with General Yur, only in reverse."

Colonel Wise flew the Thunderhead Special to Chihkiang and returned the same day. When the plane touched down, Dottie and her favorite Jeep driver raced to the plane. Dorothy wondered which of her aunts was with her Grandmother. Now she saw Auntie May with Poh-poh.

"Not now," Dorothy said when both women wanted to talk at one. She helped her Grandmother into the Jeep and they went racing toward Chungking, scattering chickens in every direction.

She reported to Colonel Wise their glorious reunion. "Grandmother is very happy. She asked me to convey her thanks and asked if there is anything she can do ..."

"She might come and visit me when I land in the brig. Dottie, this is absolutely the last time."

"Right."

Within days, bombers were flying out of Okinawa. The Fifth and Seventh Air Force utilized Philippine bases and continued to hammer Japan and Japanese occupied Shanghai. They swept the China skies clean of Japanese planes.

"Do you realize we haven't shot down a plane in aerial combat in six weeks?" Colonel Wise exclaimed. "We are moving to Chungking. The end of the war is imminent."

On the runway in Tinian, Colonel Paul Tibbets revved the engines of a B-29. The *Enola Gay* carried a 9000-pound bomb called Little Boy. The plane slowly rolled down the runway for a flight into history. In ten minutes, the plane was over Saipan, headed for Japan.

Less well known is the fact that if Tibbets suffered a debilitating bellyache or the *Enola Gay* popped a row of rivets, a backup B-29, *The City of Omaha*, piloted by Howard W. McClellan, with co-pilot Glen Jensen of Manning, Iowa, readied to complete the mission. The cards were all aces for McClellan and Jensen that fateful day. After the war, whenever kukes, pinheads, or crazies wanted to demonstrate or picket anything atomic, they sought the home or office of Paul Tibbets to create their nuisance. Had they tried that in the small town of Manning, the town with the highest per capita number of volunteers for the military in the nation, someone would have been seriously hurt.

The headquarters staff of the Fourteenth had little more than arrived in Chunking than rumors mounted. The reports were utterly fantastic.

"One bomb, a whole city is gone," Colonel Wise exclaimed in amazement. "Hiroshima gone. Nagasaki gone. We've done it!"

At that moment, Captain Cabelka came running in. "Japan is suing for surrender."

The Colonel's eyebrows rose majestically and came down with indulgence. "As I was saying …"

29

IT CAN'T BE TRUE

The cheering, the firecrackers, the drunkenness, blended into an insanity as intoxicated houseboys, now attended by their masters, spent the day apologizing, "So solly, Suh. So Solly," for having lost face.

In a massive stroke of irony, before the war ended, General Chennault was relieved of command, succeeded by General Charles B. Stone. After conferring with Stone, Colonel Wise returned shaking his head in disbelief.

"Stone wants us to maintain a thirty-day level of supplies. God dammit, Gibbens, that's contrary to purpose! We are only an in-transit depot, not a permanent storage facility."

Their presence in Chungking could be explained on paper. In early August a new unit, the Northern Sub-Depot had been created with Colonel Wise commanding, Major Earl Gibbens, executive officer, and Captain Cabelka, adjutant. Northern Sub-depot distributed in transit supplies to bases north of the Yangtze River, operated Lushien Air Base, and supplied Peishiyi; responsibilities previously handled by the 12th Air Service Group. Wise also continued to command the 12th.

Wise raged, "With the war over, people on the other side of the Hump have turned everything off; right when I have explicit orders to build up a thirty-day supply."

The insanity of idiotic and conflicting orders caused Cabelka to remark dryly, "I don't understand how we won the war."

In frustration Wise said, "Try radio. See what CASC has to say."

A prompt reply explained, "Northern S-Depot is charged with command and operation, but not administration of Base Section Number Five."

"Well that clears that up," Cabelka snickered. "Command and operate, but do not administrate."

"Dottie," Colonel Wise said. "I have to attend a policy conference in Chungking on the Twenty-fourth; Headquarters, China Theater. Make sure that everything dovetails."

"Yes, Sir."

When the Colonel returned everyone was relieved that Northern Sub Depot would continue under the command of CASC—until the staff discovered both of their truck companies were reassigned to the 10th Air Force.

"Radio headquarters," The Colonel said in disgust.

CASC radioed back, at once rescinding the order.

"Hmmm," Captain Cabelka mused as he read a report. China Theater is allocating one C-47 from the Three hundred-twenty-second Troop Carrier Squadron to the Twelfth Air Service Group."

Everyone laughed uproariously. The C-47 was the Thunderhead Special the Colonel had used ever since Liuchow.

"I wonder if we could use it for Sub-Depot." Major Gibbens said with a whimsical smile.

"Not by a dam site," erupted Colonel Wise. "The transfer order reads Twelfth Air Service Group. I don't want any screwing around in this command. Excuse me, Ma'am."

On August 29th, Colonel Wise flew to Chihkiang to raid the personnel of the 12th Air Service Group which he also commanded. Before he departed he said, "Dottie, I am sending you on an important mission to headquarters."

Briefed and ready, as Dottie waited on the apron for a plane to ferry her to Kunming, an intelligence officer approached and said, "Dottie. John has been killed."

"John who?" Dottie said.

"John Birch."

Stunned, speechless, agony jarred her brain. Dorothy felt cold as if all her blood had been drained from her. Dazed, she staggered aboard, brain numb, attempting to grasp shards of denial, trying desperately to avoid the chains of wretched reality. The engines on take-off boomed "NO!" and became a muffling blanket under which she could hide her sorrows. This was war. People died every day in war. There was no time to cry, no time to mourn.

She stumbled through her mission like a robot and when she returned and the plane touched down, she found it difficult to realize she had been to Kunming and back. She went at once to Intelligence where men shrugged sympathetically when saying they had no viable information.

Dorothy did not eat. Despite being exhausted, she could not sleep. Such a waste, John HAD SO MUCH POTENTIAL. Now all his hopes and dreams had vanished. Where once an inspiring life loomed, there remained nothing. Her eyes welled with tears; she began to weep.

A short time ago, she had put John off and delayed her answer. Now, when it was no longer possible, everything within her cried out, "*I will marry you!*" Her shoulders shook to her sobs as wept for herself.

At length her thoughts reverted to John. She had a strange vision. God was saying, "*Well, John, you arrived much too early, but welcome. Even My plans do not always reach fruition. Sometimes I wonder why I gave men choices.*" Dorothy sniffed, dried her eyes, and eventually slept. She awakened with resolve. Who betrayed John? She had to know. She knew it would take time.

With the war over, Dorothy's personal mail dropped to half. She no longer needed to spend her spare time writing. Mail Call brought in four letters. She saw one of them was from Captain John Birch! She trembled as she opened the letter and read.

---

13 August 1945
Dear Dorothy:

Thanks a lot for your kind letter of June 25 and July 13 just received. Sorry to hear about the heat and ill health in your family; trust things are better now. The summer here fell far short of last year's heat, and I am in excellent health, a little thin, and very sunburned from swimming in a river that flows by my station, and from taking several long motorboat trips on business. (Did you know I have a captured Jap boat? I'd like to take you riding in it!)

Perhaps I can find a way to see you soon again; the radio for the past thee days has been loud with rumors of Japan's imminent surrender. Please keep me informed of your whereabouts, dear. I have been unable, out here in the plains, to keep up with the new APO's; does your change to #271 mean that you have moved again?

Thanks for the word from May and Marion. Please give them my best wishes. I think of them quite often (but not so often as of you.)

It really begins to look as tho this long terrible war will soon be over. Yesterday, Sunday morning, I held a church service here, thanking God for bringing us to the eve of victory. All the men in my station attended excepting one operator who could not leave his transmitter.

I believe I shall visit my family as soon as I can, then return to China (possibly the extreme western part) to resume missionary work. Some people want me to stay in the army as an intelligence officer, but I can't escape from the conviction that God has called me to the other.

Please write me whenever you can.

Affectionately,
John

"John," Dorothy choked, helpless before a deluge of tears. Sorrow stricken, she flung herself across the bed, her body racked with paroxysms of sobbing. "John," she cried. "Why? Why did it have to be this way?"

Sharp pieced of memory flooded her mind. His face came into focus, a lean face with a gentle boyish smile. "My Lady," he said. "You have not heard the last of Captain John Birch."

His words were prophetic. She read his previous letter and sobbed uncontrollably. Through the swirling thoughts, she remembered that she had not even thanked John for saving her grandmother. She sobbed until exhausted and when able to master her emotions, asked, Who? Where? Why?

At Intelligence, men shook their heads and said, "The government has clamped a tight lid of secrecy on the whole incident."

Incident indicated the top level of diplomacy. Not be deterred, she contacted Chinese Intelligence. She learned the war was over ten days when John was killed. "It is regrettable." The man bowed. "And quickly forgotten."

She continued to press him and he used the phrase, "highway bandits," which meant Communists.

Dorothy met a man named Lou, who sometimes acted negatively to command authority. She talked at length about her past, being a radio operator.

"So that is where you met Dog-Sugar-Eight."

She had not known John's call letters but she would never forget them. "Right!"

Dorothy began pouring her drinks quietly into a crack in the floor whenever he excused himself.

"You can't trust the Communists. I knew they would start up again as soon as we settled with the Japs. The Commies were stashing bullets all along."

"Why did they kill John?" Dottie asked pointedly "How?"

Lou leaned forward and lowered his voice. "Captain Birch and a small group of officers were headed for Hsuchow when halted by a Communist roadblock. Captain Birch objected. "You have no right to stop an American military detail." The Reds thought if over and let the group lass. Soon there was a second confrontation. Captain Birch and the Chinese Lieutenant left the group and walked into the village to talk. While they were gone, the Reds disarmed the rest of the party. Before long, they heard two shots. According to reports, the villagers found two bodies. Full of bayonet holes. There were about to bury Birch when the Lieutenant stirred to life. He told the villagers that the killing was deliberate. The Commies had him in the village a couple hours before the order came down. None of the other Americans was killed. They were finally released."

"Any way to find out who they were?"

"Funny thing. They were never named."

Although Dottie had many unanswered questions, she assumed she would learn little more. In the final days at Liangshan, as they were closing the office, Captain Cabelka reminisced. "He was quite a guy."

Dottie said, "I don't suppose I will ever get over it. I am sorry the Communists killed him."

"I knew they would," Colonel Wise said.

"You what?" Dottie demanded sharply.

The Colonel's eyebrows went up at the intensity of her voice. "During the last days of the war I tried repeatedly to get him out of that area. I knew the minute the war was over the Communists would kill him, but I couldn't reach him. Captain Birch worked with us, but he didn't work *for me.*"

Dorothy pressed, "How did you know they would kill him?"

"Once the war ended I knew the civil war would resume. Only a fool would think otherwise. John knew all the Communist agents. They couldn't have a man running around who could identify all their operators. He had too much influence with the peasants. He spoke, ate, and lived with them. And there was that religion thing. There was no way the Communists were going to let him live."

"I wish I had known sooner," Dottie said sadly. She doubted if he would have listened to her.

The staff flew to Chengtu, and then transferred to Chihkiang, Hsinching and Tsingchen. Then as autumn leaves turn crimson and gold, they received orders to proceed to Shanghai.

Dottie realized the war had finally ended. She wondered if their home and her father's factory remained intact. She looked forward to the day when her family could rejoin her in Shanghai.

30

TRANSITION

During the war, Colonel Wise and his staff moved frequently, as base after base fell to onrushing enemy forces. With the arrival of peace, the group moved to Chengtu, Chihkiang, Hsinching, and Tsingchen. Then orders arrived to proceed to Shanghai. Exhilarated and overjoyed at the prospect of returning to Shanghai, Dorothy wondered if their house at 1412 Yu Yuen Road survived.

A couple months earlier, Dorothy stood on a balcony in Chungking, melancholy because the war had ended, feeling depressed because she had no future. The Fourteenth Air Force would go on without her. Again optimistic, she looked forward to seeing the Bund, the harbor with it pungent aroma of oil, fish and sweat, a place where gulls stood in the sky waiting to catch a passing cloud.

Their home had survived. Dorothy and Edna helped their father ready it for occupancy. However, Sandow's factory had been bombed, a total loss. Edna wanted to move to a place they could call their own. The Japanese had constructed a cluster of tiny homes surrounding Kiangwan. Offered at a reasonable rent, Dorothy and Edna moved in and hired a maid.

May and Marion, whom Dorothy had last seen in Kunming following their harrowing parachute escape, lived a few doors away. The Japanese forces did not evacuate at once and remained for months. The end of the war did not automatically make them friends. The Chinese kept open a wary eye. Some attempted acts of retribution. Everyone "looked over their shoulder."

Colonel Wise trained Chinese troops to take over American responsibilities and when his assignment ended, Dorothy transferred to Colonel Kinsey. Two month later, she was reassigned to Colonel Wise.

Christmas in Shanghai brought out loneliness for Dorothy, Edna and their father. Jack, Gloria and their mother remained in Chungking. A sympathetic Captain Jim Willett offered to fly to Chungking to get them for a delayed Christmas celebration.

At the appointed ETA, Dorothy and Colonel Wise sat in a Jeep at the end of the runway and waited. When the plane broke out of the haze, gliding down, the Colonel sent the Jeep racing forward. The plane rolled to a halt and Colonel Wise opened the hatch. His head jerked in shock. Wide-eyed, he recovered and slammed the hatch shut.

"Willett," he shouted. "I want to see you!"

Face livid, Wise ran to the Jeep. "Good God, it is not only your family. The plane is full of women and kids!"

"Who are they?" Dorothy asked.

"How the hell would I know? How the hell are we going to get them off the base?"

Willett approached with easy long-legged strides. "What's the problem?"

"Jim, where the hell are your brains? The inside of the ship looks like a Chinese whorehouse." The Colonel stopped. "I'm sorry, Dottie. I didn't mean that about your mother and all. But I am so damn mad at Willett." He glared at Jim. "You put us in a hellova spot. How the hell are we going to get them off the base?"

Willett shrugged. "Dottie's mother had a friend. The friend had a friend …"

"God dammit, I don't care how they got on. The question is how are they going to get off? Jeeze! All right. Now trot your ass back there and tell them to stay put until we come back. Anyone who gets off that plane before we get back will be interned as a prisoner of war. Tell them that!"

Dorothy interjected, "The war has been over for months."

"I don't care."

Willett sauntered back to the plane, attempting to appear nonchalant, and returned.

"We need to wait till dark, that's for God damn sure," Wise said with a growl. "Your family—they are American citizens—but the rest are Chinese nationals." He gave Willett a withering look. "Hell man, you could lose your bars and cost me my eagle. I hope you told them to keep those kids quiet."

Hours passed before darkness settled in. During the interval, Colonel Wise had also acquired a command car. As soon as he opened the hatch, Lillian Yuen stormed angrily, "Dorothy, what took you so long?"

"Not now, Mother."

"Do you realize how long we been waiting?' Her voice retained its cutting edge. "We had to use a helmet for a potty. We were becoming a refugee train."

"*Not now, mother.* We are on a military base. Shut up or we will all be arrested. Do as you are told!"

"American citizens in the Jeep," ordered the Colonel. "Quiet! I want it quiet!"

With children stashed under robes and luggage, they started forward at a smart pace. At the gate, Colonel Wise hit the brakes, tossed the sentry a crisp salute and roared in his finest West Point manner, "Colonel Richard M. Wise, Commanding." He reeled of some elaborate command authority. "Official convoy of two vehicles. Military personnel. American nationals. Civilian Air Force employees. Is that button on your collar open?"

"N-No sir. Proceed."

"Look sharp, Soldier."

On reaching home, Dorothy explained it all to her mother. Expecting a salty response, Lillian surprised her by tilting back her head as raucous laughter boiled forth.

At the office, Dottie typed forms allowing Colonel Wise to bring over his wife and children. Presently Willett, Gibbens and Cabelka huddled around him. "Let's make Dottie a proposition," Cabelka said.

The Colonel's palms came up to silence the laughter. "Dottie, this is on the up and up. No hanky-panky. As you know, we acquired a mansion and we want you to move in with us and run the place. Edna, too. It won't cost you a thing."

"I don't know if I can trust you," Dorothy fussed. "My job won't evaporate?"

"No," the Colonel said, seeing her concern. "This has nothing do with your Air Force job. We need you to run the house, give instructions to the servants, keep things organized. You speak their language."

Edna and I have a maid …"

"Bring her along."

The mansion rose behind eight-foot walls on Avenue Joffe Lu in the French Concession near the American Consulate. Formerly owned by a wartime traitor and profiteer, the mansion towered like a castle, surrounded by a formal tea garden and a three-car garage.

"How many servants?" Dottie asked.

"Only ten," the Colonel said with a grin. "With your girl, eleven."

The group reveled in elegant living. One of the servants was an accomplished tailor; another was a gourmet French chef. The group indulged themselves in flaming deserts, including the favorite, Baked Alaska. The parties were gala affairs. Dottie's mother, a frequent guest, thoroughly enjoyed the ballroom floor. According to popular American idiom, they were "in the groove." Edna and Dottie found some of the post-war jive talk perplexing.

In this idyllic setting, weeks slipped by, until a contention arose because the Air Force wanted to present Dottie with another medal. Dottie protested vehemently. "I certainly appreciate it and I am honored, but why can't they mail it like they did the last one?"

"This one is more important," said Captain Cabelka. "The other one was for civilian service. This one is for *meritorious* civilian service. *Superior service.*"

"I prefer to have it mailed."

"That is no way to be decorated, Dottie," Colonel Wise remonstrated. "Receiving a medal in the mail is like getting a letter. That is no way—no way at all. You talk to her Gibbens."

"Why not, Dottie?"

"I am not going to walk up there in front of everybody. All that cheering, foot stomping, catcalls …"

"It won't be like that Dottie. It will be dignified. All the big brass will be there. General Wedemeyer, General Stone, General—"

"**Wedemeyer?** Oh no!"

"Aw, c'mon, Dottie."

"No!"

"I could order you," the Colonel said.

"I won't go," Dottie insisted.

"She has you there, Colonel. As a civilian, it is within her rights not to attend the presentation."

"Who asked you to get involved?"

"You did," Gibbens said.

"Dottie," Colonel Wise fumed. "If you weren't indispensable—if we didn't need you so darn much—"

Their cajoling at the mansion spilled over to the office when the Colonel asked Sergeant Stanley Pillsbury to speak to her. "Dottie," Stanley said. "I went through an awful of work doing the research, compiling the biographical data, writing the citation—"

"I appreciate it, Stanley."

"Look at the record: China Air Service Command; Sector Three; Sector One; Twelfth Air Service group; Northern Sub-Depot, Fourteenth Air Service Group …"

"No thanks. I'm not going."

"Not even to get a medal with a silver wreath?"

"No."

"Listen to this, Dottie. Here is the way the General will read it: '*Miss Yuen's duties required her to become familiar with organization, policies and principles and to develop a detailed knowledge of administration, personnel, and logistical matters in which she had no previous training or experience. She acquired and constantly increased this knowledge by study, by unusually keen observation, and by a very retentive memory. She demonstrated great adaptability and initiative during enlisted personnel shortages by taking over various administrative tasks ordinarily performed by trained enlisted men. During the difficult and dangerous days of the withdrawal from East China, she set a high example for civilians and soldiers alike by her cheerful demeanor and devotion to duty through excessively long hours. Her calmness under frequent enemy day and night bombing and under threat from enemy agents and snipers was common knowledge of the command and inspiration to all. Of her own volition this civilian employee remained on duty in Kweilin and Liuchow until the final—'"*

"Stop," Dottie interrupted, waving her hands.

"Well, that is what it says."

"It is very nice, Stanley, and I appreciate all the work you put into it. But I can't. I am not going to listen to any more of this and I am not getting up on any reviewing stand in front of the whole Fourteenth Air Force and that's final!"

"I understand, Dottie."

Dottie remained adamant and refused to attend the ceremony. Like the first, the second medal arrived in the mail along with the citation, which she read in private without embarrassment.[1]

Later, at the mansion, the Colonel said, "We have come to depend on you."

They were alone. He sat in his favorite chair, fondling a drink, a blue-gray cloud of smoke from his cigarette coiled over his head. In a reflective mood, he confided his loneliness.

Dottie nodded. "You are just down."

"I need a drink." He rose and went to the bar. He poured some bourbon in a glass and splashed it with water. Returning to his chair, he sat down heavily. "I should have earned a star," he said suddenly. "I should have made Bee-Gee."

"Yes," Dottie agreed. His talking about himself surprised her. He never did that before.

"I would have made Bee Gee if I commanded a fighter group. But somebody has to obtain the bullets, the bombs, and the chow. The Fourteenth generated a fantastic record. During Nineteen forty-four, in aerial combat alone, our kill ratio was seven point seven to one. Nearly eight to one. I am proud of being a part of that. Our logistics kept things going when we lost base after base. Logistics!"

---

1.   A medal from the Republic of China, bearing the likeness of Generalissimo Chiang Kai-shek would take longer—twenty-nine years longer.

"Right. The men all respect you."

"I hear you."

"You will feel better when your family arrives."

"They are not coming," he said abruptly.

"Not coming? But I thought …"

"My wife wrote she would only come without the kids. Without the kids," he repeated morosely. "It is just a ruse. She knew what I would say. I told her not to come alone. It is one of her tricks. She doesn't want to leave her boyfriend."

Wise took out his aluminum cigarette case, removed the rectangular lid, shook out a cigarette, placed it between his lips and flamed it with his lighter. "You know," he said through a puff of smoke, "I have really become accustomed to having you around."

"Just don't call me comfortable," Dottie said, laughing. "One of my boy-friends did that."

"Are you still going with the sailor?"

"Not since Chungking."

"Major Cullen Brannon?"

Oh, sometimes."

"You know, Dottie, you could have anyone in the Fourteenth—" He broke off, rose and left the sentence unfinished. "What is wrong with this," he began again, making a circular gesture, indicating their present surroundings, "is that this all has to end. Before long, Captain Cabelka will be returning to the States. Jim Willett won't be far behind him."

"And you, Colonel, what are you going to do?"

He forced a laugh. "Somehow, I wish you hadn't asked."

Dottie left him sitting there and as she reached the corridor, she heard him utter a melancholy one-word expletive.

As the Colonel predicted, in June Captain Cabelka returned to the States, followed by Captain Willett. Edna and Dottie watched their maid pack; their days at the mansion were over. The three returned to the Yuen family. At home for a short time, they were treated as royalty.

Lillian did not object to having a maid. "With you prima donnas back, somebody has to do the work!"

Gloria objected because the maid slept in her room. The maid had to go.

"Just watch," Edna predicted. "Mother will start ordering us around again."

At the office, things took a surprising turn. Secret orders arrived from the State Department that detached Colonel Wise from the Air Force and assigned him to General Chennault. Chennault was back.

Replacing Colonel Wise was a man who smoked thick black cigars and rested his feet on the desk most of the time. Dorothy felt the strain. However, in early autumn Colonel Wise summed her to a meeting at the Cathay Hotel. "I want you to come and work for us. We are starting Chennault Air Lines."

"A job, not with the Air Force? I don't know …"

"This will be better. You will be Chief Secretary." His eyes sparkled. "Have you noticed the acres and acres of supplies building up around Shanghai? Tractors, plows and foodstuffs as far as the eye can see. It is part of the United Nations relief organization. They need to get these supplies inland where they are needed. So we are starting an airline. C'mon, I want you to meet the old man."

He ushered Dottie into the adjacent room. "General, this is the girl I was telling you about. You remember Dottie."

"Of course." Chennault's leathery face cracked into a grin. "I'll say I do." He squinted as he appraised her. "Didn't you come to see me once?"

"Yes."

"I thought so. Something about a hidden air strip."

"It was there all right, just where Grandma said it was. Captain Birch located it and got my aunt and grandmother out."

"I'm glad," Chennault said. "Too bad about Birch." His face became stony, eyes narrowed to slits and his jaw jutted out. "I wish I had still been here in command of the Fourteenth when that happened. I would have sent a squadron of B-25s over and blasted the Communist son-of-a-bitches and that would have been that. Well, water over the dam. Dottie, I would like you to come with us."

Colonel Wise did not wait for her response. "Dottie, I want you to take applications for pilots. Make sure they have their green cards."

"I better resign from the Air Force first," Dottie said.

No more formalities, matters moved swiftly. As a midwife presiding over the birth of an airline, Dottie experienced the pangs of birth, the joy of seeing the squalling infant take nourishment, take faltering steps, and grow.

An old friend, Colonel Chuck Hunter joined them. Later, in a café, he reminisced. "I was here in Shanghai when General Chen Tsi-tong had the Air Force. He was king of Kwangtung Province. I was there when he asked all pilots loyal to him to stand up. The very next morning they took off with every last plane and flew over to Chiang Kai-shek."

"I roomed with the woman who engineered that—the Flight Commander's lover."

"The hell you say."

"Her name was Madame Wu—or Miss Cheuk."

"Well, I'll be damned. Small World. General Chen Tsi-tong blamed it all on the man who read his prayer stick at the temple. The stick scratched a sign in the sand and the poor interpreter read the sign as opportunity. Don't loose the opportunity, instead of don't lose the planes. It is the same symbol—opportunity and planes."

"Yes," Dottie said. "The symbol 'gay.'"

"Then was then. Now is now. I never thought I would get into a hush-hush organization like this. After all, the war is over."

"Hush-hush? This is hush-hush?" Confused, Dottie furrowed her brow.

"Sure. You didn't know? I didn't think so. Remember OSS?"

Dottie nodded.

"Then you had better know this. Chennault Air Lines is operated by the CIA."

Dottie's breath caught. She remembered the secret orders from the State Department. "In that case," she said, "the less we say about it the better."

Chennault Air Lines changed its name to conform to the United Nations-UNRRA purpose and became CNNRA Air Transport, soon abbreviated to CAT. Supplies which had accumulated on the docks began to move inland ... as did the Communists.

31

NATHAN BERRY VISITS BOBBIE KUHN

During the flight to Hawaii, Nathan reminded himself that he owed Ensign Bobbie Kuhn a salute. Not long after the plane landed in Hickham Field he saw her approaching. While several paces from her, he saluted smartly. She did not return his salute and ran into his arms. "It's so good to see you," she warbled, hugging and kissing him. "How did you arrange your transfer so soon? Did you see the Commandant?"

"No, Dottie arranged it. She cut the order and had Colonel Wise sign off on it."

"You had a woman in the Flying Tigers?"

"Dottie? Sure. I'll tell you about her sometime."

Bobbie smiled her way out of an incipient frown. "You might have told me about her before. Why didn't you?"

"I needed to start work on my degree," Nathan stalled. "There really wasn't time. Do you still want to be my coed?"

"Yes! I'm glad you asked." She didn't want to scare him away. "I may not be able to get detached in time for this semester. Is that all right …? I do have credits from nursing school, and I think being a top-flight surgical nurse may qualify me for some credit. So I will catch up to you. Commander Fritchen will give me a glowing recommendation. Incidentally, he has put me in for Lieutenant JG."

"Congratulations."

"I booked us into the Alexander Young Hotel. We can dine there."

"Great. I'm famished."

Bobbie had managed to borrow a car and on the way, each avoided talking about the first time. Suddenly Bobbie said, "We can't pretend that *manage a trios* never happened."

Nathan nodded. "We have been dancing around pretending it never happened."

They laughed awkward laughs. Each managed to understand the gist of what the other had said. "That day is a beautiful memory," Nathan said. "Remembering kept me going ..." He hesitated and added, "Straight."

Her lips moved. "Then you never ...?"

"Not over there," he said. He looked away. "You know how they say, 'Sex is mental.' I found that to be true. I don't mean using your mind to suppress the urge. I mean the basics, sex per se. Sex ought to be loving, caring, giving—not taking. Sex ought to be enjoyed mentally, not just physically."

"So that is how you remained—straight?"

"Something like that. He swallowed and continued timidly, "I did slip a couple times, long before I joined the Air Corps. I thought I owed Ann her orgasm."

"I remember. I was pretty sure she went after you for that."

"It didn't happen on either occasion. The way I remember it, I broke up a lifetime friendship."

"You may be right. We are no longer close."

They checked into the Alexander Young Hotel and while Nathan washed his hands and face, they continued to talk. "Do you ever hear from Ann?" he asked.

"Almost not at all? You?"

"No. I think she found someone else to solve her problem. I was merely part of her experience. I felt used."

"This is a perfect time to admit I slipped once." Bobbie halted and bit her tongue. *Now comes trouble.*

"No kidding?"

"He was an officer, a nice guy, I thought. Maybe I drank too much. Maybe I was lonely." Her hand flew to her lips like a white dove. "I'm not making excuses."

"You needn't ..."

"I know what you mean when you say sex is mental. There was no thought to it. He jumped me like some stud. Enjoyed himself, and in a minute it was over. It was nothing."

Nathan sat down on the bed beside her. She reached out her hand. "Don't stop me. I have to say this. He fucked me."

She waited a long time for a reaction that did not come. "There, I have wanted to say that to someone for a long time. It is part of my self-prescribed therapy."

Nathan grinned. "You described it very well. As your consulting self-imposed psychiatrist, let me say it will not be necessary for you to ever admit that again; to me, or to anyone else, but especially to yourself." He massaged his chin between his thumb and forefinger. "I need to confess something too. Those pictures of you—that night at the motel. I had blowups made before I gave you the pictures and the negatives. They are in a box back home."

I didn't destroy mine either," Bobbie said. "I wanted to remember that I'm quite the *femme fatale.*"

"You certainly are that."

Nathan wore a somewhat lecherous grin and Bobbie asked timidly, "Do you still want me sexually?"

"Yes. Only a microscopic bit right now. I'm starving. You did mention they serve food here. After I have eaten, we could get around to discussing dessert."

She chortled. *I haven't scared him away.*

Bobbie led the way to the dining hall, which reflected certain elegance.

Nathan observed mostly Navy officers patronized the room. "I guess you will be safe here, from the advances of a mere Air Force Sergeant."

"Stop already. We will start with papayas sprinkled with lime juice."

"Then I will want a steak."

Conversation came easy after initial discussion about the outrageous incident that happened in their younger days. They had so much more in common. They were from the same town—attended the same high school—and had nearly identical plans for the future. It wasn't necessary to dwell on that first time.

When Nathan had finished eating his steak, he nonchalantly brushed his napkin off the table and slid out of his seat to retrieve it. On one knee, he looked into her eyes and grinned. "I missed you. I can't go on without you. My love spans continents. Bobbie, will you marry me?"

She smiled and hesitated a polite moment. "Yes. Yes, I will."

He barely heard timid applause around them. Without rising, Nathan reached into his pocked, flipped open a jewel box and placed the diamond ring in her hand. With a squeal of delight, Bobbie calmed and said with authority, "Are you going to stay down there on bended knee all night or are you going to place your ring on my finger?"

He rose and placed the ring on her finger. Their lips met. Not quite oblivious to growing applause, Nathan said, "The ring may be paste. I did shop one of the oldest jewelry stores in Kweilin. When the Japs closed in and when prices dropped to less that half I decided to take a chance. We might have the ring appraised—"

"That's not the highest priority. It is dessert," she teased. "I think you will like the pineapple pie."

"I would like pineapple pie before dessert," Nathan said, beaming.

As they strolled to their room, Nathan said, "I was thinking of an out-of-this-world Hawaiian honeymoon. Really, I don't know if it is legal for us to marry. The military has restrictions. I wish Dottie were here. She would clear it, call our chaplain, Father Buckley to marry us, and schedule a delightful party after."

Bobbie swallowed a snide remark; *does she have wings?* She managed, "She sounds interesting."

"You can say that again. When we moved in Liuchow, Colonel Wise confiscated a hotel for our headquarters. One day I walked into headquarters and Dottie was there all alone, in charge of everything: armament, medicine, food; logistics for nineteen air bases; bombers and fighters, practically the entire Fourteenth Air Force. She was running the whole damn war. Really interesting."

"If I met her, I think I would like her. But, I am already tired of hearing about her."

Bobbie may not have been the first to voice that complaint. As the months passed, more than a hundred other women probably voiced the same objection. Nathan knew it was not the right time to tell Bobbie he had a picture of Dottie. He purchased it from a photographer in Fighter Recon.

Bobbie said, "If you want a torrid Hawaiian honeymoon, you had better get started."

"I didn't say torrid."

"What if living with the Flying Tigers energized your sleeping sperm cells? I will get deliriously pregnant."

"Do you want to?" Nathan asked.

"Sure. If it happens. I am mentally ready. For everything."

Bobbie closed her eyes. This time there would be no sharing with Ann Schmitt. She loved the gentle touch of him, his exploring fingers, and his warm sensitive mouth. The way he massaged her buttocks heightened her desire. Soon she felt herself arching her back imploring, "Do it! Do it!"

"I'm supposed to be the Tiger," Nathan said, as he collapsed, out of breath, spent.

"In your dreams." A short shriek escaped her. I forgot how messy this is! Hand me that towel."

"Beside the mental, there is a physical aspect." Nathan grinned. "I love you."

"I love you right back," she called from the bathroom.

"So how does it feel to be Gertrude Solo again?" Nathan said when she returned.

"You keep coming back to that first time. I'm trying to forget it."

"It is a secret we share," Nathan said thoughtfully. "If we discuss it openly and honestly, the memory will fade in time."

"Unless you keep reminding me." She plunked down on the bed beside him and kissed him."

Nathan continued. "I am going to remind you that because of that *event*, I now have you, and I wouldn't have missed that for anything. There is one thing that troubles me—looking ahead. Some morning, ten years from now, you will wake up and find we do not have children. You will feel unfulfilled, wretchedly depressed. Have you thought of that?"

"Yes. Not having children will enable me to have a career, uninterrupted. You have given me an idea." A twinkle entered her eyes. "I'm going to ask the hospital chaplain to marry us. I will tell him confidentially that we have had—and will be having outrageous sex—and I certainly don't want to go to the delivery room with a full term infant after being married only three months."

Bobbie's pleas were persuasive. With Nathan attired in a dark business suit—which he could wear when occasions demanded—and Roberta wearing a gown that with minor alteration could be used for dancing to the big bands, the couple were married in the Navel Hospital chapel with many of Bobbie's friends enjoying the reception and party.

"You are in trouble," Nathan said seriously when they were back in their room at the Alexander Young. "When I stepped off the plane and saluted you, you did not return my salute. An officer can get in a lot of trouble if an enlisted man's salute is not returned."

"Oh, I know," Bobbie said with mock seriousness. "I plan to give you a really snappy salute when we have been married fifty years—on our golden wedding. In the meantime—" Completely nude, she slithered over him and planted an atomic kiss.

"I think I can wait until then," Nathan said.

32

SCHOOL DAZE

No one is more depraved than your average congressman. The governing body composed of knaves, scalawags, egotists and incompetents made a sudden turn-around and passed the GI bill, which afforded a virtually free education to returning veterans. Since the signing of the Constitution, that one piece of legis-lation, over time, gave congress legitimacy. It changed the woof and warp of America. Some veterans seized the opportunity to feed at the lavish public trough and entered politics. They soon learned the most important aspect of political life is—to get reelected!

William Bryte Booker did not consider a political career. He did think long and hard about furthering his education. No one would hire a chief of police who lacked education. He had dropped out of school during the second semester of ninth grade. If he wanted to be a police officer—a detective—and he certainly wanted that—he needed a formal education. With the education he had, he would be pounding a beat in the boonies until age eighty. The thought of return-ing to ninth grade with a bunch of fourteen year olds repulsed him. The school superintendent would not allow it. Booker shrugged. He had long ago cut off his nose to spite his face.

He didn't know his luck was about to change when he walked into Frank's pool hall. He overheard Skip Donovan, an Army vet who served in ETO, explaining that he finished high school in a couple hours. "I saw a sign that said you could finish high school. I went in. A couple hours later, I had passed the test. It beats sitting in high school another whole year."

A shortcut! Booker grasped the idea with enthusiasm. He planned to drive to Des Moines and check it out.

On Monday morning, wearing his uniform, Booker strode into the office of Drake University president, Henry Gadd Harmon and saluted smartly. "Sergeant William Bryte Booker, Flying Tiger mechanic, reporting for duty, Sir."

Harmon chuckled, thoroughly enjoying the salute.

Booker didn't waste time. "I didn't graduate from high school and I am here to learn if there is an equivalency examination that will enable me to gain admission." He explained how Skip Donovan had passed such an examination.

Dr. Harmon expressed an interest in the Flying Tigers and questioned him at length. "If you can obtain such a document, I am sure we can accommodate you. I am sending you to Dean Gabrielson, who will answer your questions and give you information." He handed Booker the room number in the same building. He was still on the phone when Booker departed.

The Dean obtained admission forms from the registrar. Not until Booker left the campus and reviewed the forms did he notice that on the last page where it said, "Recommended by," there appeared the names of Dr. Henry Harmon and Dean Gabrielson.

Well pleased, Booker exclaimed aloud, "Now all I need to do is take the test."

In all probability, the test could be given at any Army post. He drove south, and along Army Post Road to Fort Des Moines, WAAC headquarters. A WAAC corporal at the office desk ridiculed the idea. "Iowa is the most literate state in the union. Nearly everyone has a high school education. There is no such test."

Somewhat downhearted, Booker drove north of the capitol to Camp Dodge, where the Duty Officer slowly moved his head side to side. "I never heard of an equivalency examination."

Booker headed home. At the outskirts, he stopped at a service station long enough to find an address in a phone book. In minutes, he parked at the home of Skip Donovan. "Look at you," Skip said. "In full uniform. What did you do, re-up?"

"No." Booker drawled. "I had to make an impression. I need some info. What is the hot scoop on that high school equivalency examination you took? Where did you take it?"

"That was at Camp Atterbury near Indianapolis. I saw a sign that said a person could finish high school by taking a test. I went inside and took the test. That's all there was to it."

"What was the test like; do you remember any of the questions?"

"Some true and false, a lot of multiple choice. An equilateral triangle is? A, B, C or D. Fill in the box. An acute angle is? Who wrote the Declaration of Independence? Jane Eyre is the heroine in an Erskine Caldwell novel. True or false. I knew that was not right. I had to give a book report once. What is congruent? There were a lot of names, dates and places, stuff like that?"

"Thanks. I hope they are still doing it."

Early the next morning—Indiana was an hour earlier—Booker walked into the telephone office and spoke to the woman at the switchboard, whom everyone called "Central" and outlined his plan. In a short time, she located an officer in charge of the educational make-up program at Camp Atterbury. She nodded to Booker. "You're on."

In a low resonant voice, Booker began, "I am calling on behalf of Colonel Richard Wise, commanding, service group Flying Tigers." He explained the need and the officer agreed, "as long as there weren't too many." Booker asked, "How long will this examination be available?"

"Probably not past Labor Day."

"Thank you. Our first candidate will be Sergeant William Booker. He should be there is a couple weeks. Thank you.

Booker tuned to Central. What do I owe you?"

"For you; this one time, absolutely nothing."

"Thanks, now it's off to breakfast, then to the high school, to see if I can find a smart girl who has just finished one year at Drake University."

Without hesitation, Central said, "That would be Donna Farley. It will cost you a dime if I call her."

"I forgot you know everything that is going on in this burg. Make the call."

Donna Farley agreed to meet him. She had completed the first year at Drake toward a degree in Pharmacy. Her terms were reasonable and he liked the way she could deal. "I would rather take it out in dinners and rides back and forth to Drake."

"That's assuming I pass the examination."

"You will pass when I'm through with you. If Skip Donovan can pass it, so can you. He isn't a rocket scientist, you know."

"William Bryte Booker, rocket scientist, ready to rock!"

Booker considered hooking a ride on an Air Force plane out of Offutt and reconsidered. Wearing his uniform, he might be able to wangle a ride, but just his luck, at Atterbury, trying to come home, some tight pants Major Bull type wouldn't allow him aboard. Then he would need to hitchhike home. He decided to drive to Indiana. On the return trip to Iowa, he had better news than Gabriel Heater. Booker turned up the radio on loud and sang all the way home.

Billy Bob Jackson returned home to Birmingham with a goal achieved. He left China with four .45 caliber pistols—US government property—hoping to get one gun home. He had succeeded in getting two pistols home. He lamented the loss of two, "as pure stupidity on my part."

Deep inside, a small nut of guilt continued to disturb him. Willis Sr., his energetic father, now more sympathetic to the Klan than ever, interpreted his son's "anger," as the result of the Longstreet woman marrying someone else. Will Jackson decided the University of Alabama would be a good place for Billy Bob to further his education.

At 'Bama,' Billy Bob's reputation was soon established, as one who engaged in free-wheeling protected sex. As Billy Bob described it to a friend, "I'm making it with a bunch of empty heads." As the semesters passed, "empty-headed sex" lost some, but not all of its allure.

Part of the diversion included poker. With his experience, he did well playing poker with young college boys.

Some of the returning veterans followed serious and meaningful pursuits. Nathan and Bobbie Berry resided in Veteran's Housing at the University of Wisconsin. When an attorney friend casually mentioned to Bobbie that a well-trained nurse could make good money working with a lawyer, and testifying in court, Bobbie took courses in forensic medicine. Nathan gathered material for a doctoral thesis from Day One. He decided he would write on the psychological aspects of playing poker and balancing it with a serious study of the criminal mind. He created voluminous files in preparation. Between hours of study, he thought mostly of jumping in bed with Bobbie.

Satisfied that he could manage the curriculum at Drake, William Booker took a weekend job as a security guard. The housing boom generated building site thievery. Not content to sit reading a textbook where anyone could see him, Booker secluded himself across the road, took down license numbers when drivers seemed too inquisitive. His information led to two arrests.

A private detective approached him. "Why work minimum wage? Come work for me."

On a shadowing job, where he followed the suspect to a bar-restaurant, Booker thought he had been made. He phoned his boss, informed him of the problem, turned and said angrily to the bartender. "My wife isn't coming. Thanks for the use of the phone." Booker stormed out. He sat in his car until the boss arrived. "The suspect is still inside. If he thinks I followed him, he will be looking around for someone else who is already inside. When you casually stroll in now, he won't give you a second look."

Running a two and three man hand-off tail became standard operating procedure. One day Booker suggested having a college girl with him would allay suspicion.

"Some Hollywood type?"

"No," Booker objected. "She is level headed, smart, clean living, not a raving beauty, but nice looking. She will fit right in."

Long before the boss asked to meet Donna Farley, Booker remembered his own description. Riding with him to and from Drake several times a year, Booker had not realized where their friendship might lead.

"I think I enjoy hunting season almost as much as you," Donna said. The reason Booker returned to his hometown began and ended with hunting ducks and pheasants with a friend.

During his second year Donna asked, "Are you going home for Christmas?"

"My home is here in Des Moines now." His relationship with his father didn't amount to anything.

Booker could not remember when his feeling for Donna Farley surged beyond mere friendship. He was certain the idea to have Donna accompany him on certain stakeouts—to restaurants—had been his idea. She taught him that no one suspected people who laughed loudly and often. It was fun pretending to take her picture when he wanted to capture a suspect with someone other than his wife clearly appearing in the background.

Donna spoke to his boss. "We will not be available on those nights when big bands come to town." Booker remembered the first time they went dancing. Clyde McCoy played "Sugar Blues."

"Hey, you're leading," he complained.

"Sorry." During high school, she jitterbugged with a girl friend. In a small town, women frequently danced together. It was not because the men were away at war. They refused to be wallflowers waiting for some slew-foot to ask them to dance.

"She digs you," his boss told him. "A woman who will look out for her man is worth more than six who don't give a damn."

"I'll write that down in my Doctor Max important book."

Booker had to admit he enjoyed dancing with Donna. They enjoyed Les Brown, Boyd Raeburn, Harry James, Vaughn Monroe, Russ Morgan, Woody Herman, Pete Kuhl and Lawrence Welk.

At the completion of his second year at Drake, Donna said, "In the fall you are going to take Spanish 101. You need a foreign language to graduate. There are almost no electives in pharmacy, but I'm taking Spanish too. We will be in the same class."

Taking her home he said, "I am not going to ask you to marry me in Spanish."

"No," Donna said, matter-of-factly. "That has to be in English. You need to ask my parents first."

"They might not be happy you want to marry a juvenile delinquent."

"They are still reeling from me being a pharmacist. While I have them on the ropes—you are not a delinquent. You are a veteran of the Flying Tigers."

"If you put it that way."

Donna planned to convince Booker during their Spanish practice sessions that marriage was something to consider at the end of the next year. He surprised her with statement to her parents, "I want to marry Donna. The Flying Tigers are meeting in New York next summer. It's a splendid place for a honeymoon. Well, Sweetie, what to you say?"

"I say, I do." Donna laughed. "Are you reeling, Mother?

33

DOTTIE COMES HOME

Dottie worked long hours, hiring pilots, supervising a secretarial staff, coordinating a myriad of things with bureaus and agencies of two nations, frantically trying to keep up office demands. She worked late, oblivious of time, gulping coffee, sleeping fitfully. One day she staggered in the front door and collapsed on the bed. Weak, barely able to raise her head, a cold chill seized her.

"It looks like malaria," Lillian said. She brought a cover and another, still Dorothy remained chilled.

Struggling on the borderline of consciousness, Dorothy heard Gloria ask, "She isn't going to die, is she?"

"No," Lillian said. "She isn't. Now go away."

Dorothy felt her mother's trembling hand on her wrist. Then she fainted.

"Sandow! Get a doctor!"

Eventually, returning to consciousness, Dorothy made out the face of Dr. Wong.

"Ah," said the doctor. "You have come back to us."

Dorothy squinted. His face kept spinning in and out of focus. She heard him say through the fog, "She is completely anemic. She needs a transfusion."

"I am so cold," Dorothy whispered.

"That is normal," Dr. Wong replied. "You will feel warmer as soon as you get some blood. We need to build you up."

"I need to get up," Dorothy said. "And go to work."

"Not for a while."

A week passed before Dottie returned to work. Colonel Wise took one look and exclaimed, "My God, you're thin!"

The Colonel made a decision and said, "Dottie, I have made arrangements for you and Edna to have physicals at the base. There is a Navy doctor there."

"Do I have a choice?"

"No," he said firmly in a gentle voice.

Following the physicals, the Navy doctor said to Edna. "You have a clean bill of health." To Dorothy he said, frowning "I am not ready to make a definitive diagnosis until further consultation."

On her next visit, he said. "I'm sorry Dottie, you have tuberculosis. I advise you to seek treatment at once."

"What should I do?"

"Go to the United States to a sanitarium. You need to get it arrested."

Dottie mumbled her thanks. He had given her the news straight from the shoulder. It hit her like a sniper's bullet. A she stepped outside, shock set in. "I do not have T.B.," she cried out. "I don't want T.B." She knew TB made young bodies old inside. How long until she coughed out her lungs?

How could she go to the United States? She didn't want to go, not with Christmas coming, the first Christmas the family had together since the end of the war. She couldn't burden the family. She felt herself losing composure. There was no way she could keep her date with Major Cullen Brannon. Running to his quarters, she penned a note of regret.

Now her feet raced again. Gasping, she labored for breath. *It is happening! How many days do I have?* Tears misted her eyes and she forced herself not to cry. *Settle down. You will be okay if you settle down. Relax. You are not going to die until tomorrow. There is great joy to be found in today.* Now she walked slowly, taking tiny steps. She inhaled deeply savoring the air.

She missed a day at work and returned the next. An hour later, Colonel Wise approached and asked, "What's wrong? You are not yourself. I have never seen you like this."

As soon as she poured out her sad tale, the Colonel launched an offensive. He dispatched a cable to their former flight surgeon, Major John F. Shaner, now in private practice in St., Louis. "Make arrangements," the Colonel told him. "Cable us back."

Major Brannon stopped by. "Why didn't you tell me? Why did I have to hear it from the doctor? He saw me sitting with a long face in the mess hall after I received your note."

"I just couldn't." Dottie said. "Isn't a patient's condition supposed to be confidential?"

"You're public property, Dottie. You belong to the Flying Tigers."

Colonel Wise disrupted office procedures as he formulated plans. "You are going back to the States."

"I-I can't. How ...?"

"Leave everything to me."

Dorothy did not tell her family she had tuberculosis. With every passing hour her anxiety heightened and the task became more difficult. Finally, when she could no longer keep her secret, Dorothy blurted, "Mom, I've got T.B. I have to go to the States."

"At least we will have Christmas together."

Caught in a whirlwind of good wishes, Major Cullen Brannon asked for special privilege in order to accompany her on his way home to Albany, Georgia. "I pulled some strings," he announced. "I'm going with you."

Officer and men chipped in money. "There is so much," Dorothy exclaimed. "I will never be able to take it out of the country."

"Don't worry, Dottie," Colonel Wise said, face aglow. "I cleared it with both embassies. Don't ever worry about money. There is more where that came from."

The publicity began. A United Press release in a Shanghai paper of January 5, 1947 stated: *a young woman who used to play hide and seek on New York sidewalks, sometimes hiding with other kids amid the shadowed pews of the Hungarian Catholic Church in Eleventh Street, has set out today upon a strange, unhappy return to America.*

Monday, January 6—*The North China Daily News:* **FORMER FLYHING TIGERS SECRETARY LEAVES.**

*China Daily Tribune: **DOTTIE YUEN, HONORARY G.I., WHO RETURNS TO THE U.S. FOR T.B. TREATMENT, IS ALSO WAR CASUALTY.***

A crowd gathered at Kiangwan to see Dorothy off. He father promised to send money for her return as a CAT photographer snapped pictures.

"Mom, you always said you were going back to America as soon as the war was over and here I'm going."

Her mother gave her flowers and a box of candy. "Don't worry, Sweetie, I will be coming as soon as I can."

Dorothy noticed her father's hang dog look at her announcement. He had already stated his future lay in China.

Edna said. "Be sure to write."

"I'll write you too," said Jack." His eyes brimmed with tears.

"Oh, Dorothy," Gloria choked.

Dorothy felt Major Brannon take her arm and moved with him.

As they continued on their journey, they saw a photograph of Dorothy in the *Honolulu Advertiser.* **HOME AFTER 12 YEARS** The publicity continued to amaze her.

San Francisco Call Bulletin of January 8: *Petite Edith ("Dottie") Yuen, 24, veteran of three years service with the U.S. Army in China as a civilian employee, rested here today at the end of a 10,000 mile "flight for health" from Shanghai.*

Associated Press: **DOTTIE YUEN ARRIVES IN SAN FRANCISCO** *Bundled in a pilot's furlined jacket, 24 year old …*

San Francisco: **FLYING TIGERS' DOTTIE COMES BACK TO U.S.**

FABULOUS GIRL TO GET MEDICAL AID The heroine of the Flying Tigers was back on American soil today on her way to a St. Louis, Mo., sanatorium, where she will undergo treatment for tuberculosis … They set her down at Fairfield with loving care, for she is a legend to the men of the American, as well as the Chinese, Air Forces.

Scripps-Howard Newspapers: **HEROINE OF 'FLYING TIGERS' REACHES U.S. ILL WITH TB**

St. Louis: **SHE HELPED THE FLYING TIGERS NOW THEY HELP HER**

The darling of the Flying Tigers has returned to the United States at last. For three years Dottie Yuen braved bombs and sniper fire to work with the handful of American airmen who challenged Japan from Chinese soil. Now, she is here to battle a more insidious foe—tuberculosis. .

St. Louis *Post Dispatch: SHANGHAI GIRL, CITED BY U.S. HERE FOR MEDICAL CARE.*

Miss Edith Dorothy Lillian Yuen, Chinese-American "mascot" of the "Flying Tigers" through three years of dangerous work which undermined her health …

Dr. John Shaner waited for them at Lambert Field. Major Brannon quipped, "You didn't know I was traveling with a star, did you?"

"That's what I have been hearing."

Reporters fired questions at Dottie at the coffee shop and soon Dr. Shaner said, "It is time to go. They will take care of you at Mount Saint Rose."

Major Brannon instructed the taxi driver, "Ninety-one-oh-one, South Broadway."

At the sanitorium, black and white robed nuns scurried along the corridors. One of them brought a wheel chair. "I just traveled twelve thousand miles," Dorothy said. "I am sure I can walk to my room."

"This is where your journey ends," the stony-faced nun said with authority.

Major Brannon, allowed a brief visit, returned with pajamas, toothpaste and other supplies. He said pleasantly, "If there is anything else you need, let me know. I am staying at the Coronado Hotel."

During his next visit, their eyes met. Although they had grown fond of each other, they knew they had no future together. Dorothy explained that gently.

He said, "Going home always makes me sad."

"I don't wish to add to your burden. You have been a good friend."

"Okay, then."

A nun brought a tray and Dorothy started to swing her legs out of bed. "No," said the nun. "You can't get out of bed. You are not allowed out of bed."

"For anything?" Dorothy said dumbfounded. "Not even to go to the bathroom?"

"Not even for that," the nun said curtly.

Bedpans! The final indignity.

The sun slid over the horizon; the gloom of night approached and a dark cloud settle overt Dorothy. She had never felt so alone. If she was a casualty of the war, she wanted to be with the guys, not stuck away in a remote corner. It was too quiet. She heard the faint sound of a car protesting its way through the gears. It became the drone of a B-25 rising off the runway. If she was going to be a casualty, why couldn't she die quickly? Why didn't a bomb land at her feet?

If she had thought deep thoughts for a month, she could not have guessed nor been prepared for waking. She saw a white clad figure towering over her. As her eyes became accustomed to the light, she saw an oriental face staring at her through Coke bottle-bottom glasses. Large buckteeth filled his smiling mouth. "Hello," he said. "I'm Doctor Ohmoto."

Japanese! The enemy! She wanted to scream, to lash out.

"Miss Yuen, you really must stop crying. It is bad for your condition."

In the weeks and months ahead, they became friends.

Major Brannon came to say goodbye. They stumbled through the awkwardness of breaking off a relationship.

When he left, a nun came running in. "There is a long distance call for you. You can take it at the end of—"

"You mean I can get out of bed?"

"Just this once. We will make an exception."

"Hi," said the voice on the phone. "This is Lonnie"

"Lonnie," Dorothy scolded. "I am so mad at you. You didn't tell me you are married. I had to hear it from someone after you went home. Why didn't you tell me you are married?"

"Well," he said, groping for an excuse. "If I had told you, you wouldn't have gone walking with me. Isn't that right?"

"That's right."

"This is some greeting, Dorothy. I am not sorry. We had something beautiful. I am not ashamed of anything I did. My wife could have been looking over my shoulder the entire time."

"But you deceived ME." She could not stay angry with loveable Lonnie. "I am glad you called," she said, relenting.

In a few days, the nuns allowed Dorothy to leave her bed. A visitor appeared, unshaven, unkempt, hair mussed. "Hello, Sis."

"Bobby Roloson! How did you find me?" A half-brother, the result of her mother's prior marriage, Bobby had come all the way from New York. He promised to stay in touch.

Also from the east coast, former Sergeant Moore, who had been so hateful the first days with the Air Force, arrived for a visit.

After the initial mountain of cards, letters and flowers dwindled, a letter arrived from Shanghai. "Two new planes arrived from Manila. It was good to see our emblem and CAT painted on the side." The letter closed, "I hope that after six months you will be completely recovered and we will look forward to seeing you out here again. Most sincerely, C. L. Chennault."

The general's letter focused Dottie's attention on a decision she would need to make. She would pen an answer—eventually.

A friend stopped, bringing a completely new dimension to her life. "Hello, Dottie."

"Colonel Wise! What are you doing here?"

"I'm on the way to Washington, D.C. and my new job in the Pentagon."

Before long, she heard him say with a rapturous grin, "I am coming for something else. You!"

Her jaw dropped slack.

"Don't look so surprised. I have loved you a long time. Being away from you made me realize it. You can't know how much I missed you these past four months ..."

"I can't come between a man and his wife."

"You're not."

"You are divorced?"

"Not yet. Soon."

"Just the same, they will say I broke you up."

"They can say whatever they want. In a few weeks, I'm coming back. The next time I see you, Dottie, I am going to ask you to marry me."

Excitement welled within her as she heard him add. "I am not going to take no for an answer."

Dottie dreamed about being Mrs. Richard H. Wise. The idea dominated her thoughts.

A letter arrived from her mother. "I said I was going to America when the war ended and I meant it." She had said no to Sandow's pleading.

If her mother had said no, Dottie knew it was time for her to say yes. The owl had flown from her tree. Yet, the tree remained standing. She never looked back.

34

OBSTREPEROUS

On the morning of February 7, 1948, Harry Bratty knew the day would be memorable. He had no idea how memorable. Several Flying Tiger buddies appeared. Frank Thompson flew into Philadelphia from his home in Blackfoot, Idaho. Fred Ifft and Red Denehy arrived for Fred's wedding. Even before the ceremony Fred Ifft and Red Denehy asked, "Where's Dottie?" They finally found a knowledgeable person to answer their questions.

"Dottie wasn't invited."

"Not invited? How come?"

"Violet wants this to be her day. She does not want to compete with someone like Dottie."

Red Denehy came away with an impression. "The bride is jealous."

"I don't care if she is jealous," Fred said. "It ain't right."

At the reception, it did not take long for everyone to become aware of their displeasure. Fred Ifft said, "Dottie is really a shy person."

"You said it." The freckle-faced, Jim Denehy bobbed his red-topped head in agreement. "Dottie didn't like all the cheering and foot stomping when she arrived to eat with the enlisted men. She told me the officers were no better. One day I said, 'Come with me.' I took her to a storeroom and there we sat, just the two of us. She loved K-Rations. Can you believe that?" Red Denehy's voice rose when he noticed a cadre of listeners. "I would rather have had those moments with Dottie than to have dined with Betty Grable or Lana Turner in the most expensive restaurant in Hollywood. Motion picture stars are all publicity and hype. Their lives are make-believe. There is no publicity or hype needed to do justice to Dottie. She doesn't play roles. She is the real thing. She is better than any Hollywood star. It isn't right. She should be here."

"She should be here," agreed Frank Thompson. "You were alone with Dottie?" he whispered. "Making time?"

"Yeah. I wanted to ask her to marry me twenty-nine times. I didn't. I knew I was low on the list. She thinks I am ornery. Can you believe that?"

They enjoyed a raucous laugh.

At a Polish wedding reception, it is traditional to take up a monetary collection for the bride.

"She didn't invite Dottie," Denehy said. "No way."

"I'm not giving her one cent."

"Me contribute to her? No way!"

"No. I pass."

Guests remembered their uncharitable actions for years. "They acted terrible."

The groom attempted to calm ruffled feathers. When Harry did not return after a time, the irritated bride asked, "Where is Harry?"

She repeated her question for hours. Red Denehy, Fred Ifft and Frank Thompson had kidnapped the groom. At least four hours passed before they returned Harry to the reception.

"I guess we got even with her."

The point is arguable. For a half century, Violet Bratty would have nothing to do with the military. She refused to allow Harry to attend 14th Air Force conventions. During the annual conventions in Philadelphia in 1955 and '67, Harry did not attend. Nor did he attend the Allentown reunion in '59 and the meeting in Pittsburg in '73. Not until after Violet's death on May 27, 1996 did Harry attend. That year the 14th held their reunion in Colorado Springs. Harry and Dottie recognized each other at one and embraced. "It is so good to see you!"

A study in contrasts, when Dottie married Colonel Wise, her sister Edna attended the quiet ceremony. Other guests included the Colonel's family. Years passed and one day Dottie called her husband's place of work and discovered that he had not been working there for months. No longer necessary to maintain the pretense of going to work, he could not find employment. Counseling resorted in the end of eleven years of marriage. Dick Wise insisted on a generous settlement. Soon alcoholism took its toll and ended his life.

35

WHATEVER HAPPENED TO—?

One way to learn what happened to friends—attend the 14TH Air Force annual reunion. Joe Reilly became a New York police officer. Robert Mongell sold office supplies for the Panama Beaver Co. At the time, Charlie Nichols owned the largest bookbinder in the world. Buck Doyle returned to work for Remington-Rand. Phil Polinsky owned a taxi company. Herb Corkin ran Entwhistle, a company that supplied parts for the Navy, including catapults to hurl planes off aircraft carriers. Bob Russell purchased used planes and started a Chungking to Brisbane airline. When authorities became interested in a suspected smuggling operation, Bob sold the airline, which became Cathay Pacific. Fred Ifft purchased a tuck and established a Pittsburgh to Buffalo run. When he smashed all his ribs on one side, he sold the truck, but that came later. Barry Menchnikov drove trucks coast to coast. Harry Bratty drove streetcars, later buses for the Philadelphia Transit Company. James "Red" Denehy, became the typical—scratch that—atypical veteran who could not find work. He finally took a job as an elevator operator in a plush Boston hotel. He joked, "I always make it a point that passengers see my big diamond ring when I open and close the door." Married, with two children, Red did not live much longer than age 30.

Christmas cards afforded another way to stay in touch. Bill Booker noticed he received more greeting cards from men who still held markers than from those who owed them money. A brief note from ex-fighter pilot Hap, peaked his interest. *"At our Dayton convention, Menchnikov wrote me a check on a Chicago bank. I tried to cash it but it bounced. Damn him.*

Bill Booker decided to look into that. He wrote to Hap, and added, "See you in Chicago." During summer vacation of 1949, after completing his junior year at Drake University, Booker drove to convention site in Chicago and sought his fighter pilot friend.

246

"Hap. Did you bring that rubber check?"

"I did. I thought it was too good to be true when Menchnikov gave it to me. The little weasel."

'I'm working on something …"

"I know the Chinese Army executed a man who guarded my Lightning," Hap mused. "All the time I made Menchnikov for that shooting."

"Hunh?" Surprised, Booker's head snapped. His eyes widened. "How did you figure that?"

"Well … it was a short time after you started your book. I won a bunch of Menchnikov's markers. You left the game before I could register them. Someone said that all anyone had to do was steal the markers out of my footlocker. No way, I said. I'm storing them on my plane. I figure Menchnikov entered my plane looking for them. Chan caught him and was shot for his trouble."

"Did he find your makers?"

"No. I had them in my wallet all along. Still have them. I told Menchnikov last year I would send them when the check cleared. He wasn't happy about that."

"Interesting," Booker said. "It makes sense. Don't mention that incident to anyone else. Keep it under you hat. Here is my plan. We will casually mention to friends where we will hold the game. We will make him find us."

Nathan Berry agreed to sit in. Bobbie said, "I'll gab with the girls until you come back."

There were five players when Menchnikov timidly opened the door. "Hi. How about letting me sit in?"

Hap muttered inclemently, "Why the hell would we?"

"No markers in this game," Booker said.

"I don't think we should let him play," Hap said. "We already have five. Not after what he did to me last year."

"I know my check bounced," Menchnikov said with a lopsided grin. I'm sorry about that. I forgot about another check I wrote. Look, I will write you another check right now. I got money in the bank. In fact, I will add twenty bucks to it. I know your bank charged you for my error." He reached for his checkbook and wrote rapidly. "There."

Hap surrendered the old check and Menchnikov ripped it.

"Well, okay," Hap drawled. "That's more like it. For my part, you can sit in with us. But no damn markers."

"Take my place," Nathan Berry said. "I need to meet Bobbie. It's your deal."

"Well, all right," Menchnikov said gleefully. "It's Texas throw-down."

"That again," Hap said with a groan.

Berry changed his mind and decided to remain to gather material for his thesis. He moved behind Booker. "May I watch?"

Sure."

Booker drew a pair of 9s. The three-card throw-down showed a mixed suit 8-8-9. Booker tightened his jaw to prevent elation. *Full house!* He opened with a bid of ten. Johnson and Murray folded. Menchnikov raised ten dollars.

The way Berry saw it, Booker needed to be wary of a stronger full house. He thought Booker should turn Menchnikov's strength into weakness. Booker did just that when he raised twenty.

Menchnikov dealt a table card, the ace of spades.

Booker knew he was in trouble if Menchnikov held two aces. His thoughts wandered. If Hap held aces and eights, would his superstition force him to play it out or fold at once?

Menchnikov bet another twenty. The final table card—3 of hearts.

Booker raised forty bucks.

Menchnikov called.

Booker put down his 9-9 to go with the table 9-8-8. Menchnikov mucked his cards.

"I got to go," Berry said. "Bobbie is waiting." She would wait a bit longer, until he finished writing his notes.

"The hell with that Texas game," Hap said. "From now on it's five card stud."

At breakfast, Booker asked Nathan Berry, "How did you read Menchnikov?"

"He definitely has money in the bank. His offer to reimburse Hap twenty dollars for the bank charge was not genuine."

Booker copied the account number on the new check and handed it to Berry. "Stand by for my call."

Booker and Hap drove to a branch of the bank and approached a teller. "We are here with the Flying Tigers convention."

Hap presented his endorsed check. "It's one of yours. It's supposed to be good."

"Not quite." The teller's head slowly moved from side to side. "Sorry."

"Close?" Booker prompted. "Is it short more than twenty dollars?"

"A little less," the teller said reluctantly. "Fifteen would cover it."

"Our friend thought it would be close. He will make it good. We will be back."

"The little bastard," Hap muttered when they were outside. "He knows to the penny what he has in the bank."

"Right." Booker nodded. "That is why he added the overdraft fee."

Booker phoned Nathan Berry. "Make a fifteen dollar deposit."

With the hour, Hap and Booker returned to the branch they visited earlier. "We received a call from Menchnikov. He made a deposit at one of your other banks. He gave us the phone number. If you phone your other branch I am sure you will discover the check is good."

Verification made, the teller paid Hap $3370.

"Hot dog," Hap exclaimed when they were outside. "There is more than one way to skin a cat."

"And the cat hates them all," Booker said. "You own Nathan fifteen bucks."

"I'll gladly pay him. And here's twenty for you. I only wish I could see the little weasel's face when he finds out his account has been cleaned!"

"Keep it under you hat. Someone else may need this kind of help."

36

WONDERFUL TIMES?

In his last semester to earn a bachelors degree in psychology, Nathan Berry continued to look ahead to his doctoral thesis, which would explore the psychology of poker players compared with the psychology of the criminal mind.

He opened the daily mail. "Hey," he exclaimed. "Bill Booker is getting married. Right after the wedding, they are taking off for the reunion in New York. It will be their honeymoon."

Bobbie grinned. "Well, it's not a honeymoon in Hawaii, but the Big Apple sounds like fun."

"I didn't know he had a girl friend."

"You know how you men are. We ought to plan a reception for them."

Bobbie's plan to limit the reception to Booker's close military friends snowballed when the committee sent invitation to every member of the 14th Air Force. In a publicity note a committee member wrote, "In honor of the couple, several long-time holders of markers have agreed to accept fifty cents on the dollar. What a great idea!"

Nathan scoffed. "No big deal. Guys were willing to take fifty cents on the dollar back in China."

Booker complained when Donna said he needed to wear his wedding suit, and Donna delighted in being able to get another use out of her wedding dress. Her parents were overjoyed when they learned the New York reception wouldn't cost them a dime. The convention committee wheedled most of the costs and concluded the balance in the registration fee.

At the reception, Billy Bob Jackson could not resist teasing Booker. "So you got a ball and chain."

Booker took it in stride. He remembered he had a mission and when he estimated the liquor had taken hold, he sought Barry Menchnikov.

In a short time, Menchnikov admitted, "I never did like that damn book of yours."

"It was Colonel Wise's idea," Booker said glibly. "Without his statement, there would have been no markers of honor. Without markers, the enlisted men would not have been able to play. It leveled the field."

"I remember when he attached my pay," Menchnikov said with a bitter expression.

"I remember he attached my pay too. I stood there with you."

In the deep recesses of his mind, Booker thought that Menchnikov might have been fool enough to try to retrieve markers from Hap's plane. "Hmmm."

Bobbie Berry enlisted two friends to catalogue gifts. Among the gifts was a bunch of markers. Most envelopes did not bear the names of the donors. His book might not show who gave them but the bore the name of the debtor. Booker obtained a complete roster of members. He would send a dunning letter extending the 50 percent discount, which the committee suggested for another 60 days.

"Honey," Donna said whey they prepared to go home. "How many toasters did we get?"

"I think I loaded ninety-eight," Booker joked.

"On the way home, we can stop along the way in a string of cities, go into the stores and try to obtain refunds," his bride quipped.

"It's bad luck to return wedding gifts."

"Who said that?"

"I just made it up. We won't need to buy gifts for the next fifty years. Our children won't need to buy any gifts."

"You're terrible."

"Well, I'm a cop—or will be soon."

Nearing Des Moines, Donna said, "Don't worry about who is on first. You are my leading man. You select where you work and where we live. I will follow. That is the way it will be."

How did she know what was bothering him? "I'm glad I picked you."

Donna Farley Booker giggled.

Booker found a job with the West Des Moines Police where he was able to further his career with training in criminal investigation.

Nathan Berry earned a Doctor of Psychology degree and accepted a teaching position in a satellite College. A lawyer called him to testify. To his surprise, as the months passed he was frequently called, not only by the FBI but the defense bar. Added to the money Bobbie earned, the couple surrounded themselves with things. However, Bobbie felt a void, an empty feeling for not having children. To counter that loneliness she placed her name on the "On Call" list of surgical nurses. Nathan resumed writing—with amusement—a book entitled, "The Wicked Philosophy of Poker." In the 'Publish or Perish' atmosphere of colleges, he not only published, but also prospered from royalties to the extent that he bragged about using royalties as a down payment on a new car. Players called him to supervise poker tournaments. Nathan wisely eschewed playing for the most part. He remembered the stack of markers he accumulated during the final days of the war.

Billy Bob Willis Jackson graduated from the University of Alabama. Prior to graduation, a man named Sol walked into Will Jackson's store and lamented, "When I started my store forty years ago, it was a white community. Now it is seventy-five or eighty percent black. I'm getting out. I will stay a few months during the transition, to train the new people, to introduce them to the community, and then I'm gone. I'm getting old."

Will Jackson considered the angles. He could buy Sol's grocery at a rock bottom price. He would put Billy Bob in charge—that would get his son's angry butt out of his store. Before Billy Bob ran Sol's store completely into the ground, he would freshen up the place with paint, and sell it to some enterprising black at a profit. Maybe then, Billy Bob would be interested, settled down enough, to work in his store. Will knew it was a long shot …

Billy Bob accepted the challenge—a business of his own, out from under his father's thumb and Sol convinced him that money from blacks was as good as money from whites.

Billy Bob realized there was nothing he could do about location—location—location. However, he could concentrate on the next best thing—personnel—personnel—personnel. He hired Wilma, a young African-American woman from the community who had cash register experience and knew people. His choice of Wilma Carver was nothing less than superb.

Billy Bob failed to keep track of how many times he looked at Wilma in admiration. She had delightfully long legs made for dancing, a splendid figure, and a pleasant face. He enjoyed when she bent over and sometimes gave him a glimpse of her thighs. He liked Wilma more than he realized. His awareness heightened when he caught himself explaining to himself, *she is black but she is real light black. She is pretty.* Several times, he saw her staring at him.

One evening after the store closed, Billy Bob reached out. His hand closed over her arm. Wilma at once reached up and removed his hand. "So you feel it too," she said matter-of-factly. "Everything is right for us except we live in the wrong country. It has to stop before it even gets started."

"I know," he said.

"I don't want to find myself hanging upside down as an ornament on a tall tree and you don't either. I don't want to have your baby out of wedlock. So what do we do? I figure you need to find a white woman."

"I figure you need to find a black man. In the meantime, we need to continue our pistol practice. Right now, I want to run something else past you. Say we enlarge the place—put in a lunch counter."

"You do love to live dangerously."

Wilma was sharp, Billy Bob decided. Combining their ideas resulted in a larger store, where most of the time someone had to attend the checkout register.

Above the entrance in large letters that hollered to the world the name—EVERYBODY'S STORE. The coffee bar and lunch counter ran nearly the length of the store except for the greeting card and candy display. Tables in three sections bore "inappropriate" signs: BLACK in the front section, WHITE in the rear, and in the middle; OTHERS, with subtitles; Pink, Green, Yellow, Orange, Tan, Aliens, and Friends Loved by God. Wilma suggested The Friends tag and less than fussy people congregated there and associated with other races than their own. One lady said, "I feel pink today."

The store's in-your-face challenge of community norms resulted in a disaster plan. The back door, extra heavy and solid, had massive locks that not even a speeding truck would compromise. The entire wall would give away first. The ample parking lot was well lit, and provided a beacon for nighttime shoppers. In addition to keyed locks on the front door, Billy Bob ordered an ingenious electric closure. If at closing time, Wilma saw some tough looking individuals lurking around the front door, all she had to do was press a secret button beneath the cash register and the doors would lock.

Trouble arrived at closing time on a Saturday night with the burning of a cross on the parking lot. Billy Bob turned to Wilma and a young man, James. "It looks like our time has come. Feel like dying?"

"Not especially," Wilma said, and reached for the .45.

Billy Bob pulled on his Air Corps Jacket with all the fruit salad. He swiped on his overseas cap and stepped outside.

Men of the hooded Klan hooted and hollered. "Give us the nigger woman! Send out the black bitch!"

"Take it easy," whispered Billy Bob's hooded uncle, standing at the back of the crowd. "He will send her out soon."

"I don't think so," shouted Billy Bob.

"I'm already outside," Wilma said, brandishing her .45 automatic.

"Listen up!" Billy Bob commanded. "Keep your muzzles pointed to the moon." First one lowers his weapon gets it. I hold a government issued .45. Wilma has another with a spare clip. Maybe you didn't notice the upstairs window open. James is there with a shotgun filled with buckshot and a high-powered scope sighted rifle. James, the minute shooting starts you take out the guys moving toward the back, trying to escape. Aim high, heart shots. Wilma and I will take out the ones in front. Hear this. The way we figure it, you will kill all three of us. In the meantime, at least twelve of you will be dead as a doorknob. That's twelve at a minimum. That's just the start of it. More Flying Tigers will be after you than you can count. Some of these men could slither into a Japanese camp in the middle of the night and take out their top brass. Do you want to tangle with them? One morning at breakfast, you will be sitting there dead. It's your call."

In the back, among the hooded men, Billy Bob's uncle tugged at another's sleeve. "It ain't worth it. We have scared them enough. Let's go home."

"You are all welcome at Everybody's Store without the bed sheets," Billy Bob called out. "We are in business. Bring money."

Then he did the most courageous thing in his life. He motioned for Wilma to run inside. Then he turned his back on the remaining Ku Kluxers and strode into his store.

Presently they all disappeared into the night.

The next time he stopped as his father's store, Will said, "You'd better be careful with your gun. You might shoot someone."

"I wouldn't shoot Wilma," Billy Bob retorted. "I love her."

Billy Bob and his father had little to discuss. Billy Bob showed up at the family residence for obligatory visits with his mother on holidays.

One evening James notice activity at the rear of the store and shouted, "Beer Run!"

Wilma pressed the button locking the front door and by the time they reached it, the culprits had no place to go. Wilma approached them with a broken broomstick and rapped a boy across the head. She jabbed another with the sharp end. "Get down on the floor—face down," she ordered. She looked up and noticed an unsavory character loitering at the front door. She pressed the button. She guessed the hood who rushed in was probably the ringleader. He sneered. "Leave them alone."

"Stay out it," Wilma said sharply.

The man drew a snub-nosed revolver. "You stay out of it," he rasped.

Billy Bob had drawn his .45 when he heard James shout, Beer Run!" He crept along a display, saw he had a clear shot and with a two-hand hold, fired.

The thug's pistol flew out of his hand. His humerus shattered, blood spurted in all directions. He dropped to his haunches.

Billy Bob said, "You want to die inside the store our outside? Wilma phoned the police and requested an ambulance. A young shoplifter spied the pistol, decided to remain on his stomach and crawled along the floor toward it.

Wilma arrived first. She brought the broomstick down viciously and shattered his nose.

Presently two police officers arrived. "Why did you tie up his arm?" We have wanted him dead for a long time. The officer detained the ambulance longer than reasonable. "Take him to County. No insurance. Mark him down for amputation."

"What do you want us to do with the little punks?" asked an officer.

"Well," Wilma reasoned. "They didn't get outside with the beer. It is not an easy case. What do you say we call their grandmothers?"

The grandmothers of two boys arrived. On grandmother beat her grandson "within an inch of his life," and then the other grandmother borrowed her cane and pounded on her grandson until she nearly broke it with her exuberance. The father of the boy soon known as "No Nose," arrived drunk. His indignation, Wilma and the officer decided, was all an act.

The incident worked magnificently in Wilma's favor. She and Howard, the handsome ambulance driver, were engaged in six weeks. They had dated a couple times in high school and needed no encouragement.

When he became aware of the relationship, Billy Bob selected a gem from the pouch he had hidden and dropped it into Howard's hand. "How would you like to mount this on a ring for Wilma?"

"Man, I couldn't afford a rock like that?"

"Take it. Have it appraised at two reliable jewelers."

When Howard returned, somewhat crestfallen, Billy Bob said, "Take the lowest estimate. Cut it in half. How does that price suit you?"

"You mean it? I'll buy it!"

Billy Bob nodded approval and banished an unbidden thought.

He remembered the first time he viewed the jewels in Kunming; he thought they were costume jewelry. He had been wrong. They were high-class jewels worth a king's ransom. Why did the prostitute have them? Because they were safer in her possession than if held by her partner, her master. Unable to produce them, had the woman been killed? He forced the thought from his mind. He went through the ritual of remembering—and forgetting—every time he viewed the ring on Wilma's finger. Eventually, in time, he outdistanced the reaction. *At least I won't use one of the rocks when I get married.* He decided to save the rest of the jewels for special occasions.

Wilma read is discontent. "Now we need to get you married," she told Billy Bob.

It took some time to find a woman of patience, who claimed to understand Billy Bob, who would take no lip from him, and could hold her own in an argument. Billy considered selling a diamond from the leather pouch to buy a ring for his pride and dismissed the idea. He wanted her ring to have no connection with the past.

"Happily" married, the first thing his wife insisted on was getting Billy Bob out of the store, into a store in a more prestigious location.

Billy Bob sold Wilma half of the "First Store" and insisted on working when she needed time off and during maternity leave when her son arrived.

The second Everybody's Store, patterned on the first, proved to be profitable. It was not long before Billy Bob abandoned working in the First Store only on Wilma's day off. He preferred working there when Wilma was present.

No comments were made. A man has to run his business the best way he knows how.

37

CHANGING FAMILY TIES

To avoid the rush of holiday traffic, Nathan and Bobbie waited until after the 1960 Memorial Day weekend to begin their journey. It had rained: the Minnesota countryside appeared green and clean. Bobbie looked out the open car window and savored the freshness. There was something refreshing about rain, it washed away the detritus and made the world a better place.

During the past week, since the funeral of Bobbie's youngest sister and her doctor husband, Bobbie and Nathan had discussed everything a hundred times; up, down, and across; followed by interludes of silence. Their world had been flung upside down. Or was it right side up? The doctor liked to live fast. According to reports, he was driving 100 mph when his car hurtled off an Illinois Interstate. Fortunately, the children had not been with them and were parked with grandparents. After the funeral in Cedar Rapids, a lawyer delayed Nathan and Bobbie to read the will. They were designated to care for three-year-old Jeffrey and one-year-old Jennifer. Bobbie pleaded for a week delay to rearrange her home. The grandparents agreed they needed a week to prepare the children to receive new parents.

"Who could have imagined this?" Bobbie said for the umpteenth time.

"Not in a year of Sundays," Nathan replied.

"Our self-centered lives are over." Bobbie said.

"You always wanted children."

"We will need to hire a nanny." Bobbie said.

"Maybe two." They had argued about that.

Bobbie fingered with the radio dial seeking music. She paused at a news broadcast. "Funeral services will be held in Decorah tomorrow for prominent Northeast Iowa physician, Dr. Arthur F. Fritchen. Commander Fritchen was stationed at Pearl Harbor and was the first surgeon to operate at the outbreak of the war ..."

Bobbie's head jerked. "I know him. He was my boss at Pearl. I wonder what happened. They say bad news comes in threes. Honey ..." she paused. "Decorah is only a few miles ahead. We need to stop there. I want to attend the funeral. I will call ahead and tell them we will be a day late."

He read the intensity of her sorrow. "Fine by me."

They checked into the Hotel Winneshiek and came down for dinner. A talkative waitress answered Bobbie's questions. "Doctor Fritchen lived here in the hotel after the divorce. Their divorce shocked everyone. But not as much as his suicide."

"My goodness. What happened?"

"I really don't know. You should talk to the pharmacist at Darling Drug. It's only a couple doors down the street."

After they had eaten, Nathan and Bobbie strolled along West Water Street. They paused at the all-glass storefront of Darling Drug store. They could see no one inside. When the entered, a thirty-something pharmacist walked out of the back room pharmacy.

Bobbie seated herself at the fountain, Nathan followed. "We really don't want anything," Bobbie said. "We ate at the Winneshiek. Do you have time to talk? I served with Commander Fritchen at Pearl Harbor—I just have to find out what happened."

The pharmacist said, "Then you know on December 7th he operated twenty-four hours without stopping. Once I heard thirty-six hours."

"The legend grows," Bobbie said with a wan smile. She learned Fritchen had an abundant medical practice and was appreciated by the elderly.

The pharmacist said, "He took time to explain things. He was the doctor for the County Home and Aase Haugen Home. I think the trouble began when his wife took a teaching job way across the state in Pocahontas, hundreds of miles away. She only showed up at holidays. That led to a divorce. There was a jury trial. You never allow a doctor to face a jury trial. It is the one opportunity, people with an ax to grind, have for getting even. They sure got even. Dr. Fritchen lost the house. There the house sat; empty for months. He moved into the Hotel Winneshiek, golf clubs and all."

"I always thought she was wrong for him," Bobbie said quietly.

"He used to walk in the back door and lament, 'It isn't fair. It isn't right. I should have gotten the house.' He said it over and over, every time he walked through. In my opinion, if he had retained the house he would be alive today."

"So it was suicide," Bobbie prompted.

"Yeah. On Monday, Memorial Day, he drove his Buick into the driveway alongside the house, when he knew Ann would be home, and gulped Nembutal till it was over."

"It's sad," Nathan said.

An awkward silence, for a moment no one spoke.

Bobbie mused, "The right way, the wrong way, the Navy way, and Fritchen's way. Did you ever see him scold? His right arm would go up. His right leg would go up and down in synch for emphasis."

"Oh yeah!" replied the pharmacist. "Not only when he scolded, but when he reported that he scolded. I remember one day he came in and told how he scolded his receptionist-nurse Mary. 'Mary, you are so God-damn dumb!' His arm and leg went up and down. As you say, in synch for emphasis. This may surprise you. I think he was proudest of the surgery where he completely reconstructed a rectum."

"I'm not surprised. He did two of those at Pearl Harbor. He was proud of that at the time."

"It's all too bad," Nathan said. "He was a national hero. His death might have been prevented. But for a decision. Maybe someday my wife will decide to write his story."

"Are you a writer too?" asked the pharmacist. "After my book came out, Fritchen mentioned wanting to write his story. Twice I thought he was on the verge of asking me to write his story, or help him with it. At that point, he just couldn't go on. He couldn't swallow his pride enough to ask for my help."

"That's Fritchen," Bobbie said. "He didn't often reveal his gentle human side."

"In a small town like Decorah, a doctor is always two rungs higher than a pharmacist. That is the reality. He was also a substantial generation older. To him I was just a kid. He couldn't bring himself down to my level. He had pride. He called one doctor here a butcher."

"You wrote a book?" Nathan said.

"I'll show it to you." The pharmacist opened a drawer and handed a copy of *Journey to a Star* to Nathan. "I'm not happy about the cover. They never asked my opinion about anything."

Bobby took the book from Nathan and leafed through it. "I want to buy a copy."

The pharmacist laughed. "I knew I stayed open for a reason."

"You must autograph it for me."

When two customers entered, the Berrys made hasty farewells and returned to the Winneshiek.

Nathan observed, "Delightful sex tonight; two kids tomorrow. Gertrude Solo, you always are a miracle worker."

"I'll remember you said that."

In Cedar Rapids, the lawyer had more news. "The doctor and his wife had a second-to-die insurance policy. There is a million dollar trust fund for the children's education. When the mansion and his practice are sold, which is imminent, those funds are to be applied to current living expenses."

"We can hire a nanny," Nathan said.

"Indeed," the lawyer intoned.

With the children safely tucked in a car loaded with toys and clothing, which partially obstructed the drivers view through the rear window, they began the journey home.

"I'm glad we had foresight to completely load the car last time, or we wouldn't have been able to take it all."

"We didn't take it all," Nathan said. "They will ship the rest of it to us in boxes. Well … you always wanted children."

"Best of all," Bobbie said. "No stretch marks. Did you see the look on the grandparents faces when the lawyer mentioned the million dollar policy?"

Nathan said, "I thought they were even more surprised when he said if the youngest child has not reached the age of 7, their names shall be changed to Berry. Doc must not have shared much with his parents."

"I thought the lawyer was smooth when he explained that the names of their real parents would not change on the birth certificate A local judge didn't want the children to have to explain why their names were different from their parents every time they went to school. That was neat."

"One of these days," Nathan said, "we need to watch out what we say in the presence of OUR children."

"One of these days," Bobbie said, "YOU need to buy US a larger house."

"With Doc's money."

They laughed together.

38

1968 REUNION IN TAIWAN

On their first trip to the Orient, some of the wives viewed the little Chinese women and wondered what their husbands had been up to during the war. The others, on viewing the same women, had no concerns whatever.

A Chinese man waited patiently at the door until he identified someone. "Hap?"

"Tang?"

"My real name is Chan."

"Of course. Now I remember. It's been ages."

"I had to come," Chan said. "I wanted to meet friends." A grain of truth existed in his statement. "Is Booker the mechanic here?"

"Why yes." Hap replied. "I saw him a few minutes ago. Come along, we will search for him."

"Is it all right?" Chan asked tentatively.

"Sure."

Within minutes, they located Booker. "Look who I found," Hap said.

"Chan," Booker exclaimed. "It's good to see you."

"Mister Booker," Chan answered, bowing slightly.

"What have you been doing?"

"After the war," Chan said in flawless English, "I drifted to Hong Kong. On the strength of Colonel Fong's recommendation, I landed a job with the Hong Kong police. I must thank you for having numerous photographs made of that recommendation. Through the years, I needed them. Thank you." Chan bowed again.

"You have done well."

"I am sure you have as well." Chan knew Booker was Assistant Police Chief of Police at Council Bluffs, Iowa but allowed him to tell it.

Booker introduced his wife and Chan asked, "Is Dottie here?"

"No. She didn't come. She married Colonel Wise. They divorced in about 1959. Currently she is married to Harald Leuba, an accountant."

"Greet her for me the next time you encounter her. May I speak to you privately?"

"If there is no rush, how about after we eat? You will be my guest."

Chan smiled. "Thank you. You have a habit of providing me nourishment."

Hap strode to the podium. "We have a guest with us tonight, a man who stood guard on my Lightning, night after night. Mister Chan, please rise and be acknowledged."

Chan covered his discomfiture with a wan smile, rose and promptly sat down.

"It's Charlie Chan!" Billy Bob Jackson exclaimed loudly. "I remember Charlie Chan. We called him Poon Tang."

"Ignore the fool," Booker said.

Chan forced a smile. "It is not a title unknown to me. Colleagues and some on the other side sometimes use that name. Actually, it is not far from the way the English pronounce my name. Che-lue Chan."

Donna Booker spoke quietly. "I think I will tell all my friends I met the real Charlie Chan."

Chan accepted her compliment with a grin.

The Taiwanese government provided a sumptuous feast. When they had dined, Booker suggested they retire to his room. He had already told Donna he had business that required his attention.

Chan shook his head. "It is probably bugged. Why don't we go for a walk?"

Without a word, Chan led the way outside. "Every third person in Taiwan is an agent. The same in China," Chan said in a low voice. Without turning his head, his eyes moved. They walked to a bus stop, boarded, and found seats near the nosy motor.

"My friend," Chan began. "It has been a long and eventful journey. On arriving in Hong Kong, I secured employment and studied English."

"You speak it very well. Better than I do."

"I finally became a detective." Chan glanced around. "We get off here."

An old woman disembarked with them and shuffled in the opposite direction. Chan slowly turned toward the hotel. "No one following," he whispered. "I am certain I am being watched. You know Chairman Mao. What I wish to discuss is ancient history. I know Colonel Fong had a man shot whom he believed to be the guilty party. Perhaps that man did reverse the cartridges in Hap's plane earlier. Later, I believe my father was killed by an American."

"I believe he was," Booker declared.

"My father would not have addressed a Chinese man in English. I also believe he was killed by a .45 caliber pistol, an American weapon."

"I am positive that he was," Booker said. "I have the .45 caliber slug that was removed from his body."

"You have it?" Chan said elated, as momentary emotion overcame his normally calm and serene composure.

"It is safe in my home. I will be happy to send it to you."

Chan bowed low. I will be honored to have you keep it. Your news has warmed my ears with the music of a hundred flutes."

"You might make that two hundred flutes. I have a possible motive. Just before your father was killed, Hap won some markers in a poker game. I had departed with my book. Someone mentioned that all anyone needed to do in the meantime was snatch the markers out of his footlocker. Hap said he did not keep them there; he stored them on his plane. In reality, he did not do that, he kept them in his wallet, on his person. I believe that is what the suspect was after."

"You have narrowed the list of suspected poker players?" Chan said hopefully.

One man has come to my attention. Barry Maskoviely Menchnikov. He is now a truck driver. I have absolutely no evidence to support my suspicion. He is not here. He did not make the trip."

Chan nodded. "My father named his killer as Birry or Berry. That could mean Barry."

It could also mean Berry—Nathan Berry—or me. Billy is a nickname for William. Your father would call me Birry."

"I will keep you in mind," Chan said with what Booker interpreted as mock severity. "Perhaps I will speak with Hap."

Booker nodded. "I know you will not allude to my suspicions."

"The morning after my father was killed," Chan continued, "I found a .45 caliber shell casing near Hap's plane. Exercising great care, I managed not to touch it and in Hong Kong, I found a fingerprint expert in whom I reposed a great confidence. He lifted a partial thumb and partial fingerprint. I know the evidence is circumstantial ..."

"It might be enough."

"I have slightly enlarged photos of the partials in my jacket pocket. When we enter the hotel, I will remove the envelope. It will appear that I am showing a pass. Two steps later, you will quickly take the envelope. Perhaps you will have an opportunity to compare the prints with those of your suspect."

Booker nodded. "He does appear at conventions—mostly to play poker. I might be able to swipe his drink glass."

One moment Chan walked beside him. The next moment he was gone.
Donna asked when Bill returned, "What happened to your friend?"
"My guess—he returned to Hong Kong."

The murder of Chan's father nagged at Booker. It was not his most pressing case. He decided there was nothing he could do until the '69 convention.

At the reunion in Toledo, Ohio, he looked for Menchnikov. He asked friends, "Have you seen him?" No one had. Finally, he contacted the association secretary and learned that Menchnikov had not registered.

Home again, Booker wrote to Chan and reported that his plan had failed. "I will try something else."

He copied the partial prints and in his official capacity requested the FBI compare them with Barry Menchnikov, Billy Bob Jackson, Nathan Berry and his own. He remembered the FBI had the prints of all veterans on file.

In due time, the FBI print expert sent his report:

> *The partial print samples do not provide adequate surface to enable us to make a match. However, it is the opinion of this examiner that due to varietal difference three subjects may be excluded: Menchnikov, Berry and Booker. Similarities in the Billy Bob Jackson sample do not allow exclusion*

Seated in his den one day, Booker opened the drawer in which he stored the slug from Chan's body. Booker's eyes narrowed. His mind raced. Billy Bob might just have been foolish enough … not only to do the shooting … but to have retained the automatic pistol. The slug might be matched to a slug fired from Billy Bob's weapon. However, that presented a problem. He couldn't fly into Birmingham and say, "Billy Bob, let's go squirrel hunting with pistols!"

Booker stared at the plaques and citations opposite his office desk. He guessed that citizens thought he could take time off from the job whenever he wanted. He sniffed. *Far from the truth.* To further Chan's case, he needed the cooperation of the Chief of Police in Birmingham. Now that he had made Chief himself, he was in position to request a favor. It was a meeting not anticipated with joy. Moreover, it meant he had to miss the annual convention of the 14th Air Force. He rose and muttered, "There ain't no justice."

At the national meeting of Chiefs of Police, he befriended his Birmingham counterpart. A graying man with a hard jaw, he showed no interest in taking a government issued .45 into temporary custody, especially when there was no evidence such a weapon existed. However, when Booker mentioned Billy Bob Willis Jackson, the Chief's eyes widened and he leaned forward with interest. The Chief stared at the distant wall, not seeing it. He remembered a night when Billy Bob waved a pistol. He cleared his throat. "His uncle is a solid citizen. His father is a stand-up guy. Billy Bob has wondered off the path. He has forgotten his upbringing. He turned out to be a damned Kennedy-ite."

Booker plunged ahead. "We only need the weapon test fired into a soft solution—something that will not compromise the bullet. All you need to do is send me the slug and casing."

"And return the pistol, eh?"

"Right. The sooner the better."

"It might take some time. We don't have probable cause for a warrant."

"To rule out a weapon known to the department …"

"Precisely. I have a detective who can handle it." The Chief had already decided to send the fat boy. If something went wrong, he could take the fall.

At the cash register in Everybody's Store number one, Wilma pegged the fat man as a cop before he had taken three steps inside. She guessed he was the one folks called Fatso. She didn't need to guess about his purpose—TROUBLE.

"There's been a shooting," he said unctuously. "I need to borrow the .45 you have under the counter—so it can be excluded."

"Yes, sir."

The government issued .45 lay on a shelf below towels, hidden by a loosely hanging towel that could be easily swept aside. Fully loaded, the location was not one the average crook—or cop—would ordinarily suspect. If they pushed her away from the cash register, even if she fell, the pistol would be in easy reach. Wilma and Billy Bob had discussed situations in plain talk. Wilma asked, "What if the robber is white?"

"Shoot the sonofabitch—twice. Always twice."

Wilma reached for the weapon. "It's loaded, sir." She removed the clip and carefully presented it to the fat detective. "There is still a live round in the chamber."

Fatso ejected the cartridge so it purposely fell on the floor where Wilma would need to kneel to retrieve it.

"Please. I will need a receipt with the serial number of the piece, and your badge number, please."

"Don't get uppity."

"I said please twice, and I am cooperating one hundred percent. Make that one hundred two percent." She dropped two cartridges into his greasy palm. "You will need them for test firing. For authenticity."

Fatso grunted and scribbled a receipt. He knew he had been outclassed. *Not like the old days. Then he would have shoved her around.*

When he departed, Wilma phoned Billy Bob. He listened and said, "You did right. I don't want you there without protection. I'll bring my other one."

Fatso returned the .45 promptly. Wilma said, "Billy Bob didn't want me to be here without protection. You might want to borrow this piece too."

"Yeah."

Wilma removed the clip. She expected Fatso to eject the chamber cartridge on the floor but he allowed it to drop on the counter. Wilma gave him a second cartridge.

Fatso forced a condescending smile. "Do you think you could actually shoot some creep?"

"I would give it my best two shots."

"Hunh." He turned. *I believe you would.*

Chief Booker received twice the number of .45 caliber samples expected and sent them to the crime lab for identification. When he received the report he wrote a letter.

Friend Chan,

Is time an ally or our enemy? Do not think that I have forgotten you. The crime lab matched the slug removed from the body of your father and matched it from one of two "liberated" Government issued .45 caliber pistols nominally in the possession of Billy Bob Jackson

Another problem exists. I do not believe the matter can be successfully prosecuted anywhere but in Kunming, Republic of China. Do you agree?

I do not believe the l4th Air Force will have a reunion there any time in the near future. Even if they did, neither Jackson, Menchnikov, or other witnesses are likely to attend. Kindly share your thoughts with me.

Bill Booker

Chief Booker

There are many ancient words of wisdom extolling patience. I agree the Republic of China is the proper forum to adjudicate the matter. Of course, prosecution would generate an International diplomatic crisis. On sober reflection, the US would agree that justice demanded prosecution.

In my humble opinion, there will not be an invitation for the 14th Air Force to visit China in the foreseeable future. They have visited the land of Chiang Kai-shek. For Mao Zedong to extend an invitation would cast him as a follower, and involve a loss of face. In the present atmosphere that will not happen.

I do not expect to see the Olympics held in Kunming.

Che-lue Chan

Chan's alluding to the Olympics encouraged Booker to think beyond annual reunions, to something 'extracurricular.' That did not leave much other than independent travel, a tour of Chinese places of interest, and old haunts. The only game that interested aging Tigers had to be poker. He toyed with the possibility of a poker tournament.

With increasing popularity of poker, Nathan Berry's earlier book extolling the psychology of poker demanded up dating, especially after he psychoanalyzed the cash potential. Dr. Berry's book, *The Bizarre Strategies of Texas Hold-em,* found a waiting market.

According to Dr. Berry, Texas Hold-em generated a cadre of experts. On no-limit games, expectation centers more on the bidding than on the cards. With five players, only fifteen cards are in play. The bet sends a message. Based on bidding experience, with five cards on the table and two held "in the pocket," an expert has a good idea which two cards are in the hand of an opponent.

If a player holds pocket aces, he has to choose whether to bid with strength pre-flop, or hang back with a small bid, a feint designed to show weakness and to encourage further bidding. The same strategy is used if a player holds a full house after the flop.

According to Dr. Berry, a person holding pocket kings is a 2 to 1 favorite over a person holding A-K pre-flop. In a high stakes game, a strategy to conserve resources might include folding a 7-7-7. He asserted, young men won't let themselves be beaten by a woman. A section on body language proved useful, a splendid barometer if one becomes well acquainted with opposing players. An amateur is predictable because he plays straightforward. However, the result is as unpredictable as a bomb. His bidding defies decoding and every now and then, the last card displayed will be the card he needs. Then the experienced, opposing high roller hits a land mine and goes belly up.

In a footnote, Dr. Berry mentioned that a Texas tourist introduced the game to a young man in New York in the early Forties. The young man joined the 14th Air Force and attempted to introduce "Texas Throw-down," but after a time or two, most airmen refused to play it. Not mentioned by name, many old China hands correctly identified Barry Maskoviely Menchnikov.

39

THE VISITORS

President Richard Nixon spent a week in China in late February 1972. His visit with Mao Zedong reestablished diplomatic relations and 'opened' China to world commerce. Neither Chan nor Booker realized that the meeting would one day provide a solution to their nagging problem.

Poker historians sometime cite 1969 as the year they held a high stakes tournament game in Reno, and the World Series of Poker in San Antonio. There is more agreement relating to the seven players who vied for honors at a Texas Hold-em tournament in 1972.

Chiang Kai-shek died in April of 1975. Mao Zedong died in September of l976. By July of 1977, Deng Xiaoping assumed power.

When Booker asked Dr. Berry about the possibility of setting up a poker tournament, Nathan replied, "Funny you should ask. You always were a master of timing. I have a book out on the subject. I call it, "*The Bizarre Strategies of Texas Hold-em.*"

"Congratulations. Give it some thought. The poker tournament must be held in China. The way I see it we cannot do it in connection with our annual meeting. It has to be a separate excursion. We need a hook, some special recognition for enlisted men, something that will entice Menchnikov and Jackson to go to China."

"Let me get back to you. The idea has potential. I do see Menchnikov now and then at a game …"

Berry returned the call in a few days. "I think your idea has merit. We may have some trouble getting all the money out of China. My thought is to sell as many chips as a player wishes. Players will send me the money in escrow—I have a fund set up for the purpose. I will distribute the chips when we arrive in China. Winners may redeem them when we return Stateside—probably less a small gratuity."

"Great. You design the chips; distribute them when we get to China."

Booker selected the Far Eastern Travel Agency to conduct the tour. The agency arranged tours for veterans seeking to return to Australia, Philippines, Okinawa, and other battle sites.

Soon after the group arrived in Kunming, Dr. Berry distributed specially designed chips arrayed in a rainbow of basic colors, engraved in values of 5, 10, 20, 50, 100, 500, 1000, and 10,000 dollar denominations.

Berry opened with an announcement. "I can tell by the spread of orders that some of you have come just to play poker. Others have come to kill—winner takes all. Divide yourselves into groups; discuss what limits you wish to play. One rule—as advertised—all the games must be Texas Hold-em."

Berry assumed the role of non-playing dealer, with Menchnikov, Hap, Jackson, Wilson and Anderson playing at his table.

"It is nice to see Chan again," Hap said causally as the games progressed. "He used to stand guard on my plane."

"Yeah, Charlie Chan, old Poon Tang," scoffed Billy Bob.

Hap continued, "Chan believes his father was killed by an American. He has the .45. slug removed from his father's body and the brass shell casing he picked up. All he needs to do is have them matched. I understand some .45 pistols have already been test fired." He stared at faces and saw no reaction.

Billy Bob remembered his pistols had been tested but that involved some local shooting in Birmingham.

"Do you want to talk ancient history or play poker," Nathan said impatiently, cutting cut off discussion.

The games were routine until Hap said, "Let's separate the men from the boys."

Wilson nodded, "Yeah. Everyone kicks in a thousand and waits for the flop. Then raises come in denominations of fifty bucks."

With a $5000 pot, Menchnikov drew a 9-8 off suit. The flop came as a mixed suit Q-9-7. Each player thought he had already wasted a grand, adding fifty to it would not make any difference. The gesture told Hap and Menchnikov that no hand held much strength. The turn presented a King.

Menchnikov worried that someone might hold a J-10 and the King would give that player a flush. Holding a pair of queens prior to the flop would have given an opponent a set. However, no one had acted on it. Bluffing took about as much guts as continuing to fire at a Jap fighter on your tail that would not drop when you kept firing at it. "As you say, Hap. Let's separate the men from the boys. I raise $700."

Hap studied his at his cards. Obviously, Menchnikov held something good. Maybe three kings, three queens or a king high straight, any of which would take out his three puny jacks. *No use throwing good money after bad.* "I fold."

The bluff worked. Menchnikov raked in a $5950 pot.

Chan appeared and Berry said, "It's getting late. Big day tomorrow."

"One more hand," Wilson said. This time it's a reverse; a conservation play. Everyone kicks in fifty bucks. The first raise after the flop is one thousand.

The fifty-dollar chips came in easy. Pre-flop Billy Bob held A-A, Menchnikov K-Q, Wilson Q-Q, Hap 10-7, and Anderson 10-9.

None of them realized they had challenged the odds, not even when the flop showed A-K-J. The players remembered Wilson exclaimed, "Holy Balls," but memories differed as when he uttered it. Billy Bob, Menchnikov and Wilson each tossed in a thousand dollar chip. Like contagion, Hap and Anderson followed. Both Hap and Anderson realized that if a Queen came up on the turn or the river they would have a straight. Dr. Berry, the dealer, turned over a Queen.

"What does this raise require?" Wilson asked.

"The first raise was a thousand," Berry said, "The next one can be anything."

"Five hundred,"

"I thought you said this was a conservation play."

"I thought so at the time. Here is my five hundred."

With everyone in, Berry turned over the ace of spades

"Holy shit! Two aces on the board!"

"It's going to cost someone another thousand to see my cards," Anderson said.

Hap and Wilson each flipped in a thousand dollar chip.

"In for a thousand," Menchnikov said.

Billy Bob considered raising, but didn't. "In for a thousand. What do you have?"

"Pair of aces, pair of kings," Menchnikov said.

"It looks like my straight is good," said Anderson.

"I have the same straight," Hap said. "Now what?"

"Now—give it up to my full house. Queens over Aces," said Wilson.

"I have you all beat," Billy Bob said, grinning ear to ear. "Read 'em and weep. Four aces over a King." He reached out for the $10,250 prize.

"What the hell," Hap said. "There are 16 aces and face cards in the deck. "You dealt eleven of them in this game, Berry. What are the odds of that?"

"Monumental," Dr. Berry said. "Virtually impossible." He turned over the next five cards that might have been dealt. 2-5-7-4-8. "Well, that's poker."

"Are these Chinese cards?" Menchnikov asked somewhat insolently.

"No. Bicycles."

Hap spoke quietly to Anderson and Wilson. "We experienced something that defies logic. It is beyond probability. It shoots the odds. On the other side of the coin, are the same odds for bad luck."

"The three of us lost," Anderson said. "Is that what you mean?"

Hap's expression became grave. "There is an evil omen about. Somehow, I have a feeling it is going beyond our card games. Keep your eyes open."

In a jolly mood, Menchnikov and Billy Bob strolled to their rooms. Chan followed them at a distance. When each entered his room, Chan placed a stub of a cardboard match stick between the door and the jam. If the door opened, the stub would be dislodged and drop to the floor.

Chan walked to his room, placed a match-stub inconspicuously in the desk drawer and another in his door after he departed. As part of their plan, Booker invited him to spend the night.

They awakened early, and when they padded down the corridor, they observed the match had fallen from Chan's door. Inside, the desk drawer had been opened.

"It's gone," Chan said, peering in the drawer where he had placed the box that contained the dummy slug and shell casing, not the real evidence, only bait.

On arriving at the Great Wall, Booker and Dr. Berry caused Billy Bob and Menchnikov to lag behind the group to provide Chan the opportunity to make his great announcement. "I have solved the most important case in my career. The day my father was murdered, I found a .45 caliber shell casing near Hap's plane. Your fingerprints were on it." He dispatched a piercing stare at Billy Bob.

Billy Bob's head jerked. "That don't prove anything. That shell casing might have been lying on the runway for weeks."

"Yes," Chan continued. "We also matched the .45 caliber slug removed from the body of my honorable father to a projectile recently fired from a pistol in your possession, Mr. Jackson."

Billy Bob paled. He remembered his pistols had recently been test-fired. He whirled on Menchnikov. "You told me my .45 accidentally discharged the night Chan's father was killed." He angrily pointed at Menchnikov. "He borrowed my gun that night."

Menchnikov shouted menacingly, "Shut up. Don't try to pin this on me!"

"No wonder you were so eager to give your weapon to me when we were leaving for the States," Billy Bob retorted. "You knew that sooner or later someone might link you to it. You had to get rid of it."

"Are you gonna believe him?" Menchnikov bit out "You said his prints are on the shell casing. You said he has the .45. What else do you need?"

"Yesterday," Chan said soberly, "We allowed Hap to announce that I had a shell casing and bullet that I would send in to be matched. The killer could not have known that the match was already made. The murderer had to make one last attempt to destroy the evidence. He entered my room and took it."

"I didn't steal your evidence." Menchnikov said and pointed at Billy Bob. "Look in his room."

Billy Bob was about to enter a denial when Chan raised a silencing palm. "Not necessary. Mr. Jackson did not leave his room all night."

"That's right," Billy Bob affirmed.

"But you did, Barry Maskoviely Menchnikov," Chan said with a voice of cold steel. "I charge you with the murder of Chan Fu Lim."

Menchnikov looked around furtively. Terror filled his eyes. He swung a fist at Billy Bob who pushed him away. Thrown back, Menchnikov charged him in a blind fury. This time Billy Bob anticipated his move and ducked. When he straightened and grabbed Menchnikov, their combined energy created momentum that caused Menchnikov to be flung to the rim of the wall, where for a moment he tottered, arms flailing as he tried to catch something solid. He screamed as he fell down the far side.

The group rushed and looked over, and saw that he didn't move. "Help me down," Chan said, and Booker held him with outstretched arms until he dropped the last several feet.

"He dead," Chan called out. "It looks like he hit his head. Maybe broke his neck." He hastened to remove Menchnikov's wallet and keys.

Booker's fingers drummed Billy Bob's chest. "He attacked you! It was an accident! Now grab my arms and lower me down there."

"He's dead all right," Booker verified. Chan handed him the wallet and the money he removed from it. "I left a little. We need to get our stories straight. We need to admit he killed my father. We can't sell anything else. Too many of our friends know about the murder."

"Yeah." Booker nodded emphatically. "You got that right."

Chinese officials arrived with amazing rapidity.

Chan identified himself and presented his badge. "I have lost face," he lamented in Chinese. "I should have solved the murder of my father, not this Meghwa Chief of Police." He spoke in less than inscrutable detail.

Finally, Booker interrupted, "Would you interpret for me?"

Unnecessary," said the Chinese detective as he examined Booker's badge. "I speak English."

"We need a national favor," Booker began. "This man was a hero. Years ago, Chan's father was caught in a conflict between Americans. It was bad timing. This hero has led a good life for many years. He has paid for his crime—if by accident. The Gods are at work. It will serve no useful purpose to bring shame to a dead hero. He is also a hero in China. He was a tail gunner. The pilot would lag behind, in a lame duck maneuver. Some Jap fighter would come roaring after them, guns spitting. The bomber would roll and Menchnikov would take out that Jap fighter every time. Menchnikov had great love—for China. Dr. Berry, a world renowned psychologist who works with the FBI, witnessed Menchnikov's sudden attack on our friend Jackson."

Booker didn't suggest that the detective speak to Berry. He knew he would do just that. He also knew that Chan would speak to Berry if he managed to get to him first.

Chan assumed a pensive pose. "Would it be possible for China to honor an American hero, who destroyed so many enemy aircraft, by putting him at rest in the soil of China, perhaps near the old headquarters of the *fei hu?*"

A legend was born before the body was removed. Dr. Berry added "a fact" that Menchnikov had fallen in love with a Chinese girl and his enduring love had never allowed him to marry. He had once spoken about having his body buried in China. He had complained on the plane coming over that he had forgotten his medication.

The tour guide realized at once that he had drawn aces for continuing tours in China. Every tour—and there would be many—would include a stop at the gravesite of the romantic American hero, Barry Maskoviely Menchnikov. The tour guide worked feverishly making arrangements, enabling the tour to be at Kunming for the memorial to a fallen hero of the Chinese Republic.

When they found an opportunity, several men gathered in Menchnikov's room to assemble his gear. Booker found a switchblade knife. "I think you should have this," he said to Chan. "If you had slept in your own room last night you might have tasted this blade."

Chan bowed in appreciation.

"I found a bottle of amphetamines," Berry said.

"Get rid of them."

"These neckties would make excellent gifts for Chinese officials …"

"You're in charge of the treasured gifts from an American hero department. All the rest of this stuff we will give to the Chinese detective who understood the problem."

"What problem?"

Nathan Berry snickered. "There will be a problem if his old girlfriend shows up at the funeral with a grown child—or grandchildren."

"You invented her, Dr. Berry, I didn't."

"That's no problem," said Dr. Nathan Berry. "That's fate. We need to decide what to do with his money and all his poker chips."

"Pay off his markers." Booker turned to Hap. "Remember the convention in Chicago, back in Forty-nine?"

"Do I ever. We added fifteen bucks to his account, and I got my thirty-three hundred bucks. I wonder who else he owes?"

"There are a few." Booker spoke to Chan. "We did rather well today."

"Right, Old Chap."

"Even if we did strain ethics."

Chan modernized ancient Chinese philosophy and explained, "An ethical man knows the difference between paying and not paying his markers. A moral man would never think of not paying!"

Booker had the opportunity to repeat his words when Billy Bob sidled over to him before dinner. "Are you going to bust me for taking home two 45s."

"That's federal. The statute of limitations has run on the theft. I do not recall the Feds prosecuting a mere possession case. I will give you the serial number of the particular .45 owned by our international hero. One day you might wish to donate it to a museum with the proper inscription. We are going to pay off his markers out of his poker chips." Booker repeated Chan's words. "An ethical man knows the difference between paying and not paying his markers. A moral man would never think of not paying."

"I owe some," Billy Bob said hesitantly. "I've been slow in paying."

"Make the announcement before we eat. Confession is good for the soul"

When everyone had seated, Booker announced that Menchnikov's markers would be paid off at face value. Billy Bob rose and indicated it was long past time that his markers were paid. Dr. Nathan Berry stood and said that all he needed was for a debtor to sign off on it and he take care of it at the time chips were redeemed. "There will be a two percent surcharge due Bill Booker for maintaining the Booker Book all these years."

"Who decided that?" Booker muttered.

"A very important committee—every member has a doctor's degree in psychology."

They buried Barry Muskrat, AKA Barry Maskovielymenchnikov, AKA Alphabet, AKA Barry Maskoviely Menchnikov, international war hero, with full military honors replete with bells and firecrackers.

"Who is that over there?" Berry whispered.

"Nobody," Booker said. "Just some dude from the State Department."

40

EXODUS

Not long after she received the new 1985 calendar, Dottie and husband, Harald Leuba planned to attend the annual 14th Air Force reunion set to begin in Tucson, Arizona, and end in Taiwan. Dorothy sent a letter to her father.

Now, on the plane winging over the Pacific, Dorothy's thoughts reverted to the war, a war long past. It didn't feel like forty years ago—yet the memories were vivid. How many miles had she flown across China? How many miles had she traveled on grubby over-crowded trains? How many painful miles had she walked across the ancient land?

It was something Ed Cabelka said that made her wonder if it all been worthwhile. Communists had surged across China and taken control, forcing Chiang Kai-shek to flee to Taiwan.

Soon after the end of the war, her mother returned to New York. Sandow remained in China in the service of Chiang Kai-shek. Sandow knew Lillian would never return and married a Chinese woman. With no record of a prior marriage in China; he did not need a divorce. Sandow and his new wife left the mainland and fled to Taiwan with Chiang Kai-shek.

Dorothy thought of her family. Gloria married in Shanghai, moved to Hong Kong and had a son Michael. The marriage ended in divorce. Gloria moved to New York, married Edward Leigh, a Long Island banker and had two sons, Clifford and Lawrence. Gloria kept in contact with her father and he knew these things.

Edna also kept in contact with Sandow. She married Archibald Wong in Shanghai, had a son name Jack, obtained a divorce, and married John Chiang. Residing in Maryland, Chiang adopted Jack. The couple had four children: Vivian, Linda, Kenneth and Raymond.

Jack had come to the States with his mother, married Daisy, a Chinese woman, returned to Hong Kong, and purchased a factory. Independently wealthy, Jack and daisy had five children, Christina, Andrew, Barbara, Paul, and

Michael. Jack frequently flew to Taiwan on business and had opportunity to visit his father.

When the plane landed in Taipei, one of the men who attended the convention there in 1968 viewed the tall buildings. "This place ain't the same."

"America isn't the same either," Dottie reminded him.

She detested missing several sessions of the Air Force reunion but she had to visit her father, his new wife and their four children. Growing old, she knew her father needed financial assistance. That is what families did—they looked out for each other.

Aware of her increasing financial responsibility, Dottie returned to the convention hotel. She lamented missing several sessions. Mingled with her mixed emotions, as she looked around, she felt a pervasive sadness. Older now, the men were dwindling in numbers. Earlier, she attended many of their funerals. She realized she could no longer do that. *"Stop it,"* She admonished herself. She mounted a brave smile. "Did I miss anything?"

Dottie's marriage to Harald Leuba lasted a quarter century, until his death on October 12, 1994. On May 23, 1999, she married Clifford Phipps. As the years passed, she lamented the passing of friends and comrades.

With the millennium, she talked about the changes in her life and the life of the nation. The United States had reached its glory and grandeur in 1945. In that year and the next, the country achieved the zenith of greatness, togetherness, unity of purpose, joy, and raison d'etre. Since that moment, there began a SLOW AND PRECIPITOUS DECLINE, which continues unabated. The characteristics and facets thereof are all included in *The Decline and Fall of the Roman Empire.*

Feisty, and filled with optimism at the approaching summer of 2007, she awaited her 85 birthday anniversary, and looked forward to exchanging pleasantries with a few of "her boys" as she called the Flying Tigers, "the greatest bunch of guys in the world."

978-0-595-42451-1
0-595-42451-1

www.ingramcontent.com/pod-product-compliance
Lightning Source LLC
Chambersburg PA
CBHW030350020726
47493CB00003B/758